KINGS
ST(O)NE
AND ICE

S.J.A. TURNEY

🔟 CANELO

First published in the United Kingdom in 2025 by

Canelo, an imprint of
Canelo Digital Publishing Limited,
20 Vauxhall Bridge Road,
London SW1V 2SA
United Kingdom

A Penguin Random House Company

The authorised representative in the EEA is Dorling Kindersley Verlag GmbH.
Arnulfstr. 124, 80636 Munich, Germany

A CIP catalogue record for this book is available from the British Library.

Print ISBN 978 1 83598 046 0
Ebook ISBN 978 1 83598 047 7

Cover design by Tom Sanderson

Cover images © ArcAngel, Shutterstock

Printed and bound in Great Britain by Clays Ltd, Elcograf S.p.A.

Look for more great books at
www.canelo.co
www.dk.com

1

For Craig, editor extraordinaire, who for seven years now has taken the dusty coal of my writings and compressed it into diamonds

A note on pronunciation

Wherever possible within this tale, I have adhered to the Old Norse spellings and pronunciations of Viking names, concepts and words. There is a certain closeness to be gained from speaking these names as they would have been spoken a thousand years ago. For example, I have used Valhöll rather than Valhalla, which is more ubiquitous now, but they refer to the same thing. There is a glossary of Norse terms at the back of the book.

Two letters in particular may be unfamiliar to readers. The letter ð (eth) is pronounced in Old Norse as 'th', as you would pronounce it in 'the' or 'then', but in many cases over the centuries has been anglicised as a 'd'. So, for example, you will find Harald Hardrada's name written in the text as Harðráði (pronounced Har-th-rar-thi) but it can be read as Hardradi for ease. Similarly, Seiðr can be read as seithr or seidr. The letter æ (ash) is pronounced 'a' as in cat, or bat.

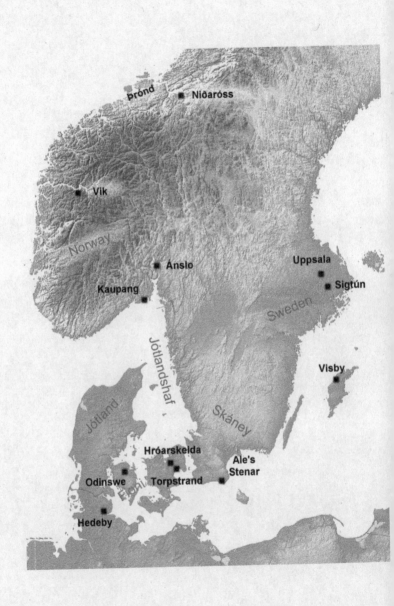

Part One

ᚹᛟᛚᚠᛖᛋ ᛟᚠ ᛟᛞᛁᚾ

Homecoming

'Brave Yngve! to the land decreed
To thee by fate, with tempest speed
The winds fly with thee o'er the sea
To thy own udal land with thee.
As past the Scanian plains they fly,
The gay ships glanced 'twixt sea and sky,
And Scanian brides look out, and fear
Some ill to those they hold most dear.'

From *King Harald's Saga* by Snorri Sturluson,
trans. Samuel Laing

Chapter 1

Hróarskelda, summer 1045

'What was the bishop's name again?' Ulfr asked.

Behind him, across the tavern, Bjorn jabbed a finger into a man's eye with glee.

'Argh!' bellowed the man, staggering back.

Leif glanced round in irritation at the scene, then turned back. 'Aage,' he said with a wry smile. 'Bishop Aage.'

'Argh!' bellowed that same victim across the room as Bjorn's big, heavy boot stamped down on his toes.

Halfdan chuckled for a moment at that, then his expression straightened, seriousness falling across it once again. 'And did you learn anything else from his priestlings?'

The small Rus warrior took a sip of his beer, smiled across the table at Anna, then nodded. 'It seems that excommunication is more powerful than we anticipated. Hjalmvigi, by all accounts, did not take the news well.'

Halfdan could quite believe that. The scarecrow priest would have been livid, he was sure. That thought warmed him a little. Snatches of history flashed through Halfdan's mind as though brought by the twin ravens of Odin, thought and memory.

Of Hjalmvigi spitting bile in a Gotland village so long ago as he damned Halfdan's father and urged Yngvar to tear down Odin's stone, and of his look of smug satisfaction as they rode away from a burning village full of corpses that had been Halfdan's friends and family.

Of the white-garbed priest beneath the hallowed roof of the palace at Kiev who had loosed arrows and snarled hate at the

3

Wolves: 'These men are pagan scum. You have no need of such animals. They should be peeled and hung from a high tower as a warning to their kind.'

Of a land at the end of the world where a tribe suffered, diseased and dying, and of the great priest Hjalmvigi's Christian *compassion*: 'They are heathen demons. No war on earth is worth such an alliance. Burn them all.'

Of the halls of the Georgian queen at Kutaisi where the white priest sneered at Halfdan: 'Run away, little heathen. Your world is shrinking fast and soon there will be nowhere for you to go.'

But he could also remember his answer to that last: 'I will find you, Hjalmvigi, for a debt is owed. We shall leave this place, but remember my words. There is no prince, priest or king you can shelter with, no land you can run to, where I cannot find you. I waited ten years for the jarl. I have become a patient man.'

Leif leaned back. 'Apparently, if rumour can be believed, Hjalmvigi beat his precentor half to death with his staff before anyone could drag him away.' Halfdan hoped his expression conveyed the fact that he had no idea what a precentor was, but Leif did not seem to notice, and continued. 'They took his robes and staff, and ejected him from his palace. Within hours, the man had fallen from being the most powerful priest in Sweden to being an impoverished vagrant. He went to the royal palace to appeal to the king, Onund Jacob.'

Again, Halfdan nodded. 'Onund would be sympathetic, I think. He had been a friend of Yngvar's after all.'

'He may have been sympathetic once upon a time,' Leif admitted, 'but no more. I do not think he can *afford* to be. Where Norway and Daneland are staunchly Christian now, Sweden is still in the process of changing, and your ways, my friend, still hold strong in some places. If Onund wants his country to stand among the other Christian nations, he will feel he must unite it behind the cross, and having a defrocked,

4

excommunicated priest as his right-hand man would hardly help matters. No, it seems that Onund greeted Hjalmvigi coldly at best, refused him aid, and had him turfed from the royal palace too.'

'I'm already warming to the new king,' Halfdan said, 'even if he does kneel to the nailed god.'

Leif threw him a withering look, and Halfdan had to remind himself once more that the Rus kneeled to that same Christ. It was easy to forget, given how much of the old north had crept into Leif's spirit and bones during his time with the Wolves. He had gone from being a quiet, bookish Rus scholar to a lean and hungry hunter.

Behind them, Ketil lurched across the room, holding a man by the neck, the lanky Icelander's height such that the man's feet swung uselessly, some way off the floor. Snarling imprecations in his sharp Icelandic accent, Ketil slammed the man into a wall, the back of his head making a bony clonking noise.

'Oi, he was *mine*,' Bjorn shouted, letting go of an unconscious man, who collapsed to the floor in a heap, and storming over toward Ketil, waggling his hand to indicate that he would like the other man too, please.

Halfdan gave his two warriors an indulgent smile, then turned back to the business at hand. 'So now Hjalmvigi wanders the streets of Uppsala?'

'Not quite. He may have fallen from grace and lost his power, but he still has his wits. No one can say with certainty where he went, but it looks very much as though he went south and west from there. One of the visiting clergymen told me that a man fitting Hjalmvigi's description tried to steal a priest's robes from a church in Skara before he was spotted and scared off.'

'What did you say?' Bjorn bellowed suddenly, turning to the table with a gasping man floundering in his grip.

'A church in Skara,' Leif repeated. 'You know it?'

'I know *Skara*,' the big albino said, his tone dark, 'and I've no wish to go back there.'

5

Leif nodded. 'I don't think we'll have to. I suspect Hjalmvigi was just passing through.'

'To here,' Halfdan said, an edge of excitement in his voice. 'No.'

'Surely he must? From Uppsala down through Skara would bring him to the coast of the Jótlandshaf, and it would not take much to cross it from there and come to Daneland. He *must* be here, or on his way, at least.'

'Bear in mind, Halfdan, that the order for his excommunication *came* from here. Yes, of course, it originally came from Jorvik in Angle Land, but it was sent on to Uppsala by Bishop Aage here in Hróarskelda. I cannot imagine for a moment that Hjalmvigi, on the run and desperate, would race straight into the arms of the man who had stripped him of it all.'

Halfdan could only nod at that. The cursed ex-priest would find no safe harbour in Hróarskelda. Bishop Aage had been surprisingly accommodating to a small group of warriors who lived by the old ways, and had been appalled at what Halfdan had told him of Hjalmvigi's past activities. The Dane had been only too happy to help bring about Hjalmvigi's removal from his Church.

'The priest fled Sweden, but not for here,' Leif said.

'No, I suppose not. Then where? Norway?'

Leif nodded. 'Magnus is king in Norway, and though he is staunchly Christian, he stands at odds with Onund of Sweden. Sveinn, the man from whom Magnus stole the Danish throne, is in Sweden with Onund now.'

'I am lost with all these people and places.' Anna sighed. 'I thought you said Magnus was king in *Norway*?'

Leif gave her an apologetic look. 'It's a complex web, my love, and it confuses even me. There are separate thrones of Sweden, Daneland and Norway, but the three realms have only two kings. Sweden is controlled by Onund Jacob, son of Olof, and no one disputes that claim. He is secure. Norway was wrested from its previous king by Magnus, and he only

6

sits upon its throne because he took it by force. Others still covet that throne, including the troublesome lunatic Harðráði, who you'll remember from Constantinople, and who is King Magnus's uncle, in fact. But, by chance, the king of Daneland died at a convenient time for Magnus, and he swept up the Danish throne too, right under the nose of Sveinn Ástríðarson, who actually had a better claim. So Magnus is currently king of both Norse and Danes, but the other men who might claim both his thrones are in Sweden with Onund. Consequently, there is no love lost between those two men.'

'So because Magnus of Norway and Onund of Sweden do not see eye to eye, you think Hjalmvigi went to him?' Halfdan pressed.

'That is my assumption. Hjalmvigi cannot have stayed in Sweden, and movement through Skara confirms that. I do not think he would dare come to Daneland, so the clear alternative is Norway, with the only man who might accept him, if only to annoy King Onund. It will not do Magnus's reputation good to have an excommunicated priest by his side, of course, but he is a shrewd one from what I understand, and I'd wager he has a way round it, or at least is working on one.'

'I'll... GAH!' shouted Halfdan suddenly as a man with a broken nose fell across his shoulder, spilling his beer across the table. The man gurgled unpleasantly in the young jarl's ear, and was gone a moment later, as Bjorn yanked him off Halfdan's shoulder.

'Will you keep your entertainment from ruining my ale?' he snapped, earning a tight smile from Gunnhild.

'I was saving you one,' Bjorn shouted, 'but now I'm not.'

There was the sound of a heavy punch and breaking teeth from behind him as Halfdan wiped the worst of the beer spillage from the table onto the floor and resettled his mug.

'Where will Magnus be?' he said, a touch of excitement back in his voice. The priest might not be in Daneland as he'd initially thought and hoped, but Norway was close, and it sounded as though he might still be almost in their clutches.

Leif shrugged. 'The geography of this part of the world is quite strange to me.'

It was Ulfr who leaned in then. 'The old king used to keep his court at Niðaróss in the north, deep in a fjord. Big Christian place. I'd wager that if Magnus is trying to promote himself as the sole legitimate, and Christian, ruler of Norway, he'll also hold court at Niðaróss.'

'Then Hjalmvigi will be in Niðaróss too. How far is that from here?'

Ulfr shrugged. 'I've not been there myself, but from what I know it's maybe twelve days' sailing from here. Half that if you're in a hurry and you want to sleep aboard and row in the dark.'

Halfdan mused on that for a moment, weighing the desire to find Hjalmvigi against his duty to the Wolves. Frankly, he'd lift the *Sea Dragon* from the water and carry it on his back if it got him to Niðaróss and Hjalmvigi faster, but he'd put the Wolves through a lot in Angle Land, and since then, too. A longer stay than necessary in Jorvik had led to a later sailing than intended, and they'd encountered dangerous seas all the way to the Frankish coast. Then, they'd had a great deal of trouble finding a port that was remotely sympathetic to their kind, for all were staunchly Christian, and many were wary of Northmen, given the chaos that was starting to spill over the borders from Duke William's Nordmandi. But finally, the Wolves had reached Daneland and the home of Bishop Aage, where they had now tarried for several very comfortable days, and so right now the crews were happy.

Those men he had picked up on the beaches of Apulia and among the violent lands of the Normans had finally truly gelled into proper longboat crews. A true hirð of Viking raiders, their sense of fraternity sufficient that Christian and Odin-son could sit side by side at the oars and laugh together, could raise sword and shield and stand as brothers against any man, for they were all the Wolves of Odin. And the new men from Swaledale were fast going the same way, too. Being children of Ash and Elm, born of the old ways, they had been quick to adapt to life with the Wolves.

Hjalmvigi was so close…

But Halfdan had to nurture this sense of unity in his hirð. If he wanted the Wolves to hold together, he had to look after them. It was part of a jarl's job. Here and now, they were happy, and making them sleep on planks and row through the night for his own personal vengeance was not a step in the right direction. He sighed.

'We can spare twelve days. More than that if we have to,' he said finally, relinquishing his desperate desire for revenge in favour of the good of his men.

'A *lot* more than twelve?' Gunnhild asked archly.

'What?'

'Pull your head out of your backside, Halfdan. If Magnus has taken in the priest, that means the man is of use or value to the king. And if that is the case, Magnus will not let him go so easily. This excommunication may have removed Hjalmvigi's personal power, but all that has happened is that instead of hiding behind Onund of Sweden, he is hiding behind Magnus of Norway. You take a longship of warriors to get at Hjalmvigi and you will be sailing them straight into the fortress of a Christian monarch, filled with his soldiers. That way, only a dark ending lies in wait for the Wolves of Odin, and I do not need to walk with the goddess to see the tangled threads of *that* weaving.'

Halfdan sagged in exasperation. 'So we are no closer, then? After everything we have done, he is still beyond our reach, even here?'

'For now. But there are ways, my jarl. Doors are opening, if we choose to step through them.'

'I'm too tired for your mystical explanations, Gunnhild. Speak plainly.'

'All right, then,' she said, leaning across the table toward him, eyebrow arching again as he deftly avoided leaning in the spilled beer. 'Hjalmvigi hides behind Magnus, because he now has no power of his own. And Magnus is too strong for the Wolves to take on, of course. We can bring down a renegade jarl and his hirð, yes, but a king and his entire nation is a little beyond even us. All this you know. But while you *listen*, my jarl, you do not *hear*. There are men out there with the power to face Magnus. And we know them already. We have a way in.'

Halfdan frowned, leaning back in his chair. 'You mean Onund Jacob of Sweden? Yes, he and Yngvar were close, but they parted long before I left Gotland. I've never even met the man.'

Gunnhild raised her eyes skyward for a moment. 'Onund of Sweden, if you only *listen*, currently plays host to the exiled Sveinn of Daneland, but also to a man whose claim on Norway is even stronger.'

'*Harðráði*,' Halfdan said, eyes bright again.

'Exactly. If my memory does not play me false, the Golden Bear himself owes us a heavy debt, both for stealing our ship and for leaving us behind in the great city. It might be time to cash that debt in to bring Hjalmvigi out where you can get him.'

'So we do not sit in Daneland and wait for Hjalmvigi to come to us,' Halfdan said, 'nor do we hunt him in his sanctuary in Norway. Instead, we go to Sweden and seek the help of three powerful men?'

'And,' Ulfr put in, wagging a finger, 'that means we will find our missing ship, too. Wherever Harðráði is, so will be the *Sea Wolf*. I miss her sleek lines.'

The glittering in Halfdan's eyes only increased at the thought. That ship had been to the end of the world with them, and had been his, and Ulfr's, pride and joy. More than that, it was a very strong symbol of what the Wolves were. To have it returned, all the way from the imperial south…

'Then we could set the *Sea Cow* free,' he said with a smile.

The others chuckled at that. When they had left Jorvik and Angle Land with the new recruits from Swaledale, there had been too many people in Halfdan's hirð for a small ship like the *Sea Dragon*. They had sailed across the sea in that ship, but also in a transport that Archbishop Ælfric of Jorvik had secured for them. At Ultra Traiectum, they had relinquished that vessel, and had shopped around for a replacement. Unfortunately, that place was part of the Holy Roman Empire, which meant there was no hope of securing a good dragon boat. The best they could find was a German sea scout, which was ugly, a funny shape, and handled 'like a brick' according to Ulfr. She had been nicknamed in line with their ships the 'Sea Cow'. The very idea of being able to sell on the cumbersome hulk, and divide the Wolves between the two sleek hunters built by Ulfr, was a tantalising one.

He looked down at the table. There were still pools of spilled beer on the wooden surface, and he dipped his forefinger into one and dragged it across the rough wood, beginning to draw a rough map of the region. A shape a little like the head of a chicken, with several small circles around it, was Daneland, where they were now. He then drew Norway, hanging above it like a limp prick, which made him smile. Then Sweden off to the east of that, the ball-sack for Norway. For a moment, he hesitated to add his home, but then he shrugged and drew a small island to the east of it all. He dotted where he thought they were now, in Hróarskelda, and then two more dots to mark Uppsala and Sigtun in Sweden. Then one in a random place up to the north of Norway for Niðaróss.

Map complete, he stabbed his finger down on their current location, and drew a line that wound around islands and head-lands, across the narrow and crucial Jótlandshaf that separated Daneland from the other nations and marked the only entrance to the great Eastern Sea. From there, rounding the south of Sweden, he moved up toward Sigtun and Uppsala, but paused as his finger traced a line past Gotland. He felt eyes on him and looked up to see Gunnhild looking at him, her gaze piercing, seeing deep into his mind.

'You have to, of course,' she said.

'There is no reason to go to Gotland,' Halfdan replied, though the thought had struck him and brought with it an unpleasant faint sense of nausea. 'When I left, I took with me everything that mattered: a sword, and my hate and determination.'

'Gotland is a draugar for you, a ghost haunting your past. You faced down and finished Yngvar, and now you hunt the last echo of your childhood nightmare, but part of all that will be seeing your home, even if it is to know that you need not go back again. The Norns have woven you a path that passes through the warp and weft of your own past to bring you home. Do not deny the weavers, Halfdan. Take it from me.'

He winced as he remembered that moment, when she had jumped from Harðráði's ship in the waters off Miklagarðr. It had cost her dearly. And then suddenly he wondered whether perhaps that weaving for her was not done. She had turned her back on her fate when she turned her back on Harðráði, and yet here they were, planning to sail straight back into his arms. Had she ever really left him, or just delayed the inevitable? For just a moment, he saw the tiniest flicker of uncertainty in her expression, just a miniscule tic, yet it was enough to suggest that she was having similar thoughts. Should he speak of it? He decided not, for he was fairly sure she would simply rebuff any comment with her usual acidic humour.

'It is odd, really.' He sighed. 'We're all coming home, in a way.' There were several nods around the table at this. 'We could have stopped by Hedeby,' he added, flicking a glance at Gunnhild once more.

'There was no need,' she replied dismissively. 'I know the fate of Hedeby. My teacher is gone, her house flattened and a nailed god temple in its place. But that insult matters not, for before a twelveyear has passed, the whole place will burn and Hedeby will be gone, a fate that I fear also faces this place. I have no need to visit, and no interest in doing so. I am home wherever I am with the Wolves.'

12

More nods, something that made Halfdan smile. 'I will visit *my* home,' he said, 'for it lies in our path.' He glanced round at Bjorn, who was busy smacking the heads of two men together in a doorway while Ketil tried to kick the men as they flailed. 'I don't know whether Bjorn ever had a home, but if he did, I don't think he would ever go back. And Ketil? Well, we know he's from Iceland, but he never speaks of it. I have the feeling he left there for a good reason. Ulfr...' he added, turning back.

'Ulfr will see his home again soon enough,' the shipwright said. 'I am a Sigtun man, born and bred, and it is there we must sail to find your kings.'

Past Ulfr, Halfdan could see two men walking toward their table. One he knew as the owner of this mead hall, and the other was big and beefy, scarred, and carrying a stout length of ash. A bodyguard? Muscle of some kind. Halfdan readied himself for trouble, checking his weapons. The men reached their table and came to a halt.

'You need to put a stop to this,' the owner said, his finger jabbing in the direction of the fighting.

'It would be easier to hold back the tide with a stick than to put a stop to a fight when those two have their blood up,' Halfdan replied with a wry smile, relaxing a little. As he spoke, his hand was dipping into the pouch at his belt, and in moments he had dropped five Byzantine coins to the wooden tabletop. 'This should cover any damage or inconvenience.'

To his credit, the owner wavered for a moment, hungry eyes on the coins, but then he shook his head. 'This is no sailor's dive, and these men of Torpstrand were here first, with good money. I am trying to run a high-class establishment here. Men of influence come to my hall, and I have a reputation to maintain. Three times already I have seen customers approach my door, but leave when they see what is happening inside. Your coins are not enough when you are costing me important custom. Call your jötnar off. Stop the fight, or I will have to ask you all to leave.'

Brave man, Halfdan thought. He looked around. Six tables of the eleven in the mead hall were occupied by men of the Wolves, all armed and all armoured. Quite apart from the danger of annoying them, the man would lose a lot of business kicking them out. Of course, three of those tables had been full of this crew from Torpstrand, too...

Halfdan looked up at the barman, then tipped several more coins out. 'I will stop it, but it will not be pretty. Take the coins.'

The owner of the hall nodded his acceptance as Halfdan rose from his chair. The fight had been inevitable. Bjorn and Ketil had been at the bar, deciding what to drink, when the men of Torpstrand had taken offence at the Mjǫllnir pendants hanging around their necks, and the mouthiest had made sure the cross at his own throat was visible when he called them a few choice names. Halfdan had sighed at the man's lack of foresight just as Bjorn had turned, without speaking a word, and thumped the man so hard on the top of the head he collapsed in a heap, unconscious in an instant. Then the man's friends had got involved, chairs scraping back as they all rose from their tables. Several of the Wolves had made to rise, too, but Halfdan had waved them all to sit down. There was no need to turn this into a mass brawl. As the fight broke out properly, the rest of the Torpstrand men had joined in, but still the rest of the Wolves had stayed seated. It was rarely a good idea to interrupt Bjorn and Ketil when they were enjoying themselves.

But the owner wanted it stopped, and there was only one way to stop a fight when Bjorn was involved, and that was to win it.

He looked around. Half a dozen bodies lay strewn across the open floor near the hall's door, none of them dead, but some probably wishing they were. There was a fair amount of blood and a few teeth and clumps of hair in evidence amid the rush mats, and perhaps half the losers were still vaguely conscious, groaning and rolling around. There were only four of them still upright, two struggling to get out of Bjorn's meaty grasp, and the other two lurking in a corner, deep in discussion, pointing at Ketil and planning as the Icelander continued to kick the pair in Bjorn's grip.

The jarl saw the gleam of a blade then, as one of the pair in the corner unsheathed a sax. Thus far, this had been a 'friendly' fight, with no weapons. To draw a sax meant a serious escalation, and would probably lead to Bjorn and Ketil brandishing their axes, at which point a punch-up would become a blood-bath, and they would all run the risk of Bjorn surrendering to the berserk. Halfdan moved quickly. Around him, the Wolves made to rise again, but Leif waved them back down, all but Gunnhild, who was at the jarl's heel even as he moved.

'That would be a bad idea,' Halfdan said to the two men, pointing at the naked blade.

The man snarled. 'Heathen dogs.'

'*Wolves*,' Halfdan said with an odd smile. 'Not dogs. Wolves.'

Even as he spoke, Gunnhild lifted her staff and jabbed out with it, past her jarl. The butt-end slammed into the arm holding the sax. It fell from his fingers and skittered across the floor. Even as the man yelped, Halfdan was on him. His hand went to the bare head, gripping a handful of hair. He yanked the head forward as his knee came up, and the two connected with a bony clonk. Given the shock to Halfdan's knee, he could only imagine how it had felt in the man's head. Still, as his leg lowered once more, and the man's head wobbled in his grip, he now slammed it backward, into the wall. He let go, and the man staggered a couple of steps, a massive red welt on his forehead and a gleaming patch of fresh blood on the back of his scalp. The man dropped and fell still, and Halfdan turned in time to see Gunnhild smash the other fellow in the cheek with a swing of her staff, sending him flying sideways, more teeth joining those scattered across the floor. The man reeled against the wall, whimpering, and then fell in a heap.

The jarl turned again, and the fight was over. Bjorn was still holding those two men, but now they were clearly uncon-scious as he continued to clonk their heads together. Ketil was arguing with him about keeping all the fun for himself, an argument which Bjorn answered with a wall-shaking fart that only incensed the Icelander more.

'Drop them,' Halfdan said to the big albino. Bjorn turned in surprise, saw his jarl, looked back to the pair of unconscious warriors in his hands, and did just that, shrugging.

Halfdan walked back over to the table, where the mead hall's owner remained, looking distinctly unhappy, his bruiser still at his side, the coins still on the table.

'There you go. It's over.'

'Out, all of you,' the owner commanded, lip curling as he pointed at the door.

'We still have gold to spend, drinks to drink, and tales to tell,' Halfdan replied.

'Then do it elsewhere.'

Halfdan thought about refusing, about arguing, but decided against it. The place was starting to smell of blood and piss from the various unconscious bodies anyway. 'Wolves, time to leave,' he called, grabbing his cloak that lay draped over the back of the chair. Opening the door he found that the clouds, which had been clustered over eastern Daneland that afternoon, had dispersed, leaving a clear blue sky and a warm sea breeze. It was too late to think about sailing today, but they would depart first thing in the morning, he decided. Behind him, the others exited the building, assembling in the street, as locals passed by, taking a wide berth to avoid the armed and armoured strangers.

'What now?' Leif asked.

'Now we find ourselves another place to relax. There's plenty of evening left yet, and we still have to eat. But I think we might want to put a limit on the drinking, else there will be a lot of sore heads in the morning when I call the Wolves to their oars.'

'Where are we bound, then?' Ketil asked, wiping blood from his knuckles.

Halfdan raised his face to the sky, took a deep breath of summer air, inflected with the salty tang of the sea, and rolled

16

his shoulders. 'In the morning, to Gotland, my home. And then Sweden, and a meeting of kings.'

Chapter 2

Leif waited as the last two men finished tying off the ropes and leapt ashore, and then looked about him, up and down the coastline and at the two moored vessels. It was unusual, possibly even a first, for him to be the last to disembark the *Sea Dragon*, as it had been with the *Sea Wolf* before that. The last ashore was almost always Ulfr, for their ships were his children, and he found it hard to leave them even for a night. The man's devotion to his ships made Leif smile indulgently, as did all the ways of his pagan friends. Some Christians treated them as demons, or as the enemy, or at the *least* as misguided fools. To Leif, they were echoes of a world fast vanishing, but a world he found fascinating and had studied during his young life in Kiev. Not that he was *always* comfortable with being surrounded by it, but he was more accepting than most.

Even now, the Wolves' heathen ways informed and guided almost everything they did. The *Sea Dragon* had departed the Danish island of Sjáland with the morning tide, employing the oars to carry them along the wide and open fjord and out to sea. The crew grinned as they worked, for they were moving at a leisurely pace, not putting their all into the rowing, since behind them the other half of Halfdan's hirð laboured along in the troublesome *Sea Cow*, working twice as hard to move half as fast. Every man aboard that fat, slow vessel yearned to reach their goal, for they'd been told that the fastest and sleekest hunter in the world waited for them there.

Once out into the blue-black waters of the Jótlandshaf, they had turned east and south, sailing past the coast of Skáney, where Daneland met the land of the Swedes and Geats and the passage at its narrowest was little more than two miles across. Over a couple of days they sailed down and round the southern tip of the Scanian Peninsula, now heading east toward the great cold sea and their first destination, Halfdan's home on the island of Gotland.

Or at least, that had been the plan.

Then Ulfr had changed it. Before they left the Scanian coast, there was a place Ulfr wanted to go, and such was his insistence that he had easily got his way. Thus it was that they had stopped here, on a windy, dry day under a bleak blue sky, seemingly in the middle of nowhere, and thus Ulfr had been the first to depart the boat for a change.

There had been a bit of a kerfuffle with the landing. The *Sea Dragon* was an old-fashioned Norse-style raiding and trading ship, shallow beamed, and could be beached safely to disembark. The *Sea Cow* was a different beast entirely, and had been forced to anchor a hundred paces from the empty, wind-blasted shore, and any who wished to join them on land had to remove their armour and weapons and dive into the water, swimming to meet the others. A few had chosen to do so. More had chosen to stay aboard the *Sea Cow* and wait.

Leif looked up. All along this coast was a reasonable, if short, beach, upon which to land, and then a terrain of hard grass that began as a shallow incline, gradually steepening into a slope. That slope only just stopped short of becoming a cliff some thirty or forty feet above them, where it seemed to plateau. What was up there, Leif was yet to learn, although there were clues. It had been referred to as Ales stennar, which, with his reasonable command of Old Norse, he knew to mean 'Ale's stones', and the fact that Ulfr had wanted to stop here suggested something powerfully pagan, of religious significance, and perhaps related to the sea, given Ulfr's vehemence.

As Leif dropped from the ship to the gravel beach with a crunch, and began to cross it and then climb the grassy slope in the wake of the others, he found himself musing on this strangely ancient pagan world, and on his place in it.

'You look like you're trying to squeeze out a fart, but you're worried it'll be a shit,' said a big, booming voice, and Leif looked up from his musing to see that Bjorn had stopped and waited for him.

'I was contemplating life, and my place in it,' Leif admitted, aware that with his big friend, such statements could often lead to ribbing.

'You think too much. I wonder if that's why you're short. You spent too much time thinking to grow.'

'That's not how it works, Bjorn.'

'Why not?'

Leif rolled his eyes. There was not enough time in the world to explain that in detail to Bjorn. Instead, he re-routed the conversation. 'There has been much talk of homecomings, since we reached Hróarskelda. Halfdan is going home soon, and we have passed Gunnhild's Hedeby, and were in her homeland for a time. Ulfr comes from Sigtun, so he will be in his childhood domain when we finish this journey. Ketil is a special case, of course, and you, I suspect, have not had a home as such for most of your life. The others joined us because their homes in Swaledale have gone, or their lives had become moot in their land of origin. I am the odd one out, Bjorn.'

As they laboured up the slope behind the others, he was impressed. Bjorn was nodding, not taking the piss. Perhaps the subject had more meaning for Bjorn than he'd realised.

'Odd how?' the big man said.

'I had a home that I was happy in. I was comfortable. And even though we sailed away from it, we sailed south to lands I knew well, and a world I understood: a land of my own people, who pray to the Christos. But now, the further we go, the further I am from everything familiar. What is home to you is the furthest removed from it to me. I am so out of my depth I am forced to tread water all the time. Do you follow me?'

Bjorn nodded. 'And you want to go home? To the Rus? To Miklagarðr?'

That stopped Leif for a moment, and Bjorn rumbled to a halt and waited. Finally, the Rus started walking again. 'That is something of a puzzle, my big friend. I may have changed too much for home. I do not think I would fit with Kiev any more. I think I would be bored, and crave adventure. Besides, I cannot see Anna being happy among the Rus. But to return to the Golden City? For much of my life that would have been my dream: to live in Constantinopolis. But I'm not sure the city is safe for us now. With Monomachos on the throne, I think our lives would be forfeit the moment our feet touched the dock. And again, I am not convinced Anna would be happy there now. She was a poor nobody in the great city until she met Gunnhild, and now she is respected, loved, even revered among the Wolves. Would she give that up?'

He sighed, stumping up the slope. 'So you see, I am not sure I have a place in *any* world now. My place has been with the Wolves, and I have been content with that since the beaches of Apulia. But now the Wolves are coming home, will there be any place *there* for me? I am troubled, Bjorn.'

There was a series of odd noises from his friend, and Leif grinned as he realised it was because Bjorn was rummaging down the front of his trousers while he thought. He continued to do so when he began to speak.

'Wherever Halfdan and his hirð go, little Rus, there will always be a brotherhood. If I thought otherwise, I would have left already. My place is with Halfdan, and with the Wolves. So is yours. And one day you'll forget this stupid notion of one god and give old One-eye his due.'

Again, Leif laughed. Sometimes it took the simplistic view of a man like Bjorn to cut away the chaff of complex emotion. If he could *not* find a permanent home with the Wolves, it would be the big albino he would miss most.

Before they could explore the subject further, though, they crested the slope, and Leif suddenly understood why they were here.

Atop the hill, the slope gave way to a wide and gentle land of green grass with a few scattered stands of trees, and a small village perhaps half a mile away. But here, close to the edge and towering above the sea, was a monument seemingly as old as time itself. Perhaps sixty stones, each at least the height of a man, stretched out to form the shape of a ship, some seventy paces long, parallel with the coast. It was a breathtaking monument, and Leif shivered.

He knew that Gunnhild felt *Seiðr*, a sort of magical aura, which pervaded some places, and Anna had told him that she too had felt it, despite her being a faithful daughter of the Church. Truth be told, Leif had thought he had felt it *himself* from time to time, and if what he had encountered that made him shiver *was* Gunnhild's Seiðr, then he had never felt it as strongly as he felt it here. There was something otherworldly at work here, and Leif would happily admit that he doubted Christianity had ever laid claim to this place. For the first time in a while, he felt a pang of uneasiness in the presence of the old world.

'What *is* this?' he asked, quietly, awe-struck.

Ulfr, standing close by, turned with a frown, as though he couldn't understand why Leif did not know.

'This,' he said, 'is the stones of Ale. I have sailed past them a few times in my life, but never had the opportunity to visit.'

'But what *is* it?'

'It is said that in the times of our ancestors, when the mountains were young, and Yggdrasil grew green and youthful, that the men of Skáney built this stone ship as a homage to Skíðblaðnir, Freyr's own vessel, the best ship in all the nine worlds. A ship that could be folded up like a scarf and put in the god's purse. The only ship,' he added with a grin, 'better than mine. This place is sacred to Freyr, but also to those of us whose destiny is tied to the whale road. To the world of the dragon boat.'

Again, Leif shivered. Freyr, brother of Freyja, two powerful gods of the Vanir in his friends' worldview. He instinctively glanced across at Gunnhild, and was not surprised to see a look of oddly serene reverence on her handsome face. This was as close to a cathedral for the *völva* as anything could be.

'It will do us all well to pay our respects here,' Halfdan said, loudly enough to be heard by all. 'The favour of the Vanir as well as of the Æsir can only be of importance when we hunt and sail.'

Leif nodded to himself at that. Whether Freyr be a god as Halfdan believed, a demon as they taught back in Kiev, or something in between, it would probably do no harm to appease him.

Halfdan gestured to Ulfr, and the shipwright moved into the stone vessel, examining the grass beneath his feet. Leif wondered what the man was looking for, but whatever it was, he seemed to find it perhaps a third of the way from the ship's bow, roughly central between the two sides. Marking the spot with the toe of his boot, he turned back to them. 'A sacrifice is called for, to Freyr, and to his golden sister.'

At this, Gunnhild turned, nodding. 'Ketil, take your bow and a couple of Wolves, and bring us an animal worthy of a god. Bjorn, Farlof and Eygrímr, find wood for a fire. Beech wood for preference, birch or hazel if not. Make sure enough of it is dry to burn. The gods like a fire, not a smouldering smoke pile.'

The men dispersed about their tasks, leaving the others standing in the billowing wind at the stone ship. Leif looked up. Without his having really noticed it, the blue sky of late afternoon in which they had arrived had slid into the mauve of early evening. And in this part of the world at this time of year, dark fell quickly, he'd already noted. After a time, waiting for all to be ready, Anna wandered over and stood beside him, taking his hand in hers.

23

'Are you comfortable with this?' he asked quietly.

She shrugged. 'I have come to terms with much in my work with Gunnhild. She persists under the illusion that she serves Freyja, without ever realising that her goddess is the Theotokos, mother of Christ, and that all her magicks are but the miraculous bounties of God.'

'God seems to take an inordinate amount of interest in poking people in the eye with a pointy staff, then.'

She gave him a strange look. 'You're in an odd mood tonight, my love?'

He was. He wasn't sure why. The sense of not belonging had been building for some time, the more time they had spent in this strange northern world of Halfdan's. He wondered at times how much of it was in his own head, struggling to come to terms with how things had changed over a few short years, but even then, tonight he was feeling it deeply. 'I think it's this place. Or at least, this place, and how disorientated I feel this far north. I think I'm just generally uncomfortable. This place and all that is happening is just a part of it.'

Anna squeezed his hand. 'I know precisely what it is, Leif. You are not useful here.'

'Thanks,' he replied, drily.

'I am not joking. When we were in the south, the Wolves needed your knowledge and your wits for their very survival. They relied upon you. And even when we moved up into the domain of the bastard Duke of Nordmandi, you were able to unpick the politics for them. But then things changed. We moved into *their* world. I have felt it too, for don't forget that I am a daughter of empire. Over in Angle Land, they were among their own, *fighting* their own. They did not need your languages, your wits and knowledge, your ability to discern the hidden things of the world. And the more we move into their world, the more familiar they are with it, and the less and less they seem to need your talents.'

'You really are *excelling* as a comfort tonight, my love.'

She gave him a playful punch on the shoulder. 'But that's the problem. You think you're done. You're not. You have the most agile mind of any man I've known. Don't feel useless. Choose not to. Adapt. Learn the ways of these places, of these people. Gunnhild has always been Halfdan's wisdom, and I think Bjorn is his strength, Ulfr his seamanship, and Ketil his speed, but you have always been his wits. His knowledge. He will always need you, just as I do.'

He smiled weakly at her. 'It sounds easy. But when you were brought up in the arms of Mother Church, this place, and the ways of our friends, are so utterly alien.'

'So was the Greek language when you were born in Kiev, yet when I first met you, you spoke it so well, I assumed you were a local. You have a talent. Learn. Become accustomed. Treat our friends as I do, as lost lambs who will eventually find their way back to God. *Powerful* lambs, I'll grant you, but you know what I mean.'

He laughed. He could only picture the faces of their friends if they heard themselves referred to as lost lambs. He subsided finally. 'I can cope with most of what we do, and offerings certainly seem a reasonable sign of respect, but I'm never comfortable with sacrifice.'

She shrugged. 'We eat the flesh and blood of Christos with every mass, do we not? And did Jacob not offer a sacrifice to God?'

Still, he stood stiff, not quite at ease, as Ketil returned with a young red fawn over his shoulder, and the others brought a collection of beech logs and kindling, some fresh-hewn, others old, seasoned, fallen wood. Gunnhild led a murmured prayer to Freyr, joined by all the non-Christian voices present, as Halfdan, being jarl here, strung the young deer from the highest stone at the ship's prow, and cut its throat, letting it bleed to the god. They stood fully half an hour, that same unearthly murmured litany flowing out across the stones over and over, as the last of the blood dripped from the animal. Then Bjorn lit the small

25

fire they had built over the spot marked by Ulfr, and the animal was burned. All through this, as the Old Norse tongue rose to the evening sky in reverence to ancient gods, Leif comforted himself by repeating the Lord's Prayer under his breath, in its appropriate Greek, of course. As the carcass rendered swiftly to ash, the Wolves of Odin sat around the flames and drank and toasted one another, chatted and made plans. By the time the fire had burned low and even the golden heart of embers had faded, the purple of evening had become the black of night.

Finally, Halfdan rose and crossed the circle to Gunnhild, who was seated beside Anna, two bodies to Leif's left.

'This place is powerful, yes?' he asked. 'Buried in Seiðr, I think?'

She nodded. 'There is power here, and it is closer to Freyja than most.'

'Will you... walk with the goddess here?'

She arched an eyebrow. 'You have questions?'

He gave her a knowing smile. 'We are on the hunt, as befits Wolves, and we hunt that most hated of all prey, the priest Hjalmvigi. But it troubles me that every oar stroke east takes us further from him.' He saw her straightening, ready to argue, and waved his hands. 'I know. You explained it all, and it does make sense, but it must be worth being sure that our plan follows what the Norns and the gods have laid out for us. Better that we know, and do not walk into nasty surprises.'

Gunnhild looked for a moment as though she might argue, but finally nodded. 'Very well.' She rose to her feet and pointed at the pile of ash and black bones in the centre of the stone ship. 'Someone dispose of those for me.'

Leif clambered to his feet and scurried across, carrying the square of old sail cloth he'd been sitting on. In moments, he was shovelling the warm remains onto the square and then folding it, enclosing them, and lifting it. He knew that most of them would simply scatter the bones to the elements now, for once the animal had been bled and burned, Freyr would have no

26

further use for it. But Leif had other plans. Carrying the bundle, he left the stones, walking away from the Wolves, toward the sea. It was not that he couldn't watch Gunnhild at her weird ways, and he'd done it plenty of times before, but this time it felt different. There was a power about this place that was making him uncomfortable. He'd felt it from the moment he arrived, and it had only made him twitch more and more as the sacrifice had been made. It would make him a little less uncomfortable to let Gunnhild's rituals go on without him. As such, he strolled out into the evening, until he was fairly close to the cliff edge, and then knelt and went to work. Using his sax, he cut a square of turf some foot and a half across, then dug under it and lifted it to one side. Then he hacked out the stony earth below and used his cupped hands to lift it and move it aside until he had a small and shallow pit.

All the time, as he worked, he felt a strange frisson of weirdness creep across his skin at the distant sound of Gunnhild singing her ancient song of power, Anna's own tones joining in from time to time in a strange harmony.

He hoped that, someday, he would feel as oddly comfortable in the presence of the old religion as his Anna. She really was a marvel. But then, she had found ways to attribute everything the Wolves did to an aspect of the divine trinity, shrugging off their pagan words as a misunderstanding of what were acts of divine grace. He smiled at that as he worked.

In no time, he had the pit ready and had dropped into it the pile of ash and bones, topping it up with some of the earth and then replacing the turf square on the surface. The deer hardly needed a proper burial, but somehow it gave Leif a little comfort that he had made this small gesture rather than attending a pagan rite. That was still going on, as was clear from the lilting song becoming ever stronger, weaving out across the evening sky like the tapestry in which Gunnhild put such stock.

His work done, Leif decided to take a short walk while the ritual was being finished. He strolled east, enjoying the battering wind on these heights above the sea, making sure to stay far enough from the edge that no sudden gust could carry him over and send him careening down the steep slope back toward the boats. He passed beyond the stern end of the stone ship, and paused there.

Ahead lay that small village, lights twinkling amid the black shapes of the houses beneath a dark sky. But, for a moment, he'd seen movement. He stopped, watching, and saw it again. Then: more movement. In the poor light it was hard to make out precisely what was going on, but then he realised the lights themselves were moving. He saw it clear, then. The villagers were coming. They had left their houses, carrying torches, and were walking in the direction of the monument. A sense of foreboding stole across him.

Were they God-fearing Christians or staunch pagans? Whatever the case, their numbers – a score or so – when combined with the waving torches, suggested anger or violence. He wavered, almost shouting a warning to the Wolves, but not entirely sure what it was he would be warning them about. Instead, he hurried back toward the end of the stone ship, moving into a position directly between the approaching villagers and the Wolves. Somehow he felt this had to be *his* task. Should these locals be left to approach the Wolves of Odin while the crew were engaged in their pagan rites and Gunnhild in the middle of her magicks, there was a good chance that violence would erupt. Bjorn, at least, would not wait to tear someone's arm off, and Ketil would be close behind.

Taking a steadying breath, he began to march in the direction of the approaching villagers. As he closed on them, getting ever further from the stone ship, he did begin to wonder about the wisdom of his actions. Still, he kept his axe and sax in his belt, remaining unprovocative. There were maybe twenty of them, while there were more than twice as many of Leif's crew up in the stone ship, and while these were probably farmers and villagers, the Wolves were warriors all, children of the cold rock, hardened by battle. If these people really were bent on confrontation, he decided, it would go very badly for them.

As he neared, and they became aware of him, the villagers slowed, and by the time he reached them, they had stopped, and fanned out into an arc, facing him. Half a dozen had torches, the rest were carrying staves or cudgels, further suggesting violent intent.

'Good evening,' he said, treating them to a calculated warm smile, which they did not return at all.

'Who is he?' someone asked.

'Dunno, but he's not local.'

'A Rus, I reckon,' another said.

Leif blinked in surprise that a farmer from rural Skáney would even recognise the Rus. 'Quite right,' he replied. 'I am Leif Ruriksson, of Kiev and formerly of the Varangian Guard in Miklagarðr. You know of the Rus?'

The man who'd spoken stepped out front. 'Rus merchants in Lund, from time to time. Weird accent. Mostly sell shit.'

Leif let the insults glance off him, for now, and bowed his head.

'I can only apologise if my friends are making too much noise and disturbing your night. I can assure you it is almost over.'

'Shouldn't be up there,' a woman said. 'Bad place that. Heathen. Devils at work there.' The woman's eyes narrowed. 'Devils at work *right now*, I reckon.'

Leif tried a disarming smile. 'Come now, good woman, my friends are just honouring the spirits of the place.'

'Devils,' the woman said again, and spat.

'Not all the ways of your ancestors are the work of the devil,' Leif replied, reaching up and moving aside the brooch that held his cloak in place so they could see the silver cross at his throat, gleaming in their torchlight.

There was a strange silence for a moment, as they took in his apparent Christianity.

'That is *heathen* work,' someone persisted.

Leif rounded on the speaker, a small woman with a face like a shrivelled prune. 'They honour the Theotokos,' he lied, glibly, trying not to remember that such skills were what had earned him the nickname 'Leif the Teeth'. He noted their bafflement, and remembered that these men and women followed the *Roman* Church, not his own. 'Maria, the mother of God. They honour her, for a priestess, a nun of sorts, leads their devotions. And while they honour the Mother, they also pay homage to the spirits of Ales stennar, and those who built this place.'

'Heathens.'

The woman would not let the subject drop.

'Have you so little regard for your forefathers?' Leif snapped, surprising himself suddenly. 'For your ancestors? Your own people? Those who carved a world out of rock and ice for you and your children? If not, do you at least follow the *commandments of your God*?' He was suddenly unaccountably angry, and it clearly showed in his tone, for the arc of locals recoiled from him. 'I,' he said, 'have studied the laws of God in our own Church of the east, and of your Romish Church of the west. And do you know what? I even read the sacred texts of the Jews, and of the Serks, far to the south, whose view of God is but a twist from our own, and all of us... *all of us*... have the same commandment: honour your father and your mother. I am *baffled* that you cannot see the importance of this monument in your own world, and that you would shun such a place. I am *incensed*!'

'God's work,' a villager began, hefting his club and taking a step forward, '*must* be done.'

'And it *will*,' Leif snarled as he grabbed the club, yanking it out of the man's hand before smacking him hard around the shoulder with it. 'God's work *will* be done. God's work is *forgiveness*. God's work is *understanding*. Do you not know your own holy book? Did Luke not tell us "Love your enemies: do good to them that hate you, bless them that curse you; pray for them that insult you. To him that smites thee on the cheek offer the other also"?'

As that man recoiled, rejoining his friends, Leif took a step forward. His thumb jerked over his shoulder up at the stone ship. 'Those people, my friends, are warriors and raiders like your ancestors of old. They could easily have come here with fire and sword. But they didn't. They came to honour an ancient place of your people, and to pray for guidance and help. And they left you to sleep in your beds. Have you any idea how *precious* that is? The things I have seen across the world, where man kills his brother for little more than a cross word? I see you, people of Skáney. I *see you*, and I tell you now that if you press this matter, each of you will die, hard. And each of you will suffer. And because those men and women atop that hill mean you neither harm nor insult, only the flames of Hell await you if you do so. Now turn around, go back to your homes and remember the words of your God, and remember those who came before you, and who gave their lives to grant you what you have.'

A few of the locals began to disperse. One who remained longer than most was the one Leif had hit on the arm. He realised he still held the man's cudgel, and smacked him with it again.

'Go!'

They fled.

Leif watched them disappear back through the dark toward their houses, and as he did so, he breathed heavily, trying to fight the urge to throw the club after them. Was this what it felt like to be Bjorn?

Something struck him suddenly. He had saved the Wolves. Oh, not from disaster. They would have won the fight anyway, and easily. But he had saved them from *needing* to. And he had saved them from killing people who did not deserve it. Moreover, he had saved those same people. Perhaps Anna was right. He did have a place in this strange northern world, after all.

31

He almost jumped his full body height when a big hand landed on his shoulder.

'Shit!'

Bjorn grinned.

'I think that's the first time I've ever seen you properly lose your temper.'

Leif frowned, twitched. 'How long were you watching me?'

'Since the moment you marched down to meet them.' Halfdan grinned. 'Gunnhild had already returned to us. You are a man of constant surprises, Leif of Kiev.'

He tried not to blush. How much had they heard? How much had they *understood*?

'What did Gunnhild learn?' he asked, changing tack to save face.

The völva gave him an unbearably knowing smile. 'I see three bears, Leif Ruriksson: a black bear, a brown bear and a golden bear. They fight to bring down a great white bear. But that is not the important part of the threads the goddess revealed. The bears struggle and fight for their victory, but it is not truly they who win. The real winners are the wolves who come after, who find the dead white bear and eat well without having to fight for it. You understand this, Leif of Kiev?'

He did. He smiled. 'Kings will fight among themselves. All the Wolves must do is wait and pick over the carcass, yes?'

'That is correct, my friend,' Gunnhild said. 'We will make a Seiðr user of you yet.'

And *that* made him shiver more than anything else that day.

Chapter 3

Halfdan looked back at the smoke hanging over the distant sprawl of buildings as they vanished into the haze behind them.

'I thought you *came* from Visby?' Farlof asked.

'I lived there for a while,' Halfdan replied. 'Until I was old enough to leave, anyway, but that was not where it all happened. I'm not even sure my home *has* a name. It was always just "the village" when I was a boy.'

The closer they came to the place where his childhood had ended, the less sure he was that he really wanted to go there. As they rode, whenever his mind drifted, it was struck by images of that day. Of Yngvar. Of the Odin stone being pulled over. Of houses burning and men and women dying. Of his father, defiant and proud to the end.

Of Hjalmvigi…

'Sometimes no good comes of wallowing in the past,' Leif advised, as if reading Halfdan's thoughts.

'And sometimes things need confronting in order for endings to be reached,' Gunnhild snapped, glaring at the Rus.

They all fell blessedly silent then, for a while, as they rode. There were only eight of them, the rest of the Wolves remaining with the ships at Visby harbour, ready to move on at a moment's notice. The heart of the Wolves came though, Halfdan and his closest companions, who had been sailing with him since the day he began to hunt Yngvar and started the blood feud, the whole cycle of vengeance that seemed set to end in the coming days. But also Farlof, who had been with them so long now that he might as well have been chiselled from the rock of the north and set among the Wolves from the start. And Eygrímr, a recent companion since Swaledale, but a man of Old Norse roots and as fitting a Wolf as any warrior, fast becoming one of Halfdan's closest men. Eight of them, only. But then, he was not expecting trouble. They had no horses of their own, of course, for ferrying horses on their ships would be impractical, but given the distances, they had bought animals in Visby, with a view to selling them again upon their return.

It took hours of travel, for these animals were not the sort used for fighting or distance riding, but slow farm horses, yet at least they were calm and good-natured. Still, the afternoon was already wearing on when Halfdan began to recognise signs of the land of his youth.

The draugr tree. He and his friends had come up with so many stories and theories about that tree when herding cattle a few miles from the village. It had never had leaves as long as he could remember, and looked like the hand of a skeleton of gnarled brown, reaching up from the turf, imploringly, at the grey sky. It was clearly a jötunn, a giant buried beneath the earth, reaching up for freedom.

He shivered. He'd always shivered at the sight as a child, and though it might seem odd to do so now as a grown adult, he still could not help but feel that same fear and power. He was not encouraged to see Gunnhild looking at the tree with narrowed eyes, as though she, too, saw more than was clearly there.

The fallow field. For some reason Asa the farmer had never put animals in it. For as long as he could remember, that field had only ever been lush grass. Why, he couldn't imagine.

The rocks of Hrungnir. A small formation that somehow resembled the pointed heart of that fabled giant.

The start of the mill race.

That meant they were close to the village. And yet there was nothing of it to see. He frowned. He should be able to see buildings from here, or the grove in which sacrifices were hung. The village had been burned, and it had been years — even the ash scattered to the winds by now — but somehow he'd expected it to have been rebuilt, reoccupied by the survivors, while Halfdan had been dragged away to live with his uncle in Visby.

Of course, he'd never gone home again.

Until now.

His sense of foreboding and unease grew steadily as they closed on the site of his childhood home. The small wooden bridge was still there. He remembered it well. He had sat beneath that bridge as a boy, pretending to be a troll to frighten Aife when she brought apples back to her mother. Whatever had happened to the rest of the place, the bridge had survived.

Little else had.

The houses were all gone. In fact, it was impossible even to identify where they had been, for the few stones and timbers that remained had been overgrown by grass and weeds and shrubs, and it was hard to tell any such remnants from the natural landscape. If he closed his eyes, he could see the houses, though, picture his home as it had been. It hurt. He'd not expected that. He had left Gotland and sought vengeance, and he'd inured himself to this loss, even from boyhood. He'd not expected actual pain at the sight of his childhood, gone.

His gaze strayed around the scene, and he stopped at a small copse of young trees. Not the old oaks and beech that had been the focus of the village's devotions when he was a boy, but new, young trees. And amid them, a stone.

His breath caught in his throat at the sight, for he recognised the shape. He knew that stone. Before he realised what he was doing, he was leaping off his horse and running across the open ground. He reached the stone and peered at it, eyes wide. He couldn't stop himself. His hands reached out, fingers dusting it, tracing the shapes.

It was so heartbreakingly familiar.

The Odin stone.

It had been damaged. The carvings on it had been hacked at roughly, and defaced, but someone had slowly, carefully, over a great deal of time, used rough tools to put the carvings back. They were far from perfect, little more than a child's scribbles, but someone had put the effort and devotion into restoring the stone as best they could, and that was worth more than all the great art in the world. More than the graceful columns of Miklagarðr, than the intricate tapestries of the castles of Nordmandi, than the bright paintings of Apulia. Because it was not well done, but it was done with care and love. Someone who respected the Allfather had done whatever was in their power to put things right.

He looked down on instinct. There were tracks. A single set of footprints, wandering hither and thither, with periodic holes as though the track-maker had been leaning on a spear.

He felt something wholly Seiðr and beyond the world of men, and turned to the thickest area of trees.

'Come out,' he said.

He was vaguely aware that his seven companions had led their horses close and some had dismounted, wandering across to stand behind him. He did not look round. Instead, he watched the faint movement of undergrowth as a figure moved through it.

The man emerged a moment later. His shirt and trousers were stained and rough, of low quality, his boots ancient and in need of replacing. His hair was wild, unbraided, and uncombed, as was his beard. He leaned on a staff some five feet long, just a straight shaft of timber, explaining the marks in the muddy ground.

His eyes were white. No pupils looked out of them.

Blind.

But none of these things were what Halfdan's attention was fixed upon.

He felt his heart flutter, his stomach freeze, his bowels loosen a little. He shivered.

36

'Ømund?'

It had been a lifetime since Halfdan had stood in this place, between his life in Visby, such as it was, his wanderings in Sweden, and then his travels across the world with the Wolves. He'd known his village was gone. He'd not expected any remains. And he would not have recognised even this one man had it not been for the pendant around his neck. It was old, and stained, and slightly damaged and worn, as carved beech wood gets when left for decades. But it was still the small, bearded, one-eyed face Halfdan had carved with a small knife during months of droving, all for his best friend's seventh birthday.

The man frowned, a strange and eerie thing with his feature-less white eyes.

'You know this man?' Leif asked from behind.

'He has the workings of Seiðr about him,' Gunnhild added, her voice strange.

'Who is that?' the man asked.

Halfdan turned to his friends. 'On the day Yngvar stole my life, and Hjalmvigi destroyed my world, I was hiding under a friend's porch. There were a few of us. Ømund and I had been stealing apples and were very pleased with ourselves. Yet we hid there, and we watched, as the priest-bastard and his pet jarl killed everyone and burned the village.'

'Not everyone, apparently,' Leif noted.

'Halfdan?' The man with the blind, white eyes, took a step toward him, free hand stretching out, coming up, fingers feeling the air. 'Halfdan Vigholfsson?'

'*That's* your name?' Bjorn said, brow creased. 'Not Loki-born.'

Halfdan ignored the interruption, concentrating on his friend. 'Ømund, what happened to you?'

The man's fingers found Halfdan, and were crawling across his face then, as though feeling for anything familiar. Halfdan let him work, despite the discomfort.

'You have changed.'

'It's been half a life, Ømund. Of course I've changed. So have you.'

'I sent a message once. Years ago. To Visby. They said your uncle was dead, and that no one could be found there.'

'I had moved on,' Halfdan said, an odd thrill of guilt suddenly there.

'Gotland is changing,' Ømund said. 'Our world is going. I save what I can.'

'You are to be commended,' Halfdan replied. 'You have worked to preserve our world while I have done nothing but settle for petty revenge.'

'There is nothing petty about revenge. I had a dream,' Ømund said oddly. 'One night, when the Seiðr swirled like the eddies of the stream, I had a dream, sent by Freyr. I saw two draugar, crumbling and diseased. And I saw one die, riven from within, falling apart as though his body was broken and ruined from the heart. But the white draugr I saw laughing and coming on. I woke before it killed me. But that day, my sight was taken from me.'

Halfdan shivered again. He turned to Gunnhild, who nodded, so he explained to his old friend. 'I killed Yngvar... the man who killed my father. I chased him to the end of the world, and I killed him. I made sure that even then, he could never sit in Odin's hall. The white draugr, I think, is the priest that drove him to it. Hjalmvigi remains in this world. But I am already on the hunt, and the priest is set before my arrow. In the coming days, everyone who did this will have paid the price.'

Ømund gave him an odd smile. 'That will be good. I remember the priest. I knew him for a sour apple at first sight. But Halfdan, that will not change the world. Even your revenge complete will not change it all. The cross of the nailed god looms over all the land. You have a hirð of your own now. I can sense them, if I cannot see them. You are a jarl?'

Halfdan shrugged. 'I am counted a jarl, though no king has made me so.'

38

'It is in the blood and the spirit,' Ømund said with a smile. Then his expression became serious again. 'Revenge can be a sweet thing, I am told. But it is not a stone block on which to build a lasting house. You have people. A hirð. A family. Our old world shrinks, Halfdan, and more important than putting right what *has* been, is putting in place what *will* be. Look to the future, old friend.'

Halfdan gave him a weak smile. 'Easier said than done. What happened to you, Ømund? When I left for Visby, you were whole, and still had your mother. You always had an eye for Aife, and I thought you would take her to wife?'

His friend shook his head. 'My past is just that. I have no wish to relive it.'

Halfdan frowned. Something had blinded his friend. When the young jarl had left, Aife was still alive and well, as was Ømund's mother. *Something* had happened. He stepped back. 'Who did it, Ømund?'

'What?'

'Who took your sight, your mother, your girl. Who took them all?'

'Halfdan, you are not listening to me. Vengeance is a poor anchor for a stable ship. A poor foundation for a house. I am content with my lot. Like Odin, I gave my eyes for *true* sight. The world has taken much from me, but I have been given gifts in return.'

'Hardly in keeping. Who *did it*, Ømund.'

His friend simply shook his head. Halfdan turned to the others. Gunnhild, surprisingly, wore an expression of uncertainty. The others were waiting, and they looked outraged, even the Christians among them. 'Somewhere round here, someone blinded my friend and ruined his life. Find them.'

Ømund shook his head for moments, then reached out and grabbed Halfdan's arm. 'It is not worth it.'

'Never let a bad man go free. Who did this?'

'The new farmer. He lay claim to all the land around the village, and now lives over by the swirl-pool. He has three strong

39

men and several thralls, and they all bow to the White Christ. They took offence at me and mine when they first arrived, but since they took my sight and my family, they are content to leave me alone. They shun this place now.'

'They'll fucking regret it,' Halfdan snarled, cheek twitching as he ran to his horse. 'Stay here. When I come back, the people who did this will have paid, and you will come with us. I will not lose you twice.'

'You never lost me, Halfdan. I was always here.' There was something oddly wistful and shiver-inducing about the way he said it.

'The swirl-pool,' Halfdan growled, pulling up a memory of the pond they'd raced stick boats in as children. 'There will be blood.'

'Are you sure about this, Halfdan?' Leif murmured as they all returned to their horses.

Halfdan just nodded. He was furious, but guilt was battering him, too, along with the hate and the grief. He had watched his father die all those years ago, and in that scene had been born a feud that had taken him to the ends of the world, and brought him back, years later, to hunt down Hjalmvigi. But he had not been the only child in the village that fateful day. Aife. Einar. Erik. Ømund. Half a dozen more. And not once since the day he had walked away, demanding vengeance, had he considered that he had not been alone, or thought about those who had cowered under the house *with him*, watching that nightmare. The others had obviously gone, or died. Ømund remained, though, an acidic reminder of his failure in that regard.

'What are we doing?' Bjorn asked as he walked his horse forward.

'We are finding the farmer and his men who blinded my friend. When we do, the halls of Hel will resound with their screams.'

He was already mounted and moving before half of his friends had shared looks and turned their own horses. Only

Bjorn, ever faithful, was right behind him. He knew the location well. The swirl-pool lay maybe half a mile from the village – from the *site* of the village, he mentally corrected. He rode steadily. Not hard, wasting the horse, for his prey were hardly likely to flee. They thought themselves the masters of this land, and had no idea what was coming for them.

He rode ahead, the others close behind, silence gripping them all. Only when he saw the farmstead did he slow and even remember that the others were with him. Ignoring the pens and corrals with their own associated structures, the farm mainly consisted of three buildings, each of timber, with a roof of turf. One was some sort of barn or outhouse, kept away from the others, while the other two sat side by side, each with a door that stood open. The larger, Halfdan assumed, was the main house.

'Bjorn and Leif: the outer building,' he said, pointing. 'Ketil and Farlof: the smaller house. Everyone else, we hit the main house.'

'And what are we doing?' Leif asked.

'Leaving no survivors.'

'Halfdan,' Leif said, quietly, but urgently.

'What?'

'Halfdan, you can't do this.'

'Watch me.'

He gripped his axe and started to march toward the door. The sound of their arrival had drawn attention, though, and figures were emerging from the farm now. Three people were coming out of the smaller central building, burly men in simple clothes, one with a staff in his hand. Ahead, from the main structure, came a better-dressed man and his wife. The farmer, presumably.

His view was interrupted as Leif was suddenly in front of him, having scurried past.

'Halfdan, *think* about this.'

'I have. They took Ømund's eyes. Killed his family. There should be redress for that. Blood will be spilled.'

41

He had to walk around Leif to keep moving, but the Rus sidestepped into his way again.

'Do not perpetuate these nightmares, Halfdan. Yngvar came to your village and killed and burned, and look what it did to you. Do you *really* want to be their Yngvar, my jarl?'

That made him stop. It was a shocking thought, a horrible comparison. For a moment, he fought through it, ready to continue, pushing aside the images that arose. But they kept coming back, and now, when he looked up past Leif at the farmer and his wife, he could see two children, a boy and a girl of perhaps seven years, lurking in the doorway, frightened, watching.

He stopped.

There *should* be redress, but it should be proportionate. He glanced back down at the Rus before him. Leif was determined, mouth pressed in a thin line as he deliberately stood in the way. Halfdan looked around at the others. Gunnhild was nodding her agreement with Leif, and if Halfdan had ever needed another opinion, it was hers. He sagged, his will to continue broken. Only Bjorn and Ketil looked faintly disappointed.

'Weregild,' Leif said, suddenly.

'What?'

'Remember Cyneric in Angle Land? He wanted Bjorn to pay weregild for damages to his man.'

Halfdan nodded slowly. 'Here we call it mangæld. But yes. Though I do not think Ømund has much use for gold.'

'Ømund did not want you to do this at *all*, Halfdan. Do not become Yngvar. You are better than that.'

He was nodding now.

'Can we help you?' the farmer called, nerves in his tone, arms spread in tentative welcome. His accent was South Gotland – from the other end of the island, but an islander, nonetheless, which further shattered Halfdan's thirst for vengeance.

Mangæld, yes. It had to be.

'The blind seiðrmaður in the old village. He was not always blind.'

'Sorry?' asked the man, apparently confused.

The Loki serpent on Halfdan's arm was starting to itch, and he looked about to see what was happening that was setting his subconscious senses off. The gathering of men at the other door had changed. Two had ducked back inside and now came out armed with clubs, like their friend. He kept them in his peripheral vision even as he spoke to the farmer.

'Ømund, the Seiðr worker at the Odin stone back near the bridge. When last I saw him he was whole, and he had not been alone. He had a mother. A girl. And there were others.'

An uneasy look crossed the farmer's face. He started to walk forward, toward Halfdan. His wife grabbed his arm, worried, trying to stop him, but he shook her off, and came on toward the visitors. He stopped almost within sword range, though he was unarmed apart from a short sax at his belt.

'Yes,' the man said. 'A terrible day. I still live with it in my dreams.'

Halfdan twitched. That sounded horribly familiar. 'You did that, though.'

The man sighed. 'We were granted this land by the jarl in Visby. He believed it empty. We settled, with our farmhands, maybe a dozen years or more ago now. This pond is not sufficient, so we needed the running water from the village stream, but it was being hoarded by a small group of locals. I tried to negotiate with them, but they were stubborn, and in the end, I lost my temper. It was no one's fault but mine. I told my men to secure the stream by whatever means necessary. I had not thought for a moment it would take what it did. The locals, they refused. They fought, even the girl. My men laid into them, merciless. When I realised what we were doing, I tried to stop them, but it was too late. My men were led by a chief farmhand called Ari, and his blood was up. I think he was killing for enjoyment. After it was over, I had him bound and sent to Visby for trial by the jarl. I believe he was sold as a thrall.'

'You see,' Leif murmured. 'Justice has already been done.'

Halfdan nodded. 'The blind man was a friend of mine. They all were. I came for revenge. But my friend here is wise,' he added, gesturing to Leif. 'He has persuaded me that mangæld is all that is really required.'

The farmer nodded. 'This is not a rich farm by any means, but we get by, and put a little away after markets. God will perhaps smile upon us if we put right a wrong from so long ago. Name your price, warrior.'

Halfdan looked to Leif, who held up four fingers.

'Four silver pennies,' Halfdan declared. It was a paltry sum, really, but now only a gesture was required. He found that in his heart he had already forgiven the farmer, and suspected that Ømund had done exactly the same.

'I will give eight,' the farmer said, expression sombre. Behind him, his wife was nodding.

'Give him nothing,' snapped one of the three men outside the other building.

The farmer turned in surprise. 'Kóri?'

'The price was already paid when you sent Ari off to Visby. No other price is owed, especially not to heretic idolaters. What we *should* be doing is going back to the bridge and tearing that fucking stone down. It is an offence against God.'

The farmer flicked a warning look at his man, then turned back to Halfdan. 'Ten pennies. Please ignore Kóri. He does not speak for us all.'

'He speaks too much,' Halfdan said, eyes going back to that man. *Never leave an enemy behind you.* An old adage. They could walk away now with ten pennies and be content, but there would always be the worry that this fanatic would take it upon himself to go for the stone, and perhaps for its guardian.

'You are their leader,' the man with the staff said, walking forward. To their credit, the other two armed men remained at the doorway, looking considerably less certain.

'I am.'

'Your presence here is also an offence before God. Take your pagan ways back across the sea.'

'You have an awfully big mouth. Be careful I do not decide to fill it with steel.'

The man was still coming. Halfdan had to hand it to him, he was brave, if stupid.

'Kóri, stand *down*,' the farmer shouted, yet the man came on.

Halfdan nodded to himself. Perhaps the weaving was how it should be. He turned back to the farmer and threw the man an apologetic look. 'Keep your silver pennies. It appears the mangæld is to be paid in blood, after all.'

The one called Kóri spun his staff in two hands in a manner he probably thought looked professional and threatening. Halfdan drew his sword, nothing else. No shield, no axe, no sax. The man saw the sword and his face twisted into a sneer. 'What is that? A *girl's* blade?'

Halfdan said nothing. He knew his treasured Alani sword was an alien design in the north, but he also knew how effective it could be. The man came on. He was quick, which surprised Halfdan, though not enough to endanger him. In a moment, Kóri went from stepping forward to lunging, stabbing out with his staff, straight for Halfdan's face. The jarl simply ducked to the side and let the staff whoosh past him, and as he did so, his sword arm lashed out in response, for the man's last move had easily brought him within range. He felt the blade sink in, meet resistance, then sink in further.

Kóri gasped, and the staff fell to the ground with a thunk.

Halfdan pulled on his sword hilt, and the blade slipped free, followed by a gout of blood and a pained wheeze. The wounded man staggered back, hands coming up to the open wound in his chest, blood beginning to pour freely from it, soaking into his shirt, a dark stain promising an end to life.

Out of the corner of his eye, he saw Leif drawing the sign of a cross in the air. 'Will you pray for him?' Farlof asked, placing a hand on the Rus's shoulder. Halfdan gave Leif a warning look, but realised he had no need. Leif's face was hard and unyielding already.

'No,' the Rus said. 'Christian or not, some men do not deserve it.'

He turned his back on Kóri as the man dropped to his knees, making a prolonged groaning noise as he clutched his chest, blood pouring out around his hands.

'The debt is paid,' Halfdan said, loudly. 'Ømund the seiðrmaður, and the Odin stone he guards, will not be harmed. Believe me that I will know if anything happens to either, no matter where I am, and half a world will not be far enough to save any man who threatens them.'

Something about his tone must have carried weight, for the farmer nodded his understanding, and there was fear in there, and absolutely no uncertainty. The other two men with clubs, he noted, had disappeared back inside and were now nowhere to be seen. There was a subdued thud as Kóri finally fell face down on the ground, dead.

A thought occurred to Halfdan, then, and he gestured to the farmer. 'There is no reason for further violence anyway. Maybe, if you make offerings to Ømund, he will grant you easy access to the stream.'

The farmer nodded. 'We have made alternative arrangements since, but that would certainly make things easier.'

Halfdan stood for a moment, looking down at the dead man, then up at the farmer, and then to the children hiding in the doorway. They might have sleepless nights, remembering the death of a farmhand, but that memory would fade with time.

Halfdan would not be their Yngvar.

He turned and mounted, the others following suit. Without a further glance back, they started the return journey to the site of the vanished village. As they rode, he could feel eyes on him, and after a while looked up at Leif and Gunnhild, both of whom were looking his way.

'What?'

'That was done well,' Leif replied.

'Thanks to you. I would never have thought of mangæld as an option. You stopped me walking a path from which I might not have come back.'

'A true jarl knows when mercy is required,' Gunnhild put in. 'And a true jarl listens to his people. It *was* done well,' she agreed. Halfdan almost smiled as they rode the rest of the way.

Ømund was seated on a tree stump, close to the Odin stone, as they slowed. He looked up at them as they reined in, clearly aware who it was. 'You let them live,' he said. A statement, not a question. Halfdan shivered. Seiðr at work.

'One man died. He needed to. It was a statement and an ending. You will have no more trouble from them. In fact, the farmer may come to you for help. It is up to you whether you grant it, of course.' He sighed. 'I had thought to ask you to come with us, Ømund. When we came here, and I realised it was you, I pictured us at the prow of a dragon ship, living the whale road. I did not even for a moment think I would leave you twice. But you will not come, will you.'

That, too, was a statement and not a question.

Ømund shook his head. 'The old world is disappearing, Halfdan, but there are still places where it holds, and people who remember it. On days of power and meaning, people come here from across Gotland. A body is hung for blood in the old way, and the grey-hooded wanderer is celebrated. While I live, it will be ever so.'

Halfdan smiled at his friend. 'I am sad to leave you again, Ømund, but I understand. And while you never left, I shall never return. I had to visit once, to understand that, I think.' A quick look at Gunnhild there, who managed not to look smug. 'Take care of yourself, old friend. May Odin always have your back.'

Ømund smiled. 'Fair winds and plenty of silver, Halfdan Vigholfsson. Farewell.'

Halfdan tore his gaze away slowly, with some difficulty, and then kicked his horse's flanks. The others joined him, then, and the eight of them rode away from the blind man and his sacred stone, from the ruins of the village, and from Halfdan's childhood.

'What now?' Bjorn asked, as they clattered across the bridge and off down the Visby road.

'Now we sail to Sigtun and take the *Sea Wolf* back from the lunatic thief-king.'

Chapter 4

Leif's eyes widened as the *Sea Dragon* moved from the last of the channels and into the lake upon which sat the capital of the King of Swedes. The journey had taken three days just from open sea, though the terrain was so well known to Ulfr that he could seemingly plot and navigate his way through the fjords, channels and narrow lakes that led all the way inland to Sigtun with his eyes closed. Leif was impressed. Kiev had been a major trade hub, but then it sat on one of the world's greatest rivers. Sigtun was seemingly hidden away inland in a maze of fjords, lakes and rivers, and yet it had achieved the status of a capital city.

But that wasn't what had opened his eyes.

That was the fleet.

Sigtun, rather unimpressive as it was to Leif's mind, sat at the northern end of a long, wide lake, but very little open water was visible toward the city end of that body of water. A fleet, mostly of good northern dragon ships, gathered there, the largest Leif had seen in many years. Larger than the Varangian fleet that had sailed to Apulia for war. Larger than the Byzantine fleet in the harbour of Miklagarðr. Probably even larger than that which Yngvar had gathered at Kiev in his bid to seek the end of the world. This was a fleet designed for one purpose and one purpose only: war.

Someone had been sensible, though, for despite the massed ships, a channel led from the open water, directly through the

49

fleet, toward the town's harbour. Presumably there still needed to be access for merchants and messengers while the fleet gathered. Ulfr led the way along that channel with consummate ease, though a glance backward suggested that the master of the *Sea Cow* was having considerably more difficulty, the big barge slewing this way and that as it closed on the city. Still, the lumbering vessel followed on without actual collision, and after an hour of navigating between warships, they were bearing down on the harbour.

Leif saw it at the same time as Ulfr, and the two of them both leapt to the sheer strake, pointing excitedly.

'The *Sea Wolf*!'

Men hurried to the side in response, for though few of the current crop of Wolves had even been around when that ship had been theirs, its reputation certainly preceded it, and it had become something of a legend and a totem of their warband.

The *Sea Wolf* had not changed. Its glorious thief of a master had apparently looked after it well. Leif drank in the sight with a wild grin. She was so *sleek*. He had forgotten just how graceful she was. *Sea Dragon* was a magnificent ship, for sure, and perhaps a match even for the vessel moored before them, but there was just something about the *Sea Wolf* that seemed divine, as though she carried with her all the dreams and glories of their travels which, to some extent, she did.

'Bastard,' growled Ulfr, pointing, and it took Leif a moment to notice what he was referring to. Near the prow, there had been one visible piece of damage that had scraped the boards and removed some of the fine carving at the top strake. It could have been war damage, or perhaps a poor attempt at docking somewhere. Whatever had caused it clearly annoyed Ulfr, but Leif could still do little more than smile. As they sailed past the anchored ship, the men aboard it looked up at the *Sea Dragon*, the only other ship on the whole lake that followed a similar small, sleek design. That they were sister vessels, built by the same shipwright, was clear. The men on the *Sea Wolf* cheered as they passed, and the Wolves cheered back in response.

Then they were past and approaching the harbour.

Of course, though Leif knew this was the place from which Halfdan and the *Sea Wolf* had set out on their great journey, and where the Wolves of Odin had been born, neither he nor Gunnhild had been with them then, and this was his first time in the place. He did not really know what to expect. As they closed on the dock, he looked back and forth, taking everything in. Ahead, the town itself stretched back up from the shore, centred upon a wide road lined by buildings, which held a bustling market, and ahead at the crest a larger structure, perhaps the palace. The town reached down to the water on the left, but to the right, as far as Leif could see into the distance, there were slipways and shipyards, all busy, all occupied. He saw Ulfr look that way, his lip wrinkling as he turned away once more. This, of course, was the big shipwright's home, the place where he had built *Sea Wolf*.

As Ulfr brought them toward the jetty with the skill of a lifelong pilot, the others moved up to join him.

'Now to find Harðráði and claim back our ship,' Halfdan said, in a determined tone.

'Where will he be?' Ketil mused.

Leif smiled. 'You remember Harðráði? Look to where the power and the gold and the prettiest girls are, and you'll find him. My guess would be that large compound at the top of the slope. It has the look of a palace to me, such as it is. We know King Onund Jacob is supposedly here in Sigtun, so he will be there, and where you find him, you'll find the thief.'

Halfdan nodded. 'The palace, for sure. Do you see anything changed in Sigtun since our last visit?' he added.

Leif looked about, though it was not a question he could answer, never having been here before.

'Too many crosses,' grumbled Ulfr.

'And a new White Christ temple,' Bjorn added, pointing.

A wooden church of ornate design, with the protruding beams variously either fashioned into crosses, or carved into dragons, sat not far from the water. There were, even Leif had to admit, rather a lot of crosses in evidence across Sigtun.

'Why so many?' Ketil asked. 'Do Christians compete like this?'

Leif frowned. 'Onund is playing host to the would-be kings of Norway and Daneland, both of which are staunchly Christian. My guess is that this is a gesture designed to show how Onund's own nation is embracing Christianity in the face of all these foreign ships and crews. Rather hiding the fact that there are still parts of his nation where the cross is yet to reach,' he added.

'Whatever it is that caused it, it makes me uncomfortable,' Ulfr said. 'The place I grew up in is almost gone. No ship is sent to water in Sigtun with a blessing to Ran and his daughters these days, you realise? The *Sea Wolf* was probably the last ship to get one.'

The conversation ended as the *Sea Dragon* came alongside the dock, bumping gently, then settling as men threw out ropes and secured her. Halfdan was the first to jump ashore, but the others followed swiftly. Ulfr set half the men to guard the ship, dispatched the other half to secure fresh supplies in the port, and then joined the core of the Wolves as they gathered on the dock.

'Let us find Harðráði,' Halfdan said.

Leif pointed at the ship. 'You're about to enter a world of kings, Halfdan. You need to arrive with appropriate show. Take an honour guard of a dozen good men.'

'We're safe here, Leif.'

'Doesn't matter. This is about show. You're a jarl, remember?'

Halfdan nodded, and chose a dozen of their best men to join them. As those warriors assembled on the dockside, weapons sheathed, but carrying shields that bore designs of Odin's wolves, the heart of the group prepared to move. Halfdan, their jarl, with Gunnhild, Bjorn, Ketil, Ulfr, Leif, Anna, Farlof and Eygrímr – a potent force.

52

As they began to walk along that great wide street that formed the core of the town, Anna fell in beside Leif with a smile. She had somehow contrived to be wearing her best clothes, all clean and pressed, with a fine cloak pinned with a Byzantine brooch, her hair neatly held back with a circlet of silver. She looked almost regal herself. He grinned, reaching out and squeezing her hand as they walked.

Sigtun was as busy a place as Leif had seen in some time, presumably partly because of the huge fleet anchored off shore, not to mention the entourages of two foreign would-be kings, and the inevitable hangers-on. The market seemed to fill almost all open space, leaving just a cart-sized stretch in the centre for the public, who milled about like ants. The Wolves had little trouble moving through the crowd, though. Even in as wild a place as this, Leif noted, the ordinary folk tended to melt out of the way of a column of men in chain shirts with shields and axes, some of them in intimidating helmets of steel, with darkened eye-guards.

And so the Wolves cleaved their way through the main street of Sigtun toward that complex up the slope like a ship cutting through the water, parting the waves and leaving a tumbling wake. As they closed on that complex at the top of the street, Leif became more and more convinced that it was a palace of sorts. A solid stockade with a manned gate separated it from the town, and he could see at least half a dozen large structures inside, one of which bore a marked similarity to that ornate wooden church down by the harbour, in that its multi-level roofs each bore protruding beams that had been carved into fantastic designs. Only a rich and powerful man could have such a home. It was almost as impressive as Jarisleif's Royal Hall in Kiev.

As they approached the gate of the place, two men stepped out with spears, forming a barrier. Before they could make any demand, though, and before Halfdan could announce himself, Leif gestured to his jarl and hurried out to the front.

In such situations it often went better when you could control the exchange from the beginning, and any man looked more powerful when he had someone to announce him.

As one of the soldiers opened his mouth to demand their identities, Leif bowed and began.

'Halfdan Vigholfsson, called the Loki-born, Jarl of Sasireti.' *A slight stretch of the truth there, but then no one here should know the place, and he'd had to pluck a name from the air, given that Halfdan was only jarl because his own people had proclaimed it.* He continued: 'captain of the Wolves of Odin, master of the *Sea Wolf* and of the *Sea Dragon*,' *and the* Sea Cow, 'former Varangian officer of the Byzantine court, friend of the bishops Ælfric and Aage, and ally of Harald Harðráði, demands admittance and an audience with the king.'

He watched the frowns, uncertainty and then wide-eyed astonishment of the two guards as he spoke, and could almost feel the grins from his friends behind him at the string of titles and impressive feats he'd pinned to Halfdan's mast. He tried to imagine the looks he'd have got if he'd added 'slayer of giants, dragons and draugar, saviour of dukes and empresses, scourge of Angle Land', and so on, to the list.

'Jarl of south-what?' asked one of the two men.

Leif allowed one eyebrow to arch dangerously, and the two guards looked at one another, then called for someone. A man in a well-tailored shirt and an expensive cloak walked over, and he and the guards had a quick, murmured conversation before he turned to the Wolves and beckoned.

'Follow me,' he said.

They did so. Now, Leif took the lead. Anna and Gunnhild walked with Halfdan, giving him that extra edge of impressiveness, something only further enhanced by the large, powerful figures of Bjorn, Ketil and Ulfr at his shoulders, then a dozen strong warriors following on. Certainly, they drew looks as they crossed the compound and made for that large and ornate hall. Leif noted those present: small bands of warriors, mostly, powerful-looking and wealthy, with knots of noblemen in rich dress here and there, thralls in tow. Palace servants and slaves criss-crossed the place, hurrying about their duties.

They were led through the large doors of the palace, which stood open, and the chamber they then entered was lit by four lamps that burned pork and beef fat, giving the room a meaty aroma that assailed the senses after the fresh autumnal air outside. The only reason the whole room hadn't filled to unbearable levels with the smell was an ingenious system of small vents in the walls beside the lamps that drew the smoke, and therefore most of the stench, away. The walls and rafters of the room were filled with shields and spears, axes and bows, a show of martial strength to impress visitors. The man leading them did not falter, and as he strode toward the next doors, equally ornate, covered with Ringerike patterns, they were opened for him.

Leif led the Wolves, following their guide, and entered the hall beyond. This great room was lit by more guttering lamps, as well as a central smoke hole in the roof in the manner of an old-fashioned longhouse. The walls were draped with banners: mainly the dragon flags of Onund Jacob and his family, and the Swedish war gonfalon that depicted a warrior mid-battle. But Leif could see others, too, in smaller numbers, presumably the banners of the visiting would-be usurpers or other various lords in Onund's service. In the corner stood one tall pike with a white flag that was tightly furled, its image impossible to make out. He could hazard a guess at its design, though. One flag that was missing here was the old-fashioned war flag, the raven banner that led any Northman to war. Had the banner been furled because of its pagan connotations, he wondered, or was it just waiting to be opened when the time came?

The hall was heated by a roaring fire that hissed and spat in a shallow stone bowl at its centre, smoke billowing up to the hole in the roof, and all around were packed tables and benches. Leif checked for Hjalmvigi's face among them, to make sure the priest had not managed to wheedle his way back into the Swedish court, but he was not present.

Then his gaze fell on the three men at the top end of the hall, where an ornate oaken throne sat at a grand table, two new chairs that had recently been re-carved and aggrandised to give them throne-like airs, accompanying it. Onund Jacob, king of Svears, Swedes, and Geats, Leif had never met, but the first figure, occupying the main throne, had to be him. Black hair tightly braided and beard plaited with silver and beads at the bottom, the man looked clever, to Leif. The unpredictable Harðráði, a man Leif remembered very well from their time in Miklagarðr, sat to the king's left. That meant the occupant of the third chair, with the short brown hair, bushy moustache and wide nose, had to be Sveinn Ástríðarson, claimant to the throne of Daneland. The man looked oddly angry, and Leif suspected he lacked both the wit of Harðráði and the wisdom of Onund Jacob. The trio's retinues stood close by – large, dangerous-looking men, with large, dangerous-looking weapons, ready to defend their lords. A chestnut-haired lady of immense grace, attended by several servants, stood close enough to Sveinn that Leif presumed this to be his wife, and a similarly impressive woman was hovering close to Onund, clearly the Swedish queen.

His gaze automatically flicked then to Harðráði, wondering what bright-looking impressionable wench the lunatic had clinging to his shirt hem this time. His smile disappeared. He blinked as he saw the immaculately dressed ash-blonde woman close by, clearly accompanying Harðráði the way the other two women did the other kings.

As if by some sort of strange Seiðr, the young woman turned at that moment and saw Leif, and her expression made it plain that *she* recognised *him* instantly too.

Ellisif, daughter of Jarisleif the Wise, prince of Kiev.

He had last seen Ellisif the day they left with Yngvar. She had always been out of his league, of course, the most eligible woman in Kiev, but he had always had that strange vain hope, and it had only ever really left when Anna had entered his life like a brightly coloured explosion of excitement. He'd never looked back since then. But a weird tumble of confusing emotions hit him at the sight of her.

He screwed his eyes shut, and the realisations of what her presence might mean. Ellisif was a clever and beautiful woman, who carried the blood of the Swedish throne as well as her own Kievan noble lineage. She bore a wedding ring, and her place in this hall made it clear that only Harðráði could possibly be that husband. Leif's eyes opened again and his gaze darted to Gunnhild, whose expression was too blank and uninformative to be an accident. She too had spotted the wife, and had slammed the shutters on any visible emotion. Leif winced again. There were uncomfortable moments coming in Sigtun, he was sure. That suspicion was confirmed a moment later when the three kings turned, and Harðráði's face lit up as his gaze fell upon Gunnhild.

Shit.

'May I present,' their guide began, then gestured to Leif, who cleared his throat.

'Halfdan Vigholfsson, called the Loki-born, Jarl of Sasireti, leader of...'

'...the most dangerous and surely the most lucky wolf pack in the *world*,' Harðráði finished, interrupting him with a grin.

'Sasireti?' Onund said, brow folding into a frown.

'It has taken you a good time to find me, my friend.' Harðráði laughed.

'We might have been quicker had you not stolen our ship and used it to flee Miklagarðr and leave us to the tender mercies of the emperor Monomachos,' the jarl said, sharply, then turned to King Onund with a less fierce expression, and nodded respectfully, his sole concession to recognition of rank, before switching back to Harðráði.

'Halfdan, my *friend*,' Harðráði said, putting immense stress on that last word this time, 'I stole nothing. Our escape from

57

the clutches of that maniac, and our flight from the city, were driven by necessity and fortune. I would have been glad to give you your ship back straight away, but unfortunately we were driven different ways. For a time, I presumed you dead, but then rumours of your exploits began to reach us via the Byzantines. Anyway, let that all be in the past. I intended no theft. I *borrowed* the *Sea Wolf*, due to unavoidable problems. She is in the harbour and I give you her back with my thanks. I have taken good care of her.'

'Apart from the damage,' muttered Ulfr, though loud enough only to be heard in their immediate gathering.

'You owe me a *double* debt, Harðráði,' Halfdan replied. 'For taking my ship, and for leaving us in the lurch in the imperial city.'

'I might actually suggest that you took from me something of greater value,' the Norseman said, his gaze slipping to Gunnhild, who had the sense and strength to meet it with an emotionless look, and silence. Leif, however, glanced across at Ellisif of Kiev, and his heart sank as he realised that she had not missed the look her husband threw at the visitor, though she too was clever like Gunnhild, and let none of it show in her expression.

'I do hope you are not about to challenge me to *Holmgång*, Halfdan,' Harðráði said in a tired voice. 'I am, in truth, not at all sure which of us would win, but I fear the world would be all the poorer, either way.'

Leif found himself smiling, then shook his head. There was something about Golden Harðráði that just made you like him. He was almost impossible to hate. Even Halfdan chuckled while he shook his head. 'No. I have ended one blood feud and look to end another now, but I do not seek blood for *our* disagreement. I do seek redress of a *kind*, though.'

'Oh? And how can I repay your kindness, young Loki-born?'

'You seek the throne of Norway, and that is common knowledge. And *I* seek a man who hides behind that throne – a priest who clings to Magnus of Norway, for no other king will have him, excommunicated as he is.'

'Hjalmvigi?' Onund Jacob put in then, leaning forward.

'The same,' said Halfdan, nodding, without looking across at the Swedish king, eyes still on the man he'd come to see.

'But I do not sit upon that throne yet,' Harðráði pointed out. 'I would willingly give you this man, if I could, but for now he is equally out of *my* reach.'

'Then you will vow to me now that when you *do* sit on that throne, you will give me Hjalmvigi.'

Harðráði seemed to consider this for just a moment, then shrugged and nodded. 'Very well. I'll make that vow in the sight of heaven and the presence of God, and before all these very powerful witnesses.' He leaned forward now. 'But *think*, Halfdan... perhaps I can go one better. Help me *take* that throne, and you will bring us closer to your goal.'

Halfdan snorted. 'You think to repay a debt to me by getting me to fight your war for you?'

Harðráði laughed out loud. 'Oh Lord, but I had forgotten what fun it was sparring with you, Halfdan. Very well, let me sweeten the pot. In return for the loan of your ship and that unfortunate business back in Constantinopolis, I vow to give you your priest as soon as he is within my grasp.' Another swift glance at Gunnhild. '*Despite* the glorious prize I, too, lost. So, I must offer you something *else* in return for fighting to help me gain my throne.'

Leif narrowed his eyes. It was at moments like this that Harðráði was at his most dangerous, for he was certainly a clever one. And the way the man was smiling, he already knew he had something that would win Halfdan over.

'Let me see if I remember how you were introduced.' Harðráði smiled. 'Ah yes... Halfdan Vigholfsson, Loki-born, Jarl of Sasireti.'

Halfdan nodded.

'I'd not known your father's name,' Harðráði said conversationally. 'Vigholf – "Wolf warrior". No wonder his son is the man he is. Still, the problem is that I *know* Sasireti. Don't forget that *I* was at that battle too, though I fought on the other side, you may remember, for Byzantium.' Leif winced as he realised that, but Harðráði was not done. 'A fictional title then, chosen, I think, by our Rus friend Leif, there, to impress those here who have never travelled in the south. I remember the Wolves, Halfdan, from our days in the Guard. You are a good man, and a good war-leader, and your men may *call* you jarl as easily as they may call you king, emperor, god, or the mangy arse-hair of a Greek stray dog, but a jarldom is *earned*, granted or bestowed by a king. It cannot simply be *claimed*.'

'Evidence suggests otherwise,' Halfdan replied archly. 'Even *crowns* can be claimed, can they not, as your nephew Magnus has shown? Has he not taken two in a row?'

'But you have no wish to be a usurper, do you, Halfdan? An outsider? No. You want legitimacy. You are a jarl born, but will never be recognised by your peers until you have the land and the power to back it up. Help me take the throne from Magnus, Halfdan, and I will grant you a *true* jarldom. A title no one can dispute. A place for you and yours, Halfdan. Think about it.'

Leif was already doing that.

A true jarldom was perhaps the equivalent of the dukedom back in Nordmandi, or one of the powerful Byzantine lords back in Constantinopolis. Certainly more than Gunnar of Swaledale, who had carved out his own land, but lost it because of such disputes. A title granted by a king, and a place of their own. The Wolves would have a home. A *proper* home.

He turned to look at Halfdan, and could see that the same possibilities were swimming through the jarl's mind, too. Halfdan's old friend Ømund had said it back on Gotland, and the words would now be swimming through the jarl's mind: *You have people. A hirð. A family. Our old world shrinks, Halfdan, and more important than putting right what has been, is putting in place what will be. Look to the future, old friend.*

'Take his offer,' a voice said, quiet, firm.

Leif turned to the speaker, surprised. It was Gunnhild. She had Halfdan in her sights, and her expression was determined, eyes gleaming.

Still, Halfdan wavered. 'I have no wish to find myself fighting wars between our own peoples, Gunnhild. Don't forget I am half Dane myself. To risk the Wolves in war for an empty title, a gilded bauble that benefits only me, would be a poor decision, don't you think?'

'He is *right*, Halfdan,' she insisted. 'At the end of all this lies Hjalmvigi, and we will not rest easy until he is with his god. To get to him, we need power in Norway, and *that* will only come with Harðráði on the throne. We should help put him on that throne, and that will bring the priest to where we can reach him.'

'And none of this is driven by a desire to see that man do well?' the jarl asked quietly, nodding at Harðráði.

Gunnhild fixed him with a withering look. 'That was beneath you, Halfdan.'

'People do odd things for love. I am just being sure.'

Halfdan turned back to the kings at the table, face straight, back straight. He folded his arms. 'A jarldom, yes, and the creature Hjalmvigi in my grip. Also, good land with a mead hall.' A long pause. 'And five marks of silver to every man who sails for me.'

'Five marks?' Sveinn exploded. 'Preposterous. I do not pay my *own* guard that much for even a season of campaigns.'

'But your guard are not Wolves of Odin,' Halfdan said simply.

Harðráði was nodding to himself. 'How many are you, Halfdan?'

'Ninety-four,' Halfdan replied, 'in two ships.'

As Sveinn of Daneland exploded once more, and Onund Jacob frowned, Harðráði simply continued to nod. 'It's a lot of money.'

'Not half as much as you took out of Miklagarðr aboard my ship,' Halfdan replied, levelly.

That made the man laugh. 'If impudence were gold, Halfdan Loki-born, you would be the richest man in the world. Very well. A jarldom, land with a hall, the neck of your troublesome priest, and five hundred marks of silver for your crewmen.' He lurched up from his seat and strode across to the Wolves, then gripped Halfdan's hand in his own and shook it, in the style of southern merchants. 'It is a deal, my friend. Your ships will be welcome among our fleet. We continue to discuss our proposed tactics, and I'm afraid this is the prerogative of kings and the men who pay for the fleet.' He turned back to the other two at the table. 'Onund, can you find fitting accommodation for our friends?'

The Swedish king nodded. 'For those present here, I can have room made in the palace buildings. The rest of their crew will have to stay aboard ship. The bunk houses, taverns and brothels of the city are already full to bursting.'

Halfdan bowed his head.

'And at some point,' Onund said, in a meaningful tone, 'I would like to discuss Sasireti.'

Leif winced again. That might not be comfortable, given their mutual history with Yngvar, but a glance across at Ellisif of Kiev told Leif that the fated jarl and his fall in the east might not be the only uncomfortable subject awaiting them over the coming days.

Chapter 5

'Tell me about Sasireti,' said King Onund Jacob quietly, his gaze, slightly irritable, darting over Halfdan's shoulder to settle on the rest of the Wolves before drawing back to his face. The invitation, or *summons* more appropriately, had been specifically for Halfdan, but he had decided to bring the others with him regardless, and the king had not argued, though he clearly was not pleased about it. But then, if it were to be a private interview, the king should not have a dozen guards, half a dozen courtiers, and several thralls with him.

And Harðráði and his man, too.

The adventurous Norseman was lounging off to one side, little more than a spectator, the bodyguard Halfdan had heard referred to as Orm Axebiter standing close to his shoulder. A glance round confirmed what Halfdan had already known. Bjorn was glaring at Orm. The two had exchanged words only once in the day they had been in Sigtun, but they had already discovered that they did not like one another at all.

Halfdan took a deep breath.

'Sasireti was a mess. A waking nightmare. The Byzantines brought their sticky fire onto the field. Kings died. Jarls died. The forest was a mass of bodies, burning or bleeding out. We lost. Liparit won. Until you have seen the Alani and the Byzantines make war, you cannot understand the level of horror. It makes the tribulations of Tyr seem as nothing.'

'And what of Yngvar?' Onund pressed.

Halfdan had been bracing himself for this. Yngvar had been a cousin of Onund's, apparently, not just a friend, and there was no telling what the king had already heard about the expedition. There had been sufficient time for all sorts of information to thread back to the north, some of which would have come courtesy of Hjalmvigi himself.

'What do you want to know?' he said, carefully guiding the conversation.

'Tell me *everything*.'

Halfdan rubbed his forehead with his thumb. Even everything that did not damn Halfdan was too much. 'That is the job of a skald,' he said. 'Yngvar's story is long and winding, and one day someone will commit it to history. I think you want to know of his ending, though, yes? He was wounded in the press of battle. An arrow. All was chaos, and he did an admirable job of extracting his people from the disaster, even with a shaft sticking from his thigh. Had Yngvar not been there, I doubt a *single* Northman would have left the field. He saved many. I took care of my own, but we were close to Yngvar as we fled, so we helped when he started to succumb to his wounds. Once we were away from immediate danger, I searched for a way to patch his wound. I wanted to find honey and clean linen to cover it until we reached true safety.'

That much was a lie, of course, but only the Wolves and a long-dead jarl knew that.

'Hjalmvigi interfered, though. He grabbed a rag I'd been using to clean my sword and used it to bind Yngvar's wound. I don't know where the rag came from. I picked it up fleeing the battlefield just to clean the mess from my blade. I think it may have been infected with something, or the man whose blood it cleaned was infected. Yngvar started to show signs of illness over the following days as we moved away from Sasireti. It *may* have been unconnected to the rag, but there had been nothing wrong with Yngvar other than an arrow wound until that rag was applied to the injury.' He thought it prudent in current

64

Christian company not to moot the idea that troublesome elves might be at the root of such illnesses…

'Gunnhild warned against just that,' he added, thumbing over his shoulder at the völva. 'She knows medicine and wounds and cleanliness, and she advised against using the rag, but Hjalmvigi was hardly going to listen to a *völva*.'

He straightened. 'Yngvar lingered for days, getting worse. He was dying a horrible death from an infected wound. In the end, in the presence of Valdimar of Kiev, I agreed to end it for him. He was just days from suffering the most unpleasant death, but I put steel through his heart to save him that agony.'

Onund, face grave, was nodding.

'That is all there is to tell,' Halfdan said. 'Yngvar was buried in the great church of Kutaisi in Georgia, by its queen. Those of us who survived went our own ways. I made for Miklagarðr and joined the Varangians with my hirð. But, as time has gone on, I have become convinced that Hjalmvigi's actions that day were no accident.'

'Oh?'

'Throughout our voyage, the priest took a dislike to us, and had very vocal ideas about what his jarl should be doing. Yngvar was forced repeatedly as time went on to bring the priest to heel and curb his viciousness. I did begin to wonder whether Hjalmvigi felt trapped enough to find a way to release Yngvar's hold on him.'

Onund frowned now. 'You really think he would kill? He is a priest, and Yngvar was a Christian.'

'Find me a Christian or a priest who says he cannot kill, and I will find you a liar.'

This made the king sit back, uncertain. 'You have any proof of this?'

'Only circumstantial. The moment the jarl was gone, Hjalmvigi was plotting. When he reached Kutaisi, he wheedled his way in with the Georgian queen, and was already commanding a unit of archers and a hall of his own, with plans to return to the north and interfere with the thrones here. This, I gather, is precisely what he did, until his own church realised the bounds of his ambition and cast him out.'

'And that is why you want him? That is why you asked Harðráði for him?'

Halfdan shook his head. 'Not exactly. In his last moments, Yngvar made me promise to bring his killer to justice. Since he cannot have expected me to know which archer among the Byzantines shot him, and the man was probably already dead anyway, I can only assume he knew that Hjalmvigi had given him the disease that killed him, and he meant for me to bring an end to the priest. It is an oath to Yngvar I now pursue.'

There was a long and uncomfortable silence. Finally, Onund Jacob nodded. 'I gave Hjalmvigi a place in my court upon his return,' he said, 'for I knew him to be a confederate of my friend Yngvar. But though I should, as a good Christian, throw my support behind the man, and even turn the other cheek now that he has been excommunicated and exiled, I cannot help but realise just how much power Hjalmvigi had accrued in the few short years he lurked beside my throne. By the time I learned of his excommunication and banished him from my lands, he was more powerful than any jarl in my court. And while Hjalmvigi may have claimed other motives for what happened, his account matches yours surprisingly closely.'

The king of Sweden exhaled, long and slow. 'Your tale has a ring of sad truth about it, Halfdan of Gotland. I may wish it were not so, but it is. Know that you have my gratitude for helping my friend in his final days, and my support in hunting the cruel priest. I am but the quiet partner in this coming campaign, for Sweden is not involved directly, but I will support my fellow kings here with men and ships and gold. I will extend that aid to you, for your wisdom and compassion in your past endeavours. And know that you are welcome in my court until the time the fleet leaves in spring.'

Halfdan bowed his head in acknowledgment and thanks and, at a dismissive wave of the hand from the king, turned with his

66

Wolves. As they made to leave, Halfdan saw the look Bjorn threw at Orm Axebiter, and knew that trouble was brewing there. Bjorn had not punched anyone in over a month, and that was almost unheard of. As they moved out into the open they kept quiet, and it was only as they made their way back into their communal bunkroom in the palace grounds that they finally spoke.

'Masterful.' Leif grinned.

Gunnhild nodded. 'You turned what could have been a disaster into a success. And with very little fiction about it. You have learned much from Leif in your time, I think, Halfdan.'

He grinned. 'We are so close. I can almost feel Hjalmvigi's neck in my hands.'

'Be prepared to be patient,' the völva advised. 'This is a long voyage. Patience and care. All will come right in time.'

'The time is coming,' Halfdan insisted, 'and soon.'

—

But it seemed he was wrong. Four days passed before, finally, the three kings had hammered out a plan and were sharing it with their jarls and skippers. Onund and Sveinn were elsewhere, speaking to their own, and Harðráði had already spoken to his most senior men. Halfdan, he had left 'til last.

'Daneland?' Halfdan said, sharply. 'But why, when Norway is your goal?'

Harðráði leaned on his elbows at the table. 'Do not forget that my cursed nephew Magnus sits upon the thrones of both Norway *and* Daneland. There are good reasons to move against Daneland first.'

'And more to move against Norway,' Halfdan argued. 'I said I would help you take the throne of Norway, not of Daneland. Hjalmvigi is in Norway. I have no interest in fighting Danes. My *mother* was a Dane.'

Harðráði's expression hardened. 'Sveinn wants to move against Daneland first, to recover his throne. And once we have

Daneland in our hands, we will have an excellent base on the western side of the Jótlandshaf from which to strike at Norway. I am willing to do this to keep Sveinn on my side. I need him. It has to be Daneland first, though my end goal is still Norway.'

Halfdan's eyes narrowed. 'If I were a suspicious man, I might wonder whether you talked your friend Sveinn into that, rather than the other way round.'

'Oh?'

'I think you want to fight in Daneland, because then all the killing, burning and looting will be Sveinn's to deal with when this is over. If we went to fight in Norway, it would be your own future kingdom we were ravaging. I know you, Harðráði, and I know you are clever.'

'That would be very underhanded of me,' Harðráði said in a tone of hurt innocence.

'It is most certainly the truth. Do not worry. I won't tell Sveinn. But you and I both know it.'

Harðráði leaned back, putting his hands behind his head, fingers interlaced. 'As soon as the spring tides are with us, we shall sail for Daneland. That gives us the winter to train, supply, and gather the last few jarls to our banners. In spring, we will make first for the island of Sjáland. We will have sufficient ships to hit the north, east, south and west coasts simultaneously. We will secure every coastal fort, port and village, and then move in from all sides, like a tightening noose, on Hróarskelda, for that is the seat of the Danish throne. Even though Magnus owns it from a distance, and has yet to visit the place, it will be a blow to him to lose his Danish capital, and it will give Sveinn the legitimacy he needs. But in this campaign, we need to do sufficient damage to anger Magnus and draw him south from Norway into our grasp. Then, we can defeat him and seize the throne, and all will be right.'

'It will also give Magnus all the time he needs to build an army and a fleet to match yours, while you will be *expending* your strength in Daneland. It makes more sense to move in winter when he does not expect it, with the fleet and army you have, which he can probably not yet match. Sail fast, find him in his own port, hit him hard and end his reign in both lands.'

Behind Harðráði, Orm Axebiter, who was standing idly by a wall and cleaning his fingernails with his sax, cleared his throat.

'Harald Sigurdsson, who you call Harðráði, is the *son* of a king, the *uncle* of a king, the *cousin* of a king, and the husband of a princess. He has fought in five wars, all on the victorious side, has captained the Imperial Guard in Miklagarðr, and sailed a thousand thousand leagues without losing a ship. He is a master tactician, a warrior, a hero, a leader of men, and a king in waiting. You, Halfdan Vigholfsson, who they call Loki-born, are an adventurous villager with a spotted history of fighting battles often on the wrong side, and of theft and flight. You call yourself jarl with no royal support, and have never led an army. You would do well to remember your place and not gainsay the plan of your betters.'

Halfdan looked across at Harðráði's right-hand man, who was still relaxed against the wall, cleaning his nails, and gave the man a hard glare.

'And you,' Bjorn shouted from behind him, addressing the man by the wall, 'Orm, who they call Arse Biter, have a back-side for a face and cannot help speaking shit out of it in a long, brown stream.'

Halfdan saw a small twitch in Orm Axebiter's face, and for just a moment the nail cleaning paused, before beginning again.

'Oxen should resign themselves to plodding after their masters and carrying heavy loads,' Orm said. 'Cattle are not bred for their opinions.'

'This fucking ox is going to cut you from arse to skull along your back, grab your dick hard, and pull off your skin,' Bjorn roared.

Halfdan turned to see that the big man was reaching to the small pouch in which he kept that precious substance that brought him to berserk. Gunnhild was faster, though. Her hand lashed out, a small, sharp blade in it, and snicked through the thongs that held the pouch to Bjorn's belt, whereupon it dropped into her hand and she whisked it away.

'No mindless violence today, Bjorn. If you must fight, you fight with what wits you have naturally.'

'Violence is rarely mindless,' Bjorn countered, still glaring at Harðráði's man.

'Keep your kill-mist down,' Orm said quietly, then turned to the others. 'Better the big ox hold his tongue and preserve a small amount of respect than he challenge me and find he is no better than a lumbering child.'

Halfdan winced at that. Men had died for saying much less.

'There will be no fighting here,' Harðráði said, loudly. 'Save your killing for our enemies.'

But Bjorn was not going to last much longer. Halfdan knew how long it had been since Bjorn had fought *anyone*, and the albino was not a man to suffer peace for extended periods lightly.

'Halfdan,' Bjorn growled, 'let me pull this prick's head off, or I might just explode.'

Again, the jarl winced. There was a good chance Bjorn would not be *able* to back down, now. He turned back to Harðráði. 'Sorry, Harald, but I think this one might be out of our hands.'

Bjorn was already stepping out of the group, moving toward Orm Axebiter.

'It is a mistake,' Harðráði replied.

'You *know* Bjorn,' Halfdan insisted. 'You know he'll kill the man. Have your guard apologise, and we might still be able to avoid this.'

Harðráði shrugged. 'Orm is his own man.'

'Not for much fucking longer,' snarled Bjorn, and he took three long steps toward him. Axebiter stopped cleaning his nails at last, wiped his blade on his thigh and sheathed it at his side again. He took a single step away from the wall. 'Back down now, big ox, and avoid embarrassment.'

Halfdan fixed Harðráði with a look. 'Do you not value your man?'

'I *know* my man. If they must do this, then they must do this. Apologies in advance.'

'And mine to you.'

Halfdan and the others backed away, leaving plenty of room around Bjorn and Orm Axebiter. The great albino was still stomping forward, arms out, ready to punch or grab, while his opponent simply took another two steps away from the wall. Halfdan found he was hardly breathing, watching.

'Two marks of silver on Orm,' Harðráði said, suddenly.

Halfdan turned to stare at the Norseman. 'What?'

'You heard me. Two marks of silver.'

'Bjorn will kill him.'

'Then you're in for a good bet.'

'All right,' Halfdan said. 'Two marks.'

They stood and watched as the two combatants closed, the larger one at a steady stalk, arms out, the smaller looking as though he were waiting calmly in the street. Halfdan had never seen such confidence in the face of his friend, and suddenly he suspected he'd made a bad wager.

'Bjorn,' he said, a touch of warning in his voice.

But he was too late. Bjorn was on Orm, roaring. His arms lashed out in a series of punches that seemed to come fast and repetitively from all sides, yet somehow Orm Axebiter managed to dodge, duck and bend away from each one with hardly any clear movement. The flurry of missed blows only ended when Bjorn's arms went round Orm in a bear hug that Halfdan knew could crush the ribs of even the toughest man.

He blinked in shock. Bjorn's arms closed in that crushing hug, but Orm was not in them any more. The man had melted away, dropping out of the big albino's grip like a slippery eel through the clutches of a clumsy fisherman. One moment Bjorn was holding the man tight, the next, Orm was crouched between Bjorn's feet as the big albino stared at his empty arms in surprise.

71

Then the blow landed. Orm made just one punch, directly upward from his crouched position, fist clenched tight. The punch struck Bjorn in the balls, hard, before Orm rolled away and then back up to his feet with the grace of an athlete.

Bjorn stared down at his nethers, and let out a surprisingly high-pitched squeak.

Then he collapsed to his knees, his big hands coming down to cradle his bruised manhood. By the time he hit the ground, Orm was back by the wall, knife coming out, finishing his nail cleaning.

'*Odin*,' Halfdan breathed. Not only had he never seen any one man get the best of Bjorn, but he'd never seen any man move so damned fast. He stared at Axebiter.

'I'll knock the two marks off your share,' Harðráði said with a smile.

Ketil and Ulfr hurried over to Bjorn and tried to help him, but the big man waved them away, and then slowly, carefully, rose to his feet with a few groans and gasps. He touched his balls a couple of times and made odd noises when he did so, then took a couple of tentative steps back, his eyes watering.

'This,' he said, gasping and pointing angrily at Orm Axebiter, 'is not over.'

'Then you are a fool,' replied the man by the wall.

'There will be times,' Harðráði said, addressing Halfdan still, 'when you need to join us over the winter for our planning meetings. I heartily recommend you leave your Wolves, or at least Bjorn, in your bunk house, when you do.'

–

Two days later, Halfdan had cause to pull Bjorn aside.

'You have *got* to drop this thing with Harðráði's man.'

The albino shook his head. 'I will get him back for that, mark my words, Halfdan.'

'Bjorn, he could have finished you the other day without even breaking a sweat. The man is a killer, and I will not have

72

my oldest friend buried with his goods on the edge of Sigtun this winter. Am I your jarl, Bjorn?'

'You know you are.'

'Then I give you a direct and unbreakable order. Until I say otherwise you are absolutely forbidden to engage Orm Axebiter in any form of fight, from arm wrestling all the way up to Holmgång. If I hear the two of you have exchanged more than an insult, I will sell you on with the *Sea Cow*. Do you understand?'

The nod in reply was sullen. Halfdan knew his big friend. Bjorn was a creature of instinct and war. He would obey Halfdan's command... but only so far. But there would come a time when Orm pushed him just too far, and no matter what promises he had made, Bjorn would snap and kill the man, or possibly be killed by him. Halfdan resigned to doing whatever he could to keep the two men apart until the Wolves moved on.

—

The following morning, a possibility presented itself.

Rain had set in, seemingly for a while, great torrents of it battering down on Sigtun from a sky the colour of a well-used cauldron. Halfdan and his friends had left the palace compound, despite the weather. Several days in a row cooped up in the palace had set them all on edge, and even in the rain, the idea of walking out in the open was appealing. Thus, Halfdan led his Wolves down that wide street, where the market had gone now the weather had changed, and to the port, to go and check on the *Sea Wolf* and *Sea Dragon*. He now had full ownership of their original ship once more, and the two sleek hunters were moored side by side at the edge of the town, on the periphery, both occupied by their Wolves of Odin crews. The *Sea Cow* had been sent off to a shipyard in the town's north, where hopefully someone would soon buy it, since they now had all the warships they needed, and they had no need of the bovine naval hulk when they had two of Ulfr's ships.

As they reached the vessels, Halfdan waved to the men aboard and had them all come to the bows where he could speak to them.

'I see that Farlof has split you well between the ships. Good. We have a few short months before we sail to war, and I want the Wolves of Odin to be the best two ships in the fleet. To that end, there will be training every day. I want both these ships out on the lake and in the fjords for at least two hours a day. By the time spring comes and we are ready to leave, I want every last man aboard trained to the oar like no other ship in the fleet, working like the perfect team. I want every man to know the sails, the hawsers, the steerboard, every plank and rib and rope in the ship, to know what to do with them, and what *not* to do. Also to know how to repair and replace any parts with speed and efficiency. When something breaks or needs doing, I want every man on both ships to be able to recognise what's wrong, be able to put it right, and to do so, without needing to be told. You have just a few short months to become the best crews in Sigtun. I want you to be able to sail these ships in any weather, in any waters, in any situation, and to be able to turn as swiftly as a bird. I want both crews to run boarding practices, from one ship to the other. Ulfr will take control of all shipboard training, and will skipper the *Sea Wolf*. Ketil will skipper the *Sea Dragon* and assist him. These are your sailing masters. They will train you up.'

He paused, and let that all sink in.

'And two *more* hours a day will be spent training to fight. Some of you came to the Wolves from military service or from other martial backgrounds, but others were shipyard workers in Nordmandi, or farmers in Swaledale. Not all of you have stood in a shield wall or watched horsemen riding at you. Some of you have never swung an axe in violence or held your ground against an angry enemy. Bjorn and I will teach you to fight

74

with sword and axe and shield, and Ketil will teach any of those who have a mind to it to shoot an arrow. Leif will teach you to throw an axe and also train you in the strategies of battles. And Gunnhild will teach you how to win the favour of the gods in your work.

'Do not shy away from this,' he snapped, watching several figures lean back. 'There are those among you who pray to the nailed god. This I know. And I have learned enough to know that there can be value in that. I am no zealot to stamp on your gods. Your ways will be neither hindered nor derided by your shipmates. But whether you pray to Thor or to the White Christ, or the Greek Christ or even the Serkish god, you are *Wolves of Odin*, and the Allfather and the weaving of the Norns ultimately guide the fate of this hirð. I care not *what* you believe, but when Gunnhild tells you something needs doing to keep the gods content, it will be done. By *all* of us.'

He rocked back on his feet. 'Training will begin this afternoon with two circuits of the lake for each ship, alternating between three different speeds of oar stroke.'

'Then all three had better be fast,' said a deep, hoarse voice from behind him. 'If they get in my way, I'll sink them.'

Halfdan turned in surprise, and looked at the five men who stood a few paces away, hands on waists as they watched with interest. It took several moments for him to realise he recognised the speaker, a big, burly man with greying braided hair and even greyer beard.

'Sæbjôrn?'

'I had heard you were here, and it didn't take much work to find your ship. She always did stand out in a crowd. Now I see she has a sister?'

'Who is this?' whispered Anna nearby.

'One of the skippers who sailed with Yngvar out east,' hissed Leif in reply. 'One of very few survivors from Sasireti.'

'I knew you came north,' Halfdan said, struggling for a moment of panic with what the man might have told the

Swedish king about the campaign and Yngvar's death, 'but I thought you were going back to your wife?'

Sæbjörn shrugged. 'I came home to find she had died in the winter. I married her sister, but she turned out to be even *worse* of a nag, so I took to the sea again.' He grinned. 'I wondered what had become of you, young Loki-born. Harðráði said you'd served under him with the Varangians, but that when he came north, you went west instead.'

'More out of necessity than choice. But it has been an interesting journey nonetheless,' Halfdan said.

'Why do you *want* to find them, Sæbjörn?' grumbled a big black-bearded man beside the skipper.

'What, Modi?'

'These men brought us nothing but bad luck in Georgia. It is the heathen fault of their big fat *berserkr* that we lost Sasireti. God was with the Byzantines because God had been shunned by ours.'

Behind Halfdan, he could hear Bjorn growling. He gave Sæbjörn a tentative smile. 'Your man had best stop making such accusations, or my big friend back there might take offence.'

'Let him, the *pagan*,' spat the black-haired man.

Sæbjörn gave Halfdan an odd look. 'Modi Wave-walker is disgruntled that we left Georgia with less than we had when we arrived.'

'Weren't we all.' Halfdan snorted. 'But *Modi Wave-walker* is pissing off the wrong man right now, and unless you want to go round picking up his teeth, he might want to apologise.' It struck Halfdan that he'd said something very similar when Bjorn had faced up to Orm Axebiter, but then this man did not exude that quiet, deadly confidence Harðráði's man had. It was a gamble. If Bjorn met two such opponents in a row, it might well ruin him. But the albino needed to let his inner bear out.

He turned to Bjorn. The facial expression he pulled, which was visible neither to Modi, nor Sæbjörn, nor their three

76

companions, was designed to carry the instruction 'Do what you have to, but do not create an *incident*'.

The way Bjorn grinned in response left Halfdan uncertain as to whether he'd understood or not, and so he stood and watched in tense silence as the big albino walked toward Sæbjôrn's man.

'I remember you at Sasireti. When we fled, you had to pull your trousers up from where a Byzantine had been buggering you with an arrow, yes?'

Halfdan winced.

The shout had very much the intended effect as Modi Wavewalker roared angrily and leapt, pushing aside Sæbjôrn and his men, who tried briefly and in vain to stop it. Modi and Bjorn met in open ground, and Halfdan watched the ensuing struggle with a level of horrified fascination. He had never seen so many varied and eye-wateringly inventive ways to injure as Modi and Bjorn displayed in combat. He watched a purse of coins pushed into a mouth and the jaw slammed shut. He watched a swinging arm deflected so that it hit its owner in the nuts. He saw eye-gouging, head-butting, and wrist-twisting, and every manner of dirty fighting that did not involve the drawing of a weapon.

Modi was good, though not Orm-Axebiter-good. Bjorn was better. The fight culminated when Modi, struggling to keep his balance with his knee, ankle and hip all injured, staggered to one side, and Bjorn simply leapt on top of him, a bear-sized, bear-torn monster with the weight of a small wagon, dropping onto the injured man. The two men hit the ground, Modi badly twisted underneath, Bjorn lying on his back on top, eyes rolling, not sure whether he had won or lost.

For long moments, the jarl worried that Bjorn had actually killed the man underneath him. Halfdan had had Bjorn's weight atop him before, and it could easily kill an injured man, he was sure. And then Halfdan heard it. For a heartbeat he wasn't sure what it was he was hearing, and then he realised it was laughter. And not from any observer, or even from Bjorn, but from Modi.

'Get off me, you big, stinky bastard,' Sæbjôrn's man said, snorting and gasping. 'You smell like Satan's own shit.'

Bjorn folded his hands behind his head, leaning back and applying a little extra pressure. 'I dunno. I rather like it here.'

The two men exploded in laughter once more, one a more wheezy, crushed laughter than the other, but both genuine.

'Bjorn?' Halfdan tried.

The big man gave his jarl a grin, then rolled off his victim, who inhaled in a huge rush. 'You don't remember Modi, then? He and I had a farting competition that last night at Kutaisi before we went our separate ways. He lost.'

'Lost? I won! In that I *didn't* smell like a draugr's scrotum!'

As the two men exploded in laughter again and collapsed in a heap, Halfdan smiled in relief. With any luck, winter would pass with that sort of humour.

Chapter 6

Leif broke off his conversation as Gunnhild tapped him on a shoulder and pointed. He turned, already knowing what he would see. Harðráði was ambling their way with Ellisif on his arm, and even as he glanced over, Leif saw the Norseman spot Gunnhild. There ought to be a word, he thought, to describe the look the man took on the moment he saw the völva. Leer didn't quite fit, for there was more than just lust there, but adoration was perhaps too much.

The Rus turned and walked toward the couple, formulating his opening line as he went.

'Jarl Harald, might I speak to you regarding the disposition of ships in the fleet?'

Harðráði frowned. 'What?'

'Ulfr is concerned that, with our ships being both smaller and faster than many in the fleet, their effectiveness will be negated should we find ourselves in a naval engagement, jammed between slower and larger vessels. The optimum placement for the *Sea Wolf* and *Sea Dragon*...'

Harðráði waved a hand dismissively. 'There is ample time to discuss such matters in the coming days, man.'

Leif dropped in beside the Norseman and very subtly steered him slightly to his left, skewing him away from the direct line he'd been making for Gunnhild and instead toward where Ulfr and Halfdan were deep in conversation with Sæbjôrn. 'You might say that, but already the skippers of the many vessels vie

79

for the best positions in the fleet and the prime targets along the Danish coast. Bearing in mind that Jarl Halfdan and his ships are only part of this fleet as a *favour*, it would serve you well to make sure that they are not lost in the mass.'

Harðráði stopped, turning to Leif. Ellisif's hand slid from his arm, unnoticed.

'Perhaps you are right, Leif of Kiev. I had best give this a little thought. You have a proposal, I take it?' he added, flicking just a brief winsome look at Gunnhild before turning fully away from her.

Leif did not. The whole thing had been plucked out of his head as an excuse as he crossed the room, but he was clever, and he would manufacture a proposal even as he put it to the would-be king of Norway. The important thing was to keep him away from Gunnhild. As he and Harðráði crossed the room, he caught an almost imperceptible nod from Halfdan, and sent one back. The jarl had been ready to intercept if Leif had not.

They were all at it. For over a month now, they had been in Sigtun, preparing, training, listening to the endless debates between the various leaders and nobles. And that meant that for over a month, they had been playing this particular game, a game of Gunnhild's devising in the first place. Leif was not at all sure how deep the völva's affections for the glorious adventurer ran, but he suspected that she was fighting her own battle not to run to him, though fighting it well. As part of this, though, she had made it clear to the Wolves that under no circumstances was she to be left alone with Harðráði.

'He will start to hound me as he did in Miklagarðr,' she'd said, 'and that is no good for either of us. I will find it distracting and irritating, and his mind will not be on this great game of 'tafl he has started.'

'Will he really pursue you like that?' Halfdan had asked. 'I mean, he has a wife now, and she is clever, attractive and powerful, after all.'

Leif had interjected then. 'That won't stop him.'

Gunnhild nodded at that. 'I task you all with this: each of you is to keep your eye on the lunatic, and if he makes for me, keep him away, until we set sail. I have no wish to find myself trapped in a corner with him.'

They had done just that. For over a month, every time Gunnhild and Harðráði appeared in any one place, a member of the Wolves would find a way to pull him aside. Leif had initially expected most of the work to fall to him or Halfdan, as the quickest thinkers of the group, but there had been surprises, and Bjorn had perhaps been the biggest of them. He had turned out to be the best of all at distracting Harðráði, for every time the man appeared in the room with his bodyguard, Orm Axebiter, Bjorn made a beeline for them and made overtures for a scuffle, which Harðráði then had to defuse by taking his man away from the scene. As well as Bjorn and Leif, Ulfr, Farlof and Ketil had managed to distract him occasionally, too. He had yet to encounter Gunnhild alone.

Taking Harðráði into a corner, Leif began to spin out a strategy that sounded to him quite reasonable, keeping the two ships of the Wolves of Odin on the left flank of the fleet, and with the front runners, because they would then be on the outside as the ships rounded the southern tip of Skáney, heading west, where their speed would best come into play. It must have been reasonable, for Harðráði nodded throughout, and then told Leif he would look at it in a grander perspective, and if it seemed reasonable, he would lobby for it with Sveinn and Onund. By the time they had finished and Leif looked around, Gunnhild had left the room, and any potential meeting had been avoided, again.

It did not escape Leif's notice that Harðráði then marched off about his business without even looking around to see if his wife was still waiting for him. Leif, on the other hand, looked across the room to where Ellisif, daughter of the prince of Kiev, stood by a wall hanging, with her arms folded and a look of carefully controlled serenity. He glanced back. Most of the Wolves were still around. Gunnhild had disappeared into another room until Harðráði had gone, but was now reappearing, with Anna at her side, safe once more.

Content that things were normal for now, Leif walked across the wide hall to where Harðráði's wife stood, stopping a respectful few paces short and bowing with just an incline of the head.

'Elisaveta Yaroslavna,' he greeted her, with her name as it was used in the Kievan dialect.

One of her eyebrows rose. 'It has been a long time since anyone has called me that. In this godforsaken land, I am Ellisif to all.'

'Not to one born of Kiev himself. I doubt you remember me, but…'

'How could anyone not remember Leif Ruriksson, spinner of enchanting tales, diplomat and scholar?'

Leif blinked. 'I…'

'Of course I remember you, friend Leif. It has not been *that* long.' She finally cracked into a smile, which warmed her face like the sun over an icy fjord. 'It is so pleasant to hear a Rus accent after the past year or so, even if your tongue has picked up some strange inflections. Byzantine I can detect and understand, but there are others.'

'We have travelled far and wide, and visited many places.'

'I have travelled not so far. I was excited at the possibility of visiting the land of my grandfather, but the place itself turns out to be not a great deal different to the land of my *father*, while the court itself is considerably less civilised.'

Leif had not really considered this, but then he had been rather busy since they arrived, what with one thing or another. He shrugged. 'It is a little… rustic, perhaps, after Kiev. But it is not without its charms.'

'Then they are well hidden.'

'The kings of the Svears and Geats have not had the luxury of the influence of Byzantium in their lands the way Kiev has.

In Kiev, a library was a place to while away the hours. In Sigtun, texts are usually written on the side of rocks.' He smiled. 'And their strange Romish Christianity is not as elegant as our Byzantine Church, not as clever. It helps to think of them like children, I find. They have infinite potential and are capable of great things, but they are still young and finding their way. It is down to those of us with a modicum of civilisation to gift it to them and help them grow.'

He looked around momentarily to make sure no locals or Wolves had heard that, for it might easily have been perceived as an insult.

'My world is shrinking, Leif,' she said. 'In Kiev I was a princess, and my authority was recognised. I could travel with my guards and attendants and be honoured wherever I went. In Sweden I am nobody. A foreign adventurer's wife. I have few attendants and no guards. I am expected to stay by my husband's side, so my world is at *best* Sigtun, but more realistically it is just this poor complex. I am bored, Leif, and my husband, glorious though he is, seems to have forgotten that I exist. He puts me on his arm in the morning like part of his clothing, and then drapes me over a chair in the evening when other matters are of interest. When we were married in Kiev, I had such grand hopes, and he was so attentive. Now he is attentive to *others...*'

Leif winced. 'Do not lay this on Gunnhild, though. Her history with your husband is long and complex, but you must believe me that she has absolutely no intention of stealing him from you.'

'Oh, that I can see from the way you all nimbly distract him. Though from the looks I occasionally catch her throwing his way, I suspect there is more there still than disdain.' She sighed. 'But it is not just your Gunnhild. For the month before you turned up, I kept finding him following the sister of one of the local jarls. Not even a *pretty* woman, either, in my opinion.'

'Yet he will stay faithful, I think.'

Ellisif shrugged. 'My husband is an adventurer, a warrior and a hunter. He is not a homebody. I think he is enticed and

83

thrilled by the chase. He pursued me for years, you know? He first tried to snare me before he went south for Miklagarðr, and then picked up where he left off when he returned. Now he has me, the thrill is gone, and he seeks a new chase.'

There was, Leif thought, probably a great deal of truth there. Perhaps if Gunnhild had let him catch her back in the imperial city, he would soon have bored of her and looked elsewhere. Instead, the chase was back on, and that had him as excited as ever. Yes, Ellisif knew what she was talking about, clearly. He looked up and noted a single tear form in the corner of her eye. Lifting his hand, he brushed it away with his thumb. 'Do not worry, Princess. Soon we leave on the great expedition to Daneland. Your husband will then be thinking only of war and thrones, and when it is over you will be with him in Norway, and then you will not be the wife of a foreign adventurer. You will be a *queen*. And queens among these people are not just expected to be a hand on their husband's arm. Your world will open up once more. This will all pass.'

'I hope you are right, Leif Ruriksson. Thank you. You have calmed my stormy soul.'

She gave him a small kiss on the cheek, then turned and drifted away toward the doorway through which Harðráði had gone.

Leif stood for a moment, then turned.

Anna was glaring at him.

Dear God, what was happening in this place? Elisaveta of Kiev despairing of her husband's eye straying, Harðráði frustrated that Gunnhild remained out of his reach, Gunnhild trying to keep the man at arm's length, Leif trying to keep everyone happy, and now Anna... jealous? Good grief.

A tiny thrill of guilt ran through him for a moment. He knew full well how it would have looked to Anna when he wiped away Ellisif's tear and she kissed him on the cheek. He knew also that there was nothing romantic in it, for all that he would have arm-wrestled a bear in the old days in Kiev for just a touch of the princess's face, let alone a kiss. No. This was platonic only, now. He loved Anna. She should *know* that.

He gave her a loving smile.

She turned her back on him and spoke to Gunnhild.

Damn it, but that was going to take some work.

A commotion in the next room drew his attention back from such worries, and he crossed the room with several others to the doorway through which the royal couple had gone. His spirits sank as he reached the opening to see Bjorn and Orm Axebiter facing each other at the far side of the room. Harðráði was ordering his man to stand down, and Halfdan was snapping at Bjorn, though neither man had moved. They were not fighting, but the air crackled with martial spirit, and it would take only one wrong word for the two men to be on one another again.

What was it with this place? As if it wasn't bad enough that the women were all complicating issues, even men with as basic a thought process as *Bjorn* could not stop causing trouble.

Leif, finding himself unaccountably angry, stormed across the room. Orm and Bjorn were trading insults, and their fingers were now dancing dangerously close to the weapons at their sides. If this went wrong, it could mean more than a bruised scrotum this time. Before he really knew what he was doing, Leif strode between the two men.

That tense martial air evaporated in a moment, as though Leif's very appearance had snapped some invisible cord holding the men together. Bjorn blinked at him.

'Leif?'

'Bjorn, you take too long to learn some lessons. Here's a hard one for you. Orm is faster than you. When you do hit him, you'll probably kill him, yes, but that's if you get the chance. And then, even if you do, you will owe Harðráði a massive debt. Back away now, and stop this stupid game.'

Bjorn blinked at him, surprised at being spoken to thusly, which had probably not happened since he was a child. Before he could reply, though, Leif had turned to Orm Axebiter.

Harðráði's right-hand man wore an unreadable expression, but Leif noted that his fingers had left his sword hilt, which was a telling sign.

'And *you*,' he snapped at Orm. 'You should damn well know better. Bjorn is a man of simple warrior spirit: a son of Thor, and a wearer of the bear shirt. You, on the other hand, have all the signs of a clever man, so perhaps you should *use* that brain. You humiliated Bjorn. He will get over that in time, if you leave him be, because he is not a man to hold unnecessary grudges. But you need to back down, and *stay* down, because I tell you now that if you ever truly *injure* Bjorn, there will be two shiploads of Odin's Wolves baying for your blood, and even your master will not stop them. Use your brain.'

He stepped out from between them.

'Now, the pair of you, piss off and stop this.'

He turned and stormed away without a further look at the two men. At other times he might have been rather proud of that, and particularly pleased at the small round of applause that broke out as he walked away. Right now, he was just irritated.

He'd thought that, with the Wolves coming home to their rightful place in the north, things would settle, be normal, natural, that they would fit in. But he was starting to think that after all their time journeying the world, the Wolves had changed. Perhaps the north was not the place for them any more. He was certainly not sure it was the place for *him*. He may have comforted Elisaveta when she felt out of place, but what she had said had oddly rung true for him, too. Their deal with Harðráði had sounded good, but Leif now found himself wondering whether their own tract of Norwegian land and a jarldom would be enough for them.

He twitched. As he reached the doorway, he spotted Gunnhild and Anna. The Byzantine woman who had stolen his heart on the far side of the world turned and gave him a look that could freeze fire embers. He sighed. A moment later Gunnhild was drawn into a conversation with some local noblewoman, and Leif leapt on the opportunity, crossing to his love. He grasped Anna's arm and turned her, gesturing away to a quiet corner. She resisted, coldly, for just a moment, then allowed him to lead her away.

'Anna, I've been thinking.'

'Yes, I'll bet you have.'

He sighed, something he seemed to be doing a lot at the moment. 'I'm not sure Sweden is a place for the Wolves to put down roots. Norway, either. Nor Daneland. It doesn't feel right, and I cannot see my future set here. You are as much a stranger to this world as I. What do *you* think, my love?'

'My place is by Gunnhild's side,' she said without a moment's hesitation. 'I stood with her in the face of death and will do it again. Wherever Gunnhild goes, *that* will be my home. If that be Sweden or Norway, then so be it. And if that does not suit you, Leif, then I am sure you will find a snug harbour among the Rus.'

She pulled her arm from his grip, turned, and marched back over to Gunnhild.

He stood there for a moment, watching her leave, and closed his eyes. He was almost certain she meant he could go home to the safety of Kiev, but from her phrasing, and given her current mood, he could not be sure she did not mean Princess Elisaveta.

He nodded quietly to himself. Anna was a woman of spirit and passion. She was angry, but that would dissipate if he gave her sufficient time to cool down. By the time of the evening meal, he would have her back. For now, though, he suddenly found himself at a loose end. The others were all busy, and he was alone in the palace.

Guidance. He needed guidance.

He'd tried thinking it through himself, and Anna was of little help in current circumstances.

A walk.

He needed a *walk*.

A quarter of an hour later, he was striding out of the gates of the palace compound. It did not escape him that he had just done precisely what Elisaveta had bemoaned her inability to do, and left the palace. Still, he was feeling unsettled, a little irritable, and uncertain, too. When that happened to those among the Wolves who still held to the old gods, they besought Odin wherever they were, for they believed the Allfather watched over them with his ravens. Or they went to Gunnhild, of course. It was different for the Christians, now a minority once more among the Wolves. For most of those men, a church was not hard to find in this world, but these churches were strange, peddling a slightly skewed version of God to that which they revered in the east. He was fairly sure he was not going to find a church of the Byzantine creed here, and so he wandered through Sigtun for a time in the chilly grey, taking it all in.

When he found himself outside the church, it came as something of a surprise. He'd not intended to go there, but in wandering down that main street, he'd eventually come to that ornate wooden building near the harbour.

He stopped, suddenly fascinated by the church doors, so delicately carved with intricate décor bearing a curious mix of Christian and pagan iconography. The frame was covered with Ringerike work, curls and swirls crossing one another, curling and interlacing in the most complex design. The doors themselves, he realised, were older. Probably considerably older than the rest of the church, and presumably belonged to an earlier building. There were crosses and Christian iconography, carved biblical scenes, but they seemed to be recent work, drowning out an older set of carvings beneath them. Yet here and there those carvings still stood clear. A stranger to this world might see them as Christian figures, as warriors of God about their good Christian business, but the student of the old world might note that the figure with the staff had only one eye, and that nearby two birds flew. Or they might wonder why a figure that could easily be an apostle was carrying a large hammer.

He realised with a wry smile that the men who'd constructed this church, who'd been given a set of ornate pagan doors and told to rework them as appropriate, had done so as much as they dared but, Christian or not, they had not had the guts to deface the old gods.

Before he knew what he was doing, he was opening the door and stepping inside.

In a way, those doors were a very good analogy for the Wolves. A veneer of Christianity but with the old gods still respected and standing proud.

As the door closed behind him, the world seemed moment-arily plunged into darkness, for outside the sky had been grey but bright, while in here the few windows that admitted any light were small and high up. His eyes adjusted slowly, and he closed them for a while to speed up the process. When he opened them again, his breath was stolen.

If he'd thought the building ornate from the outside, the interior was a whole new world. A large single room formed of arches and balconies, of criss-crossing beams and struts and rafters, all carved with beautiful designs, there was hardly a flat space in the whole church, everything complex and ornate. In some ways, he had to concede, it was arguable that this place was actually more artistic than even some of the great ancient churches of Byzantium. Certainly anyone who suggested that this world was one of crude and simple people would swallow those words when faced with this marvel. He found himself regretting some of his earlier words. Rural. Children. This building suggested something entirely different.

Perhaps Elisaveta should come here. It might change her mind about her new home. It was certainly challenging a few of Leif's preconceptions.

He walked around, studying the place, the complex archi-tecture and the designs. The altar at the far end, which was not so different to the ones he was used to. Small doors in two places led to other rooms of the church, but both were closed, so he did not try either.

Then he found it.

He stopped and stared in surprise.

A stone, not unlike a Christian tombstone, and yet different. He's seen runestones in both Daneland and in Sigtun, most of them raised since the days Christianity had taken hold, but a few, particularly here, still bore old pagan designs. He'd not thought to see one in a church, yet here it was, in an alcove seemingly designed for it. Standing perhaps to his shoulder height, the stone's carvings had been picked out in red paint, making it more legible in this dim light. The centre of the stone was a cross, while the text was cut along what looked like a long, weaving serpent coiled around it, tethered top and bottom. Again, an odd nod to the old ways around a central Christian sign.

He started to read, and as he did, a shiver pulsed through him.

> *Gunnar auk Biorn auk Thorgrīmr ræistu stæin þenna at Thorstæin brōður sinn, es vas austr dauðr með Ingvari.*
>
> '*Gunnar and Bjorn and Thorgrímr raised this stone in memory of Thorstein, their brother, who is dead in the east with Ingvar.*'

The shiver came again. He *remembered* a Thorstein from that journey. A loud, red-haired fellow from Gorm's ship. Of course, there could easily have been a dozen Thorsteins involved in their quest, but Leif found himself believing it was that one man commemorated here. *Gorm the unlucky.* Leif remembered that day, when Gorm's run of bad luck had finally come to a very fatal end, along with his ship and his crew. Burning men screaming aboard the vessel, throwing themselves desperately into the water, though the Alani fire continued to burn them even then. Thorstein would have been one of those figures.

The next shiver was different, more of a shudder.

Perhaps he needed to look at their situation from a broader perspective. The Wolves had come to their homeland in the north, and he might be unsettled by it all, but he was in a far better position than the hundreds of men like Thorstein, who had never come home at all.

'He was a good man.'

Leif started and turned at the voice. The priest stood not far behind him. The man must move like a *cat*, for Leif had never heard him open the door and approach across the church.

'Thorstein?'

The priest nodded. 'He is much missed by his family, and by our community. A fool's errand, that quest.'

'You have no idea.'

The priest gave him an odd look, part frown, but did not press the matter. 'You are my first visitor today. Are you here for silent prayer, or is it because of Thorstein?'

Leif gave him a faint smile. 'A little of both, in a way, and more besides. I think I knew Thorstein. In his last days. Loud. Red hair, yes?'

'You knew him. And in his last days?'

'Not all those who went east are lost and commemorated on runestones.'

'Then God must have preserved you for greater things.'

That made Leif chuckle. Greater things. Like saving an empress, capturing a gold-thief, aiding a duke, or removing a witch from the cold hills of Angle Land?

The priest must have misunderstood his laughter.

'God's clemency is no laughing matter.'

'For sure,' Leif said easily. 'I am a little lost, and looking for guidance. I am far from home, and I do not think I will return, but here I am not at ease, and I cannot see my path. I have a friend who is wise and who could suggest a path for me, but her methods do not sit well with my God-fearing ways, if you know what I mean?'

'Ah. Yes. I know the sort. Consider, perhaps, that they may work with God's grace, while believing it is the work of their demons. If so, then the Church should pity them, and nurture

them, bringing them back to God's embrace, rather than vili-
fying and persecuting them.'

'My… wife,' *only stretching the truth a little there*, 'is of a similar
opinion.'

'And your wife is with you?'

'She is.'

'So you are far from home and worried about your future,
but you have a wife with you, and a wise one by the sound of it,
since she agrees with me. Consider perhaps that a man's home
is not formed by the land around him. Why else would our
forebears have taken to their longships and searched for lands
a little more forgiving? So if the land is not what makes our
home, then it is our relationships and those around us that do.
Our place in society, our Church, and our family and friends.
You are not alone? You have friends or family here?'

A nod. Both, in a way.

'Then perhaps your home is wherever you are. You love your
wife?'

'I do.'

'Then I might venture that *she* is your home.'

Leif nodded. Anna had said that wherever Gunnhild went,
she would go. Similarly, wherever Anna went, Leif would go.
He frowned. Oddly, that cut through everything. It mattered
not whether he was somewhere he felt comfortable. It mattered
not if the Wolves rode the whale road forever, as long as he was
with Anna.

'That is oddly comforting.'

'The world has a way of working out for good men.'

'Apart from Thorstein.'

The priest chuckled. 'But he sits by the hand of God, and
he is remembered well. Who could ask for more? God's plan is
ineffable, but it is a plan nonetheless.'

Leif found himself smiling again now. He felt a little better
about things. And somehow this place had made it seem that
all things were possible. If the architects could make a Christian

92

door but honour the old gods as they did so, if Thorstein could be remembered on a stone with a cross, but with what appeared to be the Midgard serpent around it, if this priest, like Anna, could believe that a völva's power came from God, then who was he to say what was right and wrong, what was possible and not possible?

When it came down to it, he was a little disconnected here, but as long as he had Anna and the Wolves, he was never truly lost.

Thanking the priest, he turned and left the church to a world where the clouds had rolled back a little to allow for cold blue patches. He felt oddly refreshed and a little hopeful. Now he had to find Anna, and make sure she knew what she meant to him. Then they had just a few short months to pass in Sigtun, and they would be on the whale road once more.

Home was where they made it.

Part Two

ᚦᛟᚱᚠᛖᛗᛋ ᛟᚠ ᚨᛁᚾᛁᚾ

War

'Red flashing in the southern sky
The clear flame sweeps both broad and high
From fair Hróarskelda's lofty towers
On lowly huts its fire rain pours
And shows the people's silent train
In terror scouring o'er the plain
Seeking the forest's deepest glen
To hide with wolves, and escape from men.'

From *King Harald's Saga* by Snorri Sturluson,
trans. Samuel Laing

Chapter 7

Sjáland, spring 1046

'Odin's stinking balls, that's a small place,' Bjorn bellowed from his bench as he pulled and rolled, pulled and rolled the great oar in time with the others.

Halfdan just nodded. It *was* a small fishing village, but it did strike him that but a few short years ago, this place would have seemed quite sizeable to a farm boy from backwater Gotland. For a warrior jarl who had fought across the Byzantine Empire, had been in several wars, and had seen the greatest cities in the world, however, the village that lay ahead did indeed seem meagre.

But then they should *savour* that, since it was theirs, and *all* theirs.

The fleet had set sail with the first sign of spring, every man ready to get their teeth into the campaign. It had been a trying winter, for a number of reasons. Firstly, for Halfdan, it was the knowledge that every month they tarried allowed for the faint possibility that Hjalmvigi might somehow work his way back to power, or worse, move on out of their reach. But there was also the matter of keeping Harðráði away from Gunnhild, which they had managed on all but a couple of occasions, after each of which the völva had shut herself away for a while before returning to the fold, apparently unchanged. And then there was the matter of Leif, who seemed distracted and uncertain, not quite himself, and his relationship with Anna seemed to be a little strained, too.

Even the training for sailing and battle had been stressful, for the Wolves were of such varied origin that no two men had the same ideas or skills. They'd had some practice, of course, over the journey from Angle Land, but that was for open sailing, not war. They had rowed until the men had callouses, and were either capable of working together or had proved sufficient inability to be given lesser roles.

Ulfr taught them *racing* ships, *facing* ships, *breaching* ships and *beaching* ships, but whether his lessons would hold for such a weird, disparate crew remained to be seen. They had not even bothered broaching the subject of portage, though that would change soon enough.

The lessons in warfare had been troublesome and uncertain, too.

All in all, when the call went out and the skippers prepared their ships for departure, Halfdan was more than a little relieved, and he was not alone in that.

Every ship – Halfdan had forgotten how many there were now, but there were *many* – had been assigned one coastal target on the map of Sjáland in Onund's war room. There would be no escape for the islanders, for every few miles of coast would see a landing. Sjáland was large, and with a wandering coastline, home to many towns and villages and a few purpose-built fortresses, with the capital, Hróarskelda, a little to the north and east of centre. The fleet was to hit its targets hard, like the Norse raiders of old, killing, burning, destroying and looting, and then move inland. The whole force would be like a noose around the capital, gradually constricting.

The few dissenting voices, uneasy with such a violent assault on simple farmers and fishermen, were quelled by Gunnhild. 'Our ancestors carved out a place in the world with such ways. Do they not call the Northmen of old Vikingar, because of those raids? And those among us who follow the nailed god should remember the book of Exodus from your Bible: "the Lord is a warrior, and his name is Almighty."' That had ended

98

all argument, and surprised many, though not Halfdan, who knew of Gunnhild's study of the Bible with the empress during their time in Miklagarðr.

Still, initially, Sveinn of Daneland had assigned a quiet village each to the *Sea Wolf* and the *Sea Dragon*, but Halfdan and Leif had visited the kings and told them flatly that the two ships worked together. The two quiet fishing villages that had been allocated to them were swept away to another couple of skippers, and Halfdan had slapped his hands on the table, a wild, vicious smile on his face as the Loki serpents on his arm itched. 'There is a village called Torpstrand. We will have Torpstrand.'

Images flooded into memory of the men of that village doing their best to bring down Bjorn and Ketil in that bar in Hróarskelda. The flash of a knife as it almost turned sour.

Torpstrand.

And here it was.

Halfdan looked back and forth along the shore as the *Sea Wolf* raced through the surf. A bright white sandy beach, beyond which lay scrub grass, and then the village. The ships approached the land at the village's most northeasterly and southwesterly reaches by prior arrangement. As they'd closed on the island, they had peeled apart so that the *Sea Dragon* could hit the east, the *Sea Wolf* the west. The two crews would then launch into their land assault until they met, at which point there would be no more village. Bjorn and Ketil had not forgotten their brawl the previous autumn, and Halfdan suspected just landing those two at the village would cause nothing short of a massacre anyway, even without the rest of the Wolves.

The place had maybe twenty houses, along with a few barns, shacks and sea stores. Three small fishing boats sat pulled up on the sand. Halfdan glanced back at Farlof and could see that he was already eyeing those vessels. Each of the Wolves' ships had a small group of warriors under a capable leader whose sole role in this attack was to locate and seize all boats, holing and burning them to stop villagers escaping.

Because no one was to escape.

That was the three kings' plan: an utterly merciless assault on the coast of Sjáland, then moving inland to seize, depopulate and burn the capital. If anything was going to draw Magnus south to Daneland, it had to be something big.

'Ketil. Don't forget your task.'

The Icelander turned to him, one glittering eye, and one empty, mangled socket, and nodded. He and three men had another role here, just like Farlof and his warriors. Ketil had with him only the fastest men, who could use bows. They would not raid the houses, nor burn the boats. They would race past the buildings and take up positions where they could kill any individual who fled the village inland.

No escape...

Halfdan could hear the change in the water around the ship. The seabed was rising as they closed, just beneath the hull now. Sure enough, a moment later Ulfr bellowed the command to raise the oars, and the entire crew did just that, preventing the potential disaster of catching an oar blade on the seabed, which could snowball into a major incident on a dragon ship. Instead, the oars rose to vertical in unison, and a moment later there was a grinding noise, and the ship lurched to a halt. It was easy to tell the seasoned sailors among them, for they were ready, gripping benches and sheer strakes, and braced against the impact, while those who were relatively new to the whale road lost their footing, or were thrown against the timbers, winding them. At least no one went over the side, as they had done once or twice during those endless training sessions on the lake at Sigtun.

As he rocked back from the thud, Halfdan glanced to his right to see with some satisfaction that the *Sea Dragon* had beached almost simultaneously.

'Odiiiiin!' Halfdan shouted at the top of his voice, thrusting his glorious Alani sword in the air so that it caught the spring sunshine and shone like Angurvadal. It mattered not that there were followers of the nailed god among the Wolves, for the cry had become more than a homage to old One-eye; it had become a war cry unique to the Wolves in these times, and so every man, Christian or not, roared the Allfather's name in response as the assault began.

Halfdan made sure he was the first to leap from the boat's side, landing with jarring impact in the soft, white sand. He was off and running in a heartbeat. As usual, he shunned a helmet. Whatever protection such armour offered, it also seriously affected peripheral vision and hearing, and Halfdan preferred to be fully aware than better protected. As such, his hair blew in the wind, thrown back from his wind-tanned face as his arms came up, perfect sword in one, in the other: a shield of old design with the three wolves painted upon it, touched up by Leif over the winter to its former perfection. His chain shirt shushed and jingled and his sax clonked and flapped in its sheath at his side as he ran, continuing to bellow the Allfather's name as he did so.

Behind him, the Wolves swarmed over the ship's side and onto the beach, breaking immediately into a run. Farlof and four men peeled off, racing along the line where wet sand met dry, making for those three small fishing boats. Ketil went the other way with his speedy archers, racing for the inland side of the village. The rest were with Halfdan, Bjorn ahead, roaring, savouring the opportunity. And that had been the extent of the plan. The rest they would leave to chaos, fate and luck.

The villagers were moving now. They had not known what was happening when two dragon ships bore down on them from the open sea, but no one had expected this, obviously. It had been a long time since the days of true Vikingar, since any Northman had raided Sjáland, after all.

But the moment the ships had beached fast and hard, and armoured men had begun to pour from them, all doubt had vanished. These ships were raiders, here for violence and theft, and the villagers broke into panic. A number of them were already making for the fishing boats. They might make it there before Farlof and his men, or the matching group from the other ship, but they would never have time to get the boats to sea and safety before they were fallen upon. There would be no escape there.

Other men were running away into the countryside, but already Ketil and his men were after them, moving at eye-watering speed for men on foot, nocking and loosing arrows even as they ran. Any man who escaped them would certainly have *some* god looking out for him, for Ketil, like Bjorn, was still remembering that bar fight and seeking to finish it.

Still more of the villagers had run into their houses, terrified, as though the simple buildings might supply some form of sanctuary.

Then there were the hardy few...

By and large they were old men, who'd played a part in some war of the past, warriors emerging from their houses with spears or axes or swords pitted with rust, dusty and cobwebbed. Not many of them, maybe ten that Halfdan could see. They did not band together, but each came forth, brandishing their weapons, growling and making for the attackers threatening their home.

Halfdan nodded his appreciation. Men with such courage deserved to be respected and remembered. They would still die, but they would die well, as Northmen should.

Wolves of Odin were beside him now, running, roaring, ready for the kill. It mattered not that these people had never done anything to the Wolves, or that they were innocent. For the men of Halfdan's hirð they represented unparalleled opportunity. For their part in this campaign, the Wolves would be rich men, they would be given a home by a king, and their names would be remembered with awe. For Halfdan it meant even more. It was a critical step toward finding Hjalmvigi.

One of the brave elders had clearly made out Halfdan for the leader of this force, and was running straight for him, an old, heavy sword in his hand. Halfdan didn't need to tell his men. Those who had been running in the old man's direction veered off, finding new targets, leaving their jarl the honour of fighting a brave man.

He came to a halt as the warrior slowed, and then stopped, facing him, an oddly peaceful stand-off amid the chaos and noise of the raid.

'Why?' was all the man said.

Halfdan shrugged. 'Kings. Silver. Land. Revenge. Nothing personal. Not for me, anyway. A few of my men have unfinished business with your youngsters, mind.'

The man stood silent for a moment, flinty gaze on Halfdan. 'I will not die easily,' he said. 'I am Ivar Blackleg.'

'Good. Then I will sing your praises in Valhöll, Ivar Blackleg.'

The man gave him an odd look before straightening and readying himself. Daneland had been Christian longer than any other land in the north. This man had probably never heard a man speak such words. Still, the old warrior gave his sword a couple of experimental swings.

Halfdan shook his shield free, arm out of the strap, allowing it to fall to the sand, not because he felt that the fight would be fairer, although he was pleased at that. More because he did not want that excellent painting of wolves damaged and defaced so early in the campaign. The old man did not come for him, instead watching his eyes, anticipating Halfdan's next move. He was good, then. A trained and experienced warrior.

Halfdan made that move, not because he was eager, and he did not really want to play into the man's hands, but because the Wolves would be watching, and it would not do to have any of them see him pause and think he was uncertain about anything. A jarl needed to be confident, strong, certain, unflinching, and he needed to lead by example.

His first lunge with the short Alani sword was easily sidestepped by a man who'd been watching him, weighing him up. But Halfdan was no fool either, and he knew the man was ready for him. He'd not put too much momentum into the blow, or overextended, and even as the warrior tried to take advantage of such things, Halfdan was dancing to the side, out of the way of that great swinging sword.

The man was good, but he was old. He did not have the strength or stamina he would have had in his youth when using that blade. As such, when he swung, the blade was more in control than he, and took precious moments to bring back and ready for another move. That, Halfdan decided, was how he would win. He moved to face the man again and waited, moving tantalisingly closer, so that he was easily in reach of that swinging sword. The man, to his credit, did not attack immediately, and so Halfdan was forced to make another impotent lunge himself to draw the man forth. As he danced back from this latest failed attack, the man swung that heavy blade, and this time, Halfdan was ready for it. He dropped his Alani sword into its path, catching the larger sword and deflecting it away, but even as the two blades separated, Halfdan's was circling, rolling back, his sword's shorter reach and lighter form making it easier to handle. Even as the old man's blade still swept to the side, trying to arrest the swing and bring it back, Halfdan's smaller sword slashed out once, twice, thrice.

Each cut was precise. One to the old man's forearm, one to his chest, one to his leg.

That latter was almost a mistake. He took too long over the three blows, and was forced to throw himself back out of the way of the warrior's next swing. But as the sword whooshed past, Halfdan could see the wounds he'd caused taking effect. The man found it even harder to control the sword with the muscle in his arm cut, he winced at the pain in his chest as the swing pulled his torso round, and the leg almost gave way under the strain.

The man straightened, taking two steps back. He looked at Halfdan, eyes narrowed, then looked at his wounds, before glancing back up to the jarl. He knew he was in trouble, that Halfdan was better than him, and that the younger man had just made him weaker and more pained. To his credit, the man gritted his teeth and readied his sword once more.

'You will be wasted among the clouds with your White Christ,' Halfdan said with an odd tone of respect. 'You would be welcomed in the hall of the Allfather.'

The man said nothing, but came on once more. His sword swung. Halfdan ducked out of the way, but this time the man did not struggle to stop his swing. Instead, he spun a dizzyingly quick full circle, the sword coming round again, astonishingly quickly, only gaining momentum with the move.

Halfdan was surprised. He managed to thrust his own sword in the way to parry, but only just made it, and even then, the Dane's great blade glanced off Halfdan's shoulder, slamming into the metal links of his shirt and sending a shockwave through his body. The younger jarl reacted instantly, more out of instinct than planning. His sword lanced and danced, trying to find an opening as the warrior fought desperately with his remaining strength to keep Halfdan's blade away.

Then his leg finally gave way. The old warrior managed not to fall, but he did stagger backward, lurching this way and that, groaning and using his free hand to clutch the leg wound. Halfdan walked slowly after him.

The man's face turned upward to look at him, and Halfdan saw defeat in it. The old warrior's head twitched for a moment. It might have been a nod. Then the jarl's blade jabbed out once more, slamming point-first into the old man's chest. Even in his death moves, the warrior tried to fight back, his sword coming round in a wavering arc, gripped by a failing hand on an unsteady arm. Halfdan grabbed the man's wrist with his free hand, holding the longer sword away as he pushed, driving his own blade between ribs to pierce the heart within. He felt it touch the man's spine, then slip past, and emerge from his back. The warrior's free hand came up, gripping Halfdan's sword hand even as it held the blade that had killed him. The two men stood there for a long moment in a martial embrace, the last grasp of a dying man and his killer.

Then he let go. Halfdan released his grip of the man's wrist and pulled his sword free of the chest. The old man toppled backward with a hoarse rasp, and fell to the sand.

'Rest well, Ivar Blackleg,' Halfdan said. 'May the White Christ forget about you, and the valkyrjur come to take you home to Odin's hall.'

He shook the worst of the blood from his sword onto the white sand, then straightened. That made him wince. His other shoulder was painful. There was going to be a monstrous bruise there, and his shield arm would be weakened for a time. He looked about, spotted his shield lying some eight paces away, and walked over, scooping it up.

Now, he turned his attention once more to the rest of the fight. His men had stopped watching him when they knew he'd won, and now the raid was in full flow. Warriors and villagers tussled, ran and chased. The nearest house was already afire, flames belching from windows and roof, smoke billowing up into the clear blue. Two of the men they had acquired in Swaledale were snaking their way back toward the beach, carrying armfuls of mediocre loot they had taken before burning the place. The bodies of the house's owners lay in a heap near the door, while other villagers were suffering the same fate even now. Screams in the distance confirmed that Ketil and his men were still enjoying success at preventing escapees, and one of the fishing boats was already burning, as Wolves fought hard with the crews of the other two. For a moment, Bjorn bumbled into sight, and the man who he was busy dismembering looked suspiciously like those men they'd fought in the Hróarskelda bar. Halfdan smiled to himself at that, then looked around.

For a long moment, he could find no sign that his men had suffered at all during the raid, but then, as he strolled up the beach, he found grim evidence that not all his men would walk away this day. A warrior he recognised from the *Sea Wolf*, one of those shipyard workers Ulfr had adopted, he thought, lay in a heap, curled around a small pile of his own intestines that had slid free of his belly. His killer was only a few feet away with a huge rent in the side of his neck, lying in a veritable lake of his own blood, his skin a blotchy grey.

But fallen Wolves were few, and from a practical point of view, they still had just a few too many men to comfortably man the two ships – a small cull might make things easier in the coming days. Reaching the scrubby grass, Halfdan walked toward the centre of the village. He could see Bjorn having fun up ahead, swinging that screaming man around, holding just one arm. When the big albino let go, the man flew into the side of a building, headfirst, with an almost certainly fatal crunch. Bjorn was there a moment later, picking at his victim, irritable that he'd accidentally ended his fun too soon.

Even as he walked, men were emerging with their meagre loot, and more and more buildings were aflame. The village was done, and fewer and fewer locals remained standing every time he turned.

'The Wolves of Odin will be feared in Daneland now,' he said, with an air of satisfaction.

'How?'

He turned to see Leif strolling toward him, cleaning his sax and then sheathing it.

'What?'

'How will anyone know we were here or did this, Halfdan? If every man dies, there can be no witness, remember?'

Halfdan frowned. 'Shit, yes. But that was Harðráði's order to all the crews. Total annihilation. Leave just corpses and smoking ruins.'

He fretted. He didn't like the idea that this was all going to be forgotten. Besides, how was Magnus of Norway going to know he was supposed to be annoyed if there was no one left to tell him? He turned, head darting this way and that, and found what he was looking for: a survivor. They were few and far between, and this one had been playing dead, lying among the

107

bodies, until Bjorn trod on his leg and he yelped. The albino picked him up and casually broke the man's arm.

'Wait,' Halfdan bellowed, breaking into a jog and heading for Bjorn and his latest victim.

'You can't have him,' the albino said, a little petulantly. 'He's mine.'

'He's Magnus's.'

'What?'

'Put him down.'

Bjorn glared at Halfdan for a few moments, a battle of wills which the jarl knew he would win. Finally, the big man sighed and dropped the man with the broken arm. 'Fine, but you owe me a one-armed man.'

Halfdan chuckled, and almost laughed out loud when he saw the poor bastard's expression as he stared at Bjorn.

'You,' Halfdan said to the victim.

'Sir?'

'You heard us beach?'

A nod.

'What did we shout?'

There was another pause, and then the man spoke, his voice nervous, cracked. 'Odin?'

Halfdan nodded with a smile of satisfaction. 'We are the Wolves of Odin in the army of Harald Harðráði and of Sveinn Ástríðarson. The whole of Sjáland burns, a beacon of war for Magnus, your king. In a matter of days, his throne in Hróarskelda will be a charred mess surrounded by bodies.'

The man's eyes widened.

'Take a horse from your village,' Halfdan said to the man, 'then find a boat elsewhere. Sail away from this island of corpses, and carry word to Magnus that his lands will burn and his people die until he comes south to meet us.'

Placing a hand on the man's shoulder, which made him flinch in fright, Halfdan turned him, and pointed him away to where they could see a few horses in a field. 'Leif, go with him. Make sure Ketil doesn't just put an arrow in him for fun.'

As the man scurried away, clutching his broken arm, immensely relieved not to have simply been executed, Halfdan nodded in satisfaction. He'd broken orders, but it needed to be done. Harðráði would appreciate it in the end.

'Of course, he'll never get to Magnus,' Eygrímr said. 'Ordinary men do not meet kings.'

'It matters not,' Halfdan replied. 'He will remember this tale for a very long time, and as he moves around looking for a boat, he will see the scale of the damage, where the other ships have landed. He will cross the straight somehow, to Skáney, as he cannot stay here. He may never meet Magnus, but he will meet men across the water, and some will have the ear of greater men, and so on. The tale will pass up through the ranks of the Danes and Norse until it finally reaches Magnus. By then, it will have taken on great power and grown in impressiveness. And as the tale travels, with it will go the name of the Wolves of Odin.'

Eygrímr smiled slowly. 'You *do* have Loki cunning, my jarl.'

'I use my head for more than storing beer and growing hair.' Halfdan smiled.

Around them, the raid was over. Every building was now on fire, even the sheds and barns, and no villager remained standing, everyone, bar the chosen survivor, lay in a bloody heap. The three fishing boats were now little more than bonfires, and Ketil and his men were coming back, satisfied that no one had made it away from the village. The only activity now was Leif escorting the terrified survivor to his horse, and the Wolves of Odin carrying armfuls of loot down to the ships for storage. That would, of course, add extra weight, but it would be a negligible amount.

The next step was going to be experimental.

'How many men do we leave with the ships?' Ulfr said, wandering over and rubbing his hands together. 'I would like to be with them, Halfdan.'

'We are leaving no one with the ships,' the jarl replied.

'What? But they could be stolen or destroyed. We can't guarantee the island has been depopulated, and I tell you this, Halfdan, there are half a dozen skippers in this fleet that covet my ships, and aren't above thieving them if they get the chance.'

Halfdan took a deep breath. *Here goes…*

'Ulfr, give the order to pack and ready for portage.'

'*Portage?*'

Halfdan nodded, and Ulfr put his hands on his hips and exhaled slowly. 'Halfdan, that's eight miles with an untried crew. It's asking a lot.'

The jarl shrugged. 'Eight miles of good, relatively flat, open land – the best terrain you could hope for, for portage. And yes, this crew have not tried to carry a ship, but then we hadn't tried when we carried the *Sea Wolf* halfway across Rus lands and Georgia, and that was successful. They have to learn some time, and I want to keep the ships with us. This is a strange situation. Magnus of Norway could already be on the way, for all we know, and certainly when we sack his Danish capital, he will have incentive to come for us. I don't want to see his fleet coming down the northern fjord while we're sitting in a mead hall in Hróarskelda and our ships are eight miles away on the south coast.'

He scratched his head. 'If Magnus comes, he might bring Hjalmvigi with him, and I want our ships where we can board them in a few moments and put to sea. You understand?'

Ulfr nodded, but then he would never take much convincing to keep his ships nearby.

'How long do you think it will take?' Halfdan asked.

The shipwright folded his arms and looked about him. 'How long is a piece of rope, Halfdan? With an *experienced* crew of forty men over good land, I could get a ship eight miles in a day, if we have log rollers to take the weight. This is an *in*experienced crew. Two days at least. Maybe three. Without rollers, five, if it works at all.'

Halfdan smiled. 'We are one of the nearest crews to the capital anyway, so we can spare the time. Sæbjôrn landed way over on the west coast, so he's got thirty or forty miles to move to get to Hróarskelda. And to be honest, I'm not all that bothered about being among the front runners to sack a city I so recently enjoyed a beer in.'

Ulfr nodded at that. 'Slow and steady. There for the important bit.'

There for the important bit. Halfdan could only nod at that. The next couple of days would pass slowly, but every pace took him closer to Hjalmvigi, and when they got there, they would have the ships to hand.

Chapter 8

'The town's ahead,' Ketil bellowed, reappearing over the slight rise ahead, waving and pointing. There was something oddly ominous in his tone, but Leif heaved a sigh of relief, regardless, and could hear a multitude of similar outpourings around him. He'd known this was going to be hard work – portaging a ship was never a task to be undertaken lightly, after all – but he'd not truly been prepared for *how* hard.

The Wolves of Odin who had taken *Sea Wolf* around the rapids on the Dnieper and across the hills of Georgia five years ago had been a crew assembled by Ketil from among the born sailors and warriors of the Sigtun region, and those among them who had never tried portage at least knew the principles. They had bent to the task without fear, and had seen it through quietly and professionally. *These* Wolves of Odin were a whole new generation, with the exception of a few at its core. They consisted principally of men who had fought for the Byzantine emperor in his bodyguard, Normans from Apulia who were more at home in the saddle than on a ship, labourers from the shipyards of Nordmandi, and farmers and miners from Swaledale who had never even *seen* the sea until Halfdan brought them east.

Thank God for Ulfr and his competence and knowledge. Without him, they'd still be just a mile from that beach, two days on. The ships he had built were light enough that a crew of forty could lift them using poles slipped through the oar holes, and physically move them for short distances. Of course, that was only possible for a few hundred paces. A *single mile* would cripple them all, let alone eight of them.

That first few hours, then, the entire crew of both ships had bent their efforts to finding fifty young trees and felling them, stripping them of branches and any protuberances, forming good rollers. Of course, in that part of the task, the shipyard workers' skills shone, and they soon had twenty-five rollers for each ship. While that had happened, Ulfr used one of the village's horses to ride a mile or two north with Ketil and Halfdan, scanning the landscape they would traverse. They returned with the good news that the terrain was indeed among the best Ulfr had ever seen for portage. While eight miles was a long way, it was not the *longest* portage recorded, by far, and those men who baulked at the idea and vocally opposed it were put in their place when Ulfr reminded them that a portage of ten miles across Jótland to Hedeby was not only known, but was so well used that sometimes ships met each other going both ways. Complaints petered out into an embarrassed silence after that.

Ulfr then oversaw the positioning of the rollers on the grass above the beach. The ships would be settled onto the rollers for the journey, but the lip between beach and grassland was too difficult to manage, so the ship would have to be carried that far. By the time all was ready, the day was coming to a close and the light was beginning to fade, and so the Wolves of Odin camped on the beach of Torpstrand for the night amid smouldering huts and stinking grey bodies, recovering from their efforts and preparing for the work ahead.

The next morning, they'd begun in earnest. Both ships were slightly over-crewed still, which at least gave them plenty of manpower for the work. The masts were lowered, poles slid through the oar-ports, the men readied themselves, and on Leif's signal it began. With Bjorn leading them in an old rhythmic chant that gave the crews their timing, they heaved and lifted. Leif could only watch one ship, of course, and since Halfdan was overseeing the moving of *Sea Wolf*, Leif had taken on *Sea Dragon*. The longship rose from the sand with creaks and groans, both from the wood of the vessel and from the straining men lifting her. She held maybe a foot from the ground for as long as it took to down a gulp of beer, then crashed back to the beach with a worrying sound and the cursing of dozens of men.

Leif was just grateful that at that point Ulfr was off with the other ship and hadn't seen the failure. Several men would now be searching the beach for their teeth if they'd damaged Ulfr's ship.

The Rus took a deep breath and prepared for a second try. Control of the *Sea Dragon*'s portage had more or less come down to him by default, but he was determined to shine in the position. Halfdan was busy with the *Sea Wolf* while Ketil, being the fastest among them, ranged ahead, scouting. Ulfr kept running back and forth between the two vessels, overseeing the laying of the roller tracks, Gunnhild was too important to involve herself in such things, and no one would ever dream of putting Bjorn in charge of such work, and so it had fallen to Leif.

'Ready?' he called.

The big albino turned, nodded to him, and began the song. The words of the tale of Egil Skallagrímsson, chanted to an ancient melody, rang out in the big man's voice, and the work began afresh.

Wolf-battening warrior,
Wield we gleaming swords.

With a heave and a groan, the men lifted the *Sea Dragon* once more, this time getting the poles to shoulder height, giving the keel two feet of clearance. Leif held his breath for a heartbeat, expecting it to crash down once more, especially given the looks on the faces of some of the less able men. The ship remained borne aloft.

> *In serpent-fostering summer*
> *Such deeds well beseem.*

With another groan, the men took a single pace forward, then another with the second line of the song, the vessel moving two paces toward the rollers at the top of the beach.

> *Lead up to Lundr.*
> *Let laggards be none.*
> *Spear-music ungentle*
> *By sunset shall sound.*

By the last of those lines, the rhythm had settled in, and dozens of boots slammed down in unison, each time bringing *Sea Dragon* closer to the rollers that would save much of this effort. Leif looked down the beach at the distant shape of the *Sea Wolf* moving inland, and smiled to himself.

'The other crew are almost there. We're not going to be beaten by *Sea Wolf*, surely?'

The roar that came back to him was fed principally by the pride of the former Norman shipyard workers, whose own labour had crafted this ship from rough timbers. Bjorn laughed, and changed song, moving to a somewhat eye-wateringly crude shanty with a slightly faster, bouncy pace. The work was hard, but adding an element of competition to the onerous task made it that little bit more acceptable, and in moments the ship was jerking forward with every footstep and every off-colour melodic joke. Leif almost cheered as the *Sea Dragon* crested the slope of the beach and crossed the first of the rollers.

Of course, there was plenty still to do before the ship was even properly moving, let alone eating away the miles between the beach and Hróarskelda. *Sea Dragon* was a touch over forty feet long, and would still have to be carried that distance before she could be lowered onto the tree trunks.

Leif understood the working of the rollers, though he'd not seen them used before. When portaging the *Sea Wolf*, they had used greased beams, which were harder to prepare and maintain, but allowed a crew to lay a good track that could cope with rises and dips in the land. Rollers were easier and faster to acquire, but could only work on flattish land, for obvious reasons. He'd hoped estimates of the terrain between there and Hróarskelda were accurate, for that reason alone.

By the time Bjorn's song had offended more or less every nation in the world, and covered a number of cheek-reddening subjects, though, the *Sea Dragon* was over the rollers. They'd lost sight of their sister ship now, with the charred remnants of the village in the way, but Leif could just about hear the rhythmic tones of their work.

'Lower away,' he called.

There was a hair-raising moment when a couple of the men slipped and almost dropped the load. To do so would put sufficient pressure on the others that the ship might well just drop, and Leif sent up a small prayer of thanks when the descent was arrested and the ship fell no further, steadied by the crew. Had it fallen, it could have rolled to one side, snapping poles, or it could have knocked the rollers out of position and ruined all hope of a straightforward journey. In the end, though, the ship settled onto the rollers steadily and well.

Several men let go of the poles to spit on their hands and wipe them, and Leif jumped up.

'Get hold!' he bellowed, even as the *Sea Dragon* leaned worryingly to one side.

The rollers might take the lion's share of the weight, but while a dragon ship always had a shallow draft, the keel still came to a point, so balance remained in the hands of the men. The Wolves, chagrined, grabbed the poles once more and steadied the ship, heaving her back to the upright position.

'This is it, now,' he said. 'Ulfr says we can make Hróarskelda in four goes, and if we can't then we have no business on the whale road in the first place.'

That would cut through to the heart of each of them. The pride they all felt in being a member of the crew of either of these two ships went above and beyond that of any other vessel in the fleet. No ship that set sail from Sigtun could match *Sea Wolf* or *Sea Dragon* for speed and manoeuvrability, and the very notion that they could be considered unworthy would resound in each of them and drive them all the harder. Pride was a far stronger motivator than either fear or greed.

'We move 'til noon,' he announced. 'That's five hours of rolling this ship north. Ulfr thinks we can do two miles in five hours. Then we stop for food and rest. Then another five hours and two miles will take us halfway to Hróarskelda and our overnight stop. Tomorrow we do the same, and once that's done, we're there. All right?'

'Why aren't *you* lifting the ship?' grumbled a Swaledale man.

Leif fixed him with a hard look. 'I lifted *Sea Wolf* across the Dnieper rapids and the mountains of Georgia in the middle of a war. When you've managed more than a flat field among mates, we'll talk.'

This caused a roar of derisive laughter, and the Swaledale man received several playful slaps before he grudgingly accepted it.

With that, the ship began to move. Leif suspected that the presence of Bjorn in his group was largely responsible for the pace they managed to maintain, but he had to hand it to them: *Sea Dragon* moved with reasonable speed, north across the open grass toward the capital. While most of the crew half-lifted, half-guided the ship along the track of rollers, six men had the unenviable task of moving the timbers. Two men at a time would grab one of the heavy logs that had been half crushed into the turf and lift it with difficulty, hefting it and then jogging alongside the ship to the bow, where they would carry it to

117

the front of the track and replace it, ready to once more take the weight of the ship, while the other two-man teams circled around, doing the same.

It was hard work, but it was efficient. By late morning they had angled close enough to the progress of *Sea Wolf* that the two ships were able to move in concert, within shouting distance. At noon, they broke their journey with a meal, while rough stakes were used to prop the ships upright until they were moved once more. The meal ended with groans of dismay as the men again moved to take their place and carry the ship. Men rubbed sore muscles and winced, but at the call, they took their poles once more, and carried the ships onward.

That night was one of quiet aching and recovery, as each man nursed his bruises and ravaged muscles, drinking beer and eating salted meat, and grumbling in the knowledge that the next day was only going to be a repeat of today, but that they would start that day in an exhausted and pained state already. When darkness fell, they became aware of lights in the distance to both sides. Leif had felt heartened to realise that there was still life on Sjáland until Halfdan pointed out that the fires would be like theirs: campfires of Harðráði's other raiding parties. That had rather soured the sight.

The call to work in the morning was greeted with about the least enthusiasm Leif had ever heard from a group of men. The work seemed to go slower that day, as might be expected given the state they were now in, yet they still seemed to eat away the distance, and Ulfr reckoned they'd managed near two miles by the time they stopped for a noon meal. This news perked everyone up just a little, for it seemed that they had achieved their goal, despite everything. Leif had quietly held on to the fact that he knew they'd started that day two hours earlier than the previous one, and so the work had indeed been slower, though only a few seemed to have realised that.

This past afternoon, then, they had been on the closing stage of their journey. Six miles gone, and only two remaining to

Hróarskelda. There had been a little dismay when Ketil had returned from his scouting to announce that the land ahead rose to a gentle slope, but they had taken it relatively stoically, because the town had to be just beyond it, and the ships had crawled on slowly toward their destination.

Now, though, Ketil's latest news was being welcomed all round, and just in time, too. The sun had set perhaps a quarter of an hour ago, and there was little light left. Men had called for a halt for the day, but Halfdan and Ulfr had been insistent they push on, even into the darkness, for they had to be close.

And they were. As the crews put all their strength into a last effort to bring the ships up that slope that must loom over Hróarskelda, Leif joined Halfdan and Ulfr in hurrying ahead to see what lay before them. The sky continued to darken even noticeably as the Rus hurried up the very gentle incline to where the rangy Icelander waited, bow over shoulder and hands on hips, silhouetted against the golden light.

He reached the crest at the same time as the others, and came to a halt next to Ketil, looking down.

The slope was just as gentle as the one they'd climbed, as it fell away toward the glittering waters of the fjord, which would please the men who had to move ships down it, and the capital of the Danish crown lay between the water and the watchers.

Last time they had visited Hróarskelda, on their way from Angle Land to seek the excommunicated priest, they had simply been passing through, the town a busy trading port on their route. Now, it was something else entirely.

Leif's breath caught in his throat. As he'd approached the crest, he'd presumed the gentle golden glow in the sky to be the lights of the town. Now he knew otherwise.

Hróarskelda was aflame.

Leif shivered as he remembered Gunnhild's prophetic words the last time they'd been here: *the whole place will burn and Hedeby will be gone, a fate that I fear also faces this place.*

Clearly Harðráði had no intention of waiting for all the raiding parties to assemble from their various landing sites before launching his attack. Leif could see seven dragon boats in the fjord, one of which was flying Harðráði's flag, *Landøyðan*, or 'Land Waster', that was said to be magic. The ships were engaged in a fight with two other vessels that had presumably put to sea from the harbour at the enemy's arrival, and even as Leif watched, the invaders sank a Danish ship. The other would not last long. Others of Harðráði's army, though, had clearly already beached their ships, for flames belched from the houses of the town, and black smoke was now roiling up into the black sky. The fires had only begun recently, for he'd not seen the smoke on his approach, but they would soon engulf the whole town. He knew now that men of the invading army would be there in the streets, killing and looting, theirs the hands that had set the fires. Behind him, other members of the Wolves were coming into sight over the rise now, the rolling ships having been stopped in their tracks.

'I thought we were *waiting*,' Ulfr said quietly. 'A grand gesture to provoke Magnus?'

Leif shook his head. 'When have you ever known Harðráði to wait for anything if he could grasp it immediately? No. Rather than let the people wallow in fear for a day or more as the raiders converged, he clearly decided to start without us. The shock of a swift, unexpected attack.'

Halfdan shrugged. 'In a way, I'm not unhappy with that. I have nothing against most Danes, and there will be precious little loot to be had, given the number of men who'll be walking the streets and looking for it. Perhaps it's better that Hróarskelda burns without us. We can overnight where we are. In the morning the place will be a ruin, and we can bring the ships down to the water to be ready for the next step, whatever that might be. Hopefully it will be Magnus coming south and bringing the cursed priest with him.'

But Leif was thinking differently.

'Halfdan, the bishop…'

'What?'

'Bishop Aage. He will be in there, in his church complex, trapped. Look, the church is not on fire yet.'

'Maybe they won't burn it.' Halfdan shrugged again. 'Harðráði is a Christian, after all.'

'No, Halfdan. You heard him back in Sigtun. He didn't even think as far as leaving survivors to carry tidings. He just wanted a statement written in blood and ash: a challenge to his nephew, to bring him south to war. Harðráði wants the throne of Norway, not Daneland, so it doesn't matter to him if he turns all of Sjáland to ash and corpses, as long as he doesn't have to attack *Norway* and burn it. And I don't think Sveinn the Dane is bright enough or strong-willed enough to stop him. This town will burn to the ground, and everyone in it will die. He has his ships in the fjord to stop escape that way, and he knows his raiders, like us, are converging from all over the island, so there will be no escape on land either. Halfdan, we have to save the bishop.'

'Why?'

This rather threw Leif, as he was expecting more or less immediate agreement.

'What do you mean, why? He's a friend. An ally.'

'No he isn't. He's a friend of the archbishop in Jorvik. All he did for us was to pass on a judgement that was sent to him. I owe him nothing. *None* of us do. And as for an ally... how long do you think he will continue to throw his favour on those of us who follow old One-eye?'

Leif fretted. His gaze shot over to the town, where even now more buildings were bursting into flame. 'Bishop Aage welcomed you into his palace, Halfdan. He gave us important information for your quest, and even sided with us against another man of his Church, all on the say of Archbishop Ælfric of Jorvik, and our own accounts. He is Hjalmvigi's enemy now, and even on a basic level of logic, Halfdan, that makes him your friend. He is a *potential* ally, at the very least, a powerful man who it would be useful to remain on good terms with. But perhaps most importantly, he does not deserve to die.'

'Many who die do not deserve it,' Halfdan said, in an infuriatingly stoic manner.

Leif was beginning to feel frustrated. 'Where do I fit in among the Wolves, Halfdan?'

The jarl frowned at this. 'What?'

'How do I stand in your hirð?'

'I don't understand what you mean, Leif.'

'Really? Because you let Ulfr bring his shipworkers into the fold. Because you tarried in dangerous places in Apulia so that Gunnhild could rework her völva's staff. Because you raced off into the lands of the Pecheneg to look for Ketil, even when you thought he might stand against you. Because you let Bjorn go off on his own to seek his berserkir fight when we needed him in Swaledale. Each of your hirð you bend the warp and weft of fate to accommodate, you will sacrifice anything for any of them. Why not me?'

Halfdan stared at him, but Leif was not done.

'Is it because he's a Christian, and now that there are fewer of us among the Wolves once more, we don't matter as much? Do *I* matter that much?'

Halfdan was still staring in shock, but suddenly seemed to snap out of it. He took two steps over and came face to face with Leif, then placed a hand on each of his shoulders. 'Never doubt your value, Leif the Teeth. You have been the wit and the cleverness of the Wolves since the day we met in Kiev. And were the world to bow to the Allfather, and you alone to worship the White Christ, I would *still* seek your wisdom. I had not considered what value the bishop might be. I thought of him as a resource used and finished with. Your wisdom in the matter is clear, though. Very well, Leif of Kiev. Hróarskelda burns, and Harðráði would see it a land of corpses, but at least one man will walk away alive tonight. We shall save Bishop Aage.'

Leif pursed his lips and nodded. Oddly, once he'd started arguing, he'd expected Halfdan to argue back, and had been surprised when the jarl simply folded and agreed without further complaint.

'Bjorn, Ketil and Ulfr?' Halfdan called. 'We've a job to do. Gunnhild too.' As they hurried over, Leif spotted Anna beside Gunnhild. She was still acting a little frosty from time to time, but she seemed to have begun to overcome her thing about Ellisif now that they had left Sigtun and the princess was out of the picture.

'Farlof and Eygrímr, you're in charge of the Wolves here until we get back. Have the ships stabilised and then set up camp for tonight. We're going to rescue our friend the bishop.'

While they swiftly made ready, Leif crossed to Anna. 'I'm assuming that if I ask you to stay here, you'll tell me not to be foolish and that where Gunnhild goes, you go too, yes?'

Anna frowned. 'Yes. Why would you tell me to stay here?'

'Because Hróarskelda is burning down and is filled with bloodthirsty warriors who have been commanded to kill everything that moves without mercy.'

'And we are seven of those warriors.'

Leif sighed. There was no arguing with Anna at the best of times, but certainly not when she was in that sort of mood. Instead, he settled his weapons and tested their draw, shook out his arms and mentally prepared himself for walking into fiery disaster. He wore neither chain shirt nor helmet, though he carried a good axe at his side, a sax belted across the front and a throwing axe tucked into the back of his belt. And most of all, he had his not inconsiderable wits.

Moments later, Halfdan was waving them on.

They began the descent into Hróarskelda at a gentle jog. Despite its importance as a capital, the town had never been supplied with a defensive circuit in the way Kiev had, for the island played host to several immense fortresses into which the Danes were intended to flood in times of danger. Of course, the danger had come rather suddenly this time, but from what Leif had heard during their last visit, the place had been burned down by the Pomeranians only a decade ago, too. Clearly the Danes had not learned their lesson. At least, though, it would make ingress simple for the Wolves.

Leif found that he had moved into the lead, and half expected Halfdan to outpace him, but the jarl simply continued to run along at his shoulder, supportive, rather than commanding. This goal was Leif's in principle, and therefore Leif was being allowed to lead it. Things like that, Leif considered, were why men would follow Halfdan to the very edge of the world.

They were approaching the edge of Hróarskelda, a sprawl of houses, churches, granaries and shops arranged around a sort of grid form, more accidentally than by design, every other structure now belching out flames and smoke. Leif glanced up at the great wooden church and its associated palace and structures. They were still an island of calm amid the hellish destruction.

The town, entirely consisting of wooden structures, was not going to last very long under these conditions, and the light sea breeze only made things worse, carrying sparks in the air to ignite whole new parts of town. The two main roads into the burning centre from the south lay to either side. The left took them toward the harbour, far from the church, but an area that was, as yet, largely untouched by fire. The right would march them straight into Satan's fiery maw, but would bring them to the bishop's palace in short order. Leif fretted, unable to choose. He was clever, but it took a certain gumption to make that sort of decision. He turned to Halfdan.

The look they exchanged in that moment Leif would remember for the rest of his life. It was an exchange of ideas and theories, and he knew in that moment that Halfdan not only respected his opinion, but understood him as few did, and the young jarl took that horrible decision right out of his hands.

Halfdan took a few extra steps, putting himself out front.

'The eastern approach. It burns hot, but we can be through it fast and save the bishop. If we take the western, we risk Aage being little more than fried mutton when we reach him. Follow me.'

The seven of them raced across the slope toward the road. Leif's head spun this way and that. The Wolves of Odin stood now atop the crest, watching them, tense. Ahead, two figures came racing from the edge of Hróarskelda on horses, desperate to flee the disaster, but Leif saw a dozen of the raiders behind them, emerging from the houses. One found open ground and paused, dropping, nocking and drawing.

The first rider took an arrow in the back, body arching, then slumping, tipping and falling from the saddle. The second was only a hundred paces further when a second arrow sank into his horse's haunch. The animal bucked and threw him, but before he could struggle to his feet to run on toward supposed safety, the other raiders were on him, swords and axes rising and falling, butchering.

Leif felt his pulse race. This was what they were heading into: fiery Hell and brutal killings.

Moments later they were racing down toward the outlying houses. That they were part of the invading force was clear from their armament and the angle of their approach, and those men who'd been chasing the escapees gave them vicious grins as they neared. 'Not so much left now, eh, Odin's Sheepdogs?'

Halfdan did not even bother with a reply. His swinging right hand cuffed the man hard around the side of the head, sending him sprawling. His friends made angry noises, but were not fast enough to do anything about it, and Halfdan was leading the other six into the streets in a heartbeat, leaving the mouthy raiders behind.

The streets ahead were an inferno, with men staggering here and there in the few open spaces, some of them on fire, others swinging swords and bellowing oaths. Leif ran with the others into the outskirts of Hróarskelda, and then looked up, some supernatural sense tugging at him.

He could see the tower of the church of Hróarskelda, ornate timber carvings as he knew it to be, engulfed in a fireball.

'Hurry' was all he could think of to shout.

The bishop's palace was on fire.

Chapter 9

The first major obstacle was the cart, and the scene spoke volumes of what had happened. The main street they were following from the southern approach to the harbour had been troublesome enough so far, for every house they passed was a nightmare in itself, fire billowing out from doors and windows, burning men and women bumbling about the street, screaming in agony, others lying dead, still smouldering. Other houses were yet to burn, but from each of those issued the din of murder, screams and the sound of cleaving meat, howls of martial abandon and the clang of weapons. Harðráði's raiders were all engaged in killing and torching, barring the occasional men they saw carrying precious stolen loot with mad grins and murderous gleams in their eyes.

But the cart blocked the street as surely as any wall.

A trader had seemingly been on his way back from market, for the cart had not been particularly heavily laden. It was on its side, the rear board jammed up against a house at the street's side, the few paltry bags and baskets of vegetables and grain that had been in it now strewn across the muddy street, trodden in and forgotten. The cart's shafts reached almost three quarters of the way across the thoroughfare, forming a major obstacle, but the rest of the space between there and the building at the other side of the street was filled with the bodies of two horses, butchered needlessly in a frenzy of madness. A man in good clothes, presumably the merchant and owner of the vehicle, was draped on his back over the horses, his throat opened, face grey and lifeblood mingling with that of his animals across the street. The cart itself was already on fire, having caught stray sparks from the roof of the house next to which it lay.

Halfdan looked up over the obstacle to what lay ahead. More burning, fighting, killing and looting filled the street beyond the cart, and then, off a street or square to the right, the bishop's church compound was already blazing.

Things did not look good.

He was determined, though. He'd made a promise to Leif, probably foolishly, that they would save Bishop Aage, which might now not be possible. It was entirely likely that the churchman would be little more than a charred relic by the time they reached him, if he wasn't already, but they had to try. Leif had been right. He had given favour to all the others in their time, and somehow had not even thought to do so with Leif.

He'd pondered over that even as they pressed on through the dangerous town. It was not that he did not value Leif. In fact, it was more the precise opposite. It was not that he would not willingly grant just such favours for the Rus as the others, and the little man's religion did not bother him. In fact, rather surprisingly, Halfdan had found over their travels that he did not hate the White Christ's Church at all. Oh, he did not *trust* it, and he did not *believe* in it, and some of its followers were dangerous and needed to be dealt with. But the same could be said for some sons of Odin, while he'd learned that not all Christians were dislikeable, and in fact, Bishop Aage had been one of the better ones.

No. The reason he'd not immediately leapt to make room for Leif's needs was because he was not used to the Rus needing anything. Of all the Wolves, Leif was the one he felt could easily have walked through the world they'd travelled without them. He was clever, adaptable, spoke most languages, seemed to know everything about everything, and perhaps above all, he was utterly likeable. Everyone who met Leif fell for his unprepossessing charm. He was the only one of the Wolves who had formed a romantic relationship during their travels, and that spoke volumes, too. Even Gunnhild, who trusted Christians even less than Halfdan, listened to Leif and relied upon him. It had taken Leif shouting at him to make him realise that the Rus might actually need help occasionally.

That would not happen again.

And the first step to putting that right was saving the bishop for him.

He looked at the cart as they approached. Climbing the burning timber would be very uncomfortable and quite dangerous, but there would be difficulties climbing over the dead horses and trader too, given the slippery, sticky blood that seemed to be everywhere. That left the middle.

'Bjorn. Axe to the shafts!'

The big man did not need telling twice, pulling out his huge axe and lifting it. As he did so, Halfdan moved near to him, gripping the long wooden pole even as Bjorn swung. The axe smashed through the shaft with ease, sending splinters and debris in every direction. Halfdan felt pieces slam into his side, but ignored it, as well as the reverberation of the blow that rippled all down the shaft. The pole sheared off, and he pulled it aside and hurled it across the street even as Bjorn lifted his weapon and swung at the other shaft. He dropped and grabbed it, even as it broke free, then rose and hurled it after the first. Then he and Bjorn began to grab the various pieces of debris and fallen goods and throw them aside, clearing the way.

'Bastard,' shouted Bjorn suddenly, lurching upright.

Halfdan turned with a frown to see the big albino looking down at an arrow shaft jutting from his shoulder. Panic struck the jarl for a moment, but then he reasoned that there was no fear in Bjorn's tone, and so there was likely no mortal danger there. Indeed, the giant reached down and pulled the arrow free, holding it up to look at it, and there was hardly any blood on it, just a little on the tip, for though Bjorn had not worn his chain shirt, the arrow had thudded into the leather baldrick that carried his spare axe, and that had taken most of the blow.

'You'll have to use more than a fucking toothpick to bring down the Bear-torn,' Bjorn bellowed into the dark, fire-filled street ahead.

Halfdan had no time to marvel, though, for at that moment a second arrow thrummed out of the darkness and this one hit him in the chest, dead centre. The missile was prevented from striking home by his chain shirt, but still the blow was sufficient to wind him, and would leave a bruise and possibly even a cracked rib. He turned as the arrow fell away, grunting, and could feel the ache already, though the lack of any sharp pain suggested than nothing had been broken.

'They were too close together to have come from the same bow,' Ketil shouted, reaching them, and piling past. Halfdan took a deep breath and nodded, stepping over the few remaining pieces of rubbish. The others were with him, too, pushing on.

The arrows had to have come from one of the buildings to the right, for the view from the left had been obscured by the burning cart.

He felt a moment of indecision, then. To ignore the unseen archers would risk them being used for target practice until they were out of sight, but every moment's delay made it more likely that they would find only roast bishop at the end of their journey. His choice was made easy a moment later as Ketil turned to him, a gleam in the Icelander's eye. 'I'll deal with them. You find the bishop.'

Halfdan nodded, grateful. 'Meet us at the church.'

Ketil was off in a heartbeat, long legs whirling like a water-mill as he bounded off toward the nearest house on the right, axe and sax in hand, bow over his shoulder. Once more, Halfdan had to marvel over the Icelander's resilience. Most men, having taken a blow to the head sufficient to remove an eye, would have spent the rest of their life backing away from trouble, trying to recover. Not Ketil. He had bitten down upon the trouble it caused and forced his body to recover and rebuild.

In some ways, while he had lost half his vision, he had become *twice* the man he'd been before.

As Ketil approached the house's door, arrows came again. One whirred past Halfdan, and thunked into a shield hastily raised by Leif, while the other glanced off Ketil's armoured shoulder and ricocheted out into the dark. The Icelander bellowed something in his very thick native Icelandic, not quite Norse enough for Halfdan to catch, but it sounded distinctly like a threat, and disappeared inside.

Leaving him to it, the jarl waved on the rest of the Wolves and they ran along the street.

As they passed another building, a little further down the street, a man came out backward, hair matted with blood, eyes wild, sword raised. He was followed by another warrior in a chain byrnie, sword coming down, hammering at the retreating man. The pair stumbled out in front of Halfdan, and he and the Wolves were suddenly momentarily prevented from progressing. Growling with irritation, Halfdan grabbed the retreating man by the shoulder and yanked him, sending him falling back with a cry. His attacker, busily bringing down his own sword in a chop, was suddenly deprived of a target and fell atop the man. Halfdan ignored the struggling pair and ran on, the others at his shoulder.

Ducking and weaving between murderous assaults, crazed looters and burning figures, the six of them pressed on, and in moments reached the corner. The square, judging by the increased detritus underfoot, had presumably been the site of the market at which the trader had worked, and a couple of stalls remained, half-deconstructed, their owners caught working at the day's end when the assault began, and forced to flee without finishing the job. Though there was considerably more space in the square than in that street, there was also more activity, for, this being the heart of Hróarskelda, the buildings around the square were commercial, the best in the town, which meant that Harðráði's looters were harder at work here than elsewhere.

Halfdan ducked around a fighting pair and was then almost knocked over by a wild-eyed man hurrying across the square with large leather wine bottle over each shoulder. The man snarled something unintelligible and lurched out of the way, and Halfdan ignored him and pressed on.

The bishop's compound was not unlike the royal complex of Sigtun, though with a church at its centre instead of a palace. The two-tier stave church rose high about the surrounding palisade, visible to all. Other buildings lay around the church in a circle, butting up against the outer wall, including a dormitory for the various priests and their assistants, storerooms, a refectory, a kitchen and a wash house, as well as the guest quarters where the Wolves had stayed when they last visited. The house of the bishop himself lay at the rear, close to the church.

Three of the buildings around the periphery were already burning, and the top of the church was aflame, though most of the building remained untouched. A small group of men in chain shirts, bearing axes and swords and a couple of brands, were arguing outside the gate as Halfdan and his friends approached.

'It is a house of *God*,' bellowed one man, angrily, spittle flying as he faced off against another.

'It is a house of *Danes*,' the other man replied, equally full of ire, knuckles white on the haft of his axe.

'Step aside,' Halfdan shouted as they neared.

'No,' said the first man, turning to him. 'You will not loot a house of God.'

'I have no intention of looting. I'm here for the bishop.'

The second man turned to Halfdan now. 'He's *mine*. Think of the ransom for a bishop.'

'Fuck you,' snapped the first man, and leapt at his opponent, the two of them struggling, grappling and punching. Halfdan turned and saw Bjorn standing behind him.

'Would you?'

The big man nodded, stepped past him and reached out, grabbing each of the two struggling men by the scruff of the neck. He pulled them apart, and then slammed their heads together with a bony clonk. When he let go, both fell to the ground, unconscious. The other armed men around them, two groups facing one another, suddenly looked considerably less angry and certain as Bjorn eyed them all evilly.

'I don't give a shit whether you loot and burn the church or not,' the jarl told them all, 'but any man who tries to stop us leaving with the bishop will wish he'd never left his ship, yes?'

A smattering of nervous nods greeted this as the men pulled aside and opened the way to the gate.

The bishop's compound was walled not for true defence, but more for delineation, as a message to the people: outside it lie your mortal houses, but inside is the house of God. As such, the palisade would be easy enough to tear down for a good raiding party, and the double gate was held shut only by a single chain and padlock on the inside, rather than a stout oak beam as would be the case in a military location. Halfdan knew the system, the 'defences' and the layout from their previous visit, for he had paid attention, like all good jarls, in case he needed to know a way out with little warning. As they reached the palisade, he gestured to Ulfr and pointed to the gate's left-hand leaf. The shipwright nodded and crossed to it, pushing hard. Halfdan did the same with the right, and as the two gates creaked inwards by a hand-width until the locking chain pulled tight, the gap between the two gates brought the lock into view.

'Bjorn?'

The albino stepped forward and pulled free his large axe once more, bringing it down and shattering the chain so that the two halves of the gate swung wide under the pressure exerted by the two Wolves.

They were in. With every heartbeat, more of the church burned and as Halfdan glanced over, he could see through the small windows below the lower roofline the golden flicker of fire within. Though the church was burning from the top, the fiery debris was falling inside, so soon it would be engulfed. Off to the right, the refectory, where the Wolves had been invited to dine when they had visited, was ablaze. A dozen men in the robes of priests or the smocks of their poor helpers were hurrying from the door, faces ashen and panicked, pale and wide-eyed, as they milled about uncertainly.

Halfdan ignored them. Ahead, he could just see past the church that the bishop's house was still untouched, and that clinched a decision he'd almost made already. They needed to try the church first. Not only was it just a matter of time before the church was untouchable, while the house was fine for a time, Halfdan knew what these Christians were like. Regardless of the danger, the moment they realised trouble was striking, their first instinct seemed to be to run to the altar of a church and beg their god to save them. No true Northman would do such a thing, for Odin and Thor would just laugh at their cowardice and feebleness. But Bishop Aage would probably be there with his closest, begging.

'Come on.'

With the others in tow, he hurried across to the church. As they ran, Leif waved to the men gathering outside the refectory. 'Wait for us here in the compound. You will be safe.'

Halfdan bit down on his instinctive retort. He wanted to remind the Rus that they were here for the bishop, and that it would be hard enough to get *one* man safely out of Hróarskelda, without some sort of biblical exodus. He owed Leif, though, and he would not impose such a limit, even through common sense.

They reached the door of the church, and Halfdan took a deep breath and then pulled his scarf up around his nose and mouth. He reached for the door handle gingerly, half expecting it to burn at the touch. It was faintly warm, but touchable, so he turned and pushed. A waft of black smoke burst free, and he was immediately grateful he'd had the foresight to use his scarf. Blinking repeatedly, he pushed inside through the narrow door. Behind him, Bjorn followed, finding it difficult to fit his enormous bulk through the opening.

'Why is it so fucking small?' the big man grunted as he finally staggered within.

'To prevent any man bringing in the devil at his side,' Leif answered as he followed them in.

'I *am* the fucking devil,' said Bjorn, grinning maliciously, his hand going to his crotch as he made thrusting motions. Leif gave him a dark warning look, but Halfdan ignored the pair for now. He had other things to worry about.

The ceiling was a golden blanket of flames. These churches were made entirely of timber, right down to the nails and roof shingles, and once fire took hold, it would be fast to spread and hard to stop. Even as he looked up, a large piece of beam fell with a crash, spraying sparks and burning fragments in every direction. Halfdan slapped at one such spark that had landed on his trousers, patting it until it went out. The floor was a mess of littered fragments, some black and smoking, some seemingly untouched, many burning merrily. He looked through the smoke and could just make out a small number of figures at the far side, where the altar stood. Another fragment fell from the roof, confirming what Halfdan already knew: that crossing that open floor was at best a life gamble. Instead, he pointed to the side, and with the others in tow charged off around the southern edge. The construction of the two-tier church meant that the outer sides had their own lower roof, and were separated from the higher room in the centre by arches. As such, nothing was falling from those ceilings, yet.

He ducked into that side aisle, and scurried around to the far end. There were three men by the altar, and it was a huge relief to Halfdan to realise that one was Bishop Aage. Of his two accompanying priests, one stood, like Aage, with his vestments pulled up to his face, preventing him choking on the smoke that was rapidly filling the wide and high room. The third man was collapsed over the altar – unconscious, Halfdan realised. He sighed as he hurried across, realising that if he tried to leave the prone man, Leif would argue.

'Bjorn, pick him up,' he said, pulling aside his scarf and pointing to the stricken priest.

'Me? Why? I might catch something.'

'Pick him up,' Halfdan repeated, eyes hard.

The albino gave him an unhappy look, but walked over and lifted the unconscious man from the altar, settling him over his shoulder. Leif ran past to the bishop, lifting the scarf covering his own face.

'We have to go.'

Aage said nothing, left his scarf in place, but he nodded vigorously. All around them, fire roared and pieces fell, smacking into the floor with crashes, each time sending out more fire and debris. Halfdan turned. Gunnhild and Anna had remained by the door, and Ulfr stood part way around the circuit, for though the church was spacious, the passage around the edge not affected by falling timbers was less so, and so the three of them had left ample room for manoeuvre.

They had come round the southern edge of the church, but even as Halfdan was about to head that direction in return, Ulfr jumped and leapt out of the way, the heat of the boiling room finally too much for the windows, one of them exploding in a shower of glass. Ulfr ran back over to the door with the women, away from the danger.

Halfdan glanced to the other side, a thought occurring. He smiled as what he saw confirmed it. It was drilled into the children of Ash and Elm even as babes that the absolute north was where trolls and other dangers came from, and so only a fool angled his house with his door or a window facing north. Though the followers of the nailed god might deride such wisdom as heathen, they were not above being careful. The northern side of the church lacked the windows the southern side supported, and so, beckoning to the others, he ran around to the northern aisle. Pieces of roof continued to fall, and twice as he ran he had to brush sparks from his clothes, but within moments he had reached his three friends by the door. As he approached, Ulfr exited first, then the two women, clearing the way for the others.

Halfdan reached the door and leapt through, out into the cold night air. He turned back once he was clear, skin prickling with the sudden change in temperature, pulling his scarf back down and heaving in breaths of clear air.

He blinked and staggered as something hit him hard, and he grappled with it as he realised it was the unconscious priest, thrown through the door by Bjorn, who could not fit through while carrying him. As Halfdan righted himself and lifted the priest, Ulfr coming over to take the man's other shoulder, Bjorn squeezed through to safety, followed by the bishop and his man, and then finally Leif.

They stepped away from the church, aware of the increasing danger that it might collapse in a heap and send burning timbers spiralling out in every direction.

Even as the two conscious priests lowered their coverings and breathed in the night air gratefully, the Wolves doing the same, Leif waved to the gathering of robed men in the open, which had now doubled in number.

'Follow us.'

'Oh, no,' said another voice. They turned to see a group of warriors from Harðráði's fleet moving their way through the open gate, weapons brandished. 'Leave them for us. We were here first.' Halfdan vaguely recognised one of them from their enforced wait at Sigtun. Not the brightest, nor the most pleasant of men, though he was part of one of the more important of Harðráði's crews.

Halfdan shook his head as he handed the unconscious priest over to Ulfr and straightened. 'These men are under my protection. Back off.'

The man glared at him. 'Do you have any idea who we *are*? And you don't even pray to the White Christ anyway, pagan. What do *you* care?'

As Halfdan walked toward him, the man mirrored the move, coming close. He had a sword belted at his side, but no weapon or shield in hand, his left gripping instead a copper pot he had looted in passing. Blood spatter on his arm and leg suggested that the pot's previous owner had met a sticky end.

Halfdan knew what he had to do. These men would back down if their leader was bested; that was the way it worked with such raiders. He closed on the man, who lifted his free hand, fist bunching. Halfdan formed fists himself, but as he came close, he thrust them out to his sides. His opponent, prepared for a punch-up, faltered, frowning at the odd move. That was his undoing, for Halfdan delivered a powerful head-butt the moment he was close enough. The man yelled out as his nose exploded in a shower of blood and cartilage, and fell away to the side, his copper pot dropped and forgotten. Leaving him to it, Halfdan lifted his war-face to the rest of the raiders.

'All right. Who's next?'

He might have miscalculated, and knew in that moment that the others may well have retaliated, especially given who they were, and that their jarl was one of the top men in the fleet, but at that moment two things happened to change their minds. Firstly, Bjorn appeared at Halfdan's shoulder, stepping on the floundering man viciously, face locked in a grimace of battle. And secondly, Ketil appeared from the darkness behind them, and gave a jaunty whistle. The raiders turned to see him standing outside the gate with an arrow nocked, trained on them.

Knowing they were beaten, the men backed away to one side, opening up a passage for the Wolves to reach the gate. Leif and the bishop led the way, then, hurrying past the danger and away from the burning church until they were beside Ketil.

Halfdan waited until the last of the frightened refugees was out of the compound and in the square, then followed them, bringing up the rear with Ulfr, Gunnhild and Anna.

'You have my eternal gratitude,' Bishop Aage said, turning and directing this at all of them, but particularly Leif and Halfdan.

'Save that until we're safe,' he replied. 'It's a dangerous way back out of the town yet. The main street is chaos.'

'Then follow me,' Aage said, and turned, hurrying off into the dark. Halfdan and Leif shared a look, shrugged, and did so, the rest following on, their charges huddling close for protection. The bishop crossed the square with relative ease. Though there were still plenty of raiders and locals fighting and struggling, looting and burning, oddly the robes of a nailed god priest seemed to cut through them like the prow of a ship through water, and Aage ploughed his way through the chaos with all manner of violence simply peeling out of the way before him. Of course, it helped that they were heading not for the beating heart of the city, but into a dark corner of the square out to the east, close to the church's surrounding palisade.

There, Bishop Aage led them into a dark opening between buildings, and the alleyway that led from it. The alley was oddly peaceful after the carnage of the square and the burning church, just a dark way leading out from the town to the countryside, for as they passed the last pair of buildings, they emerged into what appeared to be woodland.

'Our land,' the bishop explained. 'The church owns four orchards of apples, pears and a few cherries.'

'Do you not have problems with theft?' Leif asked, as they moved between the trees, fires and burning forgotten, the light now that of moon and stars.

'Oh, a few mischievous children, but the locals respect the church better than to thieve her goods. "You shall not steal", the seventh commandment reminds us, after all.'

Halfdan gave a wry snort at the thought of all those Christian raiders carrying loot across the burning town. Not killing was a nailed god rule, too, he seemed to remember. Their believers apparently only believed when it was convenient.

'Get them,' a voice suddenly bellowed from the darkness. Halfdan, suddenly alert, looked about, spotting armoured figures moving their way through the trees. Even without having to get his bearings, he could see that the men were coming from outside the town. Raiders late to the party, no doubt.

'Back off,' he roared into the dark orchard. 'We are the crew of the *Sea Wolf*, in Harðráði's fleet, and these are our prisoners.'

This seemed to shake the new arrivals, and he saw most of them stumble to a halt. One man, wearing a rich, yellow cloak that made him stand out even in the dark, hurried out ahead. '*Sea Wolf*, say you?'

'Yes.'

'You taking Christians as thralls, pagan?'

Halfdan took a heartbeat to reply. He could see how many men there were now among the trees – probably forty or fifty. A full dragon ship crew, compared to seven of the Wolves and their priest charges. A fight would be nasty, and probably fatal. But it was a gamble whether claiming to have enslaved the priests would be seen as good or bad, given that these men were raiders, but also Christians.

'The bishop is to be ransomed,' he shouted to the leader of the other crew. 'The rest we will decide about when we've spoken to Harðráði.'

This seemed to suffice, for the man facing him lowered his weapon. He then sighed and rested the axe on his shoulder. 'Are we too late?'

'I think all that's left are dead dogs and bed bugs, but you can have a look.'

There was the slightest of tense pauses as the man clearly considered for a moment whether to attack the Wolves and take their prisoners anyway. In the end though, he shrugged. 'Good luck to you, pagan.'

'You too,' Halfdan replied, as the man led his crew on through the orchard toward the blazing town beyond.

They started to move again, and it was with a sense of profound relief that they emerged into open ground and could see that there were no other raiders coming their way. He turned to the right and could see a campfire blazing atop the slope, two hulking silhouettes beside it marking the location of their ships. They had made it. Half a mile up the slope and they would be back with the Wolves.

'Your lie about ransoming me came rather easily,' Bishop Aage said as they turned and made that way.

Halfdan smiled. 'Fear not, priest. You are under our protection, not our prisoner. Join us for the night, and in the morning, we will go and see Harðráði and discuss getting you somewhere safe and sensible.'

He turned, and was pleased to see that Leif was nodding at him.

Chapter 10

Hróarskelda

'Three weeks!' Halfdan shouted, his voice echoing round the warehouse, one of few intact buildings in the town that was currently serving as Harðráði's headquarters. 'Three weeks of waiting; of sitting on our arses. When are you going to accept that he's not coming, and take the fight north?'

Leif winced at the look that crossed Harðráði's face as the young jarl's angry spittle drifted in the air between them. The would-be king's fingers were gripping the arms of his chair, white and tense. Halfdan was walking close to the edge.

'The agreement was made in Sigtun, Halfdan Loki-born,' Harðráði answered in quiet, measured, but very angry tones. 'The campaign would put Sveinn on the Danish throne and bring Magnus south for war. We thought the sacking of Sjáland would be enough. Clearly it is not. We need to push him harder; to send *another* message.'

'Yes,' Halfdan snapped. 'A message that says "we are coming for you, Magnus of Norway".'

Harðráði half rose from his seat, hands still on the arms.

'Lower your tone with me, Loki-born, or Axebiter here might decide you would be better without a tongue.'

'Let the little shit-licker *try*,' Bjorn put in, stepping up beside his jarl.

Leif felt the ground opening up beneath them all. The situation was getting too tense.

He glanced across at Harðráði again, though surreptitiously, because he knew Anna would have her eyes on him. Ellisif of Kiev sat close to her husband.

The princess looked worried.

It had come as something of a surprise to find that she'd joined the fleet at all. Of course, the Wolves had been nowhere near Harðráði's flagship during the journey from Sigtun, so there was no reason they could have known, but they had all somehow assumed that the quiet, clever and sad princess would stay at Onund's court in Sigtun during the campaign. Leif ought to have realised otherwise, really. It was not Harðráði's style to go to war and leave a wife at home. For years now he had moved around from Norway to Kiev, to Constantinopolis, back to Kiev, to Sigtun, and wherever he had gone, he'd taken everything of value with him. Now that Ellisif was one of those valuable things, of *course* he'd brought her with him.

'This is getting us all nowhere,' Leif said, suddenly, stepping forward, trying to defuse the situation.

'My objective is in the north,' Halfdan snapped, rounding on him. '*Hjalmvigi* is in the north, in Norway. It's clear that Magnus is not coming south, and why *should* he? To recover a burned and dead island that he doesn't need? Better he protects Norway and stays there, eh? Norway is the *big* prize, after all. Magnus wants to protect Norway and doesn't particularly care what happens to his *second* kingdom. Just like Harðráði over there, in fact, who would rather spend years burning Daneland to a crisp than endanger his own Norway.'

Harðráði was on his feet now, a step away from his chair as he responded. 'Time and again I have outlined the strategy, Loki-born. We use Daneland to bring him out to fight. Daneland is a critical trading partner for Norway. It is through Daneland and Sweden that Norse trade reaches the south and the east. Magnus's already-cut ties with Onund means that he now has only Daneland as an outlet for his goods, so the more we make Daneland untenable for trade, the more we squeeze him and force him to act.'

He wagged a finger at Halfdan. 'And I don't care what you think of my motivations, man. The simple fact is that if we meet Magnus and his army or fleet in open territory, on our own terms, we can beat him, and with reasonable speed and efficiency. But if he remains in Niðaróss and we go to winkle him out, we will lose half the fleet and half the army before we get anywhere near the town. Niðaróss lies forty miles from open sea, up a large fjord with a narrow mouth. There is no feasible approach to the place by land for a large force, so we would have to brave that fjord. The moment he knows we're coming, he will strengthen his defences. All possibilities have been considered, Halfdan Loki-born, but a direct assault on Magnus in his capital is simply not going to happen.'

'He's right, Halfdan,' Leif said, stepping forward again. 'I know you want Hjalmvigi, but it is often better to go slow and finish the journey than go fast and risk it all.'

He stepped aside then, as Gunnhild approached them too. 'Remember what I saw, Halfdan,' she said. 'The bears and a carcass. You are not one of them. Wait for the bears' feasting to be over for the wolves to take their share.'

This earned a suspicious frown from Harðráði, though the man swiftly softened, for he could not seemingly frown at Gunnhild for any length of time. Leif's gaze slipped to Ellisif, and he was not at all surprised to find that she was the very picture of regal serenity, though there were those tiny signs of irritation at her husband's actions around her eyes that he recognised.

Halfdan sagged, clearly defeated in this. He turned a resigned look on them, then spun back to Harðráði. 'All right, if you will not take us north, and Magnus will not come south, what is the next step? Burn the fields? Mutilate the animals? Pray to your White Christ for an answer?'

The Norseman returned to his seat and sank into it as he spoke to Halfdan. 'We have annihilated Sjáland and sacked Magnus's Danish capital. That removes his access to the inner

143

sea and any political prize here. But if we wish to squeeze him, we need to cut trade off. Two of the most important trading sites in the whole of Daneland are Hedeby and Odinswe. It is they we must cut off next.'

Halfdan suddenly straightened, and Gunnhild took two steps forward. 'No,' she said.

Leif chewed his lip, momentarily confused. Yes, Gunnhild was from Hedeby, and perhaps she might not want her hometown attacked, but had she not already said she had fore-seen it burning? Why so vehement, then?

'Not Odinswe,' she said flatly, surprising him.

'It has to be,' Harðráði replied. 'Odinswe lies on the island of Fioni, a couple of hours' sail from Sjáland, and it remains one of the wealthiest trade ports in the north. More than half of Magnus's trade flows through its harbour. Hedeby will follow, too, but it is some distance southwest on the mainland, and will take more getting to. Odinswe will burn first, and when the Norse traders' ships stop leaving Niðaróss because their destinations are gone, they will turn to Magnus and he will be forced to come and deal with us.'

But as the king was speaking, Leif's mind was racing. *Odinswe*. He'd heard of a 'we' before. The term had been used for that ship of stones they had visited on Skáney, and for that stone at Halfdan's village where they had met Ømund. It had to mean some sort of ritual place, then. And that was just the end of the place's name…

Odinswe. *Odin's shrine.*

He shivered. No wonder Gunnhild was so set against it.

'I will not let you burn Odinswe,' Halfdan said, arms folded, 'and you know why. Even as a White Christ kneeler, you know why, and you will not do this.'

Given Halfdan's carefree slinging of such words, Leif was just grateful that Bishop Aage was not present to hear them. The bishop had been grateful to the Wolves for saving him and his people, but had been less than kind to Harðráði the next morning, accusing him of all manner of atrocities, which, of course, were true. Harðráði had been contrite, but only with respect to the church, which he claimed he had given strict orders not to touch. A massive donation of Byzantine gold had been sufficient to mollify Aage, who even now was sailing to Fioni to seek craftsmen and workers to build a new church.

'The war will not falter because one heathen crew want to protect their demons,' snarled a voice off to the side, dragging Leif's attention back to the present. He turned, along with the others, to see that one of the skippers had emerged from the crowd. His spirits sank as two of that jarl's men stepped out beside him, and one had a flat, broken nose, his face one massive black bruise from where Halfdan had head-butted him that night by the church. The jarl himself was an impressive man. Not young, but with a warrior's build, and missing his left arm below the elbow. Leif knew immediately that this was not a man to mess with.

'Stay out of this,' Halfdan said, giving him a hard glare before Leif could say anything.

'No,' the old warrior said. 'This war needs to move on, and if that means burning Odinswe, then Odinswe will burn, and that is not going to be changed just to protect some pagan cult.'

'We will not let that happen,' Halfdan growled at him.

'Then you'd best make sure you get there first,' the other jarl said, 'because if *I* do, I'll be carrying the first torch to touch the timbers.'

Halfdan started for him, but Gunnhild held him back, murmuring quietly in his ear.

There was a moment's uncomfortable silence, finally broken as Harðráði nodded. 'Very well. I release you from the fleet for now, Halfdan Loki-born. We move on Odinswe, but I have no interest in harming your pagan sites, and their survival will make no difference to Magnus. We need to take the fort there, destroy the harbour and burn all the store houses and docks and houses. The fleet will have their instructions to do that and only that.

Your crews can find your precious pagan shrine and protect it if you wish, but mark me, Halfdan, that the only way we will bring Magnus south is with such brutality. Odinswe *will* burn.'

Halfdan stood, locked in silent eye-to-eye warfare with Harðráði, but finally nodded.

Leif was starting to feel distinctly uncomfortable with all of this. That jarl they had already irritated once by battering his men outside the church struck Leif as a man to be wary of. Fortunately, that old warrior was the first to depart. Turning with a single look at Harðráði that seemed almost a meeting of equals, he gestured to the man with the broken nose and marched away. His hirð followed close on his heel, the injured man casting a look at Halfdan that was as black as his nose. One surprise for Leif was that a stunning, dark-haired beauty of a woman who'd been standing nearby tossed her hair like a wild horse, lifted her long skirts and turned, drifting off after him. Leif mentally weighed up their ages and decided that if she was the old man's woman, she was clearly silver-grabbing, for she was less than half his age.

One thing he did *not* miss was the look that Harðráði immediately threw after the retreating beauty. In an instant, Leif's head hurt. Anticipating what would happen, his gaze snapped from Harðráði to the woman, then back to Ellisif. The king's Rus wife was so entirely calm and inattentive that it could only be the result of careful control, for she had seen that look just as clearly as Leif had. Then Leif's gaze went to Gunnhild. He wasn't sure whether he was more surprised or disappointed to find that she looked irked at this exchange. Had she not done what she could to push Harðráði away? Yet the moment he found a new doe for the hunt, jealousy showed in the völva's face. Leif then turned to Anna to find that his Byzantine beauty was throwing black looks at both him *and* Gunnhild.

For fuck's sake! Was everyone in this world driven by their loins?

The gathering exploded like an old dandelion in a sudden gust. Harðráði rose and left the room with Orm Axebiter at his shoulder, his wife apparently completely forgotten. Gunnhild grabbed Halfdan and turned, urging him out in a different direction. Anna followed hurriedly, pawing at her mistress. Others disappeared, the meeting clearly over. One of very few people who did not move was Ellisif, who remained in her seat, her expression still carefully controlled, but her eyes dancing to a hundred different tunes.

Leif, aware that no one else he cared about was in the room now, walked over.

'For the love of God, that was difficult.'

The Rus princess nodded. 'Perhaps you need to gag your jarl?'

Leif gave a desperate laugh. 'Yes. Although I meant the others, really. You know them. I don't. Who are they?'

'You mean your jarl's new opponent?'

Leif nodded.

'He is probably the most powerful man in the army, after my husband and his fellow kings. He is Torberg Arneson på Giske, a Norwegian jarl of the Arnmødlingene. He had been Magnus's most powerful supporter until he changed sides and offered his sword to my husband. Were you gold plated and came with a tame dragon, you Wolves could never be worth half of what Arneson is to my husband. Your jarl has already provoked him twice now. I'd advise him not to do so a third time.'

'He has an interesting wife.'

Ellisif's eyes narrowed. 'You mean his daughter, Tora Torbergsdatter? She is dangerous just by existing. She is the most eligible woman in all of the north, I think. I am under no illusion that I will be cast aside in a matter of months in favour of her.'

'Never.'

'Do not be blind, Leif Ruriksson. You know I speak the truth.'

He sighed. Truly, Harðráði was on the hunt once more. 'Possibly. But there is a long way to go yet in this war, and even powerful jarls and their families can fall.'

'Do not stand in the way, Leif, you and yours. I will survive. I will be fine. But if you stand against Torberg Arneson, only bad things will happen.'

Leif shrugged with a sigh. 'I can attempt to persuade Halfdan, but it seems to me that this Torberg has already got his arrow nocked and pointed at the Wolves. I suspect confrontation is inevitable. Halfdan and Gunnhild will not let anyone desecrate the sanctuary at Odinswe, and I think Torberg is determined to do just that. A big fight is coming, and it has nothing to do with Harðráði's war.'

'Then be on the watch for Torberg Arneson.'

'Will Harðráði bring you to Odinswe, or will you stay here?'

She shook her head. 'He will take me wherever he goes until he has no further need of me. After that, perhaps I will attach myself to Bishop Aage's retinue. He is a good man, and he is already in Odinswe.'

'I do hope we don't have to run in and rescue him from a burning town for the second time in a month,' Leif said half-jokingly with a grin. In the wake of the last sacking, Harðráði had made it absolutely clear that churches and the priesthood were entirely forbidden to be harmed from then on. But in the heat of battle, men had a tendency to forget such niceties.

Their conversation drifted into matters of less import and gradually petered out, and finally Leif took his leave and departed. Outside the warehouse the world was a stark reminder of the events of a few weeks ago. Hróarskelda remained little more than a collection of shattered and blackened ruins, dotted with sporadic hasty mass burials. There had been survivors, of course, despite the mandate for genocide that had accompanied their sailing. Even had they desired complete annihilation, there would always be a few survivors, but the majority of the raiders had reasoned that there needed to be survivors in order to spread the word about what had happened. None of the others had thought to put their survivor on a ship and send him over the water to do it, though.

Consequently, hungry and homeless, often injured, men, women and children sat beside ruined walls and begged for food and goods to help them survive. Leif hardened his heart as he walked past them. He could see *Sea Wolf* and *Sea Dragon*, off to one side of the harbour, moored in an excellent spot where they were safe, comfortable, and yet in a perfect position to move to open water at speed. They were, after all, some of the earliest ships to reach the capital, having been portaged a short distance.

He took a slight detour to avoid the worst street for beggars, and found himself feeling a little more positive, despite the ruins around him. The blue sky and warm air, with enough of a briny sea breeze to overcome the smell of ash and cinders, did wonders for the soul.

'So are you Christian or not?' a voice said, suddenly.

Leif stopped, surprised, and turned.

His pulse suddenly raced as his gaze fell upon the man who'd stepped out from behind a ruined wall. He had a badly bruised face and a misshapen nose, even after three weeks. Halfdan had almost killed him with that one blow. A second man stepped out behind him, and this one held a stout cudgel. On sheer instinct, for Leif had travelled with the Wolves for *years* now, he turned. Sure enough, another man had stepped out to block the road ahead.

'I am indeed a Christian, though my devotions are held in the Orthodox manner, after the Byzantine rite. If you are here for revenge, I think you have the wrong man. Halfdan Loki-born is the one you seek, and I dare say he would be happy with a rematch. But we are all in the service of Harðráði, are we not? Shall we not simply bury the hatchet? The world has plenty of enemies for us without fighting our own.'

The man snarled slightly, though this seemed to pain him, and he reached up to his broken face and touched it gingerly.

'You are not our own. We are not the same. We are Norse, the children of Ash and Elm, sons of Mother Church in

149

Rome. Your crew are heathens, and you, if you follow heretical churches, are little better. Men like you bring ill luck to the fleet.'

'I warn you,' Leif said, 'that I may look small, but I am no easy target. Move on and find a waif or a thrall to pick on.'

'I'll move on,' the man said, 'when you give me your oath on the Almighty that you will not help your so-called jarl protect his heathen temple. When Odinswe burns, that place will burn brightest.'

Leif took a steadying breath. In some ways he would be happy not to preserve the ancient temple, and he would certainly prefer to foster good relations with these other men in the fleet.

On the other hand, this man was an insufferable prick.

'I will stand with shield and axe by my jarl when the time comes. You have been warned by Harðráði himself not to seek the sanctuary's destruction. If you do so, you defy your orders. But I will stand against you if I must.'

'Then I fear you'll not reach Odinswe,' bruise-face said, and pulled another club from his own belt. Leif was content he could hear the sound of the man behind him doing the same. Three to one. Not the best odds. Shit. Why hadn't he left with the others?

The simple fact that there were only three of them, almost certainly all men they'd met in front of the church that night, told him that this was personal, and not something done with the knowledge of Torberg Arneson – otherwise there would be more of them, and probably the jarl himself. If that was the case, then once again they would probably scatter if he could put down the main one.

They were using clubs for one simple reason, he suspected. Axes and swords tended to cause large amounts of blood, and if they returned to their ship soaked in blood, questions would be asked, which would be easily answered when Leif's body was found. Instead, they intended to beat him to death, with bruises and broken bones, and little tell-tale spray. That could give him an advantage, since *he* didn't mind turning back up at the *Sea Wolf* soaked in *their* blood. Consequently, he pulled free his axe and sax.

In a perfect world, he would be able to throw his knife and then wield his axe. Unfortunately he had discovered on more than one occasion that his sax was appallingly balanced for throwing and rarely hit the target, never point-first. The axe, on the other hand, was not a particularly large specimen, and though not designed as a throwing axe, its proportions made such a use possible. And he was going to have to close the gap in the odds straight away. Eyes still on the man before him as he and his friend moved side by side and started to advance slowly, Leif took a couple of paces forward, back, side to side, until he found the perfect spot, where he braced himself, driving his toe into the ground as if to sprint.

The two men came closer, and he could see their muscles bunching as they readied to leap. His timing had to be perfect. He was no great warrior like Bjorn or Ketil, nor protected by fortune like Gunnhild and Halfdan. He had only his wit. But he knew his wit to outshine theirs like the sun to a candle. As they moved, he suddenly kicked his foot upward. A shower of dusty earth, ash, gravel and pebbles short forward from his buried toe, right into the faces of the two men.

He didn't wait to see the result, since he knew what would happen, and time was of the essence. He turned, axe raised, and hurled it.

The man who'd been following up behind looked rather startled as Leif spun and threw with little aim. The axe was, as noted, not a throwing axe, and consequently did not embed itself satisfyingly in the man's skull. But it did hit him, and in the forehead, with the solid haft. The blow was hard enough that the man suddenly lurched and fell to the ground with a cry, club falling away as his hands came up to the welt on his forehead that was already red and bloody. He wouldn't die from it, but he would be out of action for at least a while.

Leif turned once more.

The two men were recovering, one faster than the other. The bruised and broken-nosed man had managed to close his mouth and eyes in time, and was blinking madly, coughing a little, but readying for a fight. The other man had taken dust in eyes and mouth and was bent double, gagging and crying.

Leif smiled to himself. Five years ago, he'd have thrown a book at them and run away. Look what time with the Wolves of Odin had done to studious Leif Ruriksson.

To his credit, broken-nose was not put off. He lifted his club and came on. The weapon swung forth, and Leif arced back out of the way, then stepped to the side, and struck. His sax was a close-fighting weapon, so he managed only a single slice before having to dance aside, but the blow was a good one. He'd got the man in the bicep with a cut a couple of inches long. The man yelped, but rather than pull back, he came on, club swinging and jabbing, whirling and chopping, a veritable windmill of violence. Leif had no way to parry, and so instead he continued to move, dancing back out of the way, giving ground all the time. Sooner or later, though, he would trip, and then there would be trouble.

A plan began to form as he saw one of the larger surviving charred walls off to the left. He made a quick estimate of the distance to it in short steps, and then began to turn, still ducking and dodging out of the way of the whirring club, backing now toward that wall. He was counting off the steps as he went. He had two warnings. The first almost made him laugh. He could see the triumph in the man's eyes as they neared the wall, for he was going to trap the small Rus any moment. The second came a moment later as he passed a broken barrel half-buried in refuse.

Three… step… swipe.

Two… step… thrust.

One… step… swipe.

Leif suddenly, instead of backstepping, dropped to the ground.

The man thrust out with his club as he'd been doing repeatedly, but instead of slamming it into Leif's neck, it hit solid wall, hard. The blow sent painful reverberations up through the club and into the man's fingers, hand and arm. He cursed, and numb fingers suddenly let go of the club.

Realising he'd misjudged, broken-nose looked down.

'This,' said Leif conversationally, as his sax slashed out, 'is called the Achilles tendon.'

The man screamed as the cord in his heel was severed, and collapsed in a heap.

'It is named after the Greek hero whose heel was his only weak spot,' Leif continued, sporting a vicious smile.

The man did not answer. He was busy screaming, tears in his eyes as he reached around for the ruined heel. This meant he was completely unprepared when Leif suddenly repeated the process on his other leg. He rose and stepped back as the man continued to let loose a series of blood-curdling howls.

'You'll live,' Leif said quietly as he wiped and then sheathed his sax. 'As long as you find someone sympathetic enough to bind your wounds. But you'll never walk again. Can you crawl back as far as your ship, I wonder? Or would you be better off taking a place with the beggars in the harbour street.'

'You can clearly be a vicious bastard,' said a familiar voice.

Leif turned to see Halfdan with a wry smile. Behind him, Bjorn punched the man who'd already been hit in the face with an axe haft. He turned again to see Gunnhild standing over the body of the man who'd choked on dust. Her staff, of course, had a spear point if she wished to use it as such. She had apparently wished as much, for it was red, and the man she'd dealt with was still and silent.

'I tried to talk them out of it. I think he took exception to your head-butt.'

Halfdan chuckled. 'He's been giving me dark looks for days. I've been waiting for him to come for me. Surprises me that he came for you, instead. More fool him.'

Leif shrugged. 'I suspect some see me as the weak link. I am small, educated, Christian, well spoken.'

'But you are a Wolf of Odin,' Halfdan said with a wide, fierce grin.

And somehow, everything made sense again.

Chapter 11

Odinswe, Fioni Island

'Farlof! Eygrímr! You have the ships,' Halfdan bellowed as the Wolves of Odin leapt from *Sea Wolf* and *Sea Dragon* to land on the springy turf of the riverbank.

Those two men, already treated as skippers by the young jarl, waved their understanding as the twenty men assigned to protect each ship shifted to the side and watched the rest of the Wolves move off.

They were close to the head of the attacking force. Harðráði's fleet had sailed from Sjáland, across the narrow strait and to the island of Fioni, then entered the Odinswe Fjord from the north coast, following it to the end. There lay the port of Odinswe, some two miles from the town, the rough timber jetties allowing a wide space for traders to dock, then transport their wares by cart the two miles to the town itself, or make deals in the small suburb on the shore and return to the sea straight away. The town lay beside a river too narrow and shallow for laden merchant ships, but sufficient for the shallow-draft dragon boats of raiders.

Fully two thirds of the fleet had made for the port, with the intention of burning every building, sinking every ship, and killing every soul they encountered, ruining Magnus's trade there. The rest of the fleet had entered that narrow river in single file, making for the town, where its important commercial centre would also be exterminated, and where a powerful Danish ring fort lay, which needed to be neutralised before they could move on.

By dint of being the fastest ships in the fleet, the *Sea Wolf* and *Sea Dragon* had managed to be the third and fourth vessels to enter the channel, the other two ahead of them only there by luck.

The edge of the town lay just two score paces from the river, though the gardens and orchards of the outlying houses stretched down to the water's edge in many places, and here and there they could see bridges across the flow, and even a waterwheel a little further inland. The fleet was spreading out in their landing, according to their favoured target, and so ships had been grounded all along the river, their crews leaping, howling, to the bank and then racing for murder and looting.

Many had already done so along the nearest stretches, but the lion's share of the ships had pressed on, past the edge of the town, for ahead, on the far bank and only a hundred paces from the water, lay the powerful ramparts and palisades of the fortress. The two ships of the Wolves, however, had neither landed early with intent to sack the town nor pressed on to the far end of town to take down the great circular fortress of the Danes. They had been guided by Gunnhild, who had simply gestured ahead to a wattle fence on the riverbank opposite the town, and pronounced that this was their target.

As he began to move, leading his men, Halfdan looked this way and that. Back to the northeast, along the river and toward the fjord, he could see ship after ship grounded on the far bank, their crews racing for the town, and beyond that, smoke pouring into the grey sky in numerous columns that appeared to be supporting the clouds. Each of those roiling black piles represented a burning ship or warehouse back at the port. Ahead, to the southwest, the rest of the ships were bearing down on the fortress. They clearly had their work cut out.

Odinswe's fortress was a ring of high earth banks, topped by twin concentric wooden palisades of heavy stakes, with fighting platforms. The lesser smoke of several hearths rose from within the fort, making it clear that it was occupied, probably by a number of Danish warriors, but also by whatever townspeople had had time to cross the river and throw themselves behind its defences before the dragon boats came. Halfdan was more than a little glad that they had been relieved of the need to be part of this. The port would relinquish little loot, for Harðráði had made it clear that he wanted the whole place and everything in it a charred ruin, another powerful message to send to Magnus: 'Nothing is safe.' And taking that fortress would be costly in men. Better the Wolves were not called to sacrifice themselves for Harðráði's throne there.

No. They had their own task, and it lay before them, just a couple of hundred paces from the fortress, and close to the riverbank.

To the uninitiated, it could easily have been an orchard. Stands of trees were scattered across the landscape here, between outlying farms, and this could have simply been part of that landscape, fenced in as private land. But the trees behind that fence bore no fruit for human meals, for they were of ash and oak and elm, trees of the old gods. Halfdan could almost feel the power of the place himself.

'Find the way in,' he shouted as he and the Wolves reached the fence. Ketil gestured to him and ran off to the right, along the fence in the direction of the fort and followed by grim-faced warriors, and so Halfdan took the rest and turned left, the two groups skirting the fenced enclosure in opposite directions.

It was of a roughly oval shape, perhaps two hundred paces across, and Halfdan frowned as they rounded the side away from the river and saw Ketil and his warriors ahead, running their way. The two groups met and came to a halt.

'There's no gate,' the Icelander said in confusion.

'Don't forget that Daneland has been Christian for half a century,' Leif pointed out. 'This place will not have been used in all that time, apart from perhaps a few stragglers of the old ways in earlier times.'

Halfdan nodded. 'I understand. The fence is not to keep people out of a sacred place. It is to keep that place in, and stop it interfering with their new world.'

'Hence no gate. No one is expected to go in, and certainly they don't want anything to come out.'

Halfdan chewed on his lip. Somehow it seemed wrong to simply tear down the fence. It might be a White Christ barrier to keep the old gods in check, but in some ways it also *preserved* the sacred place and kept it safe. He did consider simply posting guards all around the outside of the fence to prevent anyone going near it, but even as he began to mentally plot picket locations, Gunnhild walked past him and pointed at the fence.

'Here,' she said.

Halfdan looked about, shrugged, and abandoned plans to simply guard the place from outside. He peered at the place Gunnhild had indicated. The wattle fence had been built all in one great effort, supporting stakes shoulder-high driven into the ground a couple of feet apart for the entire circuit, and the wattle itself woven between them. But here, where they now stood, the work had both started and ended, and the wicker met between two posts without being interlaced. Halfdan approached one of the posts, gesturing to Ketil, who went to the other. They both touched the timber gingerly, for the men who had built this fence had carved crosses into the top of each upright, an extra warding to prevent the 'evil' of Odin from infecting their world. At a nod, the two men gripped the uprights and pulled, straining with teeth clenched. Slowly, and with great effort, the stakes came free of the ground, parts of the wattle cracking with the movement and bending. As the old, discoloured point came free of the grass, Halfdan pulled it toward him, Ketil mirroring the action, opening up an entrance one man wide in the fence. Job done, they slammed the stakes back into the ground as hard as they could manage, sufficient to keep the gate open for now. It was important, he felt, that when they left this place, they could put them back and make sure it was preserved once more.

As if the sacred grove welcomed them, behind the new gateway lay a stretch of low undergrowth through which a man could walk, just a foot or so deep, although as he stepped into it, Halfdan realised there were brambles within the foliage, which caught at his boots and trousers and threatened to entangle and trip him. He could not entirely escape the feeling that this was Odin's doing, that the Allfather was keeping his sacred grove as safe as possible. He faltered then, unsure as to whether pressing on was a good idea, but Gunnhild gave him a gentle push on the shoulder and he continued anyway. As he glanced back, he could not help but notice that the völva seemed to be stepping nimbly, even instinctively, *between* the brambles.

As they moved into the grove, further into the thicket of elm and oak, the undergrowth became deeper, up to the knee, the way narrower and darker, with trees crowding in and looming over them, blotting out the pale grey sky. But despite that, the way became easier, that undergrowth just grass, bracken and ferns, the difficult brambles no longer barring their path. In a way, it felt as though Odin had accepted their presence, and Halfdan began to feel less uneasy, and more fascinated, as the sense of Seiðr prickled his skin.

This place was something new.

At Ales stennar, they had been at an ancient site of power of the Norse gods, and at the old Odin stone on Gotland, too. They had felt the power at Hrafn's cottage in Angle Land, and the Seiðr of numerous ancient sites in their travels. But they had all been places that were shunned, forgotten, or even torn down and preserved with only scant measures.

This place felt *alive*.

Odinswe had been a place of power since the early days, and though the White Christ had seen it sealed in to prevent its influence being felt, the locals had been respectful enough not to simply destroy it. Thus it had lingered, a pool of Seiðr from the old days untouched and undamaged, waiting for those who sought it.

Odin was here.

He looked up, sure as anything that Huginn and Muninn, Odin's ravens, were circling above them. The sky was too obscured by the green canopy to see anything, but he was certain they were there. The Allfather watched this place; watched *them*.

As he reached the heart of the grove, Halfdan stopped in his tracks, flesh dancing with the crackle of Seiðr all around him, heart almost skipping a beat. The others came to a halt behind him, unable to pass. Gunnhild drew an impressed breath, and the only voice of dissent was Bjorn, who grumbled a little way back, wondering why they had stopped.

Halfdan drank it all in.

Did someone still live here? Did someone look after this place? Of course, the answer was no, because the fence was unbroken, and there was no sign of occupation within. But somehow the place seemed to be preserved. The grass here, in a wide clearing, was short, as though cropped, yet there was no sign of any method, whether the hand of man or the jaw of animal, by which this had happened. It looked perfect. Untouched. The clearing was circular and perhaps forty paces across. All around the edge, the trees formed a ring, each with ancient carvings in their bark. The *valknut*, the vegvisir, the ancient sign for gungnir, the spear of Odin, and runes of power abounded. They were not quite so easy to make out now as they would have been when great works happened here, when crowds of men and women breathed the name of Odin in this clearing. Then, the carved symbols would have been picked out in paint of red and white, while now they stood out only as a different tone in the wood.

But it was not these symbols, nor even the curiously well-tended grass, that stole the breath from the Wolves as they entered the clearing. As Halfdan stepped forward and aside, Gunnhild following suit so that the others could enter, their eyes were all on the tree.

They had seen oak and elm as they passed through the woodland, and even hints of ash, visible through the foliage. But *this* ash tree, which stood at the clearing's centre, was a thing of power. Old enough to be the mother of Yggdrasil, this great tree rose so high it seemed the clouds must part for it. The lowest branches began just beyond the reach of a tall man, and the immense trunk that supported them had seen the devotions of hundreds of years of Northmen. Even despite decades of disuse, it was possible to make out the stains in the wood that spoke of sacrifices hung and bloodied, of rites and rituals held here.

Once again, Halfdan knew that Odin was here, somehow.

'Odin,' Bjorn breathed as he joined them in the clearing, eyes wide. Leif, next in, drew a cross on his chest with two fingers, but his eyes were wide, and there was only respect in them, another reason Halfdan liked the little Rus.

This place was powerful, ancient, and somehow still alive, despite its neglect.

Even the raids, which were happening all around them, seemed distant and largely drowned out by the thick foliage and trees, no smoke from burning buildings visible, no roars or screams or clang of steel on steel despite the fact that some of it was happening only a few hundred paces away.

Ulfr finally made his way into the clearing, nodding in approval of the place as he brought up the rear and joined the gathering.

'I left half a dozen men at the gate,' the shipwright said, 'as guards.'

Halfdan nodded his thanks, gaze drifting over the forty-some men clustered in the clearing. 'Those of you for whom the Allfather's favour is important, now would be an excellent time for a few offerings. Those of you who kneel to the White Christ can sit and pray or whatever it is you do. We stay here and guard this place until the raid is over, and we know no one will come here. It is only noon now, and already the fortress is under attack, the port burns, and men move into the streets. For my money I cannot see this dragging on past the first few hours of darkness. Once everyone moves back to their ships, we will do the same, and only a small guard will remain here until the fleet departs Odinswe entirely.'

Plan set, they settled in. Those among them who held to the old gods paid what devotions they could, burying items of value at the base of the great tree. Four men went out for an hour and found a horse in a deserted farm, which they brought back and sacrificed to the Allfather, eight of them struggling to raise it into the branches on a rope and hang it to bleed out into the earth below. Ulfr returned to the ship briefly and retrieved the small pots of pigment he kept for touching up the paintwork on the ships' figureheads, and then went around the clearing, repainting the carvings on the trees, returning them to their ancient glory, so that the power of Odin only grew in this place. Men had trampled the path to and from the outside sufficiently now that it had become an easier way in and out. And the guards at the gate were changed hourly to give everyone a rest. A fire was built as the afternoon wore on, only from fallen deadwood, this place being far too sacred to cut the branches off. When the fire was assembled and lit, it was done so in the most open part of the clearing, and kept to a sensible size to prevent any risk of catching the other trees.

Most important of all, Gunnhild decided that it would be a waste not to walk with the goddess in such a place of power. Firstly, though, she went off on her own, communing with Odin, asking his permission to bring Freyja to this place. The Æsir and the Vanir may have been at peace for a thousand lifetimes, but it was still important to pave the way for any inter-action between the gods of Ásgarðr and the gods of Vanaheimr.

She came back with an expression of serene peace, clearly having secured the Allfather's permission. Halfdan had watched the völva in her searchings before, walking with the goddess, but he had never seen it happen in quite such a powerful place as this.

Gunnhild sang that ancient song in the language of the Vanir, the strange and enticing melody winding and twirling like the smoke that rose from the fire. Anna gave her counterpoint, adding to that melody, her own delicate tones speaking a language she did not understand, the words learned over years of listening to Gunnhild. That she was as accepted among the Wolves as any warrior, despite her gender and her faith, was confirmed by the fact that the völva accepted her part in it without comment. Since that day in Swaledale, a thread in the audio tapestry had failed, with the death of Cassandra and the loss of her voice from the melody. However, as Gunnhild gradually rose to her feet, staff twirling, those among the crowd in the clearing who still walked with the old gods joined in the more common refrains, learning them as they went.

When finally that song reached its apex, and Gunnhild suddenly dropped to the turf once more, hands opening, fingers splayed, as feathers, bones, coins and silver scattered in their strange patterns, Halfdan suddenly realised he hadn't breathed for long moments, and forced himself to do so.

The murmured strains of the song drifted to silence, slowly, as Gunnhild studied the patterns, her eyes glittering, fingers dancing, lips moving in silent speech.

'Danger comes,' she said, tone low, 'and it comes now. I see threads cut in this place, but the *We* of Odin will not fall this day, while all around it burns. I see ships in danger, too. *Our* ships. Only Wolves of Odin can save them.'

'The ships?' breathed Halfdan, worried. 'We have to go.'

'It is of no *immediate* concern. Nor is the great opportunity that comes with the dawn. A ship comes from the north, and it carries a thread of white from the disgraced priest.'

'Hjalmvigi.'

She nodded. 'But now: danger comes *here*.'

She rose, the debris of her casting ignored as she readied her staff, iron spearpoint brandished ready.

At her words, the Wolves of Odin in the clearing all drew swords, axes, spears, saxes, adjusted chain byrnies and helmets, and lifted and readied shields.

There were screams, then. A few, cut short, back along the path to the gate.

Darkness was not yet upon them, but the light was beginning to fade slowly, especially here amid the cover of so much foliage. Consequently they saw the interlopers early, burning torches dancing among the trees. Halfdan toyed with the idea of challenging them, issuing a loud threat to keep them from the grove, but then brushed the notion aside. Those screams may have belonged to intruders, but the fact that they were still coming said that the screams had also come from the throats of the Wolves of Odin guarding the gate. Blood for blood. Their deaths had to be avenged.

Every man gathered in an arc, waiting for the intruders, made his peace with his god, be that the nailed god or the Vanir and Æsir.

The first warrior came, then, bursting free of the trees. He ran out into the clearing, and then staggered to a halt, head snapping this way and that. They had obviously known that the grove was occupied, from the guards on the new gate to the well-trodden path through the trees, to the flicker of the campfire in the clearing. Apparently, though, they had not anticipated the *number* of men waiting for them here, for the warrior's expression went from furious to uncertain in a single blink.

Other men burst from the path behind him one after another, gathering together. Every other warrior held a burning torch, ready to send this sacred grove to oblivion, but none had used them en route, for they knew not what they would find and had kept them for the heart of the place.

The man who'd come first and had stopped in surprise suddenly blinked again as an arrow punched into his throat. Somewhere back and to the left, Halfdan could hear Ketil murmuring in satisfaction as he nocked another arrow.

As though that arrow had been a stick pulled that weakened and broke a dam, the interlopers suddenly burst into life. Men bellowed furiously, yelled Christian oaths, and ran at them, torches guttering and spitting, weapons gleaming. They came around that one stricken warrior, who suddenly dropped to his knees, made odd gurgling noises and then toppled to one side.

Battle was joined in that sacred grove.

A man ran at Halfdan with an axe in one hand and a blazing brand in the other. That half-moon blade of silvery steel swept down, and Halfdan lifted his shield above his head, taking the blow on the rawhide edging, feeling it bite into the wood as its momentum was halted. The man, overextended and in trouble, could do little to stop his own demise then, for Halfdan's short blade stabbed out again and again.

The man was done for by the third blow, that cutting the artery in his neck, but Halfdan pressed on, delivering stab after stab. His seventh was little more than a glancing blow as the dying man fell, the raised shield tugged downward by the weight of the axe in the falling warrior's grip, and the eighth blow barely touched the man's scalp as he toppled away. Still, risking opening himself to further attack, Halfdan bent and delivered a ninth blow. Nine bloodlettings in this sacred place, honouring the nine nights that Odin had hung on Yggdrasil.

His opponent downed, Halfdan looked up at last. Other warriors were coming now, filing from that path and into the open, but there was little danger of their victory, for their numbers were kept minimal by the narrow approach, and so no matter how many of them there might be, at any one time the Wolves of Odin outnumbered them significantly.

Another man came at Halfdan, and he ducked away from a spear thrust, then cut upward into the hand that gripped it. The man bellowed in pain but was hardened and professional enough that he did not fall or withdraw. As the spear fell from his damaged hand, his other arm came round, brandishing a sax, the tip of which bounced from the edge of Halfdan's shield, and snicked a short, thin line across his cheek, damn near taking his eye with it. Halfdan roared, partially with the soreness and irritation of the injury, and partially with anger at these people who dared to invade this place.

His sword went to work. This time, he hacked and slashed, chopped and stabbed like a man possessed, blade flashing this way and that at a dizzying speed. Nine cuts and stabs. The man fell with a cry, another blood sacrifice to the Lord of Frenzy.

As Halfdan stepped back, panting, and reached up, wiping his cheek with the back of his hand and looking down at the blood, he growled. All around him, his men were at work. Those who honoured the Allfather the old way were giving him their kills, either with nine blows, or with oaths to Odin along with every stab. The Christians were no more silent, crying out furiously to their nailed god as they fought, bringing down the intruders one by one.

The bodies were piling up already, though precious few belonged to Halfdan's crews. The enemy numbers hampered by their approach, the interlopers were getting the worst of the engagement by far.

Then suddenly there were no more. They had stopped coming. Wolves moved among the dead, grabbing the fallen torches that could have burned the trees of this sacred place and casting them into the campfire.

'Is it over?' Ketil said, shouldering his bow and fastening his quiver.

Halfdan shook his head. 'Half of you, stay here. Watch this place. The rest come with me.'

And with that, still gripping sword and shield, Halfdan began to pound back along the now-flattened path that led through the trees. His anger flared again as, ahead of his warriors, he reached the gate they had formed a few hours ago, and he noted the bodies scattered across the grass. His men had given as good as they had got, for five Wolves of Odin lay there, guts opened, eyes glassy, but twice that many of the intruders had gone to their own afterlife.

They paused then, only long enough to make sure that each of their crewmen had a weapon in hand to mark them as a strong warrior when the valkyrjur came to choose from the slain. Then they ran on, Halfdan still leading them.

'Where are we going?' Bjorn shouted from behind.

'Remember what Gunnhild said? The ships are in danger!'

And as they rounded the arc of fence that enclosed the sacred grove, that became clear. *Sea Wolf* and *Sea Dragon* had both been pulled up so that their bows were well onto the grass, in case the tidal action of the river might tug at them and pull them back out into the water. Each ship held twenty-one men, protecting them from trouble, but even now, Halfdan could see that they were swamped with twice that number of enemies.

Even as he ran, bellowing the Allfather's name, Halfdan found himself counting estimates of the dead and making mental calculations. He had known that it was almost a certainty that the crews of Torberg Arneson, of the man he had injured at the church, would come for them in the grove. Arneson had six ships in this fleet, as well as several more at home. Even if they were smallish ships, that would be three hundred men at his command, compared to less than a hundred Wolves. Counting everyone, the Wolves could not number even half Arneson's manpower.

He realised with a smile that though these were Torberg Arneson's men, they were not his entire force, and likely Arneson himself was not with them. He, and half his hirð, were either at the fortress or in the town, adding to the destruction designed to draw Magnus south. The man had sent half his warriors off to deal with the pagan thorn in their side, but had made sure that he himself would be seen in the main fight, following Harðráði's instructions, so he could not be accused of what he had clearly allowed to happen.

With a roar, the Wolves of Odin joined the fight at the ships, racing into the rear of the enemy force. Arrows began to fly from Ketil and one of his better-trained compatriots, and a couple of throwing axes spun out ahead, thudding into the backs of Torberg Arneson's warriors. It was only as men fell to these missiles that the attackers realised the tables had been turned and that the beleaguered ships' crews were not alone. Some managed to turn to face the new threat even as Halfdan and his Wolves hit them, hard.

There was no call here to make each kill a devotion, and so Halfdan simply fought, blinking away the blood that kept creeping into his eye. He hit the backs of the men with his shield held before him, braced, and heard cracks as the domed iron boss broke ribs. As the man cried out and turned, gasping, Halfdan swung his shield arm, the rawhide edge slamming across the man's face and breaking more bone in its passage. Even as the man shrieked and fell, Halfdan's beautiful Alani sword lanced out and took another man in the side, sinking deep into muscle, fat and organs. He made sure to pull it back roughly and at an angle, tearing through more organs and flesh as it came free. That man, too, fell away, howling.

Ahead, one of the attackers had somehow made it past the warriors on the *Sea Dragon* and was approaching the sail with his burning torch held high, ready to fire the ship. Somewhere close by, Halfdan heard Ulfr bellowing curses at the sight. Then, a well-aimed arrow took the torch man in the back, and he dropped, falling a full body length short of the mast and sail. Still, there was always a danger with fire on a ship, so Halfdan only breathed easy again as one of the men who'd stayed with the *Sea Dragon* suddenly dropped and then rose again with that torch in his hand, hurling it out safely into the waters of the river.

In one of those moments the gods occasionally grant men, Halfdan suddenly saw a warrior in the press turn to face him, and recognised the discoloured face and the flat nose. The man he'd head-butted in Hróarskelda let out a whoop of glee and started to run at him, sword and shield in hand, expression of determination on his ruined face.

He got halfway.

Bjorn simply stepped in from the side and lifted his foot, tripping the man. The black-eyed Norseman slammed to the ground, rolling once before falling still, groaning and shaking, trying to recover his wits enough to stand. Before Halfdan could say anything, the great albino took two steps and then slammed his boot down on the fallen man's head so hard that the skull broke and the contents burst free like an overripe melon.

Bjorn looked down at his boot in distaste for a moment, then shrugged and began to wipe it on the grass, and realised that his jarl was looking at him. The albino looked up at Halfdan with a frown as he continued to wipe blood and brain from his boot.

'Sorry. Was I supposed to save him for you, or something?'

Halfdan couldn't help but laugh.

The fight was over. A dozen or so of the enemy, maybe even a score, had managed to extricate themselves and were running, now, hurtling along the riverbank toward the great Danish ring fortress where the rest of their compatriots would be found. The rest were either dead or hopelessly injured, and even as Ketil and his friend put arrows in the backs of a few running men, the rest of the Wolves began to move around their enemies, finishing them off, making sure that anyone they thought had fought well died with a weapon in their hand, just in case.

'I don't think anyone else will come, now,' Halfdan announced.

Gunnhild nodded. 'This is over. The *We* and the ships need guarding overnight, but the danger is past. Now we can look forward.'

Halfdan felt his pulse race, remembering what else Gunnhild had seen in the grove.

A ship from the north.

A ship linked with Hjalmvigi…

Chapter 12

Off Fioni Island, summer

'Can you make out any details?' Halfdan asked, peering into the morning sunlight.

Leif pursed his lips, squinting across the glittering waves at the distant shape. His eyes were good, but it was a long way in a light haze. 'She's flying just one banner. I can't quite make out the details yet, but it's red and gold; of that I'm certain. Similar crew to ours, maybe forty at the oars, but there are half a dozen men gathered around the skipper and steersman.'

'And she's still not moving?'

Leif shook his head. They had been lucky to spot the ship at all, really. It was floating, motionless, way out to sea, at a distance that would not have been visible from the coast of Fioni. It was pure luck that anyone had come out far enough to spot them… but then it was *not* luck, really, for they were here because of Gunnhild's magicks, after all.

Halfdan had been filled with urgency after the fight at the Odin grove last night. Once both grove and ships were safe, under guard, and all Torberg Arneson's men had either been slain or retreated, the last part of what the völva had said during her communion drove the jarl on. A ship would come from the north, she'd said, and would somehow be connected to Hjalmvigi. That he had become so comfortable with Gunnhild's pagan magicks should trouble him more than it did, Leif thought. But the fact remained that she had said something would happen, and so the Wolves immediately planned for that thing as though it were a given.

Consequently, they had stayed the night at Odinswe, aboard ships and in the grove, but even before the light of dawn came up, Halfdan had assigned the *Sea Dragon* and her crew to keeping watch on the sacred wood as long as the fleet remained in the area, and had then taken out the *Sea Wolf*, splashing back into the water in the purple darkness. They had used sail only to drift quietly downstream, past the many beached ships of the fleet, and out into the fjord. Once they were out past the rest of Harðráði's fleet, and the charred remains of the harbour, where charred masts now jutted from the water's calm surface, they had dropped the oars and began to row, crossing the wide, open inlet until they reached its mouth and the open sea with the first light of the sun.

Halfdan was determined not to miss anything important.

Thus, the *Sea Wolf* had been cruising the waters off the northern headland of Fioni for hours, watching for anything out of the ordinary, which, when a war fleet was operating in the area, meant any ship at sea that was not part of said fleet, for merchants and fishermen would know better than to sail too close to Fioni while Harðráði's ships ravaged the island.

Three hours they had cruised the coastal waters with no reward, until finally Ulfr had spotted a sail way off to the north, and they had diverted to investigate. A small ship, not moving very fast or, in fact, *at all*, as they now realised. For a time they had wondered whether it was a dead ship, a deserted vessel bobbing around in the water, something draugar that had men variously gripping their Mjǫllnir pendants tight, or crossing themselves, whichever their personal faith called for. A deserted ship at sea was a cursed thing.

But as they'd come a little closer, they'd made out figures aboard, and the *Sea Wolf* resounded to the noise of relieved sighs.

'Red and gold,' Halfdan mused. 'The dragon banner of Magnus of Norway is red and gold. It has to be him. Has to be Magnus, and that means Hjalmvigi. Tell me, Leif,' he said, excitedly, 'can you see a dragon?'

Leif sighed. His jarl was always a little prone to urgency when he became animated. If he stopped to think about it properly, Halfdan would know that no king of Norway would come alone in a small vessel to talk to his enemy. If that were Magnus, there would be a hundred ships, not one.

The Rus squinted into morning light. It was impossible to tell the precise shape on the flag. *No one* could at this distance, of course. But it did appear to *resemble* a sort of animal design from what he could make out.

'Hard to tell, but I think it *is* a figure of some kind. Gold on red, for sure.'

Halfdan smacked his fist into his palm. 'It's the Norse dragon. Has to be. Ulfr, take us in.'

The *Sea Wolf* changed course immediately, angling toward the distant ship, a small vessel of a similar size to their own. Leif, his place at the oars taken by one of the two spare crewmen, stood beside Halfdan, peering at their quarry. Gradually, more details came into view. 'Definitely a dragon banner,' he confirmed.

'Just the one flag? She's not flying a raven banner too?'

Leif squinted, gaze raking the vessel from bow to stern, from yard to waterline, and shook his head. 'Just the dragon banner, no raven. Not a ship of war, then.'

Their own fleet's two flagships, those of Harðráði and Sveinn, had both borne the raven banner since the day they set sail from Sigtun, while the former had also borne the adventurer's war banner *Landøyðan*, 'Land Waster', which was said to bring only victory when shown to an enemy. Thus far it appeared to have worked.

Leif peered at the ship, still, even as Halfdan moved about, unable to stand still. There was movement aboard. They looked as though they were preparing to set sail, oars hovering above the water now, yet even as *Sea Wolf* bore down on them, they remained motionless.

'Why are they still, yet readied?' Halfdan murmured beside him.

Leif shrugged. 'By now half the world must know that the only ships in these waters are Harðráði's fleet, so we have to be seen as an enemy of Norway, yet we do not appear to be on the attack. They are cautious, I think… ready to race away if they must, but curious enough to wait until the last moment, for that looks like a fast ship to me. They do not have the look of a ship of war. See how there are no shields on the top strake.'

A courier ship, he suspected. Unarmed ships of that size, back down in the empire, were usually imperial courier ships.

'I think it's a messenger.'

Halfdan chewed his lip. 'Not Magnus? No, of course. Not in one ship.' He slumped, deflated for a moment, then straightened again. 'Can you see a priest in white?'

Leif had already looked repeatedly, for he'd been waiting for that very question. 'No. But then it is possible Hjalmvigi is not in a priest's robes, given his situation and status. He could be one of the men gathered around the steersman. But would he willingly come here? The safe money says he is not there.'

He could sense the frustration in the jarl. Halfdan had been more than hopeful that the ship would be carrying his prey, though Leif remembered a certain vagueness to Gunnhild's words. 'It carries a *thread* of white from the disgraced priest,' she had said. It was connected to him somehow, but that did not mean he was here.

'If it has no priest on board, then it is of no value to us,' the jarl announced. 'When we are close enough to be sure, we either take Hjalmvigi or, if he's not there, we sink her with all hands. Norway is the enemy, and every death could provoke Magnus himself into coming south.'

Leif winced. 'Do not do anything precipitous, Halfdan. We don't know why they're here yet. It would be foolish to sink them without knowing who they were.'

The jarl's lip wrinkled as they came ever closer to the Norse ship. 'The priest is not on board. I give you the count of a hundred to speak to them, then we attack.'

Leif glanced sideways at his jarl. Halfdan was irked, and he might well go through with that threat. The Rus, aware of his time constraint, turned and waved to Ulfr. 'Bring us close and then to a stop within speaking distance.'

Ulfr nodded and turned the steerboard, carefully bringing them parallel, just far enough away that both ships could drop oars without conflict, and then Leif stepped to the side. If Halfdan was not going to do this properly, then he would. After all, he had been an ambassador for princely Kiev at the Byzantine court. Negotiation and politics had been his very nature before setting sail with the Wolves.

'Ho there,' he called in the Norse tongue. He knew enough of the language, which was close to their own Kievan dialect, even if his own accent might make the words sound a little strange. The man at the rear with that group of men, presumably the skipper, came to their sheer strake and leaned.

'Who are you?' he called.

'We are *Sea Wolf*, in the fleet of Harald Sigurdsson, called Harðráði, and that of Sveinn Ástríðarson, king of Danes. We mean you no harm,' he said, with a sidelong glance at Halfdan, who was frowning in disapproval, and seemingly *did*.

The skipper conversed momentarily with one of the other men, then turned to shout to Leif. 'We carry a message from the king for your master, though we remain at sea for now, as sailing into the fjord is surely a death sentence. It is said that Harðráði's war banner flies, and that no ship is safe.'

'Yours is. You are not a ship of war.'

'Nor were the merchants we hear now lie on the seabed from here to Skáney,' the man said, pointedly. 'Word is that your fleet attacks first and asks questions later.'

Another sidelong glance at Halfdan, and Leif addressed the visitors once more. 'I give you my word, and the word of my jarl Halfdan Loki-born, that you will be safe. We will escort you to Odinswe, where Harðráði holds court. Sveinn of Daneland is not currently present.'

That might be a good thing. The Danish pretender had slightly different priorities to Harðráði, Leif suspected, which would gradually widen a rift between them. While Harðráði and the fleet had sacked Odinswe, Sveinn had remained in Hróarskelda, attempting to re-establish his throne. His absence might make things a little more straightforward here since, though Harðráði and Magnus were currently enemies, they were also family, while Sveinn was just an enemy, pure and simple.

There was a long pause as several of the figures on board the Norse ship went into close discussion, and finally a new figure stepped forward. This was no skipper, or sailor at all, and his rich and ornate garb and accoutrements suggested a man of some importance.

'We have the word of your jarl?' he said.

Halfdan stepped next to Leif, with a quick, unreadable glance shot at him. 'I am Halfdan Vigholfsson, called Loki-born, Jarl of Sasireti,' *the lie came easily now, clearly*, 'and leader of the Wolves of Odin. You have my word you will reach Harðráði unharmed.'

It had taken Halfdan some effort to make that promise, Leif knew. Still, even if Hjalmvigi was not on board, he was *connected* with the ship somehow, and that being the case, the only way they would find out how was to see this through.

Another short conflab aboard the Norse vessel, and the nobleman waved at them. 'We accept a truce and your protective escort to the usurper. Lead the way, Jarl of Sasireti.'

Halfdan turned to Leif. 'Let us hope this leads us north somehow, if the priest will not come south.'

Leif continued to watch the Norse vessel as they set sail once more, guiding the visitors back toward the Odinswe Fjord, and as they moved through the fjord's mouth and into the calmer waters, Leif turned his gaze toward their destination. The difference in Odinswe harbour since their passing through in the early morning was stark. Though the harbour itself remained dead and charred, the fleet was making ready for action. Ships were loading and boarding, and several had already moved out into open water, clearing the area around the port. Even as they approached, Leif saw a dragon ship emerge from the river that led up to the town, evidence that the entire force was readying to move.

The army was preparing to strike once more, now that Odinswe was gone. The next target, if Leif was any judge, would be the great trade centre of Hedeby on the mainland. He spotted the flagship, then. Harðráði's vessel remained beached, for now, a great tent that was yet to be taken down stood on the shore nearby. Ulfr gently swung the steerboard and brought them alongside the great man's ship, and the *Sea Wolf* beached with a gentle crunch. The Norse ship joined them at the shore a few moments later, expertly guided in parallel.

The crew of the Norse ship, and their passengers, waited politely until the Wolves disembarked, and Leif gestured to them, then the nobleman and his escort, as well as a few warriors clearly brought as some sort of honour guard, dropped from the ship and began to follow them toward the great tent. As they approached, Leif spotted Ellisif of Kiev, sitting on a tree stump with a handful of hazelnuts, tossing them one at a time to a black squirrel who sat nearby, remarkably tame. She looked sad; lost even, once again forgotten and ignored by her husband. He felt he should wander over and say something, but now, unfortunately, wasn't the time. He turned just in time to see Anna looking at him, narrow-eyed. He gave her an innocent smile, and then followed the others into the tent.

The Wolves had had neither the opportunity nor need to visit the leader of their expedition thus far since their arrival at Odinswe, and so as they entered Leif was surprised at the wealth and ostentation Harðráði had on display. Of course, a jarl was *expected* to show his wealth and power in public, so Leif should not have been entirely surprised, but still he blinked as they entered the tent, gestured in by a nod from Orm Axebiter, who glowered at Bjorn as he passed.

The tent was the size of a large hall, one corner curtained off as a private living area for the duration of the stay, the rest his command tent. The floor had been turned into a giant map by the clever method of cutting hides to the shape of countries and islands, and small wooden ships like children's toys marked the known position of the various forces. Leif could see their own location marked, as well as Onund in Sigtun, Sveinn in Hróarskelda, and what had to be Magnus far north in Norway. Currently, the map was ignored, though, and as the Rus's gaze swept around to the tent's owner, it took in the rest of the décor. Gold, silver, precious jewels, and rich silk hangings adorned each wall. Something that looked worryingly like the Byzantine empress's crown was on display on a cushion, and Leif wondered if, perhaps, back in Miklagarðr the great but troubled empress Zoe was bare-headed and irritated. Knowing Harðráði, Leif would not be at all surprised. Similarly a great and ornate gold cross with the extra bar of the Byzantine Church could only have been lifted from one of the great city's basilicas by the light-fingered adventurer, and several of the hangings had the look of imperial work. One was even, if Leif was not mistaken, a war banner of the imperial *excubitores*. How the man had come by some of his riches was not only staggering, but also baffling.

Amid all these treasures, and a map of war that covered three countries, Harðráði sat at a small table that held a 'tafl board. His opponent, Leif was surprised to discover, was Bishop Aage. He had worried a little last night over the bishop's safety, for the man was known to be in Odinswe, but Harðráði had been explicit in his instructions this time. Any man who damaged or stole from a church, or harmed a priest, would find himself nailed to a mast until the gulls ate him. Consequently, in all of Odinswe, the property of the Church had gone entirely untouched, and all churchmen had been located and escorted safely from the place even as it was sacked.

Harðráði had not even looked in their direction, yet. He moved a piece, and sighed. 'You are a clever opponent, my lord bishop. I have not struggled so in a game for years.'

Aage gave a snort. 'Ever the politician, eh, Sigurdsson? I know full well you could have won the game twelve moves ago, had you not been toying with me.' He chuckled. 'But I appreciate the attempt to soothe my feelings over the loss. I can only hope your war is over as fast. I would be joyful to see you enthroned, but I lament the loss of life it costs.'

At that moment, the bishop became aware they were not alone, and turned, as did Harðráði. One golden eyebrow rose quizzically.

'You have preserved your little pagan hollow, then, Loki-born?'

'The Odin grove is untouched, yes,' their jarl replied. 'The warriors of Torberg Arneson made an attempt on it, and on my ships, too, but the Wolves of Odin are made of sterner stuff.'

'I shall *suggest* to Arneson that he look elsewhere for trouble, my young friend. Sadly, he is too powerful and influential for me to dismiss out of hand. Even when this war is over, I will need him in my court. But he is a political animal, and I daresay I can persuade him to leave you alone. I would rather not have my best jarls trying to kill each other while we are at war.'

For the first time, he noticed that the small group of men standing behind Halfdan included not only the Wolves, but other guests.

'You are not alone, I see.'

Halfdan gestured to Leif, who stepped to the fore and cleared his throat, slipping seamlessly into the role of ambassador. 'King Harald, I have the honour to present to you representatives of Magnus of Norway,' he said, carefully labelling his own fleet's leader with the royal title, while omitting it from the man's nephew. 'They come alone with a message from the Norwegian court.'

'Perhaps I should leave,' Bishop Aage said quietly, making to rise.

'On the contrary,' Harðráði said, tone carefully even as he reached out to stop the priest standing. 'In such circumstances, it is often of value to have witnesses one can trust, as men of peace. And others who one can trust as the *other* type,' he added, as Orm Axebiter stepped in from the doorway of the tent, letting the flap fall closed, and standing almost offensively close to the visitors, fingers resting on the axe at his belt.

'You are the one they call Harðráði?' the nobleman asked. 'Harald Sigurdsson, brother of Olaf the Holy and uncle of King Magnus the Good?'

Harðráði nodded, again giving nothing away. Leif was impressed with the level of strained control in the room.

'My message from your nephew is for your ear alone, Harald Sigurdsson, though if you *fear* me, you may keep a guard with you.'

Now, Harðráði laughed out loud. 'You think to set conditions in my court, Olaf Ogmundsson?'

The man looked startled, and took a step back, and Harðráði laughed again. 'Yes, Ogmundsson, I know you, just as I know every clan's powerful men in Norway, those who flocked to my banner and those who clung to my nephew's. And fear you? Not precisely. In fact, I think the last time we met was at Stiklestad. You remember Stiklestad? A bloody affair, eh?'

'I pulled the leg off a man at Stiklestad,' Bjorn murmured conversationally, universally ignored by all present.

'No,' Harðráði went on. 'I think that whatever my dear nephew has to say is better spoken in front of plenty of witnesses who I trust. Say your piece.'

Ogmundsson was clearly unhappy about this, but he rallied well, placing his hands on his hips. 'Magnus, king of Norway and Denmark, sends greetings to his uncle.'

'Cut the shit,' Harðráði said in a bored tone. 'Get to the meat of the matter.'

The visitor straightened, further irritated.

'Norway is too vast a land for one man to govern successfully, especially when the Danish throne also demands attention. Thus…'

'Thus my nephew offers me a share in the power in the hope that I will let him cling on to some of it.'

'Half of Norway,' Ogmundsson said. 'Fully *half* of Norway. King Magnus offers an equal share of the throne in all parts. The land shall be divided, but along with it all goods and property of the crown. Truly equal shares. A partnership.'

'An equal part of Norway, while Magnus retains Daneland too? So what of my allies? What of Sveinn and his Danes? What of Onund and Sweden? This is not my war alone.'

The visitor shrugged. 'Onund Jacob retains Sweden already, but with a deal struck between you and your nephew, peace could then also be had with Sweden. As for the Dane pretender, his majesty sees no reason to give up the Danish throne to a usurper. This offer is made by a nephew to an uncle. As you may remember the words from the lay of Reinharð Rev: "the blood of kin is not spoiled by water."'

Harðráði sucked on his teeth for a moment, apparently deep in thought. Then he straightened and gestured to the visitors. 'Go back to your ship. I shall consider the offer and send my answer shortly. Orm?'

Axebiter bowed his head and gestured to the door with one hand. Olaf Ogmundsson gave one last not-entirely-happy look at their host, then bowed and turned to go, his escort behind him. Halfdan and the Wolves made to follow, but Harðráði beckoned to them instead. As Orm led the visitors out and back to their ship, the would-be king looked from Bishop Aage to Halfdan and back.

'Thoughts?'

'Half a throne is hard to sit on comfortably,' Halfdan said, somewhat bluntly.

'But a war avoided is better even than a war won,' Aage countered, though Leif doubted that sort of logic would appeal to either Harðráði or Halfdan.

'And by accepting Magnus's offer,' the adventurous would-be king added, 'I will make an enemy of Sveinn, which has a number of downsides.'

Leif stepped forward. 'If I might point out, you have a golden opportunity here.'

'Oh?'

'Yes, you are clearly wearing down Magnus, for he would not offer terms if he did not feel threatened. But to get terms for even *half* of Norway, you have had to burn and depopulate half of Daneland, and the level of destruction visited upon this land has not been seen for *centuries*. If you do not accept the deal, then you will be forced to continue on this path, and before long there will be no Daneland left to be king of. Then the war will have to move to Norway, because if Daneland is not worth ruling, why would Magnus bother coming south? You will then be forced to fight in your homeland, and every death and every burned house will diminish the throne you seek to inhabit. And though you say you would make an enemy of Sveinn Ástríðarson, I doubt you have missed that this is gradually happening anyway, with every Danish house we burn. That enmity will come sure enough no matter what you choose. In short, here is a way out, and if it is not taken, the result is almost certainly an echo of biblical Armageddon in the north. Would you rather be king of half of Norway, or king of a burned wasteland? You told us yourself how hard it would be to bring battle to Magnus in his own capital.'

Harðráði nodded slowly as Leif spoke. 'You may have Loki cunning,' he said, turning to Halfdan, 'but your Rus warrior there has the real wisdom, it seems.'

'And once you are on that half throne,' Leif said, smiling slowly, 'you will be very hard to remove, I think. And a man with a glib tongue could gradually bring all the more influential jarls and clans over to his banner while he sits on that throne. Why, in no time at all, it may be that Magnus finds that he is little more than a puppet of his uncle.'

That made Harðráði laugh out loud. 'Well said, Leif Ruriksson of Kiev. Yes, I think it might just be a good decision after all. But until everything is agreed and the deal is done,

181

I think it would be best if word of this were not to reach my good friend Sveinn of Daneland, eh? I do not think he will be as enthusiastic as we are. I have a few small conditions I would like to impose on any such offer, though nothing likely to break the deal, and I trust my dear nephew about as far as I could portage a ship, and Olaf Ogmundsson even less.'

His smile widened now. 'In fact, I think a little deputation of my own is in order. My lord bishop, if I could prevail on you to convey my answer and conditions to Magnus? Coming via a man of the Church there will be no argument, and should there be a trap or anything untoward awaiting a deputation, even my good Christian nephew will not harm a bishop, especially a Danish one.'

Harðráði leaned back. 'But there are difficulties, still. This message, and any deal that follows, must be struck in secret, without a hint of it reaching either Onund or Sveinn. Indeed, until the deal is done, I cannot risk word of it reaching even the jarls of my own fleet. It must be complete before it is made public. Thus, I cannot send an official representative, other than the good bishop here, who, as a Dane, is nominally one of Magnus's subjects and therefore safe. Currently, the *Sea Wolf* and the *Sea Dragon* are detached from the fleet, following your little pagan adventure, and I do not believe anyone will miss you. Halfdan, Jarl of Sasireti, would you do me a kindness and convey the bishop here to my nephew in Niðaróss? Two of you carry Danish blood, and two are outlanders anyway, from Kiev and Iceland. I see no reason Magnus would take offence at you, and you are rare in my fleet, in that I both trust you, and trust you to get things done.'

Leif glanced at Halfdan, for just a moment expecting the jarl to argue, not wanting to be sent on another errand for the glorious lunatic, but then he caught Halfdan's expression and he knew otherwise. They were being sent to Niðaróss. *Hjalmvigi* was in Niðaróss, and the jarl knew that. In essence, Harðráði was almost handing them the priest on a platter, and Halfdan was not about to argue with that.

'It shall be done,' the jarl said, with a bow of the head.

'Very well.' Harðráði clapped his hands together. 'My lord bishop, if you would commit to memory, and perhaps to paper, my response?'

He and Aage swept the pieces from the board on the table, and went to work penning the offer to Magnus. As they did so, Halfdan gestured to his friends, and they slipped from the tent into the fresh air of the morning on the beach.

'How far did you say Niðaróss was, Ulfr?' Leif asked.

'Twelve days, I reckon. Maybe ten if we rush.'

'Harðráði will have to stay here for a month, then, for us to bring back the reply.'

'Possibly longer,' Halfdan added, 'if Magnus decides to come south with us for the deal.'

Leif shook his head. 'I doubt that would happen. Magnus will be as wary of betrayal as his uncle. Any suggestion that he sail south in peace might be seen as leading him into a trap. No, I think he will accept the word of his uncle, but send us back with a reply. A month, then.'

'A difficult sail?' Halfdan asked.

Ulfr shrugged. 'I've only been halfway up that coast myself. It's not a forgiving shore, though, so I would say yes, likely a difficult sail. But we will have locals with us in a third ship, who can help guide us through the worst.'

'Frankly,' the jarl said with a dark smile, 'I don't really care *when* we come back. Getting there is the important bit. Getting there, and cutting the heart out of Hjalmvigi.'

Leif shuddered. The coming days were likely to be fraught.

Part Three

ᛈᛟᛚᛁᛏᛁᚴᛋ ᛟᚠ ᛟᛞᛁᚾ

Politics

Let no man glory in the greatness of his mind,
but rather keep watch o'er his wits.
Cautious and silent let him enter a dwelling;
to the heedful comes seldom harm,
for none can find a more faithful friend
than the wealth of mother wit.

Hávamál 6, Olive Bray trans.

Chapter 13

'Can you still see them?' Halfdan bellowed, wiping his eyes and blinking repeatedly. Beside him, Gunnhild peered into the unbreachable weather.

'No. But they were there a moment ago,' the völva hollered back over the noise of the storm.

That was little comfort to Halfdan. A moment in this could change everything. The ship being there a moment ago was no guarantee it would be there now.

'Brace,' called Ulfr from the stern, and Halfdan grabbed the sheer strake, gripping tight just as the wave hit him.

It had been an eventful journey, to say the least.

They had set off from Fioni the dawn following the visit, making sure to be out to sea before the rest of the army was moving. Harðráði would keep the fleet outside Odinswe until they returned, on the pretext that he had received rumour that Magnus was on the way, and so he would not move on to sack more of Daneland until he had confirmation one way of the other. The various jarls in the fleet would be content to spend a few weeks of downtime, since they had more or less been constantly on the move and at war since spring. And the fleet's master had vowed to make sure that no one interfered with the Odin grove in their absence, which had allowed Halfdan to take both ships.

They had slipped out of the fjord even as the first light graced the tips of the waves, *Sea Wolf*, *Sea Dragon*, and the Norse ship, named *White Arrow*, apparently. The journey across the Jótlandshaf and skirting the north coast of ruined Sjáland had been easy enough, as far as the gentle coast of Skáney, lulling them all into a false sense of security. Indeed, the sailing had been easy all along the coast, from Skáney into Norse territory. They had passed the fjord along which lay the trade town of Ánslo, where Magnus's merchants lurked safely in the harbour, unable to ply the seas for fear of Harðráði's fleet and unable to trade with their usual partners, since they were now largely ruined shells.

Beyond Ánslo, they had put in and camped for the night on a headland, on a sandy beach between two reaching arms of rock. It had been a quiet night at an easy landing, and the crews had been in good spirits throughout, though Halfdan had noticed Bjorn seeming increasingly uneasy as the evening progressed, something he'd never expected to see. When finally, as the Wolves drifted off to sleep, Halfdan had found Bjorn, he was sitting on a rock and peering out over the water at the headland they had most recently passed, a rocky and deserted place.

'You seem pensive,' he'd said.

He'd expected something ribald in reply, and his concern only deepened when the big albino turned to him and said simply, 'This place is not for the living, Halfdan,' and then rose and turned in for the night. The jarl had blinked at such a curiously deep and heartfelt sentiment from the noted teller of tall tales.

His worry had eased in the morning as they put to sea and moved away from that place, further west, and with every mile, Bjorn's spirits seemed to lift, until he was once more telling off-colour stories about improbable encounters.

From that point on they were largely in the hands of the Norse ambassador and his skipper. Olaf Ogmundsson's man chose their overnight stays, each a small town on the Norwegian coast, each feeling faintly unfriendly, and, when the locals caught sight of a Mjǫllnir pendant, usually *extremely* unfriendly.

The coastline itself was no better, and Halfdan soon began to see what Ulfr had meant by it being a difficult sail. Before long they passed away from the world of low, flat coasts, shallow, sandy beaches and rough, dry-grass dunes. The shore became craggy, with ship-killing rocks jutting up from the water's surface, way out from the land, sending white waves and spray into the air, vegetation only visible atop the rocks. Those rocks became higher as they moved north, forbidding and inhospitable, enclosing narrow fjord entrances. Here and there they put into one such place or another for the night, and each morning the Wolves' crews were grateful to be on the move again.

Norway was so very different from his homeland, despite their shared heritage, and Halfdan was starting to understand why the Norsemen were so often like their own terrain: hard, unforgiving and dangerous. This was not a world that bred comfort.

And that only became more and more evident the further north they sailed. Soon those rocks had become tors and then mountains that reached from clouded, snow-capped peaks, right down grey and gloomy drops directly to the water, with no safe place to moor. Narrow fjords wound between the high peaks, forming a coastline that was ever changing, headlands and hollows, crashing water and bleak rock. It was becoming starkly clear why Harðráði, who was a child of this very land, had no desire to bring war against Magnus here.

Day after day they moved north, each providing them with less and less accommodating locals, more forbidding and bleak terrain, and worse rocky hazards in the water. And there was more to come. On the ninth day, when they were apparently at the westernmost extreme, and the coast began to turn slightly east of north, the weather changed.

It was subtle at first, just a distant line of dark grey, far out to sea on the horizon. Halfdan would not have worried about it himself, considering a strong possibility that it would just dissipate or move off elsewhere. Ulfr, though, watched it with hawk-like eyes, tense. It boded ill for their journey, in his opinion. Ketil, used to the weather out in this part of the world, given that his Iceland home lay to the north here, agreed with Ulfr, and the warning was passed around the Wolves.

It became a race.

The next morning, that distant grey line had become darker, more solid, more threatening. Closer. But a quick discussion between Ulfr, Ketil and their guides confirmed that they were coming ever closer to the fjord that led deep inland to Niðaróss. If they could reach it before the storm broke over them, they would be safe. If not, then it was anyone's guess what might happen.

Another day's travel, and the crews beached their ships on one of the rare strands of flat, green land. The next morning, half the western sky was the colour of lead, and boiling clouds could be seen far out among it.

That evening, just a day's travel from the first stage of their entry to the Niðaróss Fjord, they decided to forego sleep and row through the night in the hope of reaching safety, for the evil grey sky was reaching out now, ready to embrace them.

The morning sun barely registered when it rose. Hidden behind the high mountains of Norway to the east, it put in a brief appearance as a pale disc glimpsed between tatters of dark grey.

'Is that the fjord?' Halfdan had asked, pointing ahead to where the land seemed to reach out to sea in a wide arm, forming a narrow waterway into which the White Arrow was steering them.

'No,' Ulfr replied. 'I spoke to their skipper about it. That is the Þrónd, a strait dozens of miles long between the coast and the islands. We need to pass through that strait to reach the fjord. Búri tells me he has known more ships destroyed in the Þrónd than in the rest of the world put together.'

Not an encouraging fact.

Even the birds now deserted the sky, knowing what was coming.

As they closed on the channel and prepared to leave behind the open sea, Halfdan could just make out the distant flashes of lightning between the dark canopy and the dark waters beneath, and he could only hope that those flashes came no closer.

They entered the troublesome strait on a morning that was almost as dark as night, the grey finally rolling right across them. The sea became black, picked out with white foam, and Ulfr began to steer very carefully, observing where the white came in crashing sheets, denoting the presence of ship-killing rocks. The current was strong, and Halfdan could feel it pulling at *Sea Wolf*, pulling her north along the strait, but also east, toward the rocky coast of the mainland. The wind, too, drove the ship ever northeast.

Then the rain started.

Even as the wind continued to strengthen, pushing them and threatening them, the rain came, hammering down from that dark, boiling sky, battering the *Sea Wolf*. Within an hour of struggling along the Þrónd, they had lost sight of the *White Arrow* ahead, and within the second hour, they could no longer spot the *Sea Dragon* either. Their world had contracted down to a stormy darkness, visible only for twenty or thirty paces around the ship, the rest rain, spray and cloud.

The wave broke across the ship now, and though Halfdan had braced as Ulfr warned, it was simply not enough. He felt his cold, numb fingers torn from the strake by the sheer force of the water smashing into him, and staggered back across the ship between swearing, struggling men, tripping over legs and tumbling into the three-inch-deep water in the bottom of the vessel. For half a heartbeat, he cursed that he'd so tripped, but then realised with a start that if he had not done so, the wave might well just have carried him over the far side and into the water. He had little doubt that they would never see any man who went overboard today again.

The ship rocked and bucked as the wave dissipated, and oars smashed into one another, men swearing and struggling, being bruised by their own oar as it was thrust into them, hard.

'Ship oars,' Halfdan bellowed, coughing out salty water as he struggled back upright. 'Ship oars. Now!'

Ulfr shouted then. 'Halfdan.'

'What?'

'Without the oars I might not be able to keep us from the rocks.'

Halfdan nodded. He'd worried about that, but he'd also seen what just happened. There would be several cracked ribs already.

'Yes, but if the waves catch the oars any worse than that, we're going to start losing men, and in numbers.' All around him the crew were pulling in the oars and dropping them into the ship, safe and sound, where they could not be thrown around by the churning waters. Off to the stern, Ulfr went silent, concentrating on one thing, now: keeping them going and upright. He gestured to Ketil, who ran over, and the two men both gripped the steerboard, working together to heave it whatever way was required to keep them away from the rocks and in the middle of the channel. Even together, both strong, powerful men were struggling, but there was no room for a third man to help.

'Everyone else, keep down, below the level of the sheer strake,' Halfdan shouted. 'Don't risk being carried overboard.'

Like me.

Another thought occurred as he sloshed through the cold seawater in the bottom of the ship. It was ankle depth already, and deepening all the time.

'Anyone with a helmet, start bailing. We need to keep the water level in the ship low.'

Everyone knew that danger, and so they began to bend and scoop up seawater, tipping it over the side between the shields that were fitted there. Halfdan looked back and forth along the ship. They'd lost two of those shields to the last wave, and they'd lose more yet. He contemplated having all the shields brought down and secured inside the ship, but they also provided just a little extra cover from the waves, and so he would allow them to stay there, even at the risk of their loss.

'Shit,' shouted Ketil, and he and Ulfr started growling as they redoubled their efforts to heave the steerboard over. Halfdan looked out ahead just in time to see a massive explosion of white foam as another wave slammed into a massive jutting rocky shelf directly ahead.

'Come *on*, Ulfr,' he said under his breath, eyes locked on that rock, watching as it slid toward them with terminal finality. The prow beast began to move, to slip a little to the left, then a little more. The rock was submerged again beneath a white wall, and then revealed once more in its grisly glory, even as the *Sea Wolf* turned thanks to the sheer bloody-mindedness and strength of the two men on the steerboard. The moment they were angled to move past without slamming into that rock, Halfdan let out an explosive breath of relief, which was clearly too soon, as just then another great wave smashed into the side of the ship, unnoticed as they all concentrated on what was ahead. With no warning from Ulfr this time, Halfdan was hit with the full force of the wave. There was no staggering or struggling now, for he was simply thrown backward, hard.

He knew he was done for as his head hit the sheer strake. His feet, whirling through the air amid the powerful torrent, slammed into one of the shields fastened there and kicked it free, out into the water, and he could feel himself being carried over after it, even through the fuzz of a half-senseless head. It came as a massive surprise, as the wave crashed back down, that he found himself slamming into the ribs of the ship and not the churning freezing cold surface of the sea. His eyes opened, looking this way and that, blurred with seawater and blood that seemed to be running into them from his scalp. He saw Eygrímr then, still holding on to his jarl's belt with one hand, the other arm wrapped around the bench below. The man had clearly saved Halfdan's life, preventing him going over. The jarl would have to thank him properly later. For now he did that with a simple nod, and vowed not to be standing in the open and waiting when the next big one hit.

'There she is!' yelled a familiar voice, and Halfdan looked forward again to see Leif stood at the fore, gripping the carved prow beast for dear life and pointing off ahead and left.

There, a short distance away, *Sea Dragon* was still moving, leaning heavily with the wind, but afloat and intact and fighting the storm.

Ulfr made damn good ships.

Good thing too. Bishop Aage was on *Sea Dragon* with two of his priests and the documentation they carried from Harðráði to the king of Norway. Halfdan couldn't decide what Magnus would do if they arrived without the deputation or the documents. He doubted it would be good.

Men continued to work, scooping up water that, despite their efforts, was now almost knee deep in the middle, and tipping it back over the side, labouring frantically. The next wave came, but they were all ready for it this time, and Halfdan dropped behind the shields with everyone else to ride this one out. It hit with a massive bang, the ship lurching to the left, almost rolling onto her side for a moment before tipping back. As Halfdan rolled this way and that with the hull beneath him, he came back up in the aftermath to see that two more shields had gone from the sheer strake on the far side, and one of the oar benches there was empty, its occupant carried over with them.

He fought the urge to run over and look for the unfortunate crewman – it was the job of a jarl to do all he could to protect his men, after all – but he also knew beyond doubt that the man was lost. He knew they would not even be able to spot him in the churning waters, let alone get to him and save him. The man would be pulled down to Ran's hall now, and there was no stopping that. Halfdan had to concentrate on the others.

'Really?' he found himself saying as, just for a moment, the path ahead became visible before a fresh sheet of torrential rain obscured it. Ahead, the strait narrowed to perhaps two thirds of a mile, arms of land reaching out from both sides toward them.

Ulfr said nothing, but he and Ketil manoeuvred the steerboard once more, angling it so that they could return to their optimum course in the centre of the channel now that they'd skirted those rocks.

Something slammed into Halfdan's leg, and he looked down to see a dented helmet rolling around in the water. He grabbed it and staggered over to that empty oar bench, then began the work of bailing, scooping up helmetful after helmetful of briny water and tipping it over the edge as the others did the same, trying to keep the water level inside as low as possible.

They paused and braced once more at Ulfr's shouted warning, and another great wave broke over them, taking with it another shield and another crewman. Halfdan paused momentarily in his work and glanced ahead. He could no longer see that narrowing of the channel through the rain and spray, despite the fact that they had to be almost upon it now. Also, they had once more lost sight of the *Sea Dragon*, though she was ahead, and must already be through that narrow gap. Then he returned to his bailing, and continued to do that as fast as he could for what seemed an eternity, trusting to Ulfr to keep them right.

When he next looked up, he could see both banks of that narrow section, to each side of the ship, close enough to make out houses up the slope on both shores, lights glimmering in the dark. Despite his faith in Ulfr, he prayed then, something he did rarely these days, offering whatever he had to whatever gods were watching for their favour, asking them to save his ships and crews.

Then they were through that narrow section, the twin arms of land falling away again behind them. The rain changed direction, rather suddenly, lashing them from head on, still not letting up, but at least there was still no sign of that lightning getting closer, and he could not make out a thunderous rumble over the rest of the storm's din.

He bailed some more, keeping *Sea Wolf* empty and afloat.

What seemed like soaked, freezing hours passed by, and finally he looked up again at an excited shout. Leif was pointing ahead, and Halfdan rose, peering past the Rus.

Sea Dragon was there again. In fact, they were catching up with her fast, for their sister ship was hardly moving, a whole bunch of men at the sheer strake, leaning over and hauling a man from the water, despite the danger this put them all in. Just as the man dropped back into the ship and the crew all threw themselves down to safety, another great wave came from ahead and right, slamming into both ships and sending them rolling dangerously to one side.

By the time they had both recovered, *Sea Wolf* was almost with them, and as *Sea Dragon* began to move forward once more, they were almost side by side. It was encouraging, and a relief, as long as they did not encounter any further narrowing of the channel. And since they'd not seen *White Arrow* since the storm came in, they could hardly ask the only knowledgeable local about what was to come.

Once more, Halfdan went to work with the others, as the ships ploughed on.

The next time he looked up, it was to see that the great island they had been following to the left fell away, with open sea visible before they met the next island.

That this might be a good thing passed through his head briefly, before he learned why it was not. With no land protecting their left side, the full force of the storm now hit. Both ships slewed right uncontrollably, and it took every bit of Ulfr's skill and his and Ketil's strength to hold them in the channel and stop them being driven against the land. The wind was appalling and powerful, and the rain seemed now to be coming horizontally. Worse still, Halfdan could hear the boom of thunder and see the flashes in the black clouds disconcertingly close, almost reaching them. How much further could they have to go?

He contemplated consulting Ulfr, but one look aft changed his mind, for the big man was using every ounce of his strength and concentration, along with those of the Icelander, to keep the ship afloat and moving in the right direction. A glance to the left worried him a little, for it looked as though *Sea Dragon* was being pushed in their direction, although they appeared to be ironing out that problem and were moving forward again, two men at the steerboard, just like on *Sea Wolf*.

The next couple of hours were among the hardest in Halfdan's life, for the winds were constant, ever in danger of driving them against the rocky coast, the rain never let up for even a breath, and the thunder and lightning continued to move toward them. All the time, they struggled and braced, were soaked and battered, lost shields, and on one occasion another crewman, and bent and scooped out water constantly, with no clear indicator of success.

Then they passed behind another island.

Though it continued to blow and rain, waves battered them, and they worked hard, it was suddenly easy to appreciate the difference the island made, and how much less dangerous it was right now than when they were exposed to the open sea.

Halfdan's spirits were still sinking, though, until suddenly Ulfr shouted, and his voice carried hope, even joy.

He was pointing ahead, along the length of the ship, to where Leif was doing the same, almost jumping up and down. Halfdan couldn't hear what they were saying over the storm, but he could just see that the mainland on their right dropped away, opening up a channel inland. That had to be the Niðaróss Fjord.

They were going to make it.

As they approached the inlet, Ulfr began to shout to Ketil, and they heaved on their burden, causing the ship to slowly angle to the right. The wind and the current were now both coming from behind, and the main danger would be over-shooting and being driven straight into the rocky northern shore ahead, and so the shipwright kept the steerboard under very tight control. *Sea Dragon's* steersman, one of those workers from the Norman shipyard, if Halfdan remembered correctly, was currently proving his worth, matching Ulfr in control as their sister ship turned in perfect unison with them, angling toward the mouth of the fjord.

Behind them, a bang that made Halfdan jump announced that the heart of the storm was upon them, and a bright flash left his eyes dazzled. When they recovered, with much blinking, he took in the scene ahead, as they turned fully into the fjord.

Another flash revealed a surprise.

Atop the rocks on both sides of the fjord's entrance stood a handful of catapults. Halfdan had seen the great siege weapons in the south, in Byzantine hands, and in Apulia, but he'd never even heard of their use up here. It seemed Magnus was equipping his people with all the latest weaponry. Though the catapults had a relatively limited range, even with their height advantage, their presence would force any attacking fleet out into the centre of the water, where they could be met and contained by another fleet relatively easily.

Halfdan was suddenly grateful that Harðráði had *not* brought the fight north. The man had been quite correct about the terrible danger any attacking force would be in as they neared Niðaróss.

The next sight that greeted him was even less welcome.

As they rounded the southern promontory and entered the fjord proper, they found the *White Arrow*.

The ship they had been escorting had been driven against the rocks at the entrance of the fjord, and all that remained of it was perhaps twenty feet of prow, wedged in rocks as waves raked and pulled at it, trying to free it from its fastness, and the mast and shredded sail that bobbed in the water at the shore. Bodies were strewn along the shoreline, and more drifted with the strong currents, floating this way and that in the fjord. Of anyone standing and waving desperately, there was no sign.

White Arrow had gone, and so had its crew, even the troublesome Olaf Ogmundsson. At least they still had the bishop. The Wolves' two ships drifted on past the wreckage in a sombre silence, broken only by the ongoing ravaging of the storm and the cracks of thunder.

'I feel we were lucky,' Halfdan said finally, as the last of the bodies disappeared from sight behind them.

'Luck, nothing,' Gunnhild said. 'We sacrificed to Freyr at Ales stennar. It was the goddess's brother whose hand held off the worst as we moved. Freyr saved us.'

'That and some bloody fine ships,' Ulfr panted from the steerboard.

Even Gunnhild had to nod at that. The less well-crafted *White Arrow* had fallen foul of the terrible conditions, but Ulfr's work had produced ships so light and manoeuvrable that they had managed to avoid the rocks both out in the Þrónd and here at the mouth of the fjord.

Some three or four miles in, away from the open sea, Ulfr left the steering with Ketil for a moment and crossed to Halfdan.

'There's a small cove up ahead,' he shouted over the din, 'with a good-looking landing beach. It's still a good twenty to twenty-five miles to our destination, and the storm is right on top of us. I think we should beach and take cover until it passes over. Then we can finish bailing, check for damage and eat a little something for strength before we press on the rest of the way.'

Halfdan nodded his agreement, and moments later *Sea Wolf* and *Sea Dragon* were grounding on a beach of gravel, scattered with head-sized rocks. A small hamlet of wooden houses sat a short way from the beach, though no one was outside in this weather, and Halfdan doubted the Wolves would be disturbed. Each vessel unloaded the spare sail kept folded in the ship at the rear, and stretched it from the sheer strakes to make an awning, beneath which the men huddled out of the rain, while the lightning continued to flash and the thunder continued to roll. At least this far into the fjord there was considerably less wind than out in the open sea.

All around him, the men stripped out of their sodden shirts and either changed into slightly drier ones from their water-proofed kit bags or at least wrung them out and shook them to get the worst off. Then they settled in to wait.

It was as the thunder and lightning moved off overland, to the southeast, that Bishop Aage found him. The man was still wet through, not having such a thing with him as a spare priest's robe, and not wishing to undress in front of heathens. His face was serious, which worried Halfdan from the outset.

'I fear we may have a problem at Magnus's court,' Aage said.

'Oh?'

The bishop lifted his hand, palm upward. In it lay what remained of the documents from Harðráði. They were sodden and limp, and even from the briefest glance, Halfdan could see the smeared stains of ink that had run.

'All of them?'

Aage nodded. 'And without Olaf Ogmundsson and his people we also have no corroboration of anything we say. It is *possible* that the king will listen and even believe us, given my rank as a bishop, but I escaped Hróarskelda with little more than the clothes on my back, and certainly none of the badges of a bishop's office. In essence, we could be any group of fools from anywhere telling lies and making up stories. We have neither evidence nor witnesses to back up the details that we *also* don't have. A problem, as I say.'

Halfdan frowned. 'Do you remember Harðráði's deal? His conditions?'

'Yes. We went over them thoroughly. I doubt there's anything that has slipped my mind.'

'Then we don't need the papers. All we need is you, and to be very convincing. Fortunately, I have a small Rus friend who has represented the prince of Kiev at the court of the Byzantine emperors. If anyone can persuade Magnus of the truth, it is Leif.'

'Then you are still determined to go on? Despite all this?'

Halfdan shrugged. 'If gods and storms and rocks and catapults cannot stop us, why should a little uncertainty? Find what you can to make yourself look as important as possible. I too will find my best gear, and will brief Leif. Once the storm is over, and that is coming in an hour or two, we'll still have plenty of daylight to make it the rest of the way to Niðaróss. Ulfr is busy checking over the ships, but apart from a few stray barnacles, I don't think there's anything wrong.'

The bishop gave him a weary smile and bowed his head. 'What a strange embassy we are, eh?'

Chapter 14

Niðaróss

In the event, their embassy failed to leave the beach before their first meeting. Even as the storm died down, the crack and boom now very distant, the Wolves of Odin had visitors.

Eight large ships hove into view around the headland, all bearing the dragon banner of Norway, all ships of war, lined with colourful shields and crewed by hard-looking men. They cut through the calm waters of the fjord until they were opposite the beached ships and then slowed and drifted to a halt, perhaps fifty paces from the shore.

'That's a serious coincidence,' Halfdan murmured.

Leif's brain was racing through connections, though, and he shook his head. 'No coincidence, I would say, Halfdan. Magnus has been expecting trouble for a while. I suspect that word of our arrival began as we pulled into the fjord under those catapults. Either a signal fire, or more likely a rider, carried that word to Magnus's assembled fleet – he has to have a strong fleet in the fjord to guard against our coming, after all – and as soon as the weather eased enough to make it feasible they sent out enough ships to make sure we were overpowered.'

'So they're here for battle?' Bjorn said.

'No. I doubt it. We bear no banners, either of war or of Harðráði. They cannot be certain we are enemies, and even if we were, what fool of an enemy would send just two ships? No, they're here to investigate, which plays well into our hands. Halfdan, I think you need to tell them that...'

But the jarl was shaking his head already. 'No, Leif the Teeth. This is *your* job. Of the eighty men on this beach, you are the only one who is trained and experienced in negotiation and embassy. We bear a message from one king to another. That's ambassador's work.'

Leif swallowed. While that was true, when he'd played such a role, it had been at the court of the Byzantine emperors. There had been plenty of danger there, of course, but less obvious than in the north. Here, one wrong word and Magnus's men might be parting his hair with an axe. Still, he knew the look on Halfdan's face. The man's mind was made up. He glanced round at Anna, and she gave him a small nod of encouragement.

'Who braves storms to approach Holy Niðaróss?' called a man from the ships out in the water.

Leif adjusted the hang of his cloak and swept it back sufficiently to make sure the axe at his side was visible. Appearance was important at times like this. Raking his fingers through his hair, he made his way between the gathered crews and down toward the waterline near the *Sea Wolf*.

'We are ambassadors,' he called back in response. 'A deputation from Harald Sigurdsson, who they call Harðráði, brother of Saint Olaf Sigurdsson. We were escorting the *White Arrow*, a ship carrying your own embassy, including the jarl Olaf Ogmundsson, but the storm caught us in the Þrónd and drove *White Arrow* onto the rocks, with the loss of all hands. Despite their absence, we still require an audience with Magnus of Norway, if you would kindly escort us to the capital.'

There was a short silence, and then a private exchange aboard the ship, before the skipper stepped forward again.

'We will take you to Niðaróss and the royal court. The king himself will decide there whether he wishes to see you. If he does not, you will leave immediately. If he does, you will present yourselves unarmed and in humility.'

'Fuck that,' Bjorn grunted nearby, Halfdan and Ketil both echoing the sentiment in slightly gentler terms.

Leif threw them a warning glance, then turned back to the ships.

'We are an embassy, not a raiding party. Weapons will be worn, but sheathed, as is fitting. As, in fact, was the case when your own Olaf Ogmundsson attended the court of Harðráði. To demand the removal of weapons is to cast dishonour upon ambassadors.'

Another quiet discussion, and then the man returned. 'Agreed. But there will only be eight of you attending. The rest can wait with your ships.'

Leif nodded again. 'Agreed. Make way for *Sea Wolf* and *Sea Dragon*.'

With that he turned to Halfdan. The jarl gave him a smile. 'Well spoken, Leif.'

The following half hour saw the dismantling of the shelters and the loading of the ships. The crew then made ready, most of them clambering aboard the beached vessels while the rest prepared and then, when all was good, heaved against the ships, pushing them back out into the water before running through the shallow surf and climbing aboard themselves.

The Wolves quickly manoeuvred the ships out into the fjord. Leif wandered over to Halfdan near the stern. 'We need to make sure everything runs smoothly. Give them the impression that we are professional and untouchable. Appearance is everything now. And, to that end, try and shut Bjorn up if you can.'

That raised a wry smile from the jarl. 'Odin himself might struggle with *that* one.'

In no time they were formed up close to the eight Norse ships, and at a signal from their leader, those ships moved off. As they sailed up the fjord, Halfdan and Ulfr continually worked with the crew, *Sea Wolf* gliding through the water, oars in perfect unison, but Leif, suddenly promoted to leader of the expedition, moved to the prow and stood by the carved beast, looking out.

He only had to get them in front of Magnus. Bishop Aage would do the rest.

The fjord and its surroundings slid slowly by as they moved ever inland. Despite the formidable mountains he could see in every direction, hazy in the cloudy distance, the land that actually surrounded the fjord itself was surprisingly fertile and low, an oasis of arable calm. Villages stood close to the shore here and there, but not all he saw was so tranquil and peaceable. He'd not recognised the warning beacons for what they were until he saw the third of them in a line, ready to carry warning of an invasion to the town. Beacons meant warriors. But the most martial thing they saw was the fleet. Perhaps fifteen miles from where they'd beached, a large inlet opened to the south of the fjord, and a cursory glance told Leif that the ships he could see there represented the bulk of Magnus's fleet. He couldn't form a precise number, but there were well over fifty ships, a fleet capable of taking on their own. Suddenly the idea of negotiating a peace with Magnus took on a new importance. Should this fleet and that of Harðráði meet in battle, the loss of life would be appalling, the most brutal battle in the north in decades.

It was almost a relief when they sailed on past that huge inlet and lost sight of the fleet, though the image of it remained ingrained in Leif's mind, a warning of what was at stake here.

Then he remembered what really was at stake here, beyond fleets and messages and kings. Why they were here in the first place, far beyond being ambassadors for the Norse usurper. He turned.

He could almost read Halfdan's mind from the look on the jarl's face. They were nearly at Niðaróss, where they would almost certainly find Hjalmvigi. Warning bells went off in his head, then. He'd seen how animated Halfdan had become at just the mention of the possibility of the priest's presence. When actually face to face with him, there was a good chance the jarl would just break and go for him. Leif chewed his lip for a moment. That would not be good. It would almost certainly scupper their mission of peace.

Leif would be busy with the bishop when the time came. Who could control Halfdan if they needed to? His gaze naturally fell upon Bjorn, but he moved on swiftly. Bjorn could hold Halfdan back with one hand, but the big man was even more impulsive and driven by battle lust than the jarl. There was more chance of Bjorn joining in than stopping it.

Ketil? No. Again, the Icelander was just too unpredictable.

Farlof would be a good choice, of course, but he was on the other ship, and Leif wanted everything prepared. Eygrímr. Eygrímr was solid, and had no personal problem with Hjalmvigi. And Ulfr. Ulfr had an embrace few men could break out of. As they sailed, the crew rowing with professional ease, Leif picked his way back between them until he reached the leader of the Swaledale men among the crew.

Eygrímr looked up as he rowed.

'We will shortly be in the court of Magnus,' Leif reminded him. 'Our jarl will see the priest that is the focus of all his hatred and anger. He may not be able to hold himself back when the time comes, so we may have to.'

The Angle warrior nodded as he worked. 'Understood. I shall remain close and ready.'

Content that he'd put something in place, Leif continued down the ship to the steerboard and, while Halfdan was busy, engaged Ulfr in the same conversation in low tones, securing the barrel-chested shipwright's support. Satisfied that all was as good as could be, Leif returned to the prow and stood beside the wooden beast, watching the fjord slide by.

Five more miles of coastline to their right, with a high, tree-covered hill beyond the narrow shore, and finally their destination slid into view. Leif was impressed. Niðaróss sat within a loop of a wide river, almost an island, connected to the other land only by a narrow spit. A dense cluster of wooden buildings surrounded a timber church that stood on a slight rise, while the nearest side of the town, facing the waters of the fjord, formed a busy port. Merchant ships were in great evidence, likely all berthed here indefinitely until the threat of war at sea was over and the southern trade centres reopened. But there were also another half dozen ships of war here, all fitted ready for action, even as they sat at jetties.

Magnus was taking no chances.

Their escort brought them into the harbour, guiding them to a free jetty. There was barely sufficient room for two ships there, and Halfdan gave the order that *Sea Dragon* remain in the water for now, along with most of their escort, while *Sea Wolf* and the ship with the speaker on both moored. As the other ship disgorged a score of men, Halfdan beckoned to the usual crowd, the core of the original Wolves, along with, at a nod from Leif, Bishop Aage and Eygrímr, and the eight of them dropped to the timbers of the jetty, adjusting their shirts and cloaks and weapons.

As they strode off to join their guide, Halfdan nudged Bjorn.

'No fighting unless I start it. And that axe stays in your belt unless you have to defend yourself. Understand?'

Leif smiled at the exchange, and then fell in beside Halfdan. He cast one look back at Anna, whose expression conveyed her irritation at being left behind, but there was nothing for it. They'd been limited to eight, and eight they had.

The Rus hardly failed to note the way their escort took position all around them so that there was little chance of any of them slipping away. Magnus was taking no chances.

The palace to which they were escorted stood out even from the grander buildings around it, in that it was a stone-built edifice to waist height, with timber and wattle and daub above. The longhouse was of a traditional, ancient design, and only the quality and sheer size of it made it clear that it was a palace, a building of high value.

Men stood on guard outside, as the small party approached, and Leif noted how, despite not being in a walled compound, the longhouse was only one part of a larger complex of a dozen or more buildings gathered around the church, linking the king with Christianity for all to see.

The men on guard nodded at the Wolves' escort and stepped aside without word, suggesting a level of importance in the speaker who'd brought them here. The longhouse had been divided, and they found themselves first in an outer chamber, from the eaves of which hung a number of banners, including the dragon pennants, various noble clans' motifs and even the raven banner of war, as yet kept inside and not affixed to a ship. That, at least, was a good sign. Their escort stopped for a moment in this chamber, in which nobles, warriors and thralls all went about their various businesses. The man spoke quickly and quietly with a servant, who slipped through the door and was gone for a short while, before reappearing for a second exchange. This complete, the escort turned to the Wolves.

'Your audience has been granted. In the king's presence you will not speak until bidden. When you do, you will be polite and deferential. Any insult given will be dealt with harshly. When complete, you will leave under escort. Do you understand?'

Though most of the Wolves answered with unimpressed glares, Leif nodded. 'Agreed.'

Moments later, the doors were pulled open. Their guide stepped through first and moved into the main hall, and behind him, Leif and the bishop walked side by side, the rest of the Wolves, led by Halfdan, close behind.

This hall was also hung with banners, with great spears and axes, swords and shields, and numerous captured trophies along the walls. One area was given over to benches, and another to a large table with a few chairs. The focus of the room, though, was the raised platform at the far end, which held an ornate wooden throne, upon which the king of Norway sat, watching them. The man was far from unprotected. Beside every upright timber along both side walls stood a warrior, armed and ready. A small group of courtiers stood atop that dais behind Magnus of Norway.

Leif's straying gaze suddenly fixed on one particular face in that group, and his heart quickened. Hjalmvigi, far from skulking like the defrocked, excommunicated wretch he was, stood proudly, close to the king, chin high, malice-filled eyes glittering. But it was not that which really shocked Leif. Hjalmvigi wore the regalia of a bishop. Leif winced.

Behind him, he heard an intake of breath, a creak and a thump, and then the low, whispered voices of Eygrímr and Ulfr telling their jarl to stand still and calm down. Leif didn't dare look. He was very much hoping that those men atop the dais had their attention on him and Aage and had not seen the brief exchange behind them. He recognised the ongoing sound of Halfdan being restrained, and they had reached the open space beneath the high throne before the other two had let go of the jarl, and Halfdan had settled, angry but silent.

'Tell me of Olaf Ogmundsson,' King Magnus said suddenly.

Leif adjusted his thinking. Oddly, he'd expected Magnus to be young and foolish, perhaps because of how Harðráði had always spoken of his nephew, as though he were a petulant child with no idea what he was doing. In truth, though, Magnus had a calm, measured, almost sing-song voice, but shrewd and observant eyes, and he had immediately launched a sharp and unexpected question at them. Leif knew the tactic from his days in Byzantium. The question was just an opener designed to throw him off his game, to put him on the defensive from the start. Fortunately, Leif knew exactly what he was doing in situations like this. The Byzantine court was a place where nothing was ever what it seemed, and no sentence ever had less than one meaning.

'As I am certain your majesty has already been informed, Ogmundsson and his entire crew were lost on the rocks at the fjord's mouth during the storm. Yet they are of little note now. They delivered their message to your uncle, and it is we who bear the response, not they.'

Magnus sat motionless for a moment, and then an odd smile cracked his face.

'You, I like. You play the game well. Almost as well as my cursed uncle. I see you are an interesting group. Your accent is Rus, I suspect, with a Byzantine inflection. I spent time in Kiev and Holmgarðr myself, learning Greek, but you I do not remember. I see beside you the Bishop of Hróarskelda, too, a good man. Some of your warriors wear openly pagan symbols despite the same being banned by law here. You come armed, which few would dare. I surmise that, in fact, you do not serve my uncle at all, but find yourself working for him anyway.'

He laughed.

'I understand. He is easy to fall in with. His way is seductive, and he tends to gather people to his banner with just a smile.'

He straightened, then leaned forward. 'What would you say if I threw in a new proposal before I even hear your message?'

Leif, eyes narrowing, said, 'I suspect it is not worth the effort, your majesty, but this is your court.'

'Ha. Yes indeed. For *now*, at least. I have been king of Norway and Denmark for some years, and even with the current proposal, I will continue to share the throne with my uncle. But I should make a few facts clear for you. My uncle is an adventurer. He relishes the hunt, and battle. He will never be content with a throne and a court, and will always want more. I, on the other hand, have created a great sanctuary to my sainted father here, have removed the threat of the Wends and the Jómsvíkings, destroying their violent stronghold and bringing peace to the region. I have grown trade and created ever stronger links between Norway and Denmark. Given time, I will be a new Cnut, pulling together the empire of the great western sea once more, bringing Angle Land back into the fold, through the careful manipulation of my friend Ælfgifu, widow of both Cnut and Æthelred of the Angles. I see and plan only great things.'

He leaned back. 'However, I see the failure of all these great things while I share the throne with a man who is only going to want more war, loot and fame. Harald Sigurdsson will also want to rule Angle Land, but he will try it in a costly way, by the sword.'

'You have a proposal?' Leif prompted.

'Simple. You throw in your lot with me instead. You see the value in my rule, and I match my uncle's offer. In return, you go back south, and instead of pouring words in my uncle's ear, you sink steel into his belly.'

Leif stared. He'd not expected something so straightforward and brutal. Yet he glanced round at Halfdan on sheer instinct. It was the sort of plan the jarl might well go along with. He had given his word to Harðráði, yes, but Hjalmvigi was almost in their grasp, and Magnus seemed to be offering just that. Halfdan was struggling with the decision. Leif closed his eyes for a moment, weighing this up. He had a horrible feeling that this clever young king was right, and that Magnus was probably the best thing that could happen for Norway, and there was a good chance that his uncle would not be anywhere near as good. And in supporting that, they would have to break their word, though they might also get Hjalmvigi in their hands this very day into the bargain.

But then in his mind's eye he also recalled that massive fleet in the inlet a few miles away. If peace could not be secured, the war that was coming would make the infamous Battle of Stiklestad look like a tavern punch-up.

Before Halfdan could speak, Leif stepped forward. 'While there may be merit to your suggestion, we are men of our word, not oathbreakers, and a peace must be sought before all of Norway and Daneland burn. As such, I give you over to Aage here, Bishop of Hróarskelda, who conveys your uncle's message.'

He stepped to the side and deliberately did not look at Halfdan, worried about what he would see. He might just have put Hjalmvigi out of the jarl's reach again.

Beside him, Bishop Aage spent a short time very eloquently putting forth Harðráði's answer. The great man would accept the throne, half of Norway, along with half all the goods and property of the crown. His various small provisos were of little

211

import until Aage reached the last one, which made Magnus frown.

'My uncle seriously expects me to sail into his arms, with all his fleet waiting, to seal the deal? Does he think I am a fool? No, no, no. That won't do. I will not walk into the bear's mouth any more than he will. He will not come to Niðaróss, and I will not go to Denmark for him. Let there be a compromise. Tell my uncle to sail to his hometown of Vik for the equinox. I will meet him there, then, and all can be agreed and sealed. We will each bring eight ships and eight ships only. This is my proposal. Take it and return south. At the equinox I will be at Vik waiting. If my uncle accepts the deal, we will meet again, there. If not, then God help all of us.'

Bishop Aage turned to Leif, then Halfdan. Leif nodded straight away, Halfdan slower, after some thought. The jarl still looked extremely angry, and his gaze continued to rest most of the time on the man in the bishop's regalia behind the throne.

The bishop frowned at the look on Halfdan's face, followed his gaze, and then nodded as he realised what was going on. He opened his mouth to address the king once more.

'These terms are agreed here, and will be conveyed to your uncle as fast as we can carry them. In the meantime, your majesty, might I bring to your attention a matter of a more personal nature, which impacts upon your vaunted piety?'

Magnus frowned. 'Go on, my lord bishop.'

'The man behind you, wearing the robes of my kind, should not be doing so.'

'Oh?'

'Hjalmvigi of Sweden is no longer an accepted member of Mother Church, let alone a priest or bishop. Though he held office in Uppsala under Onund Jacob and his father, this man has been excommunicated, by order of the Archbishop of Jorvik in Angle Land. The Church has turned its back on him, as has the king of Swedes. It is entirely unfitting for him to be in such a position of high office. Indeed, I am incensed and offended to see him in such robes. Might I enquire as to how this devil-spawn criminal has inveigled his way into your noble court?'

Leif tried not to smile. He couldn't have said it any better himself, and coming from a man of Aage's rank and reputation, it bore considerable weight. One look at Magnus, though, and he knew they were beaten. The king reacted with an easy smile.

'My dear lord bishop, it is my understanding that the offences levelled against Hjalmvigi are false, or at least hugely overstated. I might note that even your good self does not seem to be above consorting with pagans and witches? Moreover, since Hjalmvigi's arrival in Norway, he has been nothing but pious and obedient.'

'As a stepping stone to regaining his power,' Halfdan suddenly burst out behind them.

Leif turned and flashed a warning glance at his jarl, as Aage tried to smooth that over.

'Your majesty, an excommunicated man *cannot* serve in the office, or wear its robes, regardless of opinion.'

'Perhaps,' Magnus acceded. 'Though I have already sent messages to Rome some time ago, seeking an appeal with the pope, arguing the illegality of Jorvik's move and requesting its overturning and Hjalmvigi's reinstatement. I am confident that this will happen, and when it does, our friend here will serve as Bishop of Niðaróss.'

Leif winced as he heard Ulfr and Eygrímr grabbing Halfdan once more and holding him back, as the jarl let forth a blistering stream of expletives.

'I think perhaps you had best escort your friends from the palace,' the king said, his tone becoming cold. 'You have my message. Take it to your master.'

Leif lingered for a moment with Bishop Aage, bowing and taking their leave, and by the time they turned and walked back across the hall, the others had managed to bring Halfdan under sufficient control to turn him and lead him away. They passed through the doors, which were closed behind them, and into the outer chamber, where Ulfr and Eygrímr finally fully let go of their jarl. Halfdan turned. 'I was five heartbeats away from being able to stick my sword in Hjalmvigi's throat.'

'And five heartbeats later we would have all been dead,' Leif responded. 'That hall was packed with Magnus's warriors. You'd not have got to him, and we'd all have been captured or killed. Right now he is out of reach, Halfdan. You have to accept that.'

'Never. I am almost close enough to throttle the bastard.'

Leif nodded. 'I know. And I know how much self-control you have had to bring to bear in there. But for now Hjalmvigi is untouchable.'

'Only *right* now,' the jarl countered. 'He has to leave that room, and he won't always have guards and a king protecting him. At some point, he will be alone, in the shitter if nowhere else. Then, he's mine.'

Leif shook his head. 'Firstly, killing the priest will ruin everything we've done here. Even if he just washes up dead on the shore, the blame will land squarely on us. And again we'll be captured or killed, and the embassy will fail and two great armies will meet. And if I cannot appeal to you on the grounds of our own safety or of peace, perhaps I can try logic. Hjalmvigi is clever and dangerous. He's managed to rise from despised outcast to high bishop in mere months. And now that he knows you're here, there will not be a single moment where he is at risk. He will be protected at all times, even "in the shitter". He is simply out of reach for now.'

Halfdan fumed, fists balled. 'You cannot expect me to come this close and then just sail away and watch him recover all his power, becoming Magnus's pet priest.'

Leif nodded. 'Remember this, though, Halfdan, exactly what I said to Harðráði. Once he is on that half throne, he will be very hard to remove, and he will be able to build his web of power. Hjalmvigi is out of your reach while Magnus rules Norway, but Magnus's hold is slipping. Soon, he will be back within your reach, Halfdan. But do not imperil everything we do because you cannot wait.'

He glanced across at Gunnhild, and she nodded and stepped forward. 'Remember, Halfdan, that we are watching bears fighting over a kill. As Wolves, we will take the carcass when they are done. Do not defy the weaving of the Norns.'

'Personally, I'd just grab him and push a stake up his arse 'til it pricks his brain,' Bjorn said airily.

'And that is why you neither plan, nor lead,' Leif snapped.

Bjorn just snorted at that.

'We will never come back here,' Halfdan said. 'You realise that? Once we sail away we'll not be back. Unless we can beach somewhere down the coast,' he added, suddenly excitable. 'Then we could sneak back to Niðaróss unseen. Neither Magnus nor Hjalmvigi will expect that. Then we make our way into his church and butcher the prick.'

Leif tried not to take in the look of disapproval that fell across Bishop Aage's face at that.

'No,' the Rus said. 'You say you trust my judgement. You say I am your wit where Gunnhild is your wisdom, and both of us have counselled you against this. There will be another time. Gunnhild has seen that. Soon, Harðráði will sail to this Vik place to meet his nephew. I will find it an immense surprise if Hjalmvigi is not with Magnus when he comes south, just as the good bishop here will undoubtedly be with Harðráði.'

Halfdan sagged a little, defeated and well aware of it.

'Besides,' Leif said, smiling oddly, 'if your plan was to beach and then sneak back, you would have been better waiting 'til we were aboard *Sea Wolf* to say so, rather than announcing it in front of a score of witnesses in Magnus's own court.'

Halfdan looked around the antechamber, slightly sheepishly, since almost everyone in the room was looking at them with a mix of interest and suspicion, including the man who'd brought them from the harbour.

'All right.' The jarl sighed. 'We leave it to the Norns and wait for the next opportunity. So that means that for now we must continue with our own task and sail back to Harðráði with the reply.'

'Quite so. And hope that we have seen the last of northern storms, eh?'

Chapter 15

Kaupang, late summer

If there was one thing Halfdan was rapidly becoming sick of, it was hearing about three bears and a wolf. It was bad enough that Gunnhild referred back to her vision whenever she felt the need to remind him of the grand scheme of things, but now Leif and the others had started to use it, too. Twenty times a day he heard the analogy.

Deep in his heart, mind, he would have to acknowledge that the reason for that was the twenty times a day he raised the subject of Hjalmvigi. But it grated on him *so* much. He had waited years to bring down the cursed priest for his crimes: the death of Halfdan's own father, and then, oddly, the corruption of Jarl Yngvar and consequently that disaster in the east. And finally, a few days ago, he had been in the same room, and armed, not twenty feet from the man. And he'd walked away.

Oh, he knew that he'd had no choice. The others were quite right in that, had he made a move on Hjalmvigi, it would have meant the end of the eight of them right there and then in that room, and undoubtedly the death and destruction of two ships and their crews in the harbour would have followed. But that didn't make it any easier.

The bastard was a marvel.

He'd come from nowhere originally and risen to high priesthood in Uppsala, then secured the support of Yngvar, a jarl with royal blood. He'd led a scourge of non-Christians in Sweden, then influenced the jarl all the way to the edge of the world.

And when Yngvar fell and Hjalmvigi was suddenly cut loose of his sponsor, he'd managed to fall in with the queen of Georgia. Then, he'd worked his way back to Sweden and managed to inveigle his way into the court of King Onund Jacob, becoming the senior priest in the kingdom. In order to counter that, Halfdan had changed the *world* in Angle Land just to bring the bastard down, and Hjalmvigi had been stripped back to nothing, cast out of both his Church and the Swedish court. But before Halfdan could get to him, he'd managed to get a new sponsor *again*, in the form of Magnus of Norway, and once that excommunication was overturned, he would be the highest priest in the land again. No matter what Halfdan did, Hjalmvigi seemed to rise to the top, like the scum in a latrine.

So, no. Halfdan couldn't let the subject go.

And he doubted he would do so until the day came when they met again, which both Leif and Gunnhild continually assured him would happen.

He sighed as he gazed out across the water, calm for the northern Jótlandshaf. It had, at least, been a relatively quiet and easy journey back south, with the storms continuing to rage only in the far north, and a following wind carrying them easily along the coast with little need to touch an oar. A few more days, and they'd be back with the fleet.

'You'll see him again,' a voice said, interrupting his aimless musing, 'and next time you'll be holding your sword.'

Halfdan didn't turn. Leif had wandered across to the stern, where Halfdan stood, as usual, peering off into their wake, across the hundreds of miles of coastline back to Niðaróss and the bastard priest who lurked there. After a while, with no response, he heard the footsteps as Leif walked away. Then, almost immediately another set of boots, much heavier.

'Bjorn.'

The big man came to a halt beside him, swaying with the gentle motion of the ship, hands clasped behind his back. He was not currently needed at the oars, since that following wind was sufficient today to drive them on with sail alone, and the crew rested, content, as the afternoon slowly slid toward evening.

'I'm with you,' Bjorn said.

'What?'

'I would have said "Fuck the king, fuck the consequences, and fuck the lot of them", and I'd have walked past Magnus and torn the priest's heart out through his arse.'

Halfdan gave a weary smile. Bjorn. Predictable, but so very loyal, and quite comforting.

'I couldn't, though.'

Bjorn snorted. 'Maybe not. *You're* a jarl. *You* need to be careful. *I'm* not. *I* don't. No one expects me to do the right thing. You should have nudged me and I'd have done it for you. Let them try and take it out on *me*, eh?'

Again, Halfdan smiled. Bjorn would probably have done it, but it would still have come back on the jarl, no matter whether it was one of his less controllable karls that did it or not. He sighed.

'They're right. I'll get another chance. And I wouldn't have *wanted* you to do it, anyway, old friend. Hjalmvigi is mine, and mine alone. I want to watch the light go out of his eyes on the end of my sword.'

There was silence for a moment, and then another voice changed the subject. They both turned to Ulfr at the steerboard.

'We need to beach soon and settle for the night,' the man said.

Halfdan frowned. 'We've got a few hours of light yet.'

'But the wind is dropping rapidly. Soon we'll have to break out the oars if we keep going, and it might be better to let the crew have the rest before we pick up rowing in the morning. If we push tomorrow and the next two days, around the coast of Skáney, we can be back with the fleet by nightfall. Here, there are nice coves and headlands, and a few good beaches. It is the perfect time and place for an overnight.'

Halfdan nodded to him. 'All right. Find your chosen beach and we'll do that.'

'No.'

He turned in surprise to Bjorn. 'What?'

'Not here.'

Halfdan frowned. His gaze turned to the coast, sweeping across the land. Realisation dawned, then. They were back at that same headland they'd visited on their way north, where he'd found Bjorn uncharacteristically melancholy and staring out across the water. Something about this place bothered the big man, and he'd been so many places and done so many things, yet most of it remained a mystery to Halfdan.

'What is it about, Bjorn? What bothers you so here?'

The albino stood silent, staring out across the water. Ulfr threw a questioning look at Halfdan, asking whether he was still seeking a landing site, and the jarl tried to convey in his own expression the answer 'wait a moment'. He leaned his hands on the shields along the ship's sheer strake, beside Bjorn.

'Talk to me.'

'It's private.'

Halfdan fell silent, remembering how his friend had flatly refused to talk about his past when they'd been travelling up Swaledale. Was this the same? He wanted to know more, but didn't want to push it, and so he remained silent. Indeed, the whole *world* seemed silent, apart from the gentle creak of wood, the rush of water and the distant cries of wheeling gulls. Even the crew sat quiet, enjoying the rest.

Silence.

'I lived here, Kaupang, for a while,' Bjorn said suddenly, quietly.

Halfdan didn't know what to say, didn't want to push it. He stayed quiet.

'It was a bad time for me. But I lived in the ruins of Kaupang, and I found peace there. But as peace always does, it ended badly.'

Halfdan's brow creased. That was oddly philosophical for his big friend.

More silence. What to say?

Then Bjorn spoke again, turning to him. 'Did it help you?'

'What?'

'Going back to Gotland? I think that was your Kaupang. Where everything changed and ended badly. Did it help?'

Halfdan chewed his lip. He wasn't entirely sure. It had helped him learn that he would never go back again. It had been both nice and heartbreaking to see Ømund again. But there had been a certain peace in him since then. He felt he'd been tested on Gotland. In that moment with the farmer, he could have been a new Yngvar, but he'd resisted. He'd walked away and forged a new path. So did it help?

'Yes,' he said, after a while. 'It was painful, in a way. But yes, it did help in the end.'

Silence overcame them again, then. They slid past the place they had camped last time and across the open mouth of the inlet beyond which Bjorn had been gazing that night, to the place he gazed now.

'All right. Land here,' the big man said. 'But the place is important. Every man has to respect it. Anyone I find shitting on Kaupang will be looking for his teeth when I'm done with him.'

Halfdan nodded, then turned and nodded again, this time to Ulfr. He and Bjorn remained at the strake while Ulfr began to throw out commands, to both this crew and across the water to the skipper of the *Sea Dragon*, who followed on, close. The ships angled across the water, heading for the next stretch of coastline, and finally crunched up onto a narrow, shallow gravel beach. Halfdan and Bjorn gripped the timbers as they lurched to a halt, then vaulted down to the land with the others, grabbing the *Sea Wolf* and pulling her further up the beach. Then, as she was made secure with pegs and ropes by Ulfr and the others, Halfdan strolled up onto the grass to look about at their site for the night.

He'd not heard of Kaupang, but now that he was here and looking about, he realised the place had once been a sizeable town. He could see mounds and ridges that marked the sites of buildings long gone, testament to what an important place it must have been. He shivered. It was eerie. Now he was here, he felt he was beginning to understand why maybe Bjorn had not wanted to come back. What he couldn't fathom was why Bjorn had ever spent time living here in the first place, since clearly Kaupang had been gone long before the big man was born. It was another mystery to untangle.

As he settled on the best spot for a campfire, relatively sheltered, near a source of wood, and with a good view of both any land approach and of their ships, others came up, carrying gear for the night. Then he caught sight of Bjorn, who seemed to be making his way through the crowd, carrying only a bottle of drink in each hand, like a ship through a sea of people.

The jarl jumped as a hand landed on his shoulder, and turned to see Gunnhild.

'Where does he go, do you think?' she said.

'I don't know. He has a history with this place, and maybe not a happy one. I'm not sure landing here was a good idea, after all.'

'It was,' she said with certainty. 'It was important. Maybe even *essential*.'

'The place makes me shiver.'

She nodded. 'Seiðr everywhere. It feels like... like that ruin we camped at in Nordmandi. Or like the Tyche temple in Miklagarðr. Come on.'

He turned, surprised, as she started marching off after Bjorn, staff in hand. Anna was not with her for once, as the Byzantine woman was with Leif, gathering their gear for the night's camping. He hurried off after the völva and the albino, three figures cutting across the line of busy crewmen. He caught up with her as she reached an old field wall that passed around the edge of a small wood, where she had stopped for a moment. As

222

he joined her, she held up a hand to warn him to silence, and he peered out across the grassland in the waning light of late afternoon.

Bjorn, ahead, had stopped beside a mound of turf, and stood there, murmuring quietly, too quietly for them to hear. Beyond him, a field of mounds and rough stone markers stretched out into the distance. Halfdan frowned, but remained silent and still, watching as the big man finally tucked one of his bottles into his belt, and unstoppered the other, tipping the contents out onto the slope of the mound.

Halfdan shivered. A libation. An offering. To the gods? To the dead? His skin was prickling, and he could feel the Loki serpents on his arm itching. Gunnhild similarly seemed to be feeling it, for she was shaking gently, leaning on her staff.

Bjorn emptied the last of the bottle, then tucked it back into the large pouch at his belt. He then pulled the other bottle back out, removed his axe from his side, and moved to a dry patch of the mound, where he dropped to the turf and sat, cross-legged. He then placed the axe safely on the ground and opened the second bottle, taking a gulp and then sitting in silence.

Halfdan felt uncomfortable, as though he was eavesdropping on something truly private, and he was about to nudge Gunnhild and walk away when instead she began to move, beckoning to him, and rounding the wall, heading toward Bjorn. He scrambled after her, not sure this was a good idea. He caught up with her again just as Bjorn realised he was not alone, looking up at them. The big man's expression spoke volumes. For a moment, he was angry at the interruption, then oddly unsure, then settled into a calm acceptance. Bjorn and Ulfr were good friends; with Ketil he shared a warrior soul, and with Leif he had found a conversation partner, but Halfdan was his oldest friend among the Wolves, and for some reason Halfdan still didn't know, Bjorn was fiercely protective of the völva.

As they closed, the albino nodded to them and offered up his bottle.

They both shook their heads and then settled onto the grass on either side of him.

Silence reigned again for a while, the only sounds the distant lapping of waves on the shore and the hum of life back beyond the wood where the Wolves set up camp for the night. After a while, during which Bjorn continued to drink from his bottle, Gunnhild turned to him.

'Who was she?'

Bjorn coughed on his wine, lowering the bottle again and turning to her in surprise. 'What?'

'This is a burial mound. It's old enough that it blends in with the land, and is good turf, but it's too recent for trees to have grown on it or for rabbits to burrow. Maybe a dozen years ago? Or is it that even rabbits dare not burrow in this particular mound? I see deer tracks all over this place, but there are none on the mound. No flowers or weeds grow. Just grass. And even Halfdan can feel the Seiðr wreathing this place like a heavy snowfall. So I ask again, who was she?'

Bjorn looked troubled, unhappy.

'A völva. That's all.'

Gunnhild nodded. 'A völva who was important to you when you lived here. A völva who *also* lived here. Who was perhaps the *reason* you lived here?'

'I think I have said enough,' the big man murmured.

'You buried her. I wonder why you had to. It was not a calm death, was it? It shook you.'

'I don't want to *talk* about it,' Bjorn snapped, louder.

'But you need to. I want to see where she lived. I have known only two other of my kind, the one who taught me, and Hrafn the witch in Swaledale, and both were more powerful than I, for I finished my learning as best I could on my own. Some might argue that I will never truly be völva. If I ever have a chance to learn, I will continue to do so. To stop learning is to die. So where did she live, Bjorn?'

The albino growled, but before he could say anything more, Halfdan turned to him.

'You know that if anyone in the world has the right and the need to know, it is another völva, Bjorn. And you know that she will respect the place.'

The big man subsided, the growling fading. He exhaled slowly, then tipped the rest of the bottle into his mouth and rose, tucking it away in the pouch. Without a word, he walked away. Halfdan shared a look with Gunnhild, and the two of them rose and followed. Some way from the mound, yet still far from the camp, where a fire was now being set, they found the house. Bjorn walked toward the hut, then stopped. They fell in beside him.

The house was reasonably well preserved. A timber edifice, the thatched roof had grown wildly out of control, but no saplings or trees had taken root, and the building remained, in essence, intact. Outside stood a table made of four small boulders supporting a huge flat stone, and Halfdan wondered quite what had happened here that made Bjorn look almost anywhere *but* at that stone. Indeed, the big man turned his back on it now, and stood there.

Gunnhild beckoned to the jarl, and he followed as she paced past Bjorn and into the hut, through the open doorway. He entered after her and looked about, though he could see virtually nothing in the single room, for it was dark within. He jumped a little at the sound of stone and steel scraping, and then sparks leaping, before a candle started to gutter into life on a long table at one end of the hut. How Gunnhild had known where to look for both candle and lighting apparatus he had no idea, but then he had long since learned not to second guess the völva.

The room rose into view with the low, golden flame, and moments later, Bjorn edged his way inside, too. He did not look particularly happy.

Halfdan's gaze swept around the room. He could make out the vague shapes of many furnishings, but the only area well lit was the table on which the candle stood, and so he walked over to join Gunnhild, who was examining it.

'Do you think she left behind powerful things?' he whispered.

'That depends on your definition of powerful,' she replied enigmatically. 'Bjorn here buried her important possessions with her, including her staff.'

The big man blinked in surprise.

'But,' Gunnhild went on, 'to a völva many things are powerful. This very house is strong, generations of Seiðr in her walls. You can feel it, I know. We all can. Freyja has walked openly in this place many times. I can almost see the Norns at work in the very air.'

Halfdan nodded. He could hardly feel anything *but* the presence of the Seiðr. A frisson of energy danced across his skin like ice burn.

'She was powerful, your völva,' Gunnhild said to Bjorn. 'Powerful enough to see us coming, perhaps, or at least to have seen some of what would follow when she ended with no apprentice to take the house. When her time came she was prepared. She had put away all she needed to and arranged everything. Yet she left this,' she added, indicating the table with a sweep of the hand.

Halfdan paid attention to its contents now. It looked a little like an understocked herbalist's shop. At the back stood a number of containers with liquids or powders or various bits of foliage in them, some of which had survived the years well, while others had become little more than rotted powder, but the main surface of the table had long ago been cleared and laid out with six jars in a line. He frowned. 'What is it?'

Her finger began to indicate the six items. 'Dried black henbane – a minor poison. Then there is dried common mallow, which can be used in medicines. These two jars I cannot be sure of,' she added, lifting them one after the other, opening them and taking a sniff before replacing them. 'The fifth jar is a dried fungus. Not sure which one, but from the spotted appearance on a coloured cap, I can narrow it down to one of two types, both of which are quite poisonous. The last jar was, I think, fruit, though they have long since rotted away. I would say strawberries and gooseberries, probably. But since they are common in this area – I saw both in plentiful evidence as we walked – I think they were just chosen because they were the easiest option. Probably any such fruit will do.'

'Will do for *what*, though?' Halfdan said, frowning at the line of ingredients.

'Can you not guess?' she said, and then lifted a pouch from her belt and indicated it.

Halfdan blinked in surprise. These, then, had to be the ingredients of the powder she used when she walked with Freyja. And, he realised, which Bjorn used when he went battle mad. He shivered. 'She left you the ingredients?'

Gunnhild shrugged. 'Either she was incredibly prepared, and knew I would come someday,' she said, turning to Bjorn, 'or she left them for *him*, knowing that Thor took him in battle.' She indicated the albino with her thumb.

'So now, you could make more of it?'

She breathed in slowly, noisily. 'I would have to experiment. Practise. Knowing what goes into the compound is one thing. Knowing what proportions is another entirely. And what invocation should be spoken over it during preparation, what gods to seek the aid of, probably Freyja and Thor. There is plenty to learn. But this is the prime, the heart. With this I *can* learn.'

'Be careful of the mushrooms,' Bjorn said.

'What?'

'She made me learn these things once upon a time. A lot of it's gone now, after so many years. But the mushrooms I remember. I was going to cook them up once, and she stopped me just in time. She said they were never to be eaten, and that when they went into medicines they only went in very small amounts. She said if she ever put too much in, she would need to use...' he paused, scouring the table, and then plucked out another bottle, 'this.'

Gunnhild took it, and peered at it. 'Mould of some sort. Or possibly just something that has *gone mouldy* over the years.' She straightened. 'I think the Norns wove a path here for us. For me to finish my education, as your völva's apprentice come at last, and to allow Bjorn to close a door that should have been closed years ago.'

Bjorn gave Halfdan a strange look and then turned and walked out of the house. Halfdan glanced round at Gunnhild, who had found a jute bag and was loading it with the various containers she needed. She looked up at him and nodded. 'Go on. I will follow when I have all I want.'

He smiled and then followed the big albino out into the open air. In the short time they had been in the hut, the light had all but faded, and evening was settling in. A mauve sky broke into a dark gold sunset on the western horizon, out past the campsite. Bjorn had walked out past the overgrown garden and was standing, gazing out into the sunset.

'We will be gone in the morning,' Halfdan said, falling in beside him, 'but I think it was important that we came.'

The big man nodded silently.

'Come on,' Halfdan said with a smile. 'Let's get drunk.'

Bjorn rumbled something non-committal, but did not resist as Halfdan grasped his elbow and guided him back toward the glow that marked not only the sunset but the roaring fire of the Wolves of Odin.

'You have never used the brown powder,' Bjorn said as they walked.

'No.'

'Never?'

'No.'

'Ever felt tempted?'

Halfdan thought about this as they walked. 'Maybe. Once or twice over the past few years. I don't think anyone knew about it on Gotland when I was young. Berserkir are largely a thing of legend now, my friend. They exist mostly in tales of the old days. Still, *some* men were made to wear the bear shirt – you make that clear – but most are not.'

They walked on in silence, then, and when they reached the campsite, there was a roar of welcome from the two crews. They settled in for the evening as Ulfr and Farlof brewed up a cauldron of stew with the salted beef they'd stored aboard, and the singing began as jugs and bottles and flasks of ale, wine and blaand were produced, and the drinking started. Bjorn remained quiet for a time, still, which clearly concerned some of the Wolves, but soon Gunnhild reappeared from the dark, finding her way into the circle of firelight and taking a spare place left for her, depositing her bag of findings, and Bjorn finally seemed to ease a little. Half an hour later he was sipping drinks and calling Eygrímr 'nuttier than a squirrel's ball-sack'. An hour later, he was *swigging* drinks and singing a song with eye-watering lyrics about a whore who'd found a novel use for an axe haft. Three hours later, they were all asleep, all but the four men left on watch for the first shift, one of whom was Halfdan, who sat on a rock, watching the waves lapping the shore around the two ships.

From the slope he could see the glittering waters of the Jótlandshaf, but the small, rocky islands scattered along this stretch of the Norwegian coast obscured any view of the open sea, and his world was little more than a couple of miles across for now.

Somewhere beyond there, though, Harðráði waited with his army and his fleet, anticipating a reply from his nephew, King Magnus. When that reply was delivered, everything would change, and Harðráði and Magnus would hopefully both set sail for Vik, to meet and divide the world.

Halfdan was surprised to realise that the distraction of this odd stopover at Kaupang was the first time since leaving Niðaróss that he had not thought repeatedly about Hjalmvigi. Even now that he *was* thinking about the man, oddly he felt a little less angry and desperate. Things had a way of working out, and every day spent in the company of Gunnhild made that increasingly clear.

Three hours later, as he rubbed tired eyes and watched the endless waves lapping at Kaupang's shore, Thorulf came to relieve him, and he thanked the man and returned to his blankets, rolling in them and falling asleep in moments.

—

He awoke feeling refreshed and energised. Oddly almost excited. Though they'd been sailing away from Hjalmvigi for days now, they were close to home, and that was the next step in the plan, the next stitch in the weaving that would bring him to his goal. The others all seemed perky too, as they rose from their sleep around the ashes of the night's fire. Before long, all was packed and stowed once more, and in the sharply angled dawn light, they moved down to the ships and began to manoeuvre them over the beach and out into the water, leaping aboard at the last moment.

As they began to row out into the channels between the islands, Halfdan watched Bjorn, whose gaze lingered on the shore even as he rowed, head craned round, until they moved behind one of the islands and Kaupang slid from view.

The open sea was a welcome sight, and as they left the island behind, a thought struck Halfdan and he strode over to Ulfr at the steerboard.

'What do you think of the weather?'

The shipwright looked up, and then all around. 'Good. Not a hint of bad weather. It could turn in time, but not for hours, at least, I'd say. In fact, I'd be surprised if it's not clear and with a good wind for several days now.'

'And it's three days' sail back around Skáney to the fleet?'

A nod.

'How long if we cut straight south across open sea?'

Ulfr frowned, sucking on his teeth. 'We can cut out a day. We could be there by nightfall tomorrow, but that would mean

230

overnighting on the coast of Jótland. Aren't we at war with the Danes right now?'

Halfdan laughed. 'Harðráði and Sveinn are. We are just two independent crews, are we not? And two of us with good Danish blood, to boot. Let's move faster.'

And so they did. Angling south from Kaupang, they sailed straight out into open sea and enjoyed easy weather and a good following wind throughout the day, only using the oars sparingly to save the rowers. In the mid-afternoon, they passed the point of Skage in the north of the Jótland peninsula, and as the sun dipped toward the horizon, they put to shore on the island of Læsø for the night. The next day dawned just as clear and the two ships launched once more, sailing down the Danish coast toward the island of Fioni and the fleet.

It was with considerable contentment that they reached the coast and pulled into the Odinswe Fjord, between its wide, reaching arms, and even more relief that the fleet was still there. They cut their way across the calm waters and manoeuvred their way between the ships until they closed on the shoreline.

Their relief at the sight of the flagship bearing Harðráði's banner, beached close to that great tent, was tempered slightly at the realisation that it was not alone. In their absence, the fleet had clearly recombined, for the flagship of Sveinn Ástríðarson sat close by, and a second large tent had been erected beside the first. With a message of peace from their enemy for one of the two kings present, the coming days were going to be interesting, to say the least.

Chapter 16

Odinswe Fjord

Halfdan and his Wolves stood looking at the tent. Leif glanced sidelong at his leader. The jarl looked uncertain, which was never good. His optimism and unassailable confidence were part of what kept the Wolves going through endless hardships and problems. The Rus wanted nothing more than to nudge Halfdan and tell him to pull himself together, for the good of his men if nothing else. Unfortunately, such a thing could hardly be said now, with everyone within earshot.

Instead, he mentally prepared himself, for in truth he was as uncertain as the jarl.

There was a message to be delivered and a deal to be agreed, but there was also a delicacy about the situation. Since Harðráði was known to be in his tent, there was a good chance that Sveinn of Daneland was with him, and what needed to be said could not be said in front of the Danish pretender. Halfdan was unsure, clearly, how to best approach seeing one king without the other present, for a lot rode on this. If they got it wrong, they might just start a war between the two men.

At that moment, Orm Axebiter reappeared through the tent door and waved at them. As they walked over, and filed through the flap, Leif, toward the rear, let the others pass, and gestured to the great man's bodyguard.

'Sveinn Ástríðarson is inside?'

Axebiter nodded.

'How are they? Are they still close? Allies?'

'There is a strained relationship,' Orm replied. 'The Dane knows something is up, but he does not know what that something is. He suspects our king of plotting behind his back, but he has no proof, and he knows that all of Harðráði's senior jarls and ambassadors are still with him. He has yet to note the absence of Bishop Aage, I think, and I doubt you even register in his musings at all. So he ponders, and he suspects, but he knows nothing, and it is driving him to distraction. He watches Harðráði all the time. The man cannot go for a shit without Danish eyes looking to see what he's eaten. Harðráði has even taken to sleeping back aboard his ship, with his full crew aboard with him. Soon, something will happen, and there will be disaster. For one of them. It is my job to make sure it is for Sveinn, and not Harðráði.'

'Things are only about to get worse,' Leif said, then, in little more than a whisper: 'The deal is struck. Alliances are about to change.'

Orm Axebiter nodded. 'I presumed as much. A new alliance between Harðráði and his nephew will leave Sveinn Ástríðarson without his main ally in this war. Worse still, when Onund Jacob learns of the change, I have little doubt he will side with the Norse kings, and not with a man who legitimately controls nothing. Harðráði and Magnus represent possibility for him. Sveinn is little more, then, than a millstone around his neck. Sveinn is about to be on his own.'

'Perhaps you should put those you trust in the fleet on the alert?'

Orm winced. 'And risk letting the cat out of the bag? No. I think I'll wait for the order, thank you.'

Leif could hear the overtures of greeting from inside, and knew he was supposed to be there, as the main ambassador, but they were going to have trouble shifting Sveinn out of the way long enough to speak. A desperate glance around, and he spotted Bishop Aage, freshly arrived on their ship, reacquainting himself with his fellow priests. The man represented a chance.

Leif grabbed Orm Axebiter. 'Go tell the bishop that he needs to find an excuse to speak to Sveinn of Daneland. Tell him… tell him he needs to offer Sveinn the Church's support in return for his aid in rebuilding Hróarskelda.'

'What?'

'Just fucking do it,' Leif snapped, uncharacteristically short and forceful. He was out of time. Hoping Orm would do as he was told, he turned and ran in after the others.

'You have something to hide?' Sveinn Ástríðarson was saying, eyes flashing dangerously, as he looked back and forth between Halfdan and Harðráði. The king was shaking his head, while Halfdan was looking over his shoulder, waiting for his Rus companion.

'Not at all,' Leif said, forcing a tone of easy indifference into his voice and controlling his breathing as he approached the others. 'Apologies, King Sveinn, as they were waiting for me. It is *my* place to speak for this deputation as that most unusual thing: a good Christian among good pagans. There is a troublesome matter to be dealt with over the ownership and protection of a certain heathen site within Odinswe connected with Odin. There are elements in the fleet that wish to see it removed, and even some who tried to do just that during the initial landings. But though Daneland be Christian, there are those among the fleet who have yet to accept the Christ, and in the name of concord and harmony, so that our fleet is not riven and lost, these strange and pagan matters must be dealt with carefully.'

He made sure not only to be extremely verbose, but to talk fast, too, not leaving Sveinn sufficient time to question or wonder about any of it. A man racing away from a wave cannot afford to stop and consider whether it will knock him flat.

'Perhaps you might have an opinion on the matter as the new king of Daneland, Majesty. However, my tardiness is the fault of the Bishop Aage of Hróarskelda, whose church burned with the town. He has spent the past weeks attempting to drum up support for his rebuild, and he is insistent upon speaking to you with regard the remodelling of his town and church in the new Denmark you will create, so perhaps Harðráði can settle the matter, unless you feel strongly about it?'

Sveinn's eyes narrowed suspiciously. He looked around. Leif would have to congratulate his friends later over their performance. Each of them managed to radiate just the right balance of innocence and irritation that lent support to his words. There was nothing Sveinn could see that made him want to argue and disbelieve. Thankfully, Gunnhild was keeping Bjorn busy so the big man couldn't screw it all up with a poorly thought-out comment.

Sveinn Ástríðarson nodded coldly. 'Very well. I have little interest in the preservation of pagan idols.' He took a deep breath and turned to Harðráði. 'Settle this without any more burnings. We will pick up where we left off later.'

The Norseman nodded and flicked a hand dismissively, and the Dane rose and strode away from the throne, back toward the tent's entrance. Leif stepped forward now and bowed. He did not look round, but could hear from Sveinn's retreating footsteps that he had slowed slightly, paying attention as he left. Leif did a quick scan of the room to be sure one certain jarl was not present and, content that was so, he addressed the seated king.

'While we recognise that the vast majority of the fleet's crews are Christian, it appears that the men of Torberg Arneson's hirð are a little more... enthusiastic, shall we say, in their pursuit of heresy. During the sack of Odinswe, they made it their own personal goal to sack the Odin shrine for which the town is named. The crews of the *Sea Wolf* and *Sea Dragon*, as per your own instructions, had separated from the fleet and went to the defence of said site. It was hard fought, but we managed to stop Arneson's men causing any damage.'

He straightened, warming to his subject as he caught the sounds of the door being opened and Sveinn departing, speaking to his man outside. Even as the door closed again, Leif continued. 'Now I recognise that no legal protection is given to such sites in either Norway or Daneland, but the shrine's very survival thus far, fenced off as it is and kept untouched for the better part of a century, suggests that the locals, at least, if not the Danish nation as a whole, continue to respect the sanctity of the site. If an agreement cannot be reached here, we may have to wait for King Sveinn to return and…' he raised his voice slightly here, so that anyone listening outside the door could hardly miss it.

There was a long pause, and the Danish usurper failed to re-enter at the mention of his name. Leif turned to the others and gestured to Ketil with a thumb. The Icelander nodded and crossed to the door, opening it and peering out. A few moments later, he closed it again and fell back into position, nodding at Leif. Sveinn had gone.

Leif let out a sigh of relief.

'No wonder Kiev thrives, with such ambassadors.' Harðráði laughed. 'Now to the real business, eh?'

Leif bowed. 'Your esteemed nephew sits, as you suggested, in a position of great power in Niðaróss. We can confirm from what we have seen with our own eyes that any attempt to bring him to heel there would be extraordinarily costly, even if it succeeded, which it likely would not. However, despite the loss of our companions aboard the *White Arrow*, and the documents signed by yourself, during a storm, we managed to talk our way into Magnus's presence. We confirmed to him your willingness to accept his deal, and put forth your conditions.'

'Tell me, Leif Ruriksson, what you think of my nephew.'

The question seemed a non-sequitur, out of place in the current discussion, and the Rus frowned. 'It may not be what you want to hear, but I suspect he is made of the same stuff as yourself. He reminds me of you in some ways. He is, I think, less brave and less… excitable. He is perhaps a little more forward-thinking and careful. But yes, in many ways you are very alike.

He is clever – much cleverer than I expected – and clearly has a strength of will and character. Why do you ask?'

'Do you think he is lying?'

Ah. That explained it. Leif thought about it a moment. 'No. I don't think so. I think he has made a genuine offer, and he genuinely considered your own amendments, too. I will, however, qualify that. In the same way as we counselled you that once you were on that half throne, it would be considerably easier to push until you were the sole occupant, I suspect Magnus is thinking along the same lines. He cannot afford to bring this war home to Norway, and he will genuinely give you half of everything to avoid that. But I suspect that once you are ensconced in Niðaróss, you will need to start checking your bedsheets for snakes, and have someone taste your beer and food for you.'

Harðráði nodded. 'You have come to know Magnus surprisingly well in such a short time, I think. So he accepts everything?'

Leif shook his head. 'Not quite. He has a counter-proposal on only one point. In the same way as you would not accept an invitation to sail into the harbour of Niðaróss with an easy smile, Magnus similarly has no intention of sailing into the Odinswe Fjord with just an honour escort. You may be family, but familial trust at such times goes only so far. Until any deal is agreed in person, Magnus is willing to meet only in a neutral location. He proposes your hometown of Vik.'

Harðráði mused on this. 'Of course, Vik is closer to Magnus in Niðaróss than it is to us. I recognise the possibility that he could still have time to lay a trap there.' He stretched and leaned back. 'But my ties with Vik remain strong, and my name there is good. I do not think he will get the locals on his side easily in such a matter. They would, I think, rally to me.' He laughed. 'He is being clever, as you say. Because equally, I could race there and gather my own people against him, but though they will support me, I doubt they would defy the legitimate king of Norway so easily. Vik will not be easily swayed by either of us. It is perhaps the only place in all of Norway where we can meet where neither of us can guarantee the advantage. Did he give you a timescale? A date?'

'He said he would be there for the equinox. He bids you bring only eight ships, and in return promises to bring just eight himself.'

Harðráði drummed his fingers on his chair arm. 'How long 'til the equinox, you say?'

Leif shrugged. 'Two weeks and a day, if I am not mistaken.'

'For a fleet this size, Vik is the best part of two weeks' sail. Timing is tight.'

'If you are taking just eight vessels, model them on ours, fast and light, and you can shave several days off that.'

Harðráði laughed then. 'My dear Rus friend, it seems even you underestimate Magnus, despite your perceptive nature. There is more chance of a mighty oak sprouting from my nephew's scalp than him actually bringing only eight ships. His full fleet will be at Vik.'

'I detected no hint of deception in his words,' Leif replied. 'I do not think he plans a trap.'

'No. Not a trap. But I can tell you now that he will play it safe by bringing his fleet, so I must do so and ignore the eight-vessel limit. And by the same token, Magnus knows damn well I won't sail into any harbour on his word with just eight ships, and so he must bring his own fleet to be sure. We are bound by our mutual distrust. Neither of us will abide by that restriction as long as we both know the other will not. This means the fleet needs to be ready to sail as soon as possible. Fortunately I have had all the skippers and jarls in my service ready for action since the day you left. It will take little preparation to get every ship in the water and underway.'

He folded his arms and leaned back again. 'The issue will be Sveinn and his contingent. I cannot afford to simply change sides and sail away, and we cannot take the Danish ships with us. Sailing without warning to Sveinn would be tantamount to declaring war on the Dane. To keep the status quo in place, we need to part amicably if at all possible. I will attempt to persuade Sveinn to move on to Jótland and there assert his power and royal status. I will even offer him ships from my fleet in support. While he does so we shall go north and east, ostensibly to harry the coast of Skáney and the southern land of Norway. It is credible, for doing so might just have brought Magnus south anyway. I can persuade Sveinn of this course, I think. And then we are free to go north.'

Halfdan stepped forward now, the first time the jarl had spoken. 'I see your clever ruse, Harðráði. Once again you play men against one another like a giant game of 'tafl. By supporting Sveinn's seizure of Jótland, you may keep his alliance even when you ally with Magnus. But in doing so, you will also remove Daneland from your nephew's hands, thereby rendering him king of only Norway. Your equal, in fact.'

The Norseman's eyes narrowed. 'I wonder if you begin to see things that are not there, Halfdan Loki-born.' He sighed. 'But that may well be the case, intentional or not. Either way, I need one more night to keep things civil between Sveinn and I. But have your ships ready to sail tomorrow. Vik awaits us.'

–

That evening was one of strained conversation. Harðráði's tent doubled as the meeting hall for all present, since it was both larger than Sveinn's and had been here for some time. The two chairs that served as thrones for the would-be kings sat to either side of a table. The 'tafl board that usually sat upon it had been moved aside, for Sveinn had declined to play against the Norseman, and instead it held wine, taken from a fine vintner's storehouse during the sack of Odinswe. The wine sat in a bottle, but also in two cups, largely untouched.

There was no real call for the Wolves of Odin to be present, of course, though they were. As far as Sveinn was concerned, ostensibly at least, it was just another evening of planning their next moves and waiting for Magnus to react to their campaign. As far as *Harðráði* was concerned, it was their last evening at Odinswe, their last action together, and time to persuade Sveinn to split the fleet. Most of Harðráði's men had now been given the instructions to make ready to sail the next day, but the *Sea Wolf* and *Sea Dragon*, having only arrived in the harbour a matter of hours ago, were already prepared, so there was no work for them to do. Consequently most of the Wolves were on board the ships for the night now.

The core of the hirð, though, were here in the tent. Halfdan had decided he wanted to be present, to know what was said and decided. He'd made it clear to his friends that from now until the day Hjalmvigi was in his hands, he wanted to stay close to Harðráði, to be sure he missed no opportunity. Consequently, the seven of them were part of the gathering here, leaving Farlof and Eygrímr in charge of the ships.

Sveinn and Harðráði sat at their table, their wives mirroring them a little further back, relations there cold and impersonal, for the women knew each other hardly at all, and had nothing in common and nothing to say. Only relatively few of Harðráði's jarls were here, the ones whose ships were ready now, or who had trusted men doing it for them, and a few of Sveinn's jarls gave the room balance. Orm Axebiter stood close to his master, while another man with the look of a killer stood close to Sveinn, the two bodyguards eyeing one another carefully.

Leif sat on one of the benches, close to Bjorn, and next to Anna, who was busy telling him of all the things Gunnhild had found in the völva's house in Kaupang.

'...and some sort of mould, she says, which...' she continued, pressed against his side.

He'd made the mistake of allowing her to catch him looking at Ellisif of Kiev. It had been entirely innocent, of course, just part of taking in the situation in the room, but the wondrous princess had graced him in return with a smile, and so Anna had been clamped possessively to Leif's arm ever since.

Bjorn was telling stories again, and Leif was half-listening, to those as well as Anna's report, the rest of his attention on the two kings. Thus far they had danced around anything important, with carefully chosen unimportant chatter.

'So I said to the queen of Iceland,' Bjorn announced, wiping beer from his lip with his forearm, 'let go of my cock, or I'll show you what *else* I can use it for.'

'You've never been to Iceland,' Ketil grumbled.

'I went aboard a ship called *Ice Falcon*, with a skipper called Harald Bow-legs.'

'Bollocks. Iceland doesn't *have* a queen,' Ketil the Icelander replied, flatly.

'It doesn't *now*,' Bjorn replied in a tone that suggested the strained patience of someone trying to persuade an obstinate child. 'She's been gone for years. I fucked her to death.'

'When you're going to lie,' Ketil replied, 'be careful to pick places none of us know.'

'You must be from the *other* side of Iceland,' Bjorn said airily, then turned to the others. 'Now on the subject of dragons' testicles,' he began.

Leif tried to shut out the next slew of unlikely rubbish, and turned back to the two kings, in time to hear their conversation move from the banal to the important at last.

'I am aware that Denmark is not of great importance to you,' Sveinn said. 'You wish the *Norse* throne. But Denmark *is* important to *me*. I refuse to burn any more of it, for I would like to have a kingdom left to rule once I control it. The campaign has to shift focus now. Clearly harrying Danes is not drawing Magnus south, no matter how many of my trade centres you sack.'

Harðráði nodded. 'You may be right, though we still cannot risk moving against him in the north. Perhaps I should move on to the Norse coast around Ánslo, just across the border from Skáney. *That* might draw Magnus down.'

'We have a sizeable enough fleet to raise Hell there,' Sveinn said, eyes narrowing at Harðráði's sudden willingness to do what he had refused for so long.

'We do not need so many ships,' Harðráði replied. 'It is of equal importance to keep the Danish trade routes out of Magnus's hands. Instead of any further destruction, though, perhaps you should move on to Jótland and secure Hedeby by simply manning it, keeping it closed to Norway for now. That way you can also secure your crown, while I deal the next damage to Magnus.'

It sounded so feasible. So natural. Not at all as if Harðráði was carefully engineering his own future and using Sveinn as a tool of that process. Sveinn was suspicious, though, his eyes still slitted.

'So the Ánslo region is as unimportant to you as Denmark?' he said. 'I wonder, then, what *is* important to Harald the "hard ruler"?'

Harðráði sat for a moment, tapping his lip as if deep in thought, playing the game like a professional diplomat.

'My *wife* is important to me. The throne of Norway is important to me. Silver and gold, and a reputation that goes ahead of me are important. And Landøyðan, of course.'

'Land Waster?' Sveinn snorted. 'Your banner? As important as the throne, you say? As important as your wife?'

Leif's glance swept across to Ellisif at this, in time to register the briefest flicker of annoyance before that mask of careful nonchalance fell over her face once more. He moved back to the kings.

'Landøyðan,' Harðráði replied in a fierce voice, 'is the greatest banner of our age. The greatest statement a king can make in war. It is, to my enemies, what the raven banner was to our ancestors in times of war. When Landøyðan joins me in war, I cannot be beaten. The banner was gifted to me by my sainted brother, and in all the time I have borne it in war I have never lost a battle.'

242

Leif frowned, wondering if Landøyðan had been flown in the woods of Sasireti when the man had been on the other side of that great and terrifying battle.

'Horse shit,' Sveinn snorted. 'Superstitious claptrap.'

'The evidence speaks for itself. Here I sit, victor of every battle I ever fought under Landøyðan, rich beyond most men's dreams, and a short step from the throne of Norway. Land Waster wins wars. It is a fact.'

'I will believe your horse shit when Landøyðan wins you, let's say three battles against your nephew. I wonder if it works against the son of its former owner, eh?'

Harðráði glared at him. 'You do not need to remind me of our relationship every time we speak,' he hissed. 'We might be at war right now, but Magnus and I are family, and at other times we might meet instead with an *embrace*.'

Leif noticed Halfdan also paying attention now, and the jarl's hand had moved to the hilt of his sword. The conversation was becoming sharp and unfriendly, and he and Leif had both recognised that.

Sveinn's face took on an angry colour, as he leaned forward in his chair. 'And I wonder if that might be in the forefront of your mind, my dear *ally*. Before we met with Onund at Sigtun, there were those who counselled me against any deal with you. They say your contracts might as well be written in water, washing away in moments. They say that you honour deals only when they are of value to you, and cast them aside easily when they are inconvenient.'

Leif's hand now went to the hilt of the sax at his belt. This was getting very dangerous, as talks went. And the problem was that Sveinn, for all the fact that he was nowhere near as clever as Harðráði, had his ally nailed. He was absolutely correct, even though he couldn't truly know it.

Harðráði growled. 'It ill becomes you, dear *ally*, to smear my name so. My word is my bond, and ever has been. I can tell you this moment, with my hand on the holy book and swearing on the blood of my forefathers, that I have sealed no deal with Magnus and that our own alliance still stands.' Leif winced. That was, in the strictest sense, absolutely true. The deal had been agreed, but was yet to be signed, and thus no alliance had been broken. The fact that this could change in a matter of hours mattered not. 'I wonder,' Harðráði said, his tone becoming little more than an angry whisper, 'what Magnus could tell me of his dealings with *you*?'

Masterful. Leif almost smiled. Harðráði had not only managed to neatly sidestep an inconvenient probe of the truth, but with that last line, which the man knew damn well was rubbish, he had turned the table on Sveinn, an accusation of lying hanging now over the Dane's head instead.

Sveinn's lip wrinkled, a tic dancing beneath his left eye. His hand went to his side, but there was no weapon there, which was perhaps a good thing. Behind him, his bodyguard took a step forward, though Orm Axebiter did the same, forcing a stalemate.

'I think I have lost my appetite tonight,' Sveinn snarled, 'and before the food even arrives. Something in the air smells rotten, and it smells Norse to me. Perhaps I had better leave before I am forced to *defend* myself from my ally.'

He rose, face now almost puce. Harðráði simply sat there, expression unchanged, watching. Sveinn turned to the room. 'Gyda? Erik? With me.'

The Dane left the throne and walked toward the door, his slight limp more pronounced than usual since he was too angry to concentrate on hiding it, his wife and his bodyguard sweeping out at his heel. Notably, the room emptied of Sveinn's jarls in the following moments, and in no time at all, the only occupants of the tent were Harðráði's men. Orm Axebiter waited for the count of fifty, then left the place, did a quick circuit to make sure they were not being eavesdropped upon, and then returned and nodded to his master.

Harðráði leaned back and smiled widely.

'Well, well. It appears that Sveinn is even easier to manipulate than I'd hoped. The man is not the brightest candle on the shelf, is he? He is but a hair's breadth away from breaking our alliance himself. I may not need to do so, if he beats me to it. Orm, my dear fellow, do me a favour and go about the fleet this evening, chatting with people. Do make sure to tell people that Sveinn stormed out of our meeting like a petulant child after levelling false accusations at me, and that he carefully avoided answering my comment that he might have private dealings with Magnus.'

Torberg Arneson rose from a seat over to one side. 'Are you sure you want to do that, Harald? You will push him to breaking your deal. We might yet need Sveinn, for his ships if nothing else.'

Harðráði turned to Arneson, though Leif noted how his gaze fell upon Tora, the man's daughter, even as he spoke to her father. 'I suspect that Sveinn the Dane is now little more than an impediment to my campaign.'

Arneson frowned. 'Why do I suspect that the reason the fleet is ready to sail has nothing to do with taking the war to the Ánslo coast? You have other irons in the fire, Harðráði.' The king managed to maintain an expression of injured innocence, though Arneson clearly knew he'd cut to the meat of the matter. 'You will drive him to doing something foolish, Harald. There are other ways he can go rather than simply breaking off ties with you. A knife in the night is as much the Danish way as the Norse, you know?'

Harðráði nodded. 'You are quite right, of course, Torberg, and I trust Sveinn Ástríðarson about as far as I could spit a rat. It is perhaps a good thing that I sleep aboard my ship, eh?'

Leif frowned at this. 'Might I make a suggestion?'

The Norseman turned to him. 'Leif?'

'You sleep aboard your ship, but that is only so secure, for Sveinn *knows* you sleep aboard your ship. If you truly fear assassins, you would be better sleeping elsewhere for now, and not making it such public knowledge.'

The man's face slowly cracked into a smile. 'Very sharp, my Rus friend. Perhaps tonight I might sleep aboard the *Sea Wolf*, which happens to be very close to my own ship, and we shall see what we shall see.'

Chapter 17

Odinswe harbour, September

Halfdan had not slept. A sense of anticipation had stolen over him more and more as the evening wore on, and by the time the various kings, jarls and karls had all turned in, he was so alert that slumber simply would not come.

The Loki serpents on his arm had started to itch the way they often did when things were about to happen, or when something was amiss, and he had spent that evening, after the meeting between the two kings, watching the tent's interior carefully.

But there was nothing to see.

Sveinn and his people had left and gone about their own business, the parting frosty at best, and so the only people left in the room had been Harðráði's people, none of whom had any clear reason to be anything other than completely loyal. Those who were not Norse were on the whole either Swedes or Rus, drawn from the gathering at Sigtun or having accompanied the great man from either the Varangian Guard or his stay in Kiev. Nothing was amiss.

Yet something was tingling his senses, making the serpent on his arm dance with Seiðr.

It was incredibly frustrating.

He'd even posed the problem to the others to no avail. Leif had not been able to identify anything that concerned him, and Gunnhild had told him he was probably just feeling the tension of the wait for some sort of move by Sveinn, which all and sundry suspected now was coming. Ulfr and Ketil were unconvinced there was anything to worry about, and Bjorn had simply rambled away into a story about a five-legged dog until Halfdan excused himself and walked away.

But there had been *something* wrong, and whatever it was, it was not just something that would happen somewhere else, later. He felt it then and there, in that gathering. Whatever it was concerned someone there now. His eyes had passed around all present. He knew most of them by sight and quite a lot by name or reputation. All of them had been part of the campaign since the start and had proved themselves staunchly loyal, by both deed and word. And many were Norse, which meant they had *double* the reason to be loyal if they knew or suspected about Magnus. The only character in the tent who Halfdan was not entirely sure about was Torberg Arneson på Giske, who had already proved himself something of an opponent for the young jarl. But those among Arneson's crews who had truly become enemies were now dead, the grove that had been the bone of contention was safe and the trouble over, the campaign moved on. Even if Arneson still had the time and energy to devote to hating Halfdan, Harðráði had put a leash on him anyway, drawing from him an oath that there would be no infighting within the fleet. And Arneson had too much to gain from the current situation, being one of the pre-eminent jarls in Norway, to rock the boat, anyway.

No one was going to try for the Wolves, and if they did, they would regret it. And if anyone truly wanted to try for Harðráði, they would have to get past the solid, implacable and impressively dangerous Orm Axebiter first, who stood close to his master, ready for trouble at all times.

They had all eaten, all had a few drinks, and talked about the coming days and what they might hold, though in quiet and guarded terms, for it was still a thing unknown among the Danish contingent of the fleet. The Wolves had listened, watched, tried to ignore Bjorn's tall tales and sexually improbable jokes. And then, finally, all had decided to find their beds.

Like most of the fleet, Halfdan had quartered the majority of the Wolves among the ruins of Odinswe and its harbour. Tents had been made of the shells of houses using spare sail fabric, and more than half the fleet lived among the ruins. Of course, each of Harðráði's crews was packed and ready, even in their tent-houses, for their king had given the order that the fleet would sail tomorrow. Indeed, Halfdan had made sure that his crews were ready to leave at a moment's notice, quartered close to the shore and even abandoning the spare sails in favour of a speedy departure.

Each ship, though, still held a skeleton crew, guarding vessels that were ready for the off. The weather had begun to turn less clement during the evening, despite Ulfr's earlier predictions, and scattered showers at dusk had gradually evolved into a good, solid downpour that seemed to have set in for the night. Consequently, every crew had raised the cloth tent above the bulwarks of their ship for the night, covering perhaps a third of the deck and providing shelter from the rain.

Sea Wolf was no exception. Halfdan had rarely bothered with the tent, content to get wet in most circumstances, but the ships had all supplies aboard ready for the off, and so they had to be saved from the rain where possible, so he too had raised the shelter. Of course, *Sea Wolf*'s tent was a simple thing of smörred wool, plain-coloured and utilitarian, compared with the colourful and rich version that covered almost half of Harðráði's ship beside them.

Finally deciding that sleep was never coming, Halfdan rose a little from his blankets and looked about, squinting into the tent's dark interior as the downpour battered the shelter.

A score of men and women lay about the tent, fairly tightly packed in around the supplies, including all those he had known from the start. And of course, Harðráði himself, who had decided to sleep aboard *Sea Wolf* for safety that night. The king slept soundly with a slight smile, while around him the Wolves snored and breathed, farted and shuffled in their sleep. Every last one slept.

249

Trying to stay quiet, so as not to disturb anyone's rest, Halfdan rose and climbed to his feet, gathering up his sword and cloak, and slipped on his boots. Stepping to the edge of the tent, he donned the cloak and pulled it tight around him, wishing it was hooded, like the one Ketil the Icelander wore. The one sound that dominated the tent was that of water hammering at it from above as the rain drove on. But rain or no rain, he needed to move and to breathe outside the stifling atmosphere of twenty sleeping figures.

Taking a breath and bracing himself for the weather, Halfdan pushed aside the flap of wool, waterproofed with ochre and horse fat, and stepped out into the night. If anything it was even harder to see out here. Though it was a little lighter than in the enclosed tent, the driving rain obscured much beyond a few feet away. The sound of rain hitting the sea all around caused a constant din, given counterpoint by more rain pounding the timbers of the ship. It was almost deafening outside.

He looked around, and it took some work before he could see the other end of the *Sea Wolf* through the torrential water. Turning, he could just make out *Sea Dragon*, beached to their left, and Harðráði's *Silver Eagle* to their right, both ships pulled up so that the front half was solidly wedged in the sand, the water lapping around the rear. Both those flanking ships were devoid of visible life on deck, everyone sheltering in the tents.

Halfdan's heart lurched in that moment. He spun.

Sea Wolf's deck was empty, too. In his slightly tired, bleary state, and with the distraction of the weather, he'd totally failed to notice, as he emerged, the absence of the two men who should be here. Agnarr Fairhair, one of the new crewmen they had picked up in Swaledale the previous year, had drawn the black stone and been landed with first watch. He should be somewhere on deck, keeping an eye on everything, at least until halfway through the night, when he would swap with his replacement. And while it was not impossible that Agnarr was here somewhere, hunched down and asleep amid the oar benches, the fact that the other figure was missing put Halfdan fully on the alert. For the other man on watch was Orm Axebiter, set there by Harðráði himself, and told to keep close to the tent.

Neither man was in evidence.

Very quickly, Halfdan slipped and skittered this way and that across *Sea Wolf*'s deck, looking for the pair. Despite his obvious fears, he desperately clung to the faint possibility that the men were still here, either trying to keep out of the worst of the rain or keeping a low profile so that any interloper could not see them.

They were not there. The Loki serpents on his arm had gone from itching to almost burning, the sensation was so strong. Something was *very* wrong now. For a few moments, he scoured the deck, the benches, the strakes and shields for signs of trouble, for blood or debris, but the simple fact was that the downpour was hard enough to wash away any such signs in moments. The absence of the two men suggested something serious.

But what?

If they had been removed because someone wanted to get to Halfdan or his companions, then why stop there and not enter the tent and start killing? And the same could be said if somehow Sveinn had learned that Harðráði was aboard *Sea Wolf* and had sent men for him. It was a mystery.

Had someone been making for Harðráði's ship and spotted Orm Axebiter on the way? Then moved to take out the great man's bodyguard first, just to be sure? It would certainly take a skilled assassin to bring down the man. That explanation was a possibility, though, at least.

A noise drew his attention, and he turned. There was shouting from aboard *Silver Eagle*, barely audible above the hammering rain. He turned and lurched over to the sheer strake, gripping the shields there and peering out into the dark, blinking in the rain.

As he did so, he caught movement, hard to spot in these conditions.

A figure was hurtling along the deck of Harðráði's ship from the tent, racing to the beached prow. Halfdan was running a heartbeat later. He knew it was dangerous, and probably foolish. He had no idea what he was dealing with, but if he was to stand a chance of doing so, he had to move immediately. That meant moving alone. Even bellowing at the top of his lungs out here was not going to wake anyone back in the tent. And over on *Silver Eagle*, no one had yet moved out of the shelter there. For just a moment, Halfdan wondered why, but then his attention darted back to the figure.

Halfdan watched the dark figure on the other ship reach the prow and make an impressive leap to the sand. He was ahead of Halfdan by a distance, and had disappeared from sight around the prow before Halfdan copied the move, planting a foot with bent knee on an oar bench, and throwing himself over the side. He landed slightly awkwardly, but without damage, and without falling, in the wet sand, and was off running again in a moment.

A figure sprinting from the king's tent had to be an assassin. There was no other reason he could think of. Sveinn Ástríðarson had clearly done just as they'd anticipated, and sent a man to kill Harðráði. Of course, he'd failed, for the king was not there, asleep instead among the Wolves on *Sea Wolf*. But the fact that the killer had even been *in* the tent, combined with the absence of any guards on watch nearby, made it clear that the man was good, and would probably have succeeded, had Harðráði actually been there.

They'd had a narrow escape.

Now, Halfdan wanted that assassin. Partly for the simple satisfaction of having caught the killer. Partly because he took exception to Sveinn's interference here. Partly because it seemed likely that the man had also killed Agnarr Fairhair. And partly because any little extra service they could do for Harðráði at the moment would put the man a little more in debt to them, and increase the likelihood of Hjalmvigi being delivered into Halfdan's hands soon.

He panted and puffed as he ran, rain slapping him in the face like a wet glove, constantly, sodden hair plastered to his skull. As he reached the prow of the *Silver Eagle*, he undid the brooch at his throat and let the cloak fall away. It was helping keep the rain off, but the weight of the billowing wool was hindering his running speed.

Uninhibited now, he rounded the prow of Harðráði's ship and kept on running, wiping away the water in his eyes. It took him a few moments to spot the running man. He was further ahead than ever. Damn, but he was fast. He was almost at the end of the occupied area of beach already. There, where the last ships were pulled up onto the sand before the shoreline became a steeper coast of hardy grasses, a few shacks had been left standing, the stores of local fishermen, which had been impounded by the invaders. The running man disappeared behind those shacks, and Halfdan redoubled his efforts, breathing hard as he pounded across the sand and then up to the wooden walkway that ran beside the huts.

There were no other witnesses. In this weather, no one was out in the open. Back on *Silver Eagle*, men had probably left the shelter and reached the ship's strakes now, but they were too far behind to be of any help, and Halfdan simply couldn't shout loud enough in these conditions to attract attention of any of the nearby ships' occupants.

He was on his own.

He rounded the corner of the fishing sheds in time to see the figure disappear round the far end. Grimacing, fighting through the growing pain in his muscles, he ran on, turning that corner to see with dismay that the figure was, if anything, even further ahead, despite his efforts. The man was running along the coastline now, amid that calf-high hard grass. For just a moment, he looked back, clearly locating his pursuer once more. Halfdan couldn't make out enough detail to identify the man. All he saw was a momentary flash of a pale face within the dark hood of a shadowy cloak. The man's clothes were similarly dark, though a tiny gleam suggested a shirt of chain within. Then the figure turned and ran on.

Halfdan made a decision and angled slightly, running inland a little rather than following the shore, allowing him to cut across the angle and hopefully gain some time on his quarry.

His dismay returned in force as, ahead, he saw the figure suddenly disappear over the edge of the shore. A count of twenty later, Halfdan reached the spot and lurched to a halt. The high, scratchy grass reached up on a slight bluff, maybe six or seven feet above the water, which could be any reasonable depth here, since there was no beach.

He thought, just for a moment, he saw the shape of rippling waves from something entering the water, but in the blink of an eye it was gone, leaving him unsure of whether it had ever been truly there. All he could see now was that dappled surface where raindrops continually battered the sea, mixed with the white rolling waves as they struck the shore.

There was nothing.

Nowhere to hide.

Halfdan stared.

The runner had gone over the edge at this very spot. There was nowhere to lurk to either side, and nowhere he could have run. He could only have gone into the water, but he would have to have been part shark to get far enough out to sea to be out of sight in that short time. It might be *possible*, but it was unfeasible, especially in this weather. The nearest anchored ships were far enough away that the swim would be exhausting, especially after that run, and all the ships at this end of the beach belonged to Harðráði's contingent anyway, so they would hardly harbour the assassin. And most of all, the man had seemed to be wearing a chain shirt. Surely he had sunk in an instant, and was even now drowning somewhere just in front of Halfdan, under a few feet of black, foamy water.

He stood, frustrated and confused.

Then he caught sight of movement. It took him a moment to work out what it was he was seeing, but then he realised.

254

A dark, hooded cloak was drifting on the current, hammered by rain, a few feet out from the shore. Halfdan crouched and stretched out, then drew his sword to give him extra reach, and just managed to get the tip of the blade in the material, hauling it back toward him, then pulling the heavy, saturated wool out of the water.

Of course, hooded woollen cloaks were hardly rare in Odinswe. Yet it seemed impossible to believe this had not belonged to the assassin.

He stood there a while, holding the cloak, and staring down.

There was nothing he could do. In daylight, perhaps in the dry, he might have seen more. Might even have been tempted to climb down and see how deep it was, if he could maybe wade out. But not now.

He had failed to catch the man, and it seemed the only realistic explanation was that Ran had pulled him down to her dark hall. Heaving a sigh, Halfdan turned and began to stride back the way he'd come. He did not run. He was too tired. Back past the huts, he reached the beach, and there passed those slumbering ships until he found his discarded cloak. He picked it up, noting with irritation that he had somehow lost the brooch from it in the process. Perhaps he would spot it when the sun came up.

Silver Eagle was alive with activity.

He closed on the ship and made sure they knew it was him. The men of Harðráði's crew recognised him, and waved him on, so he reached up with his free hand, gripping the hands that were lowered to help, and pulled himself up onto the deck.

The crew gathered around him as he walked back toward the shelter of their tent.

'We saw you give chase. You caught him?' one man asked, eyeing the sodden cloaks in Halfdan's other hand.

Halfdan shook his head. 'The man was too fast. But I saw him disappear into the sea, and he was wearing a chain shirt. I cannot see how he could have survived. His cloak was floating where he fell. What happened *here*?'

As they reached the shelter and he pushed aside the wool, he could see for himself what had happened, though. Even as the men described it, he saw it all.

Harðráði's own bed was separate from the others, as befitted a king. It was thicker and with an actual ship-bed supporting the mattress. Moreover he had good-quality blankets in red and blue rather than drab ones like the rest of his crew. The assassin would hardly have had a problem identifying his target, even in a dark tent.

Halfdan walked over, looking at the messy bed. The blankets were rucked up over something, and as he neared it, he could see that pieces of wood had been placed in the bed beneath them, roughly in the shape of a prone man. The blankets were shredded and the wood bore three massive cuts. The assassin had actually reached his target and delivered his killing strikes, only to realise he had been tricked, and had still managed to run, getting clear of first tent and then ship, before the crew could stop him. In fact, if Halfdan had not happened to be watching him from the next deck, the man would have disappeared entirely as he reached the beach.

'Well that makes it clear. The Dane lived up to expectations.'

Leaving the scene and the crew, Halfdan walked back over to the side of the ship above the sand, promising Harðráði's men that he would rouse their king and see him back to his own ship now. He dropped to the sand and crossed to *Sea Wolf*. There, he found the lowest section of the ship's strakes and threw the two wet cloaks up over the side. He then reached up, grasping the strake in the gap between two shields, and pulled, hauling himself up and over into the ship. Straightening, he collected the cloaks and turned to stride over to the tent and wake everyone, then stopped dead in his tracks.

Orm Axebiter was standing beside the tent entrance.

The bodyguard's attention was divided, for he was watching the activity aboard his master's ship, but now was also watching Halfdan come aboard.

A horrible feeling flowed through the jarl then.

Could it be possible?

Axebiter was soaked to the bone, but then he had been stood in the rain all night, so that was to be expected. That he was standing in the downpour in just a shirt, with no armour and no cloak, *was* odd. Or would be, if he hadn't just lost them both somewhere.

Could it *really* be possible?

Halfdan had seen the man fight, that day with Bjorn. He knew just how quick Axebiter was in combat, and so it was not beyond the bounds of reason to assume he was just as fast a runner, even just as fast a swimmer. That, at least, was feasible. But to plummet into the water, flinging away a cloak, then somehow get out of a chain shirt, and swim away fast enough to be out of sight of a pursuer? That was stretching probability a bit more. Unless somehow Halfdan had missed the man come up for air for a moment. It had been torrential, and dark, with a constantly moving sea surface. And Halfdan had looked left and right, and away at the ships in the fjord.

It was *possible*. And in the most irritating way it made sense. And though there was absolutely no proof, and most people would consider it unlikely, somehow Halfdan knew without a doubt that it had been Orm Axebiter who had hacked the sleeping logs apart in the next ship, who had fled the scene before being caught, and had then been chased by Halfdan along the shore and into the sea.

His lip wrinkled.

'Nice swim?' he said in an acidic tone as he neared the bodyguard.

'This would be a foolish night to swim,' Axebiter replied, face betraying nothing.

'Would you like your cloak back?'

'My cloak is beside my bed on *Silver Eagle*, Jarl Halfdan. It is very new and the waterproofing is not yet adequate. So I make do.' He indicated his sodden state.

Halfdan's lip twitched again. Orm Axebiter irritated him. And now it seemed certain that he was also behind Agnarr's disappearance. But then, the man was only obeying the commands of his master. It was Harðráði himself who must have planned this little drama, and the reason why was clear enough.

'Where were you, then? When I arose, you were not here.'

'Every man has to piss once in a while, Jarl Halfdan.'

He ignored that. The answer was so facile it was not worth arguing. Instead he took a deep breath.

'Shall I wake him, or will you?'

Axebiter shrugged, and so Halfdan strode in through the tent door and clapped his hands. The Wolves of Odin roused, some sitting bolt upright in an instant, others slowly rousing themselves from sleep enough to pay attention. Harðráði pulled himself up, turning and pushing back his blanket. 'Trouble?'

'You could say that,' Halfdan said, gaze sliding sideways to Axebiter. 'As I expect you know, an assassin attempted to do away with you aboard your ship just now. I gave chase to the man, but he got away, and, though I cannot confirm the assassin's identity, I have a fairly good idea who it was.'

Harðráði slapped a balled fist into his palm. 'Hróaldr. Sveinn's pet killer.'

Halfdan bit his tongue in an attempt not to answer that scathingly. 'Probably best we do not delve too deeply, given that we have no proof.' Again, he glanced at Orm Axebiter, and was impressed with just how good the man was at looking entirely nonchalant. For just the blink of an eye, Halfdan caught a flicker of understanding pass between Harðráði and his bodyguard. He ignored it. Right now, he had helped attempt to capture the assassin and had therefore, unwittingly, made this little play all the more realistic. To unpick it right now would only serve to irritate Harðráði and lessen Halfdan's value. He forced himself to calm, and stood silent as the king rose to his feet. He had slept fully dressed, and only needed to slip into his boots and gather his sword and his cloak.

'It seems the betrayal we expected has come, and soon. Sveinn Ástríðarson has broken the treaty between us with a brutal act of attempted murder. We have no choice now but to divide the fleet and leave him to his own devices, seeking new alliances and a better way forward.'

Halfdan couldn't help himself, then. 'You don't need to trot out such lines for us. We were the ones who sealed your deal, Harðráði. Save your performance for your other jarls.'

The great man might have been angered at that, of course, but instead, Harðráði simply flashed Halfdan an irritating smile. 'A speech is better well practised, don't you think? I shall return to *Silver Eagle* immediately and make sail. We shall depart the fjord straight away, even in the dark and the rain, to be away from the murderous swine. Have the word passed to every other ship in the fleet. Every crew is to sail as soon as they are ready. Every ship must move at its best speed, regardless of their position in the fleet, sailing for Vik. Speed over safety, now.'

Halfdan once more fought down the anger, this time at being treated like a lackey by the man, when they had only joined his fleet as part of a deal to benefit both parties. Instead, with strained patience, he said, 'It will be done.'

With that, and a nod, Harðráði strolled out of the tent and across the *Sea Wolf*'s deck, Orm Axebiter falling in behind him, like the dog he was. Halfdan followed them out, and those of the Wolves who had risen and dressed followed on, walking out into the rain, drawing cloaks tight and pulling up hoods.

Axebiter helped his master down from the ship, then followed, dropping lightly to the sand. The two men crossed the intervening space, and then climbed aboard *Silver Eagle* with the help of the crew there. Halfdan turned to the others. Bjorn and Ketil were both with them, and he gestured to the pair.

'Go to the next ships and tell them Harðráði is taking the fleet to sea, now. Every ship is to make for Vik at speed and not wait for the others. And let Farlof know aboard *Sea Dragon*, too. Tell them to pass the word, and then get back here, sharp.

I want ours to be the next two ships to depart, leaving the fjord amid *Silver Eagle's* wake.'

Bjorn and Ketil nodded and went their own way, each dropping to the sand and running off, both ways along the beach, with the message. They were well chosen, for both men were imposing and hard, and would not be ignored or questioned, even by the seasoned skippers and jarls in the fleet.

'What really happened?' Leif said quietly, close by, once the king was long gone.

Halfdan gave a light snort. 'Can you not guess?'

Leif sighed. 'Orm Axebiter was the assassin?'

Halfdan nodded, and Ulfr frowned at that. 'What?'

'The whole evening here has been one long show, Ulfr. Harðráði already has his deal with Magnus set and needs to break with Sveinn. But if he simply switched sides and left, it would damage his reputation, would make Onund Jacob of Sweden wary of him, and would essentially put him and Sveinn Ástríðarson at war. And so he engineered an argument with Sveinn last night in the tent, and brought him to the brink of breaking the treaty. Then he made it well known that he feared an assassination attempt. Personally, though I do not think the Danish usurper is all that bright, I think he's bright enough not to try and kill his ally right in the middle of his fleet. This assassination attempt was staged every bit as much as the argument that led to it. None of this has been Sveinn's doing, yet it has left him looking like a villain, broken the alliance, and given Harðráði free rein to change his alliance however he likes.'

Ulfr exhaled slowly. 'Odin, but that man thinks in spirals.'

Gunnhild nodded. 'He certainly does. He has an agile mind and a powerful imagination. And once again, right in the middle of unparalleled violence and potential disaster, he has managed to turn it to his advantage.'

Halfdan straightened and wiped the battering rain from his face. 'Send word to the crew in the village that they need to be aboard immediately. We need to sail straight away, and it's going to be hands on oars. We are bound for Vik, and a meeting with Magnus of Norway. And that means, at long last...'

'Hjalmvigi,' Leif said, peering out into the dark.

'Exactly,' Halfdan said, excitement and anticipation creeping into his tone.

Chapter 18

Vik, Norway, just before the September equinox

Leif had to admire the way Harðráði's mind worked. The man was not averse to taking risks when the potential gain was high enough. And as often as not, for him, it paid off, because he was good at weighing it all up.

The man's ship had sailed within moments of the 'assassination attempt', and had been halfway across the fjord and on the way to open sea before any of Sveinn Ástríðarson's jarls even knew anything had happened. The crews of the *Sea Wolf* and *Sea Dragon* had been pushing the ships back down the beach, scraping through the gravel, before the king was even out of sight, ploughing his way at speed along the channel left between the ships of the fleet. The Wolves had been the next out.

Even the slowest and tardiest of Harðráði's ships was out in open water before the first of the Danish contingent's ships were even fully crewed. Sveinn may have suspected something was up, but he had clearly not anticipated his ally leaving in the middle of the night, while his own ships were not even stocked ready to sail, let alone manned or prepared. Leif could only imagine the fury and rage when the Dane learned from local rumour that he had apparently attempted to murder his fellow king, had broken his oath and the alliance, and all without any knowledge or involvement from himself.

As they sailed north, the fleet of the Norse would-be king began to stretch out across the seas. Harðráði's ship was fast, but Ulfr's two masterpieces were even faster, and so the Wolves caught up with him in the open waters north of Fioni Island. Other speedier vessels in the fleet rowed hard and joined them as they moved north, while the majority of the fleet came on more slowly. The first night, spent on the coast of Læsø Island, on the very same beach that the Wolves had used during their recent race south, another nine ships caught up with them, rowing into the evening to make it. Such was the case, then, with every stop up the coast, the more determined ships in the lagging fleet pressing on at night to rejoin their king.

Leif had wondered why this was happening. Harðráði had made clear in Odinswe his intention to arrive at Vik in force, with his full fleet and not the eight ships agreed by Magnus, and yet had then raced ahead, leaving his slower vessels to follow on, seemingly ignoring his own plan. Still, by the time they reached the mouth of the Sognefjord, along which lay Vik, they had managed to pull together eighteen ships, which looked like a sizeable enough force.

The fjord was impressive.

Since joining the Wolves in Kiev six years earlier, he had seen every sort of landscape, from dusty hot lands in southern Italy to soggy, foggy hills in northern Angle Land. He had seen mountains aplenty, from the green peaks of Georgia to the grey heights of the Alps. But nothing like the lands around the Sognefjord. Less than three miles across, the fjord lay between bleak highlands that rose like cliffs to either side, occasionally sprouting smaller side fjords that led to villages and small towns. But for all it was narrow, the great, deep channel was long enough that they had to stop halfway for the night. It was a worrying night for Leif, who was not a natural sailor. With no beach to ground on, no harbour large enough to cope with the small fleet, and water too deep to anchor in, the ships of Harðráði's fleet roped themselves together, with those who could do so tethering themselves to trees or rocks on the vertiginous shoreline.

They passed the night safely enough, and with no sign of other warships, and in the morning cut themselves loose and sailed on up the mighty fjord.

It was as they approached Vik itself, nestled at the end of a stubby side channel and filling a wide green valley between the hard mountains, that things fell into place for Leif.

It was two days before the equinox now, for the fleet had separated and the faster ships had made good time. What Harðráði had counted on, he now realised, was that Magnus would arrive *only just* in time, perhaps the next day. For all the younger man was the legitimate king of Norway, Vik was his uncle's land, and a lengthy stay in force could easily sour the locals against him. Consequently, Harðráði had timed everything in order to arrive just before his nephew. Whether this was for show or for more nefarious purposes would undoubtedly soon be revealed.

The town of Vik slid toward them, the rocky inclines to either side reaching out like a hard, cold embrace around the small fleet. The place was of a reasonable size, with good fertile fields marching off beyond, up that wide valley. A single wooden church rose above the thatched roofs, and a small harbour awaited ships, the jetties almost empty, the fleet having passed various small fishing boats over the past hour.

Then the second surprise hit Leif.

A warship sat at the dock of Vik. Just a single ship, which bore the colours of Harðráði. Leif peered at it in surprise, and realised as they closed, ready to moor close by, that it was one of their own, which had been hugging the coast with them all the way north from Daneland. Harðráði was full of surprises. Clearly, even though he had timed matters to arrive just ahead of Magnus, he had also sent a ship on ahead during the night to check the lie of the land ahead of his arrival, the sneaky bastard.

More than this, the ship had clearly also been sent to pave the way for them, for as they neared the jetty, a veritable flood of humanity moved through the streets toward the harbour, settling at the water's edge and cheering like mad men and women. Children laughed, dogs barked, and off to one side, tumblers threw themselves around with wild abandon as a small group of musicians filled the autumn air with melodies by pipe and lyre and drum.

It was a celebration of the town's most famous son coming home. If Leif had not believed that Harðráði was especially popular here, he certainly would now. The place was alive with activity and atmosphere, and he had to force himself to remember that though this felt so peaceful and joyful, it was, in fact, a massively important political meeting in order to stop a war that had already killed thousands and burned a hundred towns and villages.

His smile faltered at the thought.

Still, it was hard to be maudlin with such a carnival atmosphere going on around them. Even the rest of the Wolves around him looked cheerful as they slowed their oar strokes and then lifted the great timber lengths to allow Ulfr to drift them gently into place on the jetty. Halfdan looked eager, his smile slightly predatory, for this would be the closest they had come to their goal since Niðaróss. Bjorn, he knew, from hours of drivel, was looking forward to stopping in a 'proper town, with proper beer and proper whores'. Ulfr was pleased that his ships had been pre-eminent among the fleet, sailing in the lead with the king. Ketil was feeling more at home than usual. His origin in Iceland made him more comfortable the further north they went, and this cold land of high rocks and icy waters was more like his birthplace than anywhere they had been. Gunnhild had that self-satisfied smile she wore when she knew that things were panning out just as she'd predicted. And they were.

He hated that he was starting to believe her magicks, but there was no denying it. She had seen three bears fighting over a fourth, which was very clearly Onund, Sveinn and Harðráði over Magnus, four great king bears in the north. And though it had not gone the way Leif had expected, their campaign had brought Magnus to the point of submission. The white bear was down. And best of all, now that he was down, Onund would be content to stay in Sweden and make treaties with them, Sveinn would rant and rage for a while over the way he'd been treated, but in the long run he would realise he could have Daneland back, and would be out of the way. And Harðráði would be paramount, and would owe the Wolves. The body of the white bear would be theirs for the picking, just as planned.

It was all working out.

The *Sea Wolf* thumped into the jetty gently, then came to rest, and Ketil and Sten leapt from the ship and tied her off to the cleats. Harðráði had come to rest against the timbers just behind the ship he had sent ahead, while *Sea Wolf* and *Sea Dragon* were now nestled on the other side of the wooden walkway that marched out into the sea.

Other ships were docking at the jetty to their left, though not at the one to the right for some reason, while further skippers approached the narrow stony beach further along, where they would presumably ground for the duration. Off in that direction too lay a wide grassy swathe where a couple of fishing boats had been pulled up far from the water.

The identity of the man who'd gone on ahead should have come as no surprise to Leif, and Torberg Arneson stepped from his vessel to the dock, with his stunning daughter and a couple of powerful karls at his side, to await the new king's presence. Even as the Wolves began to drop to the timbers, Harðráði stepped off his ship and down to the jetty. At the far end, on the dock, the people of Vik cheered.

Leif, again, smiled to himself. Harðráði had arranged everything so neatly. In many ways he should be the *lesser* party in this meeting. Magnus was still acknowledged as king in Norway, he had a powerful fleet and army, an unassailable fastness in the north, and still sufficient power and poise to be the one setting the main terms. Harðráði, on the other hand, was a usurper, with a strung-out fleet, tired from a season of war, no home base to call their own, and coming to demand something from the other party. Yet now, here they were in a town cheering them, ahead of Magnus, spirits high and all falling into place. And even though their fleet was mostly still on the way, they would arrive in time to block Magnus in, should everything go sour.

Another thought struck him, and he looked about, laughing. Despite Harðráði bringing north every ship he had, and even quite a few here in the lead flotilla, there would be precisely eight ships moored in Vik's harbour, four at each jetty. Even now, those that were beaching further along were disgorging men and rollers, ready to pull them up onto that grassy area, away from the water. When Magnus appeared, it would look very much as though Harðráði had stuck to the deal.

The clever bastard.

Behind the king, Ellisif, his wife and soon-to-be queen consort, was being helped down from the ship. Normally, he would march ahead and leave her to her own devices, as Leif had seen time and again over the months, but his arrival in Vik was all about pomp and show, and the beauty of the Kievan princess would only enhance his aura to the locals. Sure enough, he gestured and she stepped to his side, hand on his arm as he led her toward the town. Leif could not help but notice, however, how the man's eyes strayed first to Tora Torbergsdatter, standing just behind her powerful father, then to Gunnhild, where they lingered for a time. The man's gaze was hungry. Though ongoing events kept the king too busy to stray from his wife and hunt another, clearly the subject was never too far from his mind, and all it would take was sufficient time at leisure. He'd not been close enough to Gunnhild for long enough since Sigtun to press her, and it was likely he was being carefully circumspect around Tora, for fear of offending her father, whose support had brought him more than a third of his fleet for this war.

'Does Gunnhild know he lusts after her?' a voice asked close by.

He turned to see Bishop Aage, smoothing down his robes after descending from the king's ship. Leif gave a mirthless laugh. 'That particular Greek tragedy has been going on since Miklagarðr, four years ago. He will grow a second head before he gets her, though.'

The bishop frowned. 'I suspect *he* does not think so. Many men who wear the look I just saw on his face end up in speaking to me in confessional.'

That made Leif laugh – the very idea of Harðráði confessing his sins!

'The Church rather frowns on infidelity,' Aage said quietly, 'though obviously in these modern times, we are forced to look the other way when men of power falter. Perhaps I need to have a quiet word with him?'

'Good luck.' Leif smiled. 'Trying to talk Harðráði out of anything is like trying to cut down a tree with a herring.'

'Where are the whores?' Bjorn asked loudly, then belched, stepping next to them.

Leif rolled his eyes. 'Please, Bjorn. There is a man of the Church present.'

'I don't care *where* he's from, he can stand in line like everyone else. I'm sure there'll be whores for all.'

With that, the big man stomped off down the jetty in the wake of Halfdan, who was following Harðráði, singing a loud ditty about a fisherman's fight as he went.

Eg rodde meg ut på seiegrunnen
Det var om morgonen tidleg
Så kom han Olav frå Kårelunnen
Og lagde båten for ile
Så dro eg til han me fiskestangji
Så n datt i uvite att i rongji
Eg vart så gla, tok til å kva
Eg rådde grunnen åleine
Sudeli dudeli dudeli dei ho

Still rolling his eyes, Leif walked on, beside Bishop Aage.

Approaching the end of the dock, everyone slowed. Harðráði was at the fore, of course, with Ellisif on his arm, and Orm Axebiter at his shoulder. Behind him came Torberg Arneson with his daughter and senior karls. Then Halfdan and the Wolves, with Bishop Aage along for the ride. The rest of the crews were busy with the ships, securing everything and simply resting after the journey for now.

The cheering crowd parted as the new arrival approached, like the Red Sea for Moses, and Harðráði passed through it like the king he was about to become. Leif's gaze moved briefly to Halfdan, and he could see the anticipation in the jarl's eyes. Tomorrow Magnus would arrive, and then the deal would be done. Harðráði would be king of Norway with his nephew, and then the Wolves of Odin could call in the debt. Not only Hjalmvigi for Halfdan, but also his jarldom in Norway, land and a longhouse for the Wolves.

Oddly, the uncertainty Leif had felt early in the year seemed to have abated. While he still felt a little out of place this far north, he was rapidly becoming used to its bleak, stark beauty, and the simplicity of the life here. And the sense of uselessness and ennui he'd experienced as they moved back into the northern lands had evaporated with the evidence that he was needed and important just as much here, where he was a stranger, as he'd been in the familiar south. He might not here be the man required to teach them about the world around them and how to communicate in it, but once more, he had fallen almost seamlessly back into his more traditional role of diplomat, or ambassador. It was starting to feel comfortable. Anna had got over her petty jealousies, everyone still deferred to Leif, and all was feeling right. Those who had told him that home was simply wherever the Wolves of Odin were had been correct, it seemed.

He was still smiling about this, and pondering on how life changed you as you sailed through it, *or sometimes changed itself to suit you*, as they walked through the town, between the cheering crowds. His gaze played across the gathering, and it was almost heartwarming to see so many people of all social status, and all ages, shoulder to shoulder and cheering for their would-be king.

He frowned.

For just a moment, he thought he'd seen something out of place. Then it was gone, lost among the crowds. A single figure. A figure in a hooded cloak might not seem strange in the mountainous north of Norway in autumn, when the rains continued to hover on the periphery, threatening, yet oddly this one did. It was simply a matter of difference. Almost everyone here was in bright colours, wearing their best for the occasion, and they were cheering, clapping, straining to see over one another, smiling. The one figure had stood dour in a dark cloak, arms by its side, watching the visitors as they passed through the crowd.

He was about to dismiss it as a figment of his imagination when he saw the figure once more. Just a fleeting glimpse again, lost in the throng a moment later, but having seen it twice, he knew it for reality and not some illusion or mistake.

As they moved off into the rear of the town, he craned his neck, trying to see any further sign of the figure, but it was now properly lost. He tried to fix it in his mind, in case he saw it again. It was a man, he thought. He'd only seen the person briefly, and the face had been largely in shadow because of the hood, but he thought he'd seen a small, neat moustache. And a prominent nose, for that had protruded far enough to catch the light. He was not tall, nor short, and of slim build. That was all. But Leif made sure to commit every detail he could to memory. Something about the figure disturbed him.

Close to that great wooden church, they finally stopped, and Harðráði was introduced to the lendrmaðr of Vik, Bodvar Biarnisson, who stepped forth, all gold and velvet in bright colours, hair braided intricately and beard combed well, and spent far longer than necessary expounding on Harðráði's brilliance, and the importance of Vik in the world. Leif spent the entire time only half-listening, watching out for any reappearance of the hooded man, but even after the lengthy diatribe, he'd not seen him again.

By the time they were finally able to breathe, the sun was already dipping behind the highest of the peaks to the west, and Harðráði was forced to apologise to those in the crowd waiting to greet him, noting that he had yet to even sit down after a long voyage, and with sunset on the cusp, he would see many of them at the feast that had been provided this evening, and any others in the morning. They were then shown to accommodation. Bishop Aage and his companions to the church, of course, Harðráði to a longhouse owned by his family and until recently occupied by a distant cousin who had perished the winter past.

Provision had been made for half a dozen of the more senior jarls and their men, with various available buildings in the town and, though Halfdan could hardly claim to be one of the more important among the fleet, his close links to Harðráði saw one such house assigned to him and his top people. There were, in fact, only four beds in the place, but with Ulfr, Farlof and Eygrímr staying with the ships and their crews, those present numbered only six. Leif and Anna announced they were content to share one bed, and Bjorn snorted and declared that by the time he'd swived every available woman in town and drank a mead hall dry, he would be able to sleep on a plank.

With that, they left their gear, locked the house, and went out for the evening, Bjorn to explore the streets of Vik, looking for things to fuck, fight or gulp, the rest of them to the square, where tables had been laid out and a banquet was in preparation, hogs and goats and locally caught coalfish and halibut roasting over open fires.

Anna was at her best during the occasion, her more bubbly personality coming to the fore, which meant that she talked as though words were going out of fashion, but was happy and fun to be around, and that attracted her much attention and interaction. Early on in the evening, Harðráði had been watching Gunnhild closely, though less so as time wore on and his attention was required by others. Leif smiled to see Bishop Aage as one of those, speaking to the great man in low tones, presumably reminding him how, as a king of Norway, he could certainly not afford to be seen to be consorting with a pagan woman in flagrant disregard for his good Christian wife. Certainly, Harðráði's expression suggested that this had been the subject of the priest's conversation.

Leif initially felt a little out of place again, despite Anna's constant involvement of him, and his eyes continued to play across the gathering, looking for the hooded man. But as the meal went on, he found that he had become a constant source of information for people. Whenever either Harðráði or Halfdan were asked by one of the locals about their glorious travels or the events of the past few months or years, both men directed them to Leif as their de facto skald, leaving him with an almost constant series of questions, stretching from the time of the Georgian civil war, through Miklagarðr, all the way down to the burning of Hróarskelda.

In fact, he was kept so busy regaling enthralled locals with tales of their exploits that by the time the feast ended, and only the hardened drinkers remained in the square, determined to see it through to the dawn, he was quite hoarse. Anna retired back to their house before him, along with Gunnhild and the others, and even Bjorn, who had turned up later in the evening with a wide grin and an armful of bottles. As a drunken native finally thanked Leif for his time and tottered off to find something else to consume, Leif looked around to see that not only was he the last of the Wolves in the square, but even Harðráði and the lendrmaðr had gone to their beds now.

He stood, stretched, and looked about. Maybe a score of men remained here, roughly half of them from the fleet, the rest locals, all laughing and drinking, none of them men Leif knew. He looked up into the sky and realised with a start that he could see the faintest of glows in the east, announcing that the night had passed speedily, and dawn was not far off.

He would have to hurry, for even then he would only manage to squeeze in a couple of hours of sleep before he would need to be up and about again. As he turned and clambered over the bench on which he'd now been sat for the past three unbroken hours, he realised that he must have had a lot more to drink than he'd thought. His legs felt distinctly shaky, and he almost fell face first for a moment, tottering, keeping his balance with only great effort and concentration. He gave his leave to a square full of people who were paying him no attention anyway, and wandered off.

He only got lost a few times, unfamiliar with the streets, and finding it surprisingly hard to focus as he pushed on, looking for home. Finally, he spotted a familiar building, and behind it a high peak with a waterfall running down it in an almost straight vertical line toward the town, a landmark he'd noted when they first arrived.

He ambled toward the house, only bouncing off a wall once on the way.

Such was the fug in his brain from the late night and the copious drink, that he didn't notice there was anything wrong until he was almost in it. As he rounded a corner, finally something reached his nostrils, and he frowned. Had the smell of the roasting pits in the square followed him? He looked around.

Then up.

Half an hour ago, he may not have seen it, but with the sky lightening by the moment, he could make out the thin column of black smoke as it coiled up into the air.

Shit.

He found he was suddenly sober. Much more so than he really wanted to be, as he caught sight of the first orange flame on the roof amid the smoke, and registered that the Wolves' house was on fire. His head was spinning suddenly. He looked about. No other buildings were smoking, so this was not a town fire. It was just their house alone. And the weather was cold and still, with virtually no breeze and so little chance of the fire spreading to neighbouring buildings.

It was not an accident.

Oh, there were perhaps a dozen ways a fire could start on a dry day in a town made largely of wood, especially when many of the occupants had had more to drink than they needed. But somehow, Leif doubted this was anything but a deliberate attack. He could see the fire spreading across the roof at a frightening rate. Whoever had done this must have thrown a burning brand up into the dry thatch, and can only have just done it, else the fire would be far more advanced already. Quickly running around the other side, he found the front door blocked, a large, chest-height barrel standing in front of it. Closing, he realised the barrel was, ironically, full of water. He knew the futility of it, of course, but with panic setting in, he rushed over to the barrel and put his shoulder to it, trying to heave it or just tip it. He might as well have tried to lift the *Sea Wolf* on his own.

He'd known that, of course. That quantity of water weighed a huge amount. It would take him so long to find a bucket and empty it down to a movable level that the house would have burned down by then. A frightening creak from high up suggested that the roof was close to collapse, and then there was a damn good chance that everyone inside would die.

There were two other ways in and out, both windows, but they were high up, one at each end, close to the burning thatch. They would be too hot and dangerous to use, and would take too long anyway. There was no other hole.

One would have to be *made*, then.

The main part of the house was wattle and daub. He ran to the wall and smacked it with his palm, then moved a little to the left and repeated the move, continuing to do so along that wall and then round the corner to the next one. As he did so, he shouted. 'Halfdan? Anna? Bjorn? Can anyone hear me?'

274

He would be hard to hear over the roar of flames, but the occupants must be awake now, and know their peril. Then, between his knocks, he heard them shouting, just, their yells almost submerged beneath the roar of fiery thatch. He couldn't hear what they were saying, but then a moment later, he heard something else, the other thing he was listening for. Wattle and daub could be good and solid, but over time it often became crumbly and weak in places, and he heard then the difference in sound as he slapped the wall. Leaning close to it, he took a deep breath and bellowed.

'Bjorn! Get your axe and hit the wall where you hear my voice.'

There was some sort of reply, though he couldn't make it out. Hoping against hope they could hear him, he repeated that command over and over, marking the spot and trying to be heard at the same time.

The shock he suffered when an enormous axe blade smashed through the wall an inch from his nose made him dance back in terror, eyes wide. Two more thuds, another blow of the axe, and then two more of them joining in, and suddenly the weak section of the house wall exploded outwards like a smashed eggshell. The Wolves of Odin came barrelling out of the house like a tidal wave. Each of them had had the forethought to grab their kit bag, and Anna, third to emerge, was bringing Leif's for him.

'Shit,' Ketil said suddenly, 'my cloak!' He turned and dived back toward the hole in the wall, but Bjorn grabbed him and held him fast just as the roof finally collapsed, sending a massive shower of burning timber and thatch down into the room below. Even as Bjorn dragged the Icelander away, Ketil was clawing at him, eyes on the house, barking angrily about his cloak.

'Well now,' Halfdan said, 'that is a curiously specific fire. And we couldn't get out because the door was blocked.'

Leif nodded, straying eyes picking out the shape of a dark hooded cloak, discarded in the street only a few paces from

275

the house. 'This was planned and executed slowly and carefully. Whoever did it has been watching us since we arrived, and thought we were all in there. Thank God Almighty that I am the least memorable and recognisable of you all. They even took the time to fill a barrel with water to block the door shut.'

'I don't suppose you saw who set the fire?'

Leif shook his head, but even as he did so, he couldn't fight the image of a thin man in a that discarded hooded cloak, lurking among the crowd.

'Well, I think we return to *Sea Wolf* until full morning and stay there until Magnus arrives.'

'Then I don't think we'll have long to wait,' Ketil said, pointing up at the hill above the town. A beacon up there was blazing away.

Magnus of Norway had come.

Part Four

ᚹᛟᛚᚠᛖᛋ ᛟᚠ ᛟᛞᛁᚾ

Justice

'The far-known king the order gave,
In silence o'er the swelling wave,
With noiseless oars, his vessels gay
From Denmark west to row away;
And Olaf's son, with justice rare,
Offers with him the realm to share.
People, no doubt, rejoiced to find
The kings had met in peaceful mind.'

From *King Harald's Saga* by Snorri Sturluson
trans. Samuel Laing

Chapter 19

Vik, September equinox

Halfdan stood in his best blue shirt and dun-coloured cloak, faintly irked that his good brooch had been lost in the dark on a Danish beach. By the simple fact that he had been quartered among the more important jarls of the fleet, he had found himself standing among the highest men of Norway, close to Harðráði and Torberg Arneson, and was relieved that he had dressed for the occasion. So had the rest of the Wolves, who were gathered close behind him, although dressing for the occasion meant different things to different people. Gunnhild was stunning and incredibly impressive in an emerald-green dress that matched her eyes, while Bjorn had simply combed his hair for a change and still looked more like a troll than a man as he farted loudly in the expectant silence.

As the ships slid toward the jetty in front of them, the young jarl looked this way and that across the waiting crowd. It was pointless, of course. He had only Leif's description of the man believed to have burned down the house, attempting to kill the Wolves, and even that was very vague. He'd not have really been able to identify the man, even had he still been wearing his hooded cloak, and that was not going to happen, since the cloak had been abandoned in the street.

He wanted to get to the bottom of that. Someone had deliberately targeted the Wolves, or at least one of them. Magnus and his people had not arrived yet, and none of the Wolves had any connection to the people of Vik, which lent a heavy suggestion to the notion that the culprit had come north with them as part of the fleet. The only element there who'd been known to have trouble with the Wolves were the crews of Torberg Arneson, but since the attack at Odinswe that seemed to have calmed, and Arneson had been coldly aloof in their presence, Halfdan simply couldn't see Arneson being bothered going to such efforts to deal with him.

So who?

His gaze continued to play pointlessly across the crowd, and only returned to the arrivals as the ship thumped against the jetty. While two of the three great wooden walkways out to sea still held eight of Harðráði's vessels, the one that had been left for local fishermen had now been cleared to allow space for four of Magnus's ships.

The red and gold dragon banner of Norway snapped in the breeze as the ship came to a halt and men leapt ashore to tie her up.

Halfdan tensed. This could be an occasion of any manner. The two men meeting here were family, and in theory were here to create peace and unity, but both had so recently been at war, and both were clever and wary, each having broken their own accords, for Magnus too had arrived with a sizeable fleet.

The young king of Norway reached the sheer strake of his ship and dropped lightly to the timbers, taking a moment to find his land legs. Then he stopped, turned and eyed the waiting would-be king with a curious expression. Harðráði remained still, silent. In fact, silence reigned, then, the only sounds the lap of waves, the creak of ships, the distant cries of sea birds and the distinctive sound of hundreds of people trying not to make a sound.

Magnus took three steps forward. His hand fell to his belt, close to the hilt of the sword strapped there, but instead reached the leather, thumb curling into it. Behind him, his senior jarls dropped to the jetty, along with half a dozen very strong-looking warriors.

And then a priest.

Halfdan fought the urge to say anything, even to break into a run and barge the bastard from the jetty into the water and drown him.

Hjalmvigi turned, and his expression fell almost immediately upon Halfdan, as though none of the other people here mattered, and it was Halfdan alone for whom he'd come. The smile the priest issued at him then carried all the warmth of Fimbulwinter. Predatory. Cruel. And with absolutely no fear. Hjalmvigi was not expecting to find trouble here, only satisfaction, which worried him. The man should be frightened.

His gaze moved back to Magnus, with difficulty. The young king took several steps more, slowing. His expression was carefully neutral.

Harðráði walked forward, then, out onto the jetty, and came to a halt just a dozen paces from his nephew. The two men stood facing one another, neither speaking.

Another two steps each. Another step.

The sense of relief that swept across the gathering as the two men suddenly leapt forward into an embrace was palpable.

'You old dog.' Magnus laughed. 'I knew you'd bring your fleet.'

'Just as I knew you'd bring yours,' Harðráði replied genially. 'I have a tent being raised for us. It should be ready by now, in fact. You will no doubt want to rest and eat after your journey.'

Magnus turned and waved to his ship, and two more men dropped from it, each carrying something bulky and heavy, wrapped tight in blankets. Harðráði gestured, and Magnus joined him, the two men turning and walking back toward the town. The crowds parted for them, and Halfdan stood aside with the other jarls, letting them pass. With the two kings went Magnus's guards and his two men carrying the parcels, and then, in a moment that made Halfdan's lip wrinkle with distaste, Hjalmvigi. The priest did not even spare Halfdan a glance in passing, and he fought the urge to lunge again. Instead, he quietly fell in with the others as they strode toward Harðráði's great tent that had now been raised in an open space not far from the harbour.

His eyes occasionally darted to the two leaders, but most of the time they rested on the priest in his bishop's robes, a sight that only served to inflame Halfdan all the more. As they passed through the crowd, two men also in priest's garb stepped out of the mass and fell in alongside Hjalmvigi, who nodded his acceptance to the pair.

Halfdan started as something tugged at his sleeve, and he turned as he walked. Leif's expression was thunderous.

'What is it?' Halfdan hissed.

'Those men. The one on the left with the big nose. I'd swear he was the man watching us yesterday, wearing the cloak.'

Halfdan's lip twitched again, then. A priest. And an ally of Hjalmvigi's apparently. The hypocrisy of the White Christ knew no bounds, it seemed, for he had heard many times how their holy words told them not to kill. Yet it seemed an inescapable fact that one of those priests had attempted to burn the Wolves of Odin alive in their guest house.

Was it possible? Yes. Likely, even. Hjalmvigi knew Halfdan was after him, and close, for they had met at Niðaróss. He had known that Harðráði would be coming to Vik, and therefore that Halfdan would come with him. It would not have taken a great deal of effort to get a message to a cruel priest of the nailed god here to do away with the troublesome crew before Magnus arrived.

He filed that away in his mind. There would be a price paid for that before the sun rose once more. But for now, he had to play the good jarl, for he was close to sealing his agreement with the new king.

They followed the procession of the mighty and the wealthy into the tent, where tables and benches had been set up ready for a feast, and all Harðráði's usual ostentatious show of wealth was on display. Two thrones had been set up side by side, and

Harðráði dropped easily into one of them. Magnus followed suit beside him, and as they sat side by side, Halfdan realised just how similar the two men were. With only a decade between them, he could imagine Magnus looking almost identical to Harðráði once ten years had passed.

The various jarls took their places at the tables, filling the benches around the large tent, and Halfdan was angered to see Hjalmvigi being given a place of honour close to his king. At the younger king's gesture, then, the two men following him placed their packages on the table before the two thrones and began to unwrap them. Inside, each contained a small trove of treasures, from delicate, decorative sax daggers to rich, velvet cloaks, to gold cups and more. At another wave from Magnus, the two men lifted their burdens once more, with difficulty now they were not wrapped, and carried them to the lines of jarls, each taking one side.

'Gifts from your kings,' Magnus announced loudly. 'Claim what takes your fancy.'

The two men moved down the lines then, each seated jarl taking an item from the pile. When it reached Halfdan, he peered into the goods, and with a grin grasped a silver brooch of intricate Ringerike design. As the man moved on, he swapped the beautiful item for the plain one holding his cloak in place, then returned his attention to the meeting in general.

The two kings smiled as the gathering of jarls each took something. Halfdan decided that later he would have to give something to each of his friends, since they, not being jarls, were not included in this gathering, and instead stood at a distance with the other crews. Once the last seated lord had taken an item, the two men gathered up what remained and placed the rest on another table.

When things settled once more, Magnus gestured again, and a man hurried over, carrying two lengths of wood. As they were handed to the younger king, Halfdan could just make out that they were both carved with runes and decoration. Magnus gripped the two sticks and turned to Harðráði.

'I offer you two worlds. Which will you take?'

Harðráði sucked on his lip for a moment, and then reached out and grasped the nearest one, taking it, and reading the runes thereon. He nodded.

'With this baton,' Magnus announced, loudly, addressing all present, now, 'I grant you half the wealth, power and lands of Norway. In all the land, whether within your domain or mine, you shall be counted as king, and accorded all appropriate honours.'

Halfdan smiled at Harðráði's expression. The man looked smug.

'I impose only these slight conditions,' Magnus said then, and Harðráði's eyes shot to his nephew at the unexpected comment. 'When we are together,' the younger man said, expression serious as he turned to his uncle, 'I shall be counted the senior, and all first salutations and dignities shall come to me. And when we meet with any third king, I shall seat myself in the centre.'

Silence fell, and it was an oddly dangerous silence. There had been various small concessions added by each of the kings before their meeting, but this was sudden, unexpected and as yet not agreed. Halfdan watched Harðráði wrestle with himself for a moment, fighting the urge to explode with indignation. He saw the older king master himself and push down the anger, sealing it in with a tight smile. He turned to Magnus and rose.

'Thank you, nephew and brother-king, for your generous words. I accept all with gratitude. Let there be peace and concord between us, and no more war in the north. Let us have three days of celebration here in this glorious place.'

Magnus laughed. 'Indeed. But let it begin with ceremony. All has been agreed and accepted, but to be law, there must be a Thing. Let the Thing be held here tomorrow, and all be made legal and certain.'

The two men nodded at one another, and a cheer went up around the tent. Halfdan's gaze strayed once more to Hjalmvigi

284

then, for the grim priest was giving a half-hearted cheer simply for the look of things, while his gaze fell upon Halfdan, and rested there, carrying hatred his way. The local priests on either side did much the same.

The feast began then, food and drink brought in for the guests. Outside, provision had been made for the rest of the visitors, and once Halfdan was content that no one cared about him, he slipped away from the table of noisy, eating noblemen, and dipped out into the colder world to find his friends. The Wolves were seated to one side, laughing and drinking, and Halfdan crossed to them and pulled Leif aside.

'How sure are you about that priest?'

'I'm certain, Halfdan.'

He nodded.

'What are you going to do?' Leif asked quietly.

'Better you don't ask,' he replied, aware of how Leif might take the answer, being a Christian himself. With that he walked away. As he returned to his seat in the tent, he glanced across and found that priest with the long nose watching him, a sight sufficient to convince Halfdan that he was right.

He joined in the festivities then, for the rest of the afternoon, though he was not feeling particularly festive himself. As the sky outside began to lose its light, evening marching their way with all speed, the great meeting gradually broke up. Jarls announced the need to get back to their ships and make ready for the next day, for a Thing was an important affair, and every man wanted to be at his brightest. The end of the festivities came really when Magnus said as much and rose to leave.

The kings having departed, finally Hjalmvigi and his fellow priests rose.

As he left the tent, the robe-clad villain gathered half a dozen of Magnus's guards that had been left for him. The man was in the same town as the Wolves of Odin once more, and was not about to take any risks, it seemed. The priests marched off and made their way to the church in the heart of Vik. Halfdan slipped out of the tent after them, and as he emerged into the evening's cold air, the Wolves remained at their place, laughing and drinking. Gunnhild glanced his way for a moment, gave him a single nod, and then looked away again.

Halfdan turned and hurried across the square. Clearly the priests were not expecting trouble, for the three of them conversed in low tones as they walked through the town with their armed escort. Halfdan followed at a distance, having no difficulty trailing them, for their robes stood out easily.

They reached the church, and there separated. Hjalmvigi himself entered the main building, the guards taking up positions by the church doors. The man Halfdan neither knew nor cared about wandered off into the town, heading further inland. But the priest with the big nose walked across the open space by the church and opened the door to a small, plain house, disappearing inside. It was a humble cottage, as should befit a humble priest.

Halfdan waited for a while, then gradually moved around the house, viewing it from various angles as he found several places to stand unobserved. Once he was content the priest was alone in the house, he crossed to the single door and tried it gently. It had not been locked, and swung inwards with the quietest of creaks. He slipped into the gloomy interior and closed it behind him, then stopped and listened. The building was just one storey high, and divided into two rooms with a wattle screen, the doorway in it covered by a draped curtain.

Halfdan crossed to it and peeked through the gap to see the priest standing at a bowl on a table, washing his face, the gentle splash of the water accompanied by one of their nailed god dirges, hummed in a tuneless voice. Smiling menacingly to himself, Halfdan slipped through the curtained doorway, his soft footsteps unheard over the splashing and humming, and slipped his sax from his belt. As he crept up behind the priest, he brandished the blade, knuckles white on the hilt. Then, at the last moment, a thought struck him, and so did a vicious smile as he reversed the knife in his hand, lifted it, and brought it down on the back of the inattentive priest's head, hard. The priest crumpled with just a sigh.

The following half hour was busy, as Halfdan prepared, and finally, when all was ready, he dipped a wooden cup into the bowl of water and threw it into the man's face.

The priest blinked awake with a start, coughing.

'What? Where am I?'

Halfdan waited for the man to register the answer to that. His house probably looked a little different upside down. He gave the man a prod, and the tethered priest swung slowly back and forth on his rope like a pendulum.

'You.'

Halfdan nodded. That, for him, was all the confirmation he needed, on top of Leif's certainty. The priest's expression was one of both recognition and utter hatred. There was no doubt now in the jarl's mind that this was the man who'd attempted to kill them. Of course, he seemed a little small and reedy to have moved and filled a water barrel on his own, so he was likely not alone in the work. Perhaps that other priest had been involved, but only this one's involvement could be proved, and Halfdan was not about to go out and kill a man who might or might not have been involved.

'What are you doing?'

'I've never read your nailed god book,' Halfdan replied quietly. 'I never felt the need or the urge. But my friend Leif has, many times, and he tells me things occasionally. I don't remember it word for word, of course, but certain parts stand out. I *do* remember the line "an eye for an eye and a tooth for a tooth".'

The priest's eyes widened as he realised what Halfdan meant, but before he could scream or beg or whatever it was he was planning to do, Halfdan jammed a rag into his mouth, filling it, and muffling him. He twirled gently on the rope from which he hung, looped around his ankles and thrown over a beam.

His hands worked feverishly to free themselves from the bonds behind his back. Halfdan grasped him and set him spinning slowly, then crossed to his other preparations. He'd found lard and fat in bowls in the small kitchen area, and had used a wooden spoon to smear them on the curtain between the two rooms and on the blankets of the bed and the priest robes hanging on a peg.

It was when he picked up the stinking tallow-fat candle that guttered on the table that the gently rotating priest's eyes really widened in panic.

'I hope you enjoy meeting your joyless god,' Halfdan said quietly, as he touched the candle to the bed, watching as it caught and roared into golden life, then repeated the process on the priest robe.

The dangling man choked and coughed, trying to scream through the rag jammed in his mouth. Halfdan nodded at him once, then lifted aside the curtain and moved into the outer room before touching the candle to that drape too. As it began to roar, he cast aside the candle, left the house and closed the door behind him. There was no one in the small square, and so he crossed and disappeared into an alley between houses, then began to scurry back toward the harbour as behind him a huge bang announced that the house had truly caught in the grip of inferno.

As he reached *Sea Wolf* finally and climbed aboard, he received solemn nods from several of the others, even Leif, which relieved him, for he'd not been sure the little Rus would approve. Turning, he could see the column of smoke from the burning house across the roofs of the town, black against a dark purple sky. He'd been pleased to find the priest's residence had been sufficiently far from any other, with the breeze only the gentlest, as to make it unlikely the fire would spread.

He retired for the night, then, and slept soundly.

–

288

The morning was a dreary one when he awoke from slumber to the blaring of a horn. The sky had come in with deep grey clouds, and though it was yet to rain properly, there was a cold dampness to the air, promising a downpour soon enough. Once more, he dressed in his best, with the brooch that had been a gift from the king of Norway, and the others made themselves presentable. Then, they dropped to the jetty and joined the flood of humanity heading inland, and left only a half dozen men aboard each ship, in the same manner as every other skipper in the harbour.

The horns continued to blare calling every king, jarl, karl and free man and woman in Vik to the grand Thing. The populace of the city moved through the streets, and it was with a certain satisfaction that Halfdan and his friends passed the burned-out shell of a building beside the church. The Thing would be held in the fields beyond Vik, for with almost every soul in the valley attending, there needed to be plenty of space.

Arriving at the site, Halfdan was impressed. Harðráði and Magnus had clearly had their people working on this through the night. Benches and logs formed three sides of a great open area, in four concentric rows. The last side was occupied by the two thrones, with a great table between them, both chairs draped with red and yellow cloth. The whole thing was worked around a gentle natural hollow, which allowed all the seats and gathering crowd a reasonable view of the main event. The two kings were already in place, with their best men around them. A man with a horn continued to blare the warning, and a man with a great drum stood ready, waiting. Behind the two kings, alongside their guards of honour, stood Hjalmvigi, accompanied now by only one priest. The Christ-villain's face was twisted in an expression of vile hatred as it fell upon the young jarl and his friends arriving at the meeting.

Halfdan took his seat with his closer companions, many of the Wolves relegated to standing with the crowd around the edge, looking on from behind. He glanced at the two kings almost in passing, for his attention was locked on Hjalmvigi now. He was as close to getting his hands on the priest as he had ever been, and he could feel Odin watching now, waiting for the world to change.

The crowd gradually assembled, and the horn blasts ended. The drum banged out rhythmically, calling the Thing to order, and a law-speaker lendrmaðr was chosen: Bodvar Biarnisson, the lendrmaðr of Vik, out of deference to their location. Still, Halfdan paid little attention. He was watching Hjalmvigi instead. He was vaguely aware of the declaration of a shared kingdom, and of all legal matters being passed to allow Harðráði and Magnus to rule together. He heard in passing the division of all goods, including, something of a surprise, Harðráði's offer to share his own personal treasure, amassed from his time in the south and east, with his nephew. That did draw his attention for a moment, and he realised, as he caught the look on Harðráði's face, what this was. He himself might be a decade older than Magnus, but he was married and secure, Magnus not so. The look in the older man's eye spoke poorly for the likelihood of his nephew seeing out the year. And with no wife or children, Harðráði would slip seamlessly into sole rule. He was giving away half his fortune to buy Magnus's goodwill and perhaps lull him into a false sense of security, for he knew that when his nephew died, possibly even *accidentally*, it would all come back to Harðráði anyway.

As matters drifted off into other legal minutiae, he stopped really listening again, and returned to watching his quarry, and it was only when Leif and Gunnhild nudged him that he suddenly returned to the present.

'What?'

'You were called,' Leif said, pointing at the kings, who, Halfdan now realised, were both looking directly at him. Uncertainly, frowning, Halfdan rose to his feet and strode over toward them. He did not speak. Wasn't sure what to say, or how to address them. It mattered not, because then, Harðráði broke the silence.

'This man, Halfdan Vigholfsson, called the Loki-born, I have known now for some five years. He has served me, and served alongside me, in the guard of the emperors in Miklagarðr, and has been at the very forefront in Denmark. He has been a man upon whom I have relied, along with his hirð, as warriors, messengers, explorers and diplomats. But to this day, he owns naught that he cannot carry with him in his magnificent ships. But Halfdan Vigholfsson has been accounted a jarl by his people since the first day I met him, and he has always carried himself with the power of one. As such, and with the right and authority of a king of Norway, I hereby name him jarl by royal design. I shall retain the jarldom of Vik, but now I give the villages of Dragsvik and Tjugum across the fjord to Halfdan to be his jarldom. Let this be witnessed by all present. And as a gift for his many services, I grant him a bag of silver the size of a man's head with which to settle his hirð and build his longhouse. Let this be recorded by the law-speaker.'

Halfdan nodded slowly, then fixed Harðráði with a direct look. 'We had a deal, King Harald, though, did we not?'

Harðráði had the grace to look uncomfortable, then. 'You would press for *every* condition?'

He shook his head. 'I would give you back everything you offer, but one condition must stand.'

Harðráði sighed. He turned to his nephew. 'You have a priest with you who was excommunicated.'

Magnus frowned. 'He remains so until I receive word of his reinstatement from Rome.'

'There will be no need for that. I agreed with Jarl Halfdan that in return for his services, I would give him the priest, Hjalmvigi.'

Halfdan looked past the kings then, half expecting to see shock and panic on the priest's face. He was slightly disconcerted to see that all Hjalmvigi did was nod slowly to himself, one eyebrow slightly raised.

'The priest is my bishop in Niðaróss,' Magnus said, tone tight and dangerous.

'I gave my word.'

'The priest is not yours to give, dear uncle. You own only *half* of Norway, after all.'

'True,' Harðráði replied, then turned to Halfdan. 'Which half of the priest would you like? Top or bottom? Front or back? Left or right?'

Despite everything, Halfdan almost burst out laughing at that. Instead, he kept his level gaze fixed on the king, and Harðráði sighed, nodded at him, and turned to his nephew. 'You would have me break my word? Bear in mind that upon our meeting yesterday, you imposed a condition upon our shared throne that had not been agreed, and which I had not anticipated. And yet I accepted it, for the sake of peace. Do not test me on this, Magnus, for I value that peace, but I will not go back on my word. Hjalmvigi is Jarl Halfdan's, to do with as he pleases.'

There was a sudden squawk of alarm, and Halfdan glanced past them to see that Orm Axebiter had appeared behind Hjalmvigi, and now had an arm round his neck, pressing dangerously on his throat. It would not take the man much to kill the priest from that position, and from the questioning look Orm threw at his king, he was ready to do so. In return, Harðráði threw a similar look at Magnus. The younger king clenched his teeth, angrily, fingers curling around the arms of his chair. He glanced at the trapped priest, then at Halfdan, then at Harðráði, and fretted in silence, struggling with a decision.

Halfdan tensed.

'Very well,' Magnus of Norway conceded, irritably, but with a beaten tone. 'I recognise your acceptance of certain necessities, and it is only fitting that I also be willing to sacrifice things to keep the peace.' In the background, even as the kings agreed the priest's fate, Halfdan saw Hjalmvigi dragged from view by Orm Axebiter. The other priest stood transfixed, staring in shock.

'In a way,' Magnus said with a sigh, 'perhaps it is a good thing. My relationship with Onund of Sweden was going to be rocky as long as I harboured the priest he ejected.'

Harðráði laughed mirthlessly. 'It may be better for the priest, too. Even if his fate is to meet the edge of a sword blade, at least he might avoid burning his own house down, eh?'

The way the man's eyes narrowed as he turned to Halfdan left the new jarl in no doubt that Harðráði was entirely aware of how one of the town's priests had met his end last night.

'Thank you, my king,' he said, and bowed, then stepped back and returned to his seat, noting the looks of triumph and elation among his friends as he did so. Harðráði had lived up to every part of his side of the bargain. The Wolves were to have a home, here in this place, and Halfdan was now a jarl by royal decree, with which no man could argue.

Best of all... Hjalmvigi, at last, was his.

Chapter 20

Leif rubbed bleary eyes, and then quickly corrected his step as he almost walked into the harbour in the process. He yawned. It had been a long night. The great Thing of the two kings had been reason enough for the whole of Vik and its surrounding area – the whole of *Norway*, really – to celebrate, and the drink had flowed easier than the water. In fact, it was doubtful there was anything more intoxicating than seawater left in Vik now. Despite the threatening weather of the afternoon, the rain had held off, and even patches of black sky sprinkled with stars had appeared above the roaring laughter and copious drinking of the valley. The moon had been already past its peak when the majority had turned in, including the two kings.

The Wolves, of course, had gone on a little further. The main celebration had been just for the cessation of a war, the crowning of a king and the reconciliation of a family. For the Wolves, though, it also meant the culmination of a hunt that had begun in the forests of Georgia six years ago and had taken them across the world and even against a witch, a warlord and a berserkr in the moors of Angle Land. Hjalmvigi was theirs now. It was over.

Naturally, the priest had been one of the main topics of conversation during the raucous celebrations. It was Halfdan's decision, of course: the fate of Hjalmvigi. Even had he not been the jarl, and now a *true and official* jarl with the ear of a king, this quest had been his from the start. Halfdan did not know what he would do yet, though. Hjalmvigi had to die, of course, unless the young jarl suddenly thought of something *worse* than death, but he had to suffer in the process. The priest was currently confined in a cage usually used to hold vicious animals captured in the lands around the village, under royal guard, and it pleased them all to think of the anguish and panic the man must be enduring there, waiting to face his fate.

And should any of them falter in their hatred and start to feel sympathy for the damned priest, it did not take much to recall the man's villainy in all its forms.

'*Your presence offends us,*' Hjalmvigi had said. '*Begone before you are flayed.*' His first words to the Wolves, back in Kiev, before they sailed and when Leif had not even yet joined the crew.

And then there was that moment with the priest spitting bile and urging Yngvar to do away with Serkish merchants, watching them pushed over violently, their lives threatened, the innocent southerners only saved by the arrival of the Georgian queen.

'*Heresy will be stamped out,*' the priest had snarled, threatening to convert the whole of Georgia to his brand of Christianity, by the sword if necessary, regardless of the fact that many of the fleet were Rus and shared the Georgians' faith. An image rose of the priest in the woods of Sasireti, then, white robe soaked red with the blood of others, sword in one hand, cross in the other, bringing his own faith on a razor's edge to men of the Orthodox Church.

Then there was the '*cleansing death*' Hjalmvigi had advocated for the suffering cadavers at the edge of the world.

And had Valdimar of Kiev not been a patron to the Wolves on their return from the east, Leif was under no illusions that Hjalmvigi would have had them all burned for heresy in Kutaisi. Even closer to home, the would-be bishop had set his priest in Vik to burning the Wolves to death in their house. Hjalmvigi would love nothing more than to watch the Wolves burn.

And for Halfdan it had gone back so much further, to his father's death and the defacing of that stone of Odin in his village.

No, Hjalmvigi had plenty of crimes to pay for, and Halfdan would have the man pay.

'Sleep on it,' Gunnhild had advised. 'As often as not, answers come in the night. Tomorrow you will know what to do with him.'

And that had been the end of that. But the celebration had gone on, for they had a village, a jarldom, a king. The Wolves of Odin had a home, and even Leif felt that this might be a place he could settle. The *sumbl*, the celebratory drinking feast, went on for some time, until eventually, the town already mostly abed, the Wolves had retired. Many went back to the ships, while the core of the hirð had gone to their accommodation in the town. Following the burning of their house, they had been given another, a farmer's barn on the edge of town, where wicker screens and drapes had been supplied to create rooms within.

Everyone had gone home, with two exceptions.

Bjorn, of course, was not done and, despite being told it was fruitless by the others, insisted that somewhere there would be another drink and a hospitable woman waiting for him, and had gone to search for them.

And Leif. His head appeared to be full of wool, his mouth tasted like the sole of a shoe, and his eyes had gone blurry during the later evening. The drink had flowed just a little too freely, and he had decided to walk it off before bed. He'd done half a circuit of the town, then come down to the water's edge for fresh sea air in the hope that it would clear his head and make sleep more likely. He was starting to feel better all the time, yet the moment he stopped, he could still feel the alcohol coursing through him. He felt odd. Bolder perhaps than usual.

Straightening, he turned away from the water. The town was a mess, but then at least it was a *festival* mess, so that was all right. Recently the only towns Leif had seen had been left as charred ruins, so a little lively mess was a vast improvement.

He smiled as he walked through the town, and not only because of the sense of relief and closure he felt at their success and reward, but also at the various figures he saw lying at the side of the street as he went. For months when he'd spotted such figures, they'd had their bellies slit open or their heads caved in, or were black and burned. Here, they were snoring and clutching jugs of ale as though they were loved ones.

He passed the church and the burned-out house nearby, and that gave him just a moment of dour recall, but once the sight was behind him, his mood improved again almost immediately. Alcohol did that for Leif – made him easy prey for emotion, but also reduced his attention, so that he changed fast. His head was clearing a little, and his eyes. He still felt hazy, but in a good way, now. The farm appeared ahead as he passed the outskirts of the town, the sprawling agricultural complex lying not far from the site of today's Thing. The buildings were all dark, now, and there was no activity. Almost everyone was abed by this time. He wondered idly whether Bjorn had given up his pointless search for flesh and beer and gone home while Leif had been wandering around town.

As he rounded the corner of the barn, heading for the door, he was surprised, and a little concerned, to find Orm Axebiter standing in the dark, silent, watching. He frowned. The man spotted him, nodded a greeting, said nothing. Leif returned the nod, nothing more. If Axebiter was here, then the new king of Norway was almost certainly here too. Leif braced himself and pushed open the barn door.

The locals had done an excellent job of dividing up the great space with wicker screens and hangings. A separate room on the left had been put aside for Halfdan, being a jarl, and another room had been portioned off on the right, for the women. The rest was one large open common room, with a passage leading to it from the door, between the other two rooms.

He could hear Halfdan snoring gently on his left, though only just, over the louder snores from ahead. But it was from the right-hand side that the sounds were *interesting*. Conversation. Leif screwed his eyes tight. That was not good. If Harðráði was here, in Gunnhild's room, realistically there could be only one reason. He thought for a moment of Ellisif, somewhere back across town, lying alone, probably well aware of where her husband was. The beautiful princess of Kiev, and now queen of Norway, deserved more than that.

The voices stopped for a time, and Leif winced again, wondering what that meant. Then, quietly, they resumed, low murmurs that he couldn't quite make out, even with only a curtain for a door. He wrestled with himself, then. He was a master of etiquette, from the days of his service in Constantinopolis at the Byzantine court, and he knew it was not done to disturb a lady in her bedchamber. Moreover, it was simply *unheard of* to interrupt a monarch, unless you were part of his retinue or staff, or perhaps involved in saving his life. Despite that, Leif found himself at the curtain door a moment later, rapping on the wattle wall beside it. The silence seemed to loom, then, deeper, more meaningful. Then Anna appeared, pulling aside the curtain.

Good. Anna. At least nothing too untoward would be going on if the couple were not alone in there.

'Leif? Why are you up?' she said with a frown.

'I might say the same.' Leif smiled.

'Yes, but *I* did not drink myself into insensibility, and have already had half a night's sleep. You, on the other hand, look like you've drunk a taverna dry. And you smell like... I just don't know. It's indescribable.'

'The king should not be in there,' Leif said very quietly.

Anna gave him a sharp look, then pushed him back and stepped out, letting the curtain fall behind her, as though it might do more than slightly muffle the sound.

'That's none of your business, Leif Ruriksson. None of mine, either, but Gunnhild woke me as a witness to make sure there was no funny business.'

'I honestly thought he'd mostly moved on to other prey, apart from a leer here and there. That Tora woman, for a start.

He could concentrate on her instead. Or maybe, and it's just a suggestion, his *wife*?'

'Ah yes, looking after the Rus princess again,' she replied with an edge of ice in her tone.

Leif sighed. 'For the last time, Anna, I have no interest in her other than feeling sorry for her. But you know as well as I that nothing good can come of what's happening in there.'

She seemed a little disarmed at this. 'Gunnhild knows what she's doing. And the two of them are going to have to work this out, if we are to stay in this place.'

'He needs a few truths handing to him,' Leif said. 'I thought Bishop Aage had done that the other day, but I suspect the man was too careful and polite to have made much of a dent. Harðráði doesn't always notice such things unless they are hammered home. Sometimes he needs to be slapped in the face with them.'

He stepped round Anna. She turned. 'Leif...'

But he was past her and lifting the drape out of the way to step into the room beyond.

Gunnhild sat cross-legged on a low mattress of straw and blankets, staff across her knees, fully dressed and with a serene expression. Harðráði sat opposite, on one of the two chairs in the room. He had his hands on his knees and a curiously conspiratorial expression on his face.

'Go to bed, Leif,' Gunnhild said quietly, and not unkindly. Harðráði just nodded.

'I'm afraid not. I watch you all dance carefully around this subject. Halfdan, you, the bishop, all of you. You amble around the matter without confronting the bare truth. Without making the *king* here confront the bare truth.'

'And what truth is that, then?' Harðráði said, tone cold as he turned to the new arrival. 'I know you for a clever man, Leif Ruriksson, and I'd have thought you cleverer than this.'

'Ignore him,' Anna said, stepping in beside Leif. 'He's still drunk from the festivities.'

There was an element of truth to that. He felt emboldened the way he probably wouldn't when completely sober. He was more content to step forth and confidently confront matters that he'd probably think twice about at other times. But the fact that it needed to be said remained, even if the reason he was saying it was a consequence of the drink.

'Think, king of Norway. You have a wife, and she is a Christian, the daughter of a powerful prince, and the niece of Onund of Sweden. Any dishonouring of her will endanger everything you have sought to gain. And though you now have half of Norway, it is still new, and your grip on it is fragile. You need to be *strengthening* your position right now, *consolidating* your hold on power.'

Harðráði's expression took on a hard edge.

'You are very lucky to be so valued. A less valued man might regret speaking thus.'

Leif snorted. '*Listen* to me. You are a good child of Christ. I know this. I know you believe. I know you walk with God, as does your nephew, and all your fellow monarchs across this world. Norway is Christian. All of it. There might be small pockets of paganism, including just on the other side of that wall, but you yourself have to be seen to be above such things, a model leader for your Christian populace. If you want to be king of a Christian nation, you simply *cannot* chase someone like Gunnhild. In the end, it will cost you your throne, and it may well cost her her life into the bargain.'

There was an uncomfortable silence, then, for this was plain truth, and there was little about it Harðráði could argue with... or so Leif thought.

'I think you overstate the case, Leif,' the man replied. 'Look at your Wolves of Odin. You have maintained a strong position in the fleet, achieved land and title here in Norway, you have the ear of a king and a powerful bishop, and all without most of you kneeling to the Lord. You would be surprised how readily people will look the other way when things are inconvenient, and if they are avid enough not to, it is often the case that a few silver coins can change a mind more readily than any sermon.'

Leif sighed. This was ridiculous. Harðráði could not have Gunnhild. They all knew it, but he simply would not let go. Leif breathed slowly. Perhaps, if he could not persuade the king that *he* could not have *her*, he could persuade Harðráði that *she* could not have *him*.

A thought occurred to Leif, then. He was astounded he'd never thought it before. Perhaps it was the drink giving him less tight control on his wandering imagination than he usually maintained. The idea had arisen as an excuse to use in this argument, but the more he thought about it, the more it seemed to be true.

He took two steps toward Harðráði and put his hands on his hips.

'All right, Harald Sigurdsson, king of Norway, if I cannot appeal to your own sense of security and logic, I must lay out the facts for you.' He thrust a finger back toward the room's other occupant.

'Gunnhild is no ordinary woman. Not even a *noblewoman*. She is *völva*. Have you any idea what that means? Have you ever met another völva? I have met *three* now, and I will tell you this: none of them had a man. And I have heard and even read of tales of the völvas of old, and neither did they. The goddess they worship, Freyja? She does not have a husband or consort. Perhaps it is not a rule. Perhaps Gunnhild here can take a lover. Perhaps she even will someday, but I tell you now, she will never take a husband.' He straightened. 'If she *could*, do you not think that *Halfdan* would be with her by now?'

A shocked silence descended suddenly.

Leif realised he was trembling. He stared in panic, now unsure whether it had been wise to voice the thought that had come to him. Damn the wine and beer that were still troubling his senses.

Harðráði was staring at him, and then slowly, pale-faced, he rose. He turned and bade Gunnhild a very formal goodnight, nodded at Leif and Anna, and then swept out. They heard him speak tersely to Orm Axebiter outside, and then the pair walked away.

Leif stood trembling, regret at having said such things flooding him. He hardly dared turn. He closed his eyes.

'How did you know?' a calm voice enquired.

He opened his eyes again and turned to Gunnhild. 'I only just realised, but the more I look back on things, the more it makes sense. I have Anna. Bjorn finds every warm bed he can, and Ketil and Ulfr find solace in such activity when we have time. But I have never seen Halfdan even *look* at another woman. Not even the queen of Georgia.'

'But he knows he cannot have me.'

Leif nodded.

Gunnhild rose slowly, leaning on her staff to do so. 'Upon a time, I *could* have been Harðráði's. I was not truly völva when we met in Miklagarðr, and the Norns had woven me a path with him. But I defied that. I walked away from him and chose the goddess, and now? Now I am völva, and will be no man's.' She sighed. 'Much as it might have been nice.'

'One day, Halfdan will find someone else.'

'I hope so, Leif. For now, I think you have done enough. For good or for ill, I suspect that is the last time the king of Norway will look at me so. You have put up an impenetrable barrier in the form of Halfdan. I think that even if Harðráði thought to fight him for me, he would shy away from such a challenge.' She frowned suddenly. 'Is Harðráði coming back?'

Leif blinked. 'I rather doubt it. Why?'

'Because I hear boots on hard ground.'

Leif felt a chill run through him. He turned to Anna. 'Stay here. Arm yourself.' Then he ducked under the drape and ran into the room, shaking each slumbering figure he found. 'Wake up. Wake up.'

'To arms!' he said, louder, as the Wolves stirred from sleep.

At that moment the door of the barn burst open, and men barrelled through it. Fortunately, the narrow approach limited their number, and they could come only two at a time. The front pair ran for Leif, swords bared, and behind them, two more entered. One of these second rank fell immediately as the pointed iron end of Gunnhild's staff tore through the drape and slammed into the man's temple, plunging deep into his brain before being pulled clear, allowing him to collapse to the floor, shaking wildly.

Leif readied himself, pulling free his axe and his sax as the two men ran toward him. He wished the others were up and ready. The Wolves were moving now, some up and about, rushing to grab weapons and get to the trouble, but no one would be in time to help immediately.

Leif knew he was not a born warrior. He had trained now, and had fought time and again with his friends, against terrible enemies. But he was not a *natural* soldier. He was a scholar, and a skald, who *happened* to be able to swing an axe.

Against two opponents simultaneously, he was in trouble. The two men, both with swords in hand, were already pulling them back and wide for a swing. The chances of parrying both blows were low. All he had to do, though, was buy sufficient time for the others to join in.

He was probably not a lot less surprised than the two attackers when he suddenly dropped to the ground. It was a last-moment decision, driven far more by desperate necessity and inebriated invention than tactics. But it worked. He hit the compacted earth and immediately rolled forward into the legs of the two men. With cries of dismay, they tumbled over him, collapsing to the ground themselves.

Leif prayed his friends were ready now, for he could do nothing more about those two men. The one behind them, whose companion had been felled by Gunnhild, was right in front of him now. The attacker swung down his sword in a massive chop, and Leif desperately rolled out of the way, the blade biting into the earth mere inches from him. Had Leif been a better warrior, he may well have been able to capitalise on that. Indeed, he had to admit in that moment that he might even have been able to do so had he not been still under the influence of the beer. Instead, he lay, stunned, for a moment. The man wrenched his sword free of the ground and stabbed down. Again, Leif rolled out of the way at the last moment, and the sword tip slammed into the dirt.

The Rus then swung with his axe, but he couldn't reach to get the man in the legs, and that sword came again a moment later, forcing him to roll to the side once more.

Again and again the sword came down, and Leif could do little more than react, rolling this way and that, away from the shining weapon as it repeatedly plunged toward him. Then, suddenly, by sheer chance, he found that he'd rolled close to his attacker, and took the opportunity. His hand came up and back down, sax held in it, slamming into the man's foot. The blade broke several small bones as it plunged through the soft leather boot, the wool sock, and the foot. Then it punched on through the sole and into the dirt, sliding deep until only the hilt stood free of the foot.

The man screamed, and the flurry of sword blows stopped.

Leif left the dagger in the foot and scrambled back, panting, away from his opponent, then realised he was backing toward the two men who'd tripped over him. He looked around sharply, and realised with some relief that Ketil and Ulfr were busy laying into them, and that they would in no way pose a danger to him.

He turned back, rising to a crouch. The next two men had met with disaster, for not only was Gunnhild stabbing out through her curtain and killing and maiming as she went, but now Halfdan had emerged from the doorway opposite, and was slashing and jabbing with his Alani blade.

Leif strode over to the man with the crippled foot. With a roar, he pulled back his axe and swung it. The man was still too busy hollering in agony at his foot to realise the danger he was in. He looked up at the last moment, too late, as the axe slammed into him. It bit into his unarmoured ribcage, smashing bones and cleaving the organs inside. He screamed again and fell away, and Leif lost his axe, torn from his hand as it remained lodged in his victim.

He panted and staggered, then reached down and pulled his sax free of the man's foot, which had torn horrifyingly as he fell. He leaned the other way, and tugged his axe free of the quivering body. Rising, he realised that all six men were down. Just in case, he lurched along that short corridor, nodding to Halfdan as he passed, blood running from the blades he held in both hands, and reached the barn door.

As he looked out, he ducked, by some unidentifiable instinct which saved his life. The six men were not alone, and one man remained, standing outside, beside the door. He'd not followed the others in, presumably once he realised the Wolves were not all asleep and vulnerable as they should have been, and that his friends had met disaster instead of finding easy victims.

The man grunted as he swung his blade, but thanks to Leif's low stance, it thrummed across above his head. In response, Leif slashed out, but the blow was wild and random, and the man easily jumped out of the way.

Leif pulled himself upright, and the man started to run, apparently deciding that his life was worth more than valour. Leif raced after him, but even within four footsteps it became clear that the Rus was never going to catch his prey, who was taller, more refreshed, and less crippled by drink.

His heart skipped as something thrummed past him, and then an arrow slammed into the running man's back. The attacker fell forward with a cry, a second arrow thumping into him even as he fell. A third slammed home into the prone body a moment later, and Leif turned, not at all surprised to see Ketil standing in the barn doorway, bow in hand, head turned slightly to allow him to sight along the arrow with his one remaining eye.

He glanced round and a few moments later, Ketil jogged past him at speed until he reached the body, which he then scooped up and threw over his shoulder, turning and running back with his prize. The man was draped, dead and limp, and Ketil favoured Leif with a slightly worrying grin as he ran back past him.

Heaving in a sigh of relief, the Rus followed the Icelander back into the barn, in time to see Ketil dump the body in with a pile of the other six. They had been very lucky, really, firstly that there had been anyone awake to warn the others, and secondly that the access had limited how many of them could get in at a time.

Seven. There were nine Wolves in the barn, for Ulfr, Farlof and Eygrímr and come from the ships to join them for the celebration. Seven men set to kill nine was perhaps a foolish number, but then they had clearly at this time of night, and after drunken revelry, expected the Wolves to be asleep and vulnerable. Had that been the case, they could have crept in, cut nine throats and been out in a matter of moments, with no one the wiser.

They had failed.

Halfdan and Ketil were now searching the bodies, going through their effects. Finally, the young jarl straightened.

'Had anyone asked me who might send assassins after us, I could only find one answer.'

Leif nodded. 'Hjalmvigi, yes. But he is *captive*.'

'He is far from alone. He still has at least one priest ally in Vik, and maybe more.'

'It need not be him,' Anna replied. 'Remember that we are not universally popular.'

Halfdan tossed a coin to her, a silver thing that gleamed as it spun. She caught it and looked down at it. 'So?'

'Swedish money. From the priest.'

Leif shook his head. 'The fleet came from Sigtun in the spring, Halfdan. There will be Swedish coins in *every* man's purse.'

'But how many men are carrying one of *these*?' Halfdan replied, repeating the gesture, tossing a coin over to Leif. The

Rus caught it, then opened his fist and looked at the contents. Another silver coin. An image of the Theotokos, the mother of God, hand raised with two fingers extended, looked back at him, a most Byzantine image if ever he saw one. He frowned, for as far as he knew, Hjalmvigi had returned from Kutaisi to the north, and had been nowhere near Constantinopolis. Then he turned the coin over, and realised he could not read the various legends on the other side. The coin was very reminiscent of Byzantine issues, but it wasn't one.

'This is *Georgian*.'

'Quite. And apart from ourselves, the only people in this town that I know were in Georgia are Sæbjôrn and his crew, who I can see no reason to want us dead, and Hjalmvigi. Indeed, Hjalmvigi, being the one who dined at the palace in our last days there, is the only one I can imagine walking away with their coins.'

'So this *was* Hjalmvigi's doing,' Leif mumbled. 'The man proves extremely dangerous, even disarmed and imprisoned. Do we hunt down his friends? Should we go and see the priest of Vik in his church?'

Halfdan shook his head. 'They are just tools of the false priest. Just blades he wields. When a man comes after you in the night, do you destroy the sword that strikes at you, or the fist that wields it?'

'Does that mean you've decided what to do about Hjalmvigi?'

Halfdan took a deep breath. 'I don't know how, as yet, but he has to die, and now. Let's go find him.'

Chapter 21

Halfdan approached the guards, anger boiling up in his chest, threatening to explode. Half a dozen of Harðráði's strongest and most trusted men guarded the wooden cage, which itself sat within a small, fenced compound on the edge of town and close to the steep slope of the Reindalsfjellet that rose to the east of Vik. The men there closed together, sealing the gap and preventing access as he neared. Halfdan's eyes narrowed dangerously as he came to a halt in front of them.

'Stand aside.'

'We have orders from the king. No one goes near.'

'The king *gave* him to me,' Halfdan snapped. 'He is *my* prisoner, not Harðráði's.'

'Orders are orders,' the guard said. 'You want to see him, you ask the king.'

Halfdan stood silent for a moment. He could argue, of course, and he rather felt like doing so, but unless he was willing to actually assault Harðráði's men, it seemed unlikely they were going to submit. In a way, that was good, he had to admit. If they wouldn't let *him* near Hjalmvigi, then no one else would get close. That being said, *someone* had. He turned to the others behind him, each of whom wore an expression similar to his own, angry and expectant. 'Find Harðráði. Bring him.'

Leif and Bjorn nodded, jogging off together to fetch the king, and Halfdan turned back to the men on guard.

'Who has seen the prisoner since you locked him up?'

The two men at the fore looked at one another, brows creased. One turned back to Halfdan, shrugging. 'No one, I think. I only came on guard two hours ago, and no one has been in since then, but there are standing orders not to let *anyone* near.'

'*Someone* has been in,' Halfdan replied, 'and I think I know who. Which of you has been here the longest?'

A tall man with receding hair and a scar across his cheek stepped forward. 'I missed much of the evening for this.'

'So who has been allowed near Hjalmvigi?'

'The prisoner has had no visitors,' the guard said, and just as Halfdan was about to argue angrily, the man frowned. 'Apart from his confessor.'

'The confessor... this is a priest, yes?'

'Yes.'

'The one from the church in the town?'

'Yes.'

Halfdan turned to the others. 'And there is the connection. The priest visits Hjalmvigi in prison and coins change hands. The coins then find their way into the purse of some local curs with no sense of honour, and murder is attempted. Even locked up, Hjalmvigi is dangerous.'

The guard frowned. 'Murder?'

'Not important right now. How is the prisoner?'

'In good spirits,' the guard said. 'Oddly, really.'

'That will be because he thinks we are dead. When this local priest came, there was an exchange, yes? Hjalmvigi gave him a purse?'

'I don't think so,' the guard replied. 'But the confessor came with food to keep the man going. Bread, cheese, mushrooms. We checked his basket in case he brought a weapon, but we let the rest in. We have orders to feed him after all, and keep him alive.'

'But you didn't check the basket when he left. And that was when it contained bread, cheese, mushrooms *and plenty of coin.*'

The guard had the sense to look embarrassed, and the jarl nodded slowly.

'What will you do with him?' Ketil asked.

Halfdan chewed his lip. 'I still have not decided. It needs to be slow, and meaningful. He puts such stock in his crosses, maybe we should nail him to one, like his precious White Christ.' He caught the dark, disapproving looks of the guards, but they didn't concern him too much. 'Or maybe it would be better to hang him from a tree like Odin, to see if he gains any wisdom?'

Ulfr chuckled darkly. 'Bit late for wisdom now.'

'Maybe it would just be better for all of us if you cut off his head and be done with it?' Ketil put in.

Halfdan continued to muse. There was a certain logic to that. The priest deserved the worst of deaths, but in some ways, was doing so bringing Halfdan down to his level? Was he really not better than that? Was he not able to mete out merciful deaths as well? It would look better as a jarl to give the priest a quick death, for all the lack of satisfaction it would bring.

'Offer him up to the gods,' Gunnhild said quietly.

Halfdan turned to her. 'What?'

'You heard me.'

'Yes,' Halfdan said, musing now on that idea. 'Hanging by the feet in a sacred grove. Drained of blood and offered to Odin. Perhaps that is the way, if there is any such sacred grove around Vik.'

'No,' said a new voice, and the jarl turned to see Harðráði, king of Norway, walking toward him, looking bleary and rubbing dishevelled hair, just awoken from his bed.

'What?'

'I draw the line there, Halfdan. I have kept my part in the bargain and given the priest to you, but I am trying to rule a Christian nation here. It will be difficult enough to bend laws to allow you and your people to live here as you do, and yet I am willing to do that, for I prize both your friendship and your support. I will even protect your right to make horse and other animal offerings in the old way, but sacrificing *people*, no matter

310

how corrupt they might be, is going too far. There will be no such pagan horrors in Norway. Kill him if you will. Kill him *slowly* if you really must, but not like that. Not a sacrifice.'

Halfdan paused then. Bjorn and Leif had returned, too, and Bjorn looked rather scathing over the matter, for he would be quite happy to bleed Hjalmvigi in a grove, but Leif's own expression matched the determination of Harðráði's. The Rus disapproved, and after what Leif had said that day at Hróarskelda about being given the same trust and support as the other Wolves, despite his religion, there was no way he could refuse that. Halfdan took a deep breath. 'Yes. Agreed. No sacrifice.' He turned to see Gunnhild with just one eyebrow arched. He would explain later, if necessary.

'You want to see him?' Harðráði asked, blinking and rubbing sleep from the corner of his eye as he pointed into the compound with the other hand.

Halfdan nodded, and so the king waved the guards aside and he and Halfdan, with the Wolves close behind, walked in through the gateway. The surrounding fence was just high enough to keep prying eyes away from the prisoner, and the cage was large enough only for two or three wolves or a single bear. Hjalmvigi sat cross-legged in the dark cage in his white robe once more, the bishop's regalia having been removed when he was incarcerated. He looked up as they approached, pale features and slightly hooked nose catching the faint moonlight. Halfdan felt a chill. The man did not look remotely worried, which came as more than a little surprising.

'Your little game failed,' Halfdan said, coming to a halt before the cage and addressing its occupant.

'Game?' Harðráði asked.

'Our friend here managed to retain the services of some local killers, and sent them to our house in the middle of the night. Fortunately some of our people were still awake, so the bastards did not get to kill us in our sleep as planned. Instead, they lie rotting in a pile outside the barn.'

Harðráði's eyes widened. 'How? No one was supposed to go near the prisoner.'

'The local priest did. Your guards let him in. There's your connection.'

The king frowned. 'Am I to expect another priest to accidentally burn down his house now?'

Halfdan shot him a look. 'I leave this one up to you. He broke your rules, after all. Deal with him as you see fit. Hjalmvigi, on the other hand...'

The priest rose to his feet now, in the cage, and took a couple of steps forward. 'You cheat death at every turn, heathen. But you cannot do so forever. Your hateful, sick, perverted world is gone, and you will follow it soon enough. And when *you* are gone, and I am free, I will make it my life's work to pull down every one of your obscene idols, to burn every grove you have ever desecrated with your devilish rites. I will plough up your "ship burials", and I will shatter your stones. I will hammer flat your precious bronzes and burn your decorated doors. There will be no more images of demons when a cross should hold sway. I will go to my rest only when I know that the word of Christ reigns supreme in the north, and that your offensive heresy is no more. Only ghosts will remember your gods, heathen.'

Halfdan was impressed, in a way. 'Bold words for a caged man looking at a falling blade.'

'You think I *fear* you?' Hjalmvigi spat. 'You think I worry about my fate? My fate is in God's hands, and God will not let me fall to the likes of you.'

'You are about to be sadly disappointed,' Halfdan answered quietly.

'I think not. I challenge you to Holmgång, heathen.'

Halfdan blinked in surprise, stepping back. 'What?'

'You heard me,' the priest spat. 'Holmgång.'

'On what grounds?' Harðráði put in, similarly surprised.

'This heathen accuses me of paying assassins to murder him. I say he lies. He has offended me and questioned my moral strength. To this, I say I demand justice. I demand Holmgång. Let him meet me on the green with three shields to defend his claim.'

Halfdan was shaking his head. 'That is ridiculous, priest. I could kill you five times with just my thumb before you lifted a sword. Unless you intend to find someone to stand for you? But I cannot see a soul in Vik stepping forward and facing me to save *your* sorry hide.'

'I need no second,' Hjalmvigi spat. 'God is my sword, and God my armour. He will protect me and guide my hand, and with His power, I will strike you down, pagan dog, and see you gutted and hollowed. There is no room in this world now for your magic and your demons.'

Halfdan turned to look at the king. Harðráði shrugged. 'The laws of Holmgång still stand in Norway, Halfdan. Any man can claim the right against any other. Refuse and you are a níðingr, shamed and honourless. There is little I can do. It is not my place to deny it.'

Halfdan breathed deep, stepping back. 'Then I accept the challenge, priest. Holmgång it is. At least it removes the difficult decision of your fate.'

'Then I shall set the Holmgång for three days' time,' Harðráði said, 'though after the usual custom. In Norway, a second is a requirement, so I shall select them myself. But Holmgång calls for the first wound. The first blood spilled on the ground wins the bout.'

'No,' said both Halfdan and Hjalmvigi at the same time.

'These are not the lawless days of death duels,' Harðráði replied. 'First blood is standard.'

'But death is an option if agreed by the fighters, yes?' Halfdan urged.

'Strictly speaking, yes.'

'Then to the death it is.'

Harðráði pondered on this for a moment, then finally nodded. 'Very well.' He turned to the guards. 'Hjalmvigi of

Uppsala will remain in his cage, in custody, until that time. He will be given two meals a day, and not physically damaged by anyone. Other than my guards or Halfdan's hirð, the priest will be allowed no visitors, and so there will be no opportunity for any underhanded business. The usual rules will apply.' The king straightened. 'This is my ruling.' Then he yawned. 'And now, if you don't mind, I'm going to sleep for a couple more hours.'

With that, Harðráði nodded at his men and turned to depart. 'No visitors for the prisoner other than those now present,' he reminded them as he walked away.

Moments later, Halfdan stood with the Wolves, watching the caged priest. The white-robed man seemed oddly predatory, perhaps *because* of the cage, and as he started to walk slowly back and forth inside, chanting one of his nailed god prayers, he reminded Halfdan very much of a caged wolf.

'I don't know what you plan, Hjalmvigi, and I don't know what's going on in your head, but I will kill you in Holmgång, and that I *promise* you.'

The priest made no reply, and did not even look at Halfdan, no interruption in his pacing and praying. After a pause, the jarl turned and walked back through the gateway in the fence, his friends gathering around him.

'What's he up to?' Ketil hissed.

'I don't know.'

'He'll not last ten breaths against you,' Bjorn added.

'No.' Halfdan turned to Gunnhild as they walked back toward the farm. 'Is it possible?'

'What?' she replied.

'You protected us from elves when we were in Georgia, to keep us safe from that plague that killed Yngvar in the end. Half the fleet fell to the sickness, but we were saved by your marks. Can the White Christ do the same? Hjalmvigi seems to think his god will save him. Can he paint crosses on his skin like runes of power?'

Gunnhild sucked on her teeth. 'I have not heard of such a thing. And I think if they could, then we would have seen it done during that time in Miklagarðr. But I do not know everything about their strange religion, so I cannot say for sure. And Hjalmvigi is a wily dog.'

'He actually seems to think he will beat me.'

They walked in silence for a while, then, all the way back to the farm. At the barn, the question of sentry duty was raised. There were only a few hours of darkness left, and there was precious little chance of a repeat of the earlier attack, with everyone so aware and Hjalmvigi under ever tighter guard, but there was no need to take extra risks. Besides, something about the air of confidence the priest exuded, even knowing he was outclassed and had agreed to his own death, made Halfdan feel edgy and uncertain. As such, he took the watch, knowing that sleep was unlikely anyway.

The barn had only the one entrance, and so he sat outside it on a tree stump, reasonably alert, glancing round from time to time, keeping an eye on every approach, ears pricked, listening. That latter was how he knew that Gunnhild too was awake. They had not been back long before he heard her voice, along with that of Anna, raised in that ancient song of discovery, and he knew she was consulting the goddess.

Perhaps half an hour later, he heard her approaching. She sat on one of the fallen logs from the recently felled tree, close to him.

'It is hard to hear the goddess here,' she said quietly.

'Oh?'

'This place rings endlessly with the bells of the White Christ, and they drown out the voices of the gods. But with effort, even here, Freyja still favours me.'

Halfdan turned, then, interested.

'I could not see the threads,' she said. 'Could not see them end, and so I cannot be certain of the outcome of your meeting. The nailed god's influence clouds the Norns' weaving so much, here. And what I *did* see confuses me. I am not at all sure how it fits together.'

'Tell me.'

'I saw two figures in a square.'

'Holmgång. Me and Hjalmvigi.'

She nodded. 'I presume so. Beyond that, though, I cannot be sure. I could not see the end, who fell, any more than I could see a thread cut short. But more than that, I could not work out who was who in that square. One figure I saw was a shieldmaiden, which confuses me, for even though Hjalmvigi may wear the womanish robe of the White Christ priest, I can find no reason to see him as a shieldmaiden. The same, of course, I say for you. You too are no shieldmaiden. The other figure in the square wears the bear shirt, which I find no less confusing than the shieldmaiden. Hjalmvigi is as far removed from the berserkir as any I can think of, and you have never shown such tendencies.'

Halfdan nodded. 'I cannot think to go berserk. I value my mind too much, and I cannot give over my thoughts to Thor, and allow him to control me. I need control of my own actions in *any* fight, let alone one as important as this.' He folded his arms. 'Is it possible that, in the same way as you cannot see the weaving of the Norns or hear the voice of the goddess because of the White Christ here, you also cannot see your casting properly?'

Gunnhild pulled a face. 'I had considered that, and I cannot discount the possibility entirely, but I do not think so. I could feel the Seiðr, and I could sense Freyja, even if I could not hear her. The image has relevance, I just do not know what it is. Perhaps its meaning will unfold in the coming days.'

'I am troubled by the priest's challenge, Gunnhild.'

'I can imagine.'

'If it were a desperate last-moment attempt by Hjalmvigi to at least have the smallest chance of survival, or at least to receive a good death and not a hard one, then I could see it and understand it. But he truly seems to think he will win, and the way he challenged me... I think he had already been planning to do so.'

316

'Perhaps the stakes are sufficient that he is willing to gamble,' Gunnhild noted. 'I do not know what the local laws of Holmgång are in Gotland, but I understand that here, in Norway, the winner can take all of the loser's possessions.'

Halfdan felt his stomach lurch at that. No such condition had ever been practised to his knowledge in Sweden, and no similar rule had been applied in Angle Land. It did not make Hjalmvigi any more likely to win the duel, but it did, as Gunnhild had said, perhaps make the gamble worthwhile. If, by some bizarre and unexpected twist of luck or fate, Hjalmvigi *did* manage to overcome and kill Halfdan, not only would he almost certainly walk away a free man, waiting to receive a reprieve from Rome through Magnus and become a bishop, but he would also inherit the best two ships in Norway, the title of jarl, a swathe of land with two villages, and enough gold to bury a man beneath. Hjalmvigi would inherit the *Wolves of Odin*.

He shivered.

'He will not win. He *cannot* win.'

'But regardless,' Gunnhild replied, 'I recommend you spend the next three days practising and preparing. Train with your sword, make sure your strength and your balance are up to the mark, limit your ale, and eat well. Be ready.'

Halfdan nodded. 'And while I do that, you do what you can to learn more of what is coming. Perhaps there is more to discover?'

She nodded, and, laying a soothing hand on his arm for a moment, she turned and walked away, back inside the barn. He looked down at that arm for a moment, as the flesh tingled where she had touched it, and then sighed, and checked the approaches again before settling down to wait out his watch.

Chapter 22

The day had dawned cold but bright, with high, light cloud patched intermittently across the blue, contrasting against hills of green and yellow, the leaves now turning with the autumn weather.

The Wolves had been up since dawn. The *whole of Vik* had been up since dawn, of course, for word of such momentous events spread rapidly in a place like this, and every last man or woman in the valley, be they sailor in the fleets or resident of the town, wanted a good view of the action.

For three days now, the Wolves had remained at the farm, with Halfdan training daily, keeping up his strength with good meals and clear mountain water, making sure his sword edge was as sharp as ever, his skills even sharper. Leif couldn't be much help in the training, and so, while Ketil and Bjorn had sparred with their jarl, the Rus had set about creating a regime of exercise and good solid food and drink, making sure Halfdan was abed in good time and up sharp in the mornings.

On the surface of things, it seemed ridiculous, really, a trained warrior as accomplished as Halfdan facing a priest, whose weapon of choice was spite and self-importance. But there had to be more to it than that. Hjalmvigi was confident, which was a worry, and which suggested that a surprise was coming, and so Halfdan could hardly rely on simply being better. He had to be ready for anything.

Of course, when Leif thought back over the years, it had occurred to him that maybe Hjalmvigi was not as weak and unprepared as most would think. The Rus had a distinct memory of the priest in the woods of Sasireti, soaked in blood and screaming outrage as he waded across the battlefield, sword and cross in hand. Although there he had been in comparatively slight danger, really, with Yngvar and his men around to protect him. But still, it proved that Hjalmvigi at least knew which end of a sword to hold.

'What are you doing here?' Ulfr barked suddenly, turning from the fire he'd been feeding close to the Rus and his cook pots.

Leif looked up from his work, past the shipwright, to see an unexpected figure in the middle distance. The local priest from the church in Vik was hovering at the edge of the farm's yard. Roused by the shout, Ketil and Bjorn jumped to their feet from the log on which they'd been sitting and waiting to break their fast, and pounded off toward the priest, who turned, face paling, and ran.

Leif frowned after the receding figure. In the aftermath of the night attack, Harðráði had decided to deal with the priest, as Halfdan had suggested, but Magnus had stepped in with an objection. There had been three priests in Vik, he pointed out, but one had mysteriously burned to death in his house, and another was now in a wooden cage, waiting to fight a jarl to the death. If the kings executed or imprisoned the third man, who would tend the church and its flock? And so, for now at least, the priest had escaped punishment. Why he would choose to come to the Wolves' barn was a mystery, but it was one they were currently unlikely to solve, since the man had run away immediately.

Leif returned to his stirring in the smaller of the two iron cauldrons that hung, bubbling, over the fire, finishing preparing dagmal, the first meal of the day. The previous night's lamb stew had left little in the pot, for Bjorn's appetite was as enormous as the rest of him, and so Leif had needed to cook up some extras to add to the reheated meal. Even then there was little more than a single large portion left, and so he had set that meaty one aside for Halfdan, while cooking up a new fish stew for the others. It seemed only right, with Halfdan needing more energy and strength than the others in the coming hours.

Across the open ground, Halfdan finished whetting his blade and then wiped it down and sheathed it, just as Leif tipped a sizeable portion out into a wooden bowl for him, then passed it over. The jarl tucked in hungrily as the Rus put aside the small, empty cauldron and returned to stirring the larger one, the pungent aroma of boiled herring rising from it.

'Where is it to be held?' he asked, as he stirred.

Between mouthfuls, Halfdan answered. 'Harðráði wants it to be visible to all, so he's had one of the jetties cleared of ships and the ground marked out there.'

'Good job you're not wearing armour,' Anna said. 'One wrong step and you'd be in the sea and sinking.'

Ketil frowned at her. 'If he steps out of the marked ground he loses anyway. He'd be níðingr. If a man should step out of Holmgång, it would be better to drown than to live with the shame.'

'Sorry, I didn't know,' Anna said. 'I've only ever seen the one Halfdan fought in Swaledale, and no one explained the rules to me.'

Halfdan shrugged. 'They vary from place to place, but always there is a boundary outside which you cannot step.'

Leif gestured to Ulfr, who carried across a stack of wooden bowls, and the Rus began to ladle the fish stew out into them, then filled his own at the last and wandered over to take a seat beside Bjorn.

'Will they restrict weapons, do you think?' Ketil mused. 'Axes are better for shattering shields, after all.'

Halfdan shook his head. 'I made it clear to Harðráði that I would be using my sword. In a way it's a shame. The image of Hjalmvigi, with his reedy arms, trying to lift and swing a Dane axe I find quite humorous. But no. I think we shall both use swords.'

'Then you'd best get planning.' Ketil grinned. 'The priest will use a big boy sword, not your little darning needle.'

Halfdan chuckled. 'I am not worried about Hjalmvigi's weapon, or his skill in using it. I should outclass both. I am worried about what we *cannot* see. What trick the priest has planned that is giving him such confidence.'

At this they all nodded, Leif more than most. It was a question that had been vexing him. Hjalmvigi was sealed in a cage. He might have had access to his fellow priest before, when he paid the mercenary killers, but since then that avenue had closed. The only people to see the priest at all were his jailers. And they knew he had nothing in his cage other than the clothes he wore, a shit-bucket, and periodically a wooden bowl with his food in it. He could not get out, no one could get in, he had nothing secreted about him, and had access to nothing. He would leave his cage for the first time in about an hour, when he was to be brought to the jetty for the fight. And then what could he do? He would be surrounded by enemies, in full view. All he would be given were the weapon and shields for the Holmgång, and then surely it would be too late for tricks.

Just to be sure, Leif had checked in daily with the guards, to make sure there had been no visitors, and every time Hjalmvigi was fed, they search both him and his cage.

Could it possibly be that the priest was so utterly deluded with regard to his piety and self-worth that he actually believed that God would protect him?

Leif shivered. Frankly, despite his faith, Leif would be prepared to put more stock in Gunnhild's magic runes than hoping the divine would sweep down and shield him in a fight. The Rus was a Christian, but he was not an idiot.

He continued to fret over the subject for the following half hour, while they finished eating, and then he and Anna took the bowls and spoons over to the stream that ran by the farm and washed them all. He continued to fret as they gathered everything they valued and prepared to move back across town.

Nothing was left at the barn. All the Wolves would need to watch, for it was the time of their jarl's revenge, and so no one could be spared to watch their kit. Everything went with them.

He continued to fret as they started to walk through Vik, into the sprawl of houses, past the burned building by the church, through the wide square where they had feasted on their first night here. He began to fret on the matter even more as the bell began to toll, calling all to attend the Holmgång.

It was as he was approaching the harbour, where the crowds were already gathering, that Leif began to worry about something else. He didn't feel quite right. Couldn't quite put his finger on it. A little bit sick, but only a little. And with a fluffy head, as though he'd been drinking, which he hadn't. He was shivering. A little cold. And all this had come on as he walked through the town, as though he'd passed through an invisible barrier and into something awful. He nudged Bjorn beside him.

'Are you feeling all right?'

Bjorn slowed, clenched his fists, and let out a fart of such volume that it echoed from house wall to house wall, ending with a sort of wet sound.

'Better now.' The big man grinned.

'No, honestly. I don't feel well. I wondered if it was the fish, since we bought it in town and didn't catch it ourselves.'

Bjorn shrugged. 'Nothing wrong with me.' He turned and tapped Ketil. 'You got the shits or anything, Icelander?'

Ketil shook his head, brow furrowed at the strange question.

Leif sighed and kept walking. He still didn't feel right. If anything it was getting just a little worse. Was he ill? Had he caught something?

'Are you all right?' Anna said, next to him.

'I don't know. I don't feel quite right.'

'Probably nerves,' she said. 'I'm a bit twitchy myself.'

He nodded, leaving it at that, as they came to the waterfront. The crowd had made way for Halfdan, who led them, wearing just a shirt and trousers, boots and a belt. He had his sword in his hand, unsheathed, ready.

322

Leif felt the tension rise again. Ahead, the rightmost of the three jetties had been cleared of ships and laid out ready for Holmgång. It was just wide enough to accommodate the bull-hides that stretched in a square, each side half as long again as a man was tall. Outside the hides, three concentric squares of rope had been pegged a foot from the timbers and a foot apart, marking the three lines which would warn a man he was about to step outside the given area and forfeit. Of course, the ropes were only really of value on one side, since the others meant a six-foot fall into cold seawater. Two of Harðráði's men stood at the near end of the jetty, preventing anyone passing, while two more stood at the edge of the roped square: the seconds who would pass the shields to the fighters when required.

The people of Vik were gathered as best they could all along the seafront and on walls, in house windows, wherever they could get even a poor view of the jetty and the action thereupon. The men of the fleet were doing the same, from the decks of their ships, and Leif had not seen so many vessels pulled into one small area of water since the day Yngvar's fleet had assembled at Kiev for his expedition. The nearest places in the water were given to the ships with a vested interest, of course, and so *Sea Wolf* and *Sea Dragon*, both crammed with the Wolves, joined the flagships of Magnus and Harðráði, bobbing gently, motionless otherwise, just twenty paces from the ropes on the jetty.

Leif had talked to the lendrmaðr of Vik about the coming fight. It seemed Holmgång was becoming something of a rarity in Norway these days. Half the matters that would once have called for a square of ox hide were now settled with words, mediated by the courts of either crown or Church. Bodvar Biarnisson was a man of fifty-two summers, and he could not remember Holmgång taking place in Vik since childhood. Ahead, Halfdan spoke to Orm Axebiter, who was close to the jetty's end, representing Harðráði should he be needed. Leif waited for him to finish, and then pushed between the others to speak to the jarl.

323

'If you spot anything out of the ordinary, if you suspect anything untoward, hold off the duel and step back down the jetty. I don't trust Hjalmvigi, and if we cannot be there with you, you need to be alert and ready.'

Halfdan nodded, seeming not to be paying him much real attention. Leif put it down to nerves, and stepped back, leaving his jarl.

Halfdan walked down the jetty, and as he did, Leif's eyes narrowed in suspicion. There was something off about Halfdan's step. Only slightly, and no one else seemed to have noticed. His fretting came back aplenty, then. Unfortunately, he was given precious little time to do anything about it as, a moment later, the crowd began to roar. For a while, Leif could not decide whether the sound was one of approval or hatred, but as Hjalmvigi was led closer to the jetty by a rope that bound his hands, it became clear that the crowd was booing. The people of Vik might be Christian, but a priest who sent assassins in the night was something they could not countenance. After all, if a priest would dare do such a thing to a jarl, what might he do to ordinary folk he took against?

By now, Halfdan had reached the far end of the jetty and was standing beside his second and the pile of three shields that lay just inside the outermost rope. Hjalmvigi was roughly pulled and dragged to the jetty, and there Orm Axebiter removed the looped rope from around his wrists. The priest rubbed his hands and arms vigorously, then rolled his shoulders and his neck, working out the stiffness from his confinement.

Axebiter gave the priest no options, holding out a straight, basic sword of war, which the priest took. His arms dipped a moment with the weight, sending a wave of laughter through the watching crowd, but he soon recovered and lifted it.

'With this,' he said, loudly, though apparently addressing the sky as he looked up, 'I will vanquish heresy and demons, and bring the light of God into even the darkest of places. Let heathen blood wash away the past and make way for the righteous.'

He lowered the sword. A strange silence descended, broken a moment later as Bjorn shouted, 'Up your arse, pillow-biting fuck-badger.'

Leif wasn't even really sure whether the sentence made any sense, but he just couldn't help laughing, as did half the assembled crowd. Hjalmvigi glared daggers at Bjorn and the rest of them, and then, at a gesture from Orm Axebiter, began to stride down the jetty toward his opponent.

'Maybe we should make good use of the holm,' Bjorn announced, looking over at Orm. 'When Halfdan butchers the priest, you and I could resume *our* contest.'

'Any time,' Axebiter replied easily, then turned away.

A roar from the crowd drew Leif's attention once more, and he turned to the end of the jetty to see Halfdan down on one knee. He rose unsteadily, with the help of his second, but then settled into a reasonable stance.

'What happened?'

Gunnhild was frowning now. 'He almost fell from the jetty. Something is wrong.'

Hjalmvigi reached the rope, and took his place by the other pile of shields. Harðráði started to speak then, announcing the reason for the duel, making sure to highlight the perfidy and wickedness of the priest and the affronted honour of the jarl. After all, he himself had sponsored Jarl Halfdan. He had to back up his decisions, or look like a fool with poor judgement. How much he must be feeling the nerves, Leif thought, given that Halfdan had just almost fallen in the sea before they started.

There was a hum of background noise all across the harbour, the low murmuring of people, the creak of wood, the lap of waves, the cries of birds and, over all that, the voice of King Harald the Third of Norway, reciting the rules of Holmgång to all who were not aware. Next to Leif, Anna was listening intently, taking it all in, unaware that anything was wrong. In fact, only Leif and Gunnhild seemed to realise that. And Halfdan, presumably. And probably Hjalmvigi...

'How do you feel?' he asked Gunnhild.

'Fine. A little nervous perhaps.'

'I feel ill. Not at all right. I... I can't describe it. But I think it's affecting Halfdan too. I don't know what it can be. No one could have got to us, surely. And we both ate different meals this morning. So what could have happened?'

It was baffling. He spun, and almost fell, his brain whirling wildly, eyes blurring. Was this what had just hit Halfdan and almost sent him into the sea? If it was, then there was little chance of the jarl surviving what was about to happen. Leif could hardly imagine lifting an axe right now, let alone fighting with it.

'I fer... I angaboo... I...' He didn't seem to be able to find the words. 'I?'

He staggered again, then.

Panic was gripping him. He forced a little focus into his eyes and peered down the jetty, just in time to hear some great shout from Harðráði and to see Halfdan and Hjalmvigi both step across the ropes into the square of battle.

Shit. It had started.

Halfdan was swaying, like a narrow tree in a high wind. He lifted his sword and his axe, shook his head a couple of times, and then stepped unexpectedly sideways, dangerously close to leaving the rope.

'We haf supput,' Leif managed, grabbing Gunnhild desperately.

'What?'

'Supput. *Supput!*' He straightened, pushed every ounce of control into his mouth, and tried again. 'Stop it.'

'We *cannot* stop it. It is Holmgång.'

'Gunnhi... Ee bee pussun.'

'What?'

'Pussun! Poisoned!'

The völva stared at him wide-eyed. 'Poison?'

She grabbed him and half walked, half dragged the Rus over to Orm Axebiter.

'Let us past.'

The man shook his head. 'This is Holmgång. Sacred law of the ancestors. No one approaches.'

'*They* fucking do,' shouted Bjorn, as he landed a punch right in the middle of Orm's face, the blow coming unseen and unexpected.

'That felt good.' The big man grinned as he stood over Axebiter, who was quickly recovering. By the time he was coming to his feet, though, Gunnhild and Leif were barrelling down the jetty toward the duel, other Wolves right behind them. Shouts were going up all around the fleet and harbour now at the unexpected interruption.

Leif blinked, forced his eyes to open. His gaze fell on Hjalmvigi, and he felt a sudden and irresistible urge to stick a sax in the man's head and see if he could scrape out the contents.

Somewhere inside the strange haze that seemed to have settled into his head, a thought began to grow in Leif Ruriksson. He turned. He could see Bjorn following them now, Axebiter, angry and with a bloody nose right behind him. Beside Leif, though, even as he stumbled on, was Gunnhild.

'When you... doatoodo.'

He took a breath, steadying himself. 'When you do... what you do... with the goddess. How doesitfeel?'

'I don't understand.'

He concentrated. He *needed* her to understand. 'Do you *imagine* things. *See* things. Is the world blurry? A funny colour. Do you feel cold? Even a bit sick?'

'Sometimes. A little. Why?'

'I feel like that. I feel weird. I think it's a berserk thing. And I think that's what Halfend... Halfdan... is going grue. Through. Going through.'

Gunnhild's eyes widened. 'How did he get the powder.'

'Not pder.' Leif heaved in a breath. 'Shrooms? You told me about shrooms from völva's hut. This time shrooms.'

'The fungus from Kaupang. But how?'

Leif winced. It was getting quite hard to concentrate and talk. He started to flail and use his hands to accompany his words. He wanted to explain. He'd worked it out, at last, but now he couldn't tell her.

That was why Hjalmvigi was so confident. He didn't need to be a great warrior to beat Halfdan. Right now a *six-year-old child* could probably beat Halfdan. The priest from the village, when he took Hjalmvigi's coins for the mercenaries, had also brought him food. Among the things the guards said he had in the basket, were mushrooms. That same priest had been hovering at the edge of their camp this morning as Leif cooked the food. No one else was suffering because they had all had fish stew, made fresh by Leif. But when he'd warmed up Halfdan's lamb stew, he'd supplemented it with vegetables and mushrooms to bulk it out. And, of course, he'd touched the mushrooms plenty while cooking. That was why only he and Halfdan were feeling it. If the jarl felt anything like Leif, he'd be useless in the fight. And Halfdan had eaten chunks of it, rather than just sucking fingers covered in it.

He suddenly realised that, though his subconscious was piecing together puzzles and solving problems, what his mouth appeared to be doing was flapping around and making unintelligible sounds as his arms windmilled pointlessly.

He spun, which was not a good idea, for he felt quite dizzy, and dropped to his knees, throwing up quite copiously onto the boards. As he gagged and choked, a seemingly endless torrent of stuff rising up from his gut to pour onto the jetty, and down between the planks into the water below, he managed to raise his head.

Even defocused as he was, he could see there was trouble. Halfdan was crouched, using both knees and a hand as a tripod to stop him falling prone, the other hand holding up one of the three shields that was already little more than a few pieces of splintered board, loosely held together by a dented boss

328

and some straggly rawhide, as Hjalmvigi of Uppsala, God's representative in the north, officially, hammered down at the shield again and again with his heavy, long sword. Halfdan was done for. He didn't even have his sword any more. He was just crouched in disappearing shelter, waiting to die.

Then, for some reason, the fight came to Leif of Kiev, too. Someone was pulling at him, pushing, shoving. He tried to fight back, but neither his body nor his brain seemed to be functioning properly. Something was in his face then, fighting, pulling at his nose, his jaw. All he could taste was vomit. Something was crammed into his mouth.

He heaved. Tried to spit. He was choking. This was appalling. He was going to suffocate. Who was torturing him? What was going on?

'For fuck's sake, swallow,' came an irritated voice, and such was the suddenness and the command in the tone that Leif did just that without actually intending to. He swallowed. Then he fell. Things went black.

—

He woke.

He felt very strange. His body was trembling gently. He felt very cold. But he didn't feel sick. Oddly, he felt hungry. And as he thought this, he realised with some surprise that he *could* think. His mind seemed to be his again, although it was still a little fuzzy, and he had a seven-drum hangover going on.

'I… am I all right?' he managed.

'Thought we'd lost you for a while, there.' Bjorn grinned. 'But you're back. Now I owe Ketil two jars of wine.'

'Thank you for your confidence,' Leif replied bitterly, as he tried to sit up.

Gunnhild was there, then, grabbing him just as his strength failed and he fell back, and lowering him to the ground. 'You are weak. It will take time for the rest of the poison to work its way out of your system. You were very lucky, I think, in that

329

you threw most of it back up. That may have saved you. The rest is down to this.'

The völva held up a jar, and Leif focused on it, brow crumpling.

'What is that?'

'An anti-poison. When you described what was happening, as though it were what I take to walk with Freyja, and what Bjorn takes to rage with Thor, I suddenly realised. It was the fungus. The one that is used to make the compound. That is why it felt a little like the Freyja-song or the bear-shirt battle madness to you. And the fact that Halfdan was suffering too… well I had seen in a vision the berserkr within the ropes. Halfdan would not wear the bear shirt by choice, but he had it thrown over him.'

'How is he?'

She ignored the question. 'Once I knew it was the fungus, presumably brought by the priest, I remembered the völva's hut in Kaupang. There was a warning of what to do if you used too much fungus. Ridiculously, it was Bjorn here who drew it to my attention. He may well have saved your life. Incidentally, I also realised why the other combatant, Hjalmvigi, was a shieldmaiden in my vision. Hjalmvigi is Borghild, using a feast to poison Sinfjötli.'

'How is Halfdan.'

Her face took on a troubled aspect, then.

'He's not good. He ingested a lot more than you, and it worked on him for longer. He's alive. Fortunately we managed to call a halt to the Holmgång just as Hjalmvigi was about to gut him. Now, the priest is back in his cage for the night. If Halfdan makes it 'til morning, he should recover well. Then the fight can be recalled. If not, then Hjalmvigi wins, officially, though I doubt the two kings will consider it a win.'

'If he does *not* last the night, the last thing Hjalmvigi will have to worry about is kings,' Leif replied, darkly.

He turned his head, and for the first time, saw Halfdan lying across the room, groaning and rolling around in sweaty blankets.

330

'Hjalmvigi's plot is foiled,' Gunnhild said. 'Undone. The only question is whether it was foiled in time.'

'No wonder the bastard was confident,' Leif growled. 'In what kind of a world do we go around telling people that Christ is the way, and that the Church is the future, bringer of light in the darkness, when its bishops slink around the place poisoning good men?'

He tried to sit up again, but failed. A little bracing, and preparing, and the third time, he managed to get upright. Taking a deep breath, he turned sideways.

'What do you think you're doing?' Gunnhild snorted.

'What has to be done.'

'You can't walk, Leif Ruriksson.'

'Watch me.'

'If Anna knows you're out and doing things, she will be furious. She will talk at you for weeks. At me too.'

'Let her.' Leif turned to the other side and waved to a big figure. 'Bjorn!'

'Yes?' the albino answered, walking slowly across to the table on which the Rus lay.

'I seem to be a little weak. I might need your help.'

Bjorn shrugged, and started picking Leif up, before he waved the effort aside. 'No, not in *carrying* me. Come with me.'

He slid from the table, letting his feet land on the ground, then slowly pushed himself upright. He wobbled. Tottered. Almost fell. But Bjorn grabbed his shoulder and steadied him. 'What now?'

'Come with me,' Leif said again, and began to walk.

It was a slow and troublesome journey. He could do maybe six or seven steps before he staggered and Bjorn had to grab him and put him right, but slowly and surely they made their way out of the house that had been given over to them for the night and into the street outside. Steadying himself, then, Leif looked for the landmark he sought, and, spotting it over the roofs, started moving again. The two of them moved through quiet streets. It was, by the look of the light, late afternoon, heading into evening. He must have been unconscious for the better part of a day.

Through the town the pair walked, until finally they came to their destination. Leif looked up at the church. It was a simple, wooden affair. Not one of the grander examples he had seen, with just a small wooden belfry at the end, and half a dozen windows to each side, beneath the eaves. A light glowed within. Of course it did. The house the priests of Vik used had burned, with the man's friend in it. And the priest was not the most popular man in the town now. He had already been despised for days, once it had become public knowledge that he had been part of an attempt to assassinate a jarl and his people. Then, when it also came out that he had further compounded matters by trying to *poison* that jarl, the remaining tattered shreds of his reputation faded away. The people of Vik would not have him. He couldn't get to Hjalmvigi now. Harðráði was already prepared to kill the man for his crimes, and now Magnus would not protect him, probably. The priest had nowhere to go but his church, no one to plead to but God.

Approaching the doors, Leif gestured to them, and Bjorn walked forward and pulled them open. As it happened, they were locked, though that did little to stop the big albino, and the doors simply exploded outwards as he pulled one from its hinges.

Leif might have laughed another time at the sight of the priest, kneeling at the altar at the far end of the church, almost leaping out of his skin in fright. The man was on his feet a moment later, backing away against the altar, eyes wide, face pale.

'This is a house of God,' the priest said, somewhere between defiance and desperation.

'Not *my* fucking god,' Bjorn grunted.

'God looks *away* from this place,' Leif growled in reply. 'For the priests here have turned their back on *him*.'

'I am under the protection of King Magnus,' the man breathed.

'I doubt that is now the case. If it is, I will pay mangæld to him for what is about to happen.'

'What...' the priest began, licking his lips nervously, '*is* about to happen?'

'I am going to ask my big friend here to get creative.' Leif turned to Bjorn. 'He's all yours. I just want something recognisable left at the end.'

The albino grinned at him, as though Leif had given him a birthday gift.

Leif habitually looked away when Bjorn was at his most inventive, and especially when the big man's victim might be a Christian. Not this day. He watched as Bjorn grabbed the man and pushed him face down over his own altar. Then the albino turned him over so that the man was leaning very painfully backward over the edge. The priest tried to fight him off, then, and received a punch in the face for his efforts, which sent him reeling. Leif was impressed that Bjorn had pulled his punch sufficiently to simply stun the man and not knock him out. He watched as Bjorn slammed a hand onto the man's bloodied forehead, while his other one fumbled at his belt.

'God will curse you,' the man coughed through blood.

'Good,' Bjorn growled. 'Let him.' Then he made two swift moves. His left hand reached into the mouth and grabbed the wagging tongue, while his right brought up a sharp sax and snicked it straight through the organ. As the priest gave a gurgling scream, hands going to his face, Bjorn looked at the severed tongue, and then, in a move that further impressed the Rus, used the bloody end to mark a design on his own white forehead. A bloody valknut, Odin's sign.

The priest had collapsed into a sobbing wreck by the time Bjorn came back to him. The big man systematically started to break the joints in the man's arms and legs, then, until all they were left with was a torso, topped by a crimson mess coughing

333

and gagging, sprouting misshapen, spindly limbs like a crane fly's, with shards of bone jutting from the skin here and there.

Finally, Bjorn seemed satisfied.

'For the fire you helped set to burn my friends,' Leif said quietly. 'For the assassins you hired to butcher them in their sleep. For the poison fungus you slipped into our gear to ruin our jarl, this is retribution.'

He turned. He was starting to feel stronger, steadier. He was content that he could walk safely now. He was recovering rapidly. He turned to Bjorn. 'Please, deliver the priest to Hjalmvigi. Do not let the guards stop you. Leave them together to chat. I'll see you back at the house.'

Bjorn gave him a nasty grin, and then turned and reached down, grasping what was left of the priest and none-too-carefully throwing it over his shoulder.

Leif left him to it, content that Bjorn would achieve his task easily enough. Face set in a satisfied grimace, he wandered back through the streets of Vik as the sun disappeared finally behind the hills, and soon, he came back to the house.

He opened the door, waved aside Ketil, who leapt up to their defence, and walked inside. Across the room, Halfdan slowly, gently, lifted his head from the table on which he lay.

'Where have you been? I'm hungry.'

Chapter 23

Halfdan straightened. 'I think I'm ready.'

Gunnhild's eyebrow peaked as she eyed him. 'What *you* think is of lesser importance. I think you need another day, maybe two.'

'I am holding down food and drink. I can walk. I don't feel bad. Just a little weak and shaky.'

'And in two days that will go, too.'

'It's an honour thing, Gunnhild. The laws here state that Holmgång should take place no less than three days following the challenge, but no more than seven. It has been six days now. Three of training, then three of recovery. I'm out of time.'

'Such rules are pointless now,' Gunnhild said. 'Once poison had been used, and its culprit identified, the fight was called off, and no one will expect it to resume until you are back to good health.'

'Nevertheless, the rules…'

'No longer apply, Halfdan. Neither king will hold you to them now.'

Halfdan fixed her with one of few looks he knew she would not dismiss out of hand. 'You *know* Hjalmvigi. The man is a serpent. He will find a way out – he always does – and every time he worms his way from trouble, he comes back stronger, more powerful. I cannot allow that to happen again. If I do not adhere to every rule, I give him an excuse. I give him something he can use to get out of the fight. Right now, he's made a fatal miscalculation. He thought I would die from the poison. That he would kill me that first day. He would never have to face me properly, so the whole Holmgång thing was unimportant to him. Unfortunately for him, I am still alive, and now he is trapped in this duel. I cannot – *will* not – allow him any chance of getting out of it.'

She stopped for a moment, watching him carefully. 'You are not at your strongest. And, as you said, Hjalmvigi is a serpent. There may still be a way he can trick you. Are you sure about this?'

'I need to end this. I cannot sleep another night with that creature, that draugr, walking the world. You've not *seen* anything?'

She shook her head, but he noticed that there was a strangely evasive look to her face.

'What is it?'

Gunnhild sighed, leaned against the wall and folded her arms. 'Hjalmvigi does not die today.'

'What?'

'I cannot see *beyond* today, but his thread goes on for now. Unless you can keep the Holmgång going on into the morning, you will not kill him today.'

'Yes I will.'

'No, you won't.'

He stared at her. She was wrong. She *had* to be. He was going to fight, and to kill the priest. He turned away.

'I advise against it. That is all I will say,' she called after him as he started to walk.

He nodded. 'Noted.'

He had to do this, and do it now. And she did not sound as sure as she usually did. If she was convinced she had the right of it, she would have been far more forceful, but in this place of crosses and churches, she was finding it harder to hear Freyja. As such, perhaps she was wrong.

He walked across the room, noting the looks the others gave him as he went. Anna disapproved, purely because Gunnhild did, and that was good enough for her. Ketil gave him a single nod, one warrior to another, a slight gesture that suggested Ketil knew precisely what Halfdan was going through. That he would do the same. That Ketil was at his back throughout this. How odd, from the days of old, when the Icelander had been an unpredictable and untrustworthy ally, always on the edge of vying for leadership of the Wolves. And the loss of an eye may have brought him wisdom, but simply being part of the Wolves seemed to have done the rest. There were few men Halfdan would trust more. He nodded back, their exchange unspoken, yet no less important for it.

Ulfr gripped his Mjǫllnir pendant as Halfdan passed, grinning and making the valknut sign in the air. Staunch, dependable, ever-loyal Ulfr.

Bjorn turned as he approached. 'You need a stand-in? I've been practising. I think I could pull his brain out through his dick hole. That would be good for a crowd. Lots of cheering, I think.'

Halfdan laughed. 'From any other man, I might think that an idle boast, Bjorn, old friend. But you had your Holmgång in Swaledale against a giant. I will need no replacement here.'

'You *do* need a *second*, though,' Farlof noted, as he and Eygrímr polished their swords, two men who had joined the Wolves late, but who had become as much a part of the crews as any; trustworthy, the heart of the hirð, the skippers of his two ships.

Halfdan nodded. He knew that. It was a legal requirement. The second was there in support, to pass shields across and warn when the ropes were close — eyes, ears and an extra pair of hands. Harðráði had chosen seconds the last time, but this time, he wanted someone he knew and trusted with him.

He opened the door and walked outside into the morning air.

Leif was leaning on a rail, looking out to the sea ahead. The Rus turned his head, without straightening. 'You look good,' he said. 'Maybe not quite good *enough*, but better than you have any right to be.'

Halfdan smiled and leaned on the fence next to him.

'The fight is back on.'

'I assumed that would be the case. If you do not kill him this time, I will take it as proof that you were right, and that my God does not exist.'

The jarl chuckled. 'I never claimed he did not *exist*, Leif, just that so did others.'

It was the Rus's turn to chuckle then. 'We make a strange pair, my jarl. You, a country boy, hardened by war into a leader and a fighter, respected by all, an echo of the men who fill the tales of old. A Sigmundr or a Beowulf, a Ragnar Lothbrok or a Bloodaxe. And here am I, a scholar and translator of texts, a courtier of the Kievan Rus and an ambassador to the Byzantine emperor. And here we are side by side in a land neither of us know, watching the world change.'

Halfdan nodded. 'It would be a terrible world, I think, where everyone was a Sigmundr. Who would grow the crops or sing the songs or make the ships or brew the beer? The world needs every type of man, Leif, and it is slowly becoming clear to me as we watch the world change that it needs a lot more of your sort than mine.'

Leif made to argue, but Halfdan waved it down.

'You asked me once, earlier in the year, where you fit in among the Wolves. Over the past months, I have watched you, and something has become clear to me. I lead this hirð, a jarl now in more than just name, but that is an easy thing, and requires no great skill. Gunnhild guides us with her wisdom, but her power is innate. Her skill is in *interpreting* it all. Ulfr is the best shipwright in the world, and that is his thing. Ketil and Bjorn are warriors. They are content as long as I can find men for them to fight. Even Anna, who has come to be far more than just a girl we picked up along the way, is part of this hirð, but she is Gunnhild's second. What *you* are is something different. You are the… You are the caulk that stops the ship leaking, Leif. You are the glue that holds the shield together. When things start to

338

fall apart, it is always you who finds the way to put them back together. When the way seems impossible, it is you who finds the answer. I am slowly forming the opinion that we are all but pieces on the 'tafl board, but it is you who *plays*. I do not think there would *be* Wolves of Odin without Leif Ruriksson of Kiev. *That* is where you fit in, and that is why you will always be part of this.'

Leif was looking at him in surprise, and Halfdan straightened, stepping back from the rail. 'I go to fight Hjalmvigi, and I go *now*, but I need a second, and I want that second to be you.'

The Rus nodded. Nothing more. Nothing needed saying. Economy of words could be as important as florid speech, and only a man of Leif's quickness knew that. The two men strode over to the corner of the house, which stood close to the harbour, and Halfdan waved to Harðráði's man standing near the water.

'Call the kings forth, and have the priest brought out from his cell. Holmgång will be fought this morning.'

The man gestured his understanding and turned, jogging away.

'I'll rouse the others,' Leif said, 'then meet you at the jetty. Go steady. Be safe.'

Halfdan smiled and nodded as the Rus wandered back over to the house, slipping through the door, and then turned and walked down to the waterfront. Already, a number of locals had gathered, and several of the ships' crews were at the sheer strake in anticipation.

Orm Axebiter was at the end of the jetty, guarding the site for Holmgång, making sure no one could interfere with it, and Halfdan nodded to him.

'I had a feeling you would fight today,' the bodyguard said quietly. '*I* would have done, were it me.'

Halfdan strode on, clomping across the boards, heading for the pegged-out hides at the far end. His legs were slightly shaky, and he was ravenously hungry, stomach eating itself. He'd had only bread and water so far since his recovery, and even those only this morning. He was not at his strongest, and he would certainly have thought twice about picking a fight with any warrior today. But Hjalmvigi was no warrior, and if Halfdan could not beat the priest today, then he did not deserve to lead the Wolves.

The memory of Gunnhild's prediction continued to nag at him as he found his place and stepped across the outer rope, into the holm. He stood there for a time, looking around. Nothing had changed here since the fight, the setup precisely the same... with one exception, he noted. Where they had each had three shields, they had not been replaced yet. Hjalmvigi's pile still had three, for Halfdan had been barely able to swing a sword by the time the bout had started, but only one shield remained on the jarl's side, for two had been battered to pieces by the exultant priest.

He stood for a time, swinging his sword, testing moves, his muscles, his reflexes, his strength. He could do this. Gradually, as he waited and exercised, more and more people appeared on the harbour and on the ship decks. Then, Harðráði arrived. The new king was quartered in the town's best accommodation, and so the Norseman strode down the jetty with Bishop Aage, this time ashore, and not watching from his ship, like Magnus. The two men halted a respectable distance from the ropes, and Harðráði gestured to him.

'I have bad news for you, Halfdan, I'm afraid. The Holmgång will resume, of course, and Hjalmvigi is ready. *All* is ready, in fact. However, the priest has requested that the duel return to the standard form, to first blood.'

'What?' Halfdan blinked, not quite believing what he'd just heard.

Harðráði nodded. 'The first blood to hit the ox hide decides the winner. And I'm afraid it's been agreed already.'

Halfdan's eyes blazed angrily. 'Why?'

'Because for Holmgång to be to the death, both duellists have to agree. And now that Hjalmvigi opposes it, that option has been removed. I tried to argue your position, but Magnus was firm on it, and the bishop here confirmed it with the law-speaker. It cannot be avoided. The duel is to first blood now, and not the death.'

Hjalmvigi does not die today.

Halfdan seethed, trying to find the words he needed through the consuming anger, and Harðráði had the grace to look apologetic. 'It cannot be changed,' the king said, 'but bear this in mind, Halfdan: first blood could be a killing blow *anyway*.'

Still too angry to speak safely, Halfdan latched on to that point. A thought occurred. 'And if I win, Hjalmvigi is mine anyway. You gave him to me.'

Again, that apologetic look. 'That would be my stance on the matter, yes,' the king replied. 'Magnus, I think, is of another mind, but that is a fight to get to *after* this one.'

Halfdan ground his teeth. Damn it, but the priest was on the verge of a way out again. Trying to finish Hjalmvigi was like trying to nail fog to a door. Before the jarl could think of an argument, Harðráði turned and walked away with the bishop, part way back down the jetty to a position where they would get a good view of the fight. Moments later, Leif walked past them carrying two shields, on his way to join his jarl, the rest of the Wolves lining up on the dock, close enough to watch.

'I've heard,' was all the Rus said as he came to a halt beside the shields.

'This is not right,' Halfdan growled. 'He manages to change things even as they happen.'

'On the bright side, it was mooted that you begin with only one shield, since it is the same Holmgång. I managed to overturn that,' he said, dropping two extra shields to the pile. 'And as for the outcome, just make sure that your strike for first blood *counts*, if you know what I mean.'

Halfdan nodded. He would do just that. He would make sure not to just nick or puncture the priest. When he drew

341

first blood, it would be a death blow. The nagging memory of Gunnhild's words struck him again, though, suggesting that such a thing could not happen.

All these thoughts trailed off, then, as the figure of Hjalmvigi reached the end of the jetty. Orm Axebiter left someone in his place, guarding the wooden walkway, while he accompanied the priest and his assigned second to the holm, being especially alert as he passed the king. Only when they reached the ropes did the bodyguard hand over a sword to the priest and then step back.

'God grant me the strength and the will to draw the heathen's wicked, black blood first this day,' Hjalmvigi said, eyes raised to the sky.

'I will kill you today,' Halfdan told him, quietly enough that only the four men at the holm and Orm Axebiter nearby could hear.

'I think not, heathen animal.' The priest almost leered with smugness over his perceived victory.

'Whether I kill you inside these ropes or I beat you to blood and then kill you later, when Harðráði hands you over as per our agreement, the end is inevitable, Hjalmvigi.'

The priest's smile faltered for a moment, then, though it came back, tinged with disbelief a heartbeat later. His precious King Magnus would save him.

'You all know the rules,' Orm Axebiter shouted, interrupting their exchange. 'The first blood to touch the hides decides the winner today. The winner's good name and reputation over any insult shall be restored, and he shall gain the right to take from the loser any and all possessions. The loser of the Holmgång shall be considered níðingr.'

The man paused, to let this sink in, and the crowd to murmur back down to silence, and then resumed. 'Each fighter has three shields. They will trade blows in sequence, with Halfdan Vigholfsson striking first as the challenged party. Blows will continue to be struck until blood is drawn, and once all three shields are gone, the defender must rely upon parries alone. Each contestant's second is permitted to step over the outer ropes but not into the central square. They are permitted to hand over replacement shields and take ruined ones, and to warn their fighter if they are inadvertently coming too close to the rope boundary. That is the limit of their interaction. Any attempt on their part to interfere or distract will be punished harshly. Should either combatant step across the outer rope, the fight will be terminated immediately with them accounted the loser. Any attempt to fight out of the ordered sequence will be considered a breach of the rules, and will indicate defeat. Have you any questions?'

There was a resounding silence as Halfdan and Hjalmvigi glared at one another across the square of ox hide.

'Very well. Let Holmgång commence. First to strike is Halfdan "Loki-born" Vigholfsson.'

Halfdan took a breath, grasped the shield Leif held out to him, and stepped across the ropes into the central square. Hjalmvigi followed suit, the watching crowd silent, the Wolves at the water's edge and aboard their two ships, the locals across the harbour, the fleet crews aboard their vessels, Magnus on his flagship and Harðráði with the bishop on the jetty. The only sounds were those of gulls, timbers and waves, squawking, creaking and splashing.

The jarl examined his opponent. Hjalmvigi held the sword well enough, though he was not adopting any combative stance, suggesting a lack of martial ability. The shield was up and ready, and held as though the priest was trying to fit his entire being behind it.

Halfdan had no doubts about his own ability. He knew he could beat Hjalmvigi, and easily. Were this to the death, he would simply wade in and finish the priest. But it was *not* to the death, and that was where the difficulty lay. He did not want to accidentally cause a light wound and win too easily. He had to make sure that the first blow he struck home with was the killing one. That would be difficult, and the presence of the shields made it all the more so. It would be all too easy to glance off the shield and draw blood. He needed the priest's three shields out of the way.

A traditional northern long sword was, in principle, better for this. Their sheer weight could smash the boards of a shield apart when swung hard enough. By contrast, Halfdan's sword was smaller and sharper, better for stabbing, but less likely to shatter a shield.

As he reached the central area, where Hjalmvigi stood, waiting now, eyes betraying just a little nerve amid their crazed zeal, he took note of the priest's first shield – the direction the boards went in, the relative thicknesses of the edging on the entire circumference, the fastening of the boss at the centre. The design on the surface mattered not. Wolves or dragons, or runes of power, none of that would make a difference for a White Christ priest.

Halfdan lifted his sword, braced, and slammed it downward, angled slightly to his right, and Hjalmvigi lifted his shield to take the blow, just as the jarl expected. The sharp edge of the Alani blade bit beep into the rawhide edge, shearing through it, in perfect line with the angle of the parallel boards that made up the shield.

He almost won in that moment.

As the shield fell apart from the cleverly aimed blow, the priest yelped and leapt back. He held up his hand, expression a strange mix of panic and triumph. Halfdan's blade had hit him where he held the shield grip inside. Fortunately for Halfdan, he had only grazed the man's knuckles, leaving a tiny red line that disgorged no blood.

The crowd roared all around them at this first, very successful, strike.

The shield was done, hanging in two halves only loosely held together by the rivets in the boss. Since Hjalmvigi seemed uninclined to deal with it, his second came to the inner rope

344

and leaned far enough over to grab the shield and remove it. He then passed a second one to the priest and stepped away again.

Halfdan watched as Hjalmvigi's lip wrinkled. The man placed his shield on the ground, and gripped the large sword in two hands, lifting it. When he swung, Halfdan had been half tempted to dodge out of the way, but he knew that was bad form. The watchers would disapprove. Avoiding the blow was a coward's way. So, instead, he lifted the shield, angling it carefully, ducking his head to the right, behind it. Hjalmvigi's blow was strong, given gravity and the use of two hands, but it was also basic and inexpert, badly controlled. The blade hit the boss of Halfdan's shield, just as planned, scraped the edging, and then swept off into the air, above his ducked head.

Again, the crowd roared, gleeful at the action, even if it had failed.

The two men stepped apart once more. Hjalmvigi lifted his shield ready. Halfdan looked at it carefully, chose his place once again, and then struck, sword coming round in a backhanded slash from left to right this time, once again in line with the angle of the shield's individual boards. Hjalmvigi had apparently not learned his lesson, for the blow hit home, shredding the edging, and drove apart the boards again, though this shield was clearly of better construction, and the boss continued to hold it together for now.

They parted again. Then the priest struck his second blow. He tried to jab low, this time, the blade lancing out, trying to hit Halfdan under the shield's lower edge, but Halfdan had anticipated it, seeing the man's stance, and even as the sword came, the shield slammed down, knocking it aside.

Hjalmvigi braced again, holding his damaged shield up.

Halfdan could see his next target. Where the boss held the boards together, one of the four rivets that attached it was loose, rattling in its hole in the boss.

He pulled his sword back and left as though going for another backhanded swing, but then slammed out with the eagle-shaped pommel first instead. The result was everything he'd hoped for. The blow struck the boss just where it met the wood, and the board came detached and swung about, unwieldy. As the priest lifted it and moved it, the shield creaked as more timbers shifted. Snarling angrily, Hjalmvigi threw the shield away, where it fell over the edge of the jetty and disappeared with a plop, to the ongoing roar of the crowd.

Halfdan braced with his own shield then, as Hjalmvigi repeated his earlier procedure, not taking the proffered shield yet, instead gripping his sword with both hands. This time, he swung sideways, and the jarl dropped the shield in the way once more. The sword slammed into it, and he felt the edging break. The shield was still intact, though, and he decided not to take the replacement Leif was already offering. Better to save shields just in case.

Hjalmvigi, on the other hand, had reached out now and taken his last shield.

The jarl eyed his opponent warily. Hjalmvigi must have noted by now how Halfdan kept hitting his shields in the same place and tearing them apart. Only a fool would not notice by their third shield. It was extremely unlikely the same blow would work once more.

Halfdan struck so anyway, another overhand blow, and sure enough, Hjalmvigi caught it better this time, deflecting the hit without ruining his shield. He then swiped at Halfdan again, a wild, angry blow that sent splinters and shards of wood flying as the first of the jarl's shields finally gave up. Accepting the second shield from Leif, he disposed of the first into the sea, and readied himself. He could see the scratch and dent from his last blow, and aimed carefully now. His swing was on target, and his sword bit into the same place as before, this time shearing through the rawhide. The shield remained intact, but its integrity was failing, bit by bit. Another blow, maybe two, and the priest would lose his last shield. Halfdan smiled grimly to himself at that. He was content that, once the shields were gone, he would be able to disarm Hjalmvigi without too much difficulty, which should, then, leave the man unharmed and completely defenceless. At that point, delivering a killing blow should be a simple thing.

He braced himself behind his own second shield as Hjalmvigi came once more, sword slamming inexpertly into the boards. The shield held, and Halfdan danced backward to the sound of thousands of people cheering. Hjalmvigi's eyes had narrowed.

The jarl eyed his opponent's shield once more. It was damaged. Intact, but starting to come apart. It would not take much. A well-aimed blow might just do it. He took a breath, eyes locked onto that weak spot he'd already battered, following its movements even as its bearer shifted.

He swung.

He realised his mistake mid-swing, when it was too late.

Hjalmvigi did not use the shield to block this time, nor did he jump out of the way. Instead, he turned slightly, so that the shield was at an angle. Halfdan saw it coming, and tried to pull his blow at the last moment, but the sword was moving, unstoppable. It struck the edge once again, but this time glanced across and smacked into Hjalmvigi's arm where it held the shield. The priest cried out, a sound that cut through Halfdan's soul, and the jarl watched in horror as the red flow of Hjalmvigi's lifeblood welled up out of the long cut and fell in large drips and gobbets, hitting the hide below with what sounded to Halfdan like a tomb door slamming shut. He stared at the fallen blood, face paling.

Gunnhild had been right. Gunnhild was *always* right. He'd done everything he could think of to avoid wounding the priest until he could deliver a killing blow. It had not occurred to him for even a moment that Hjalmvigi would deliberately *get himself* wounded, just to end the duel without a death. The wily bastard, ever a step ahead.

'Victory to Halfdan Vigholfsson,' cried Orm Axebiter, holding up both hands.

347

The crowd, aboard ships and on land, all exploded in a din of cheers and shouts and whistles. Arms waved above wide grins. To them, Halfdan had won. Only he, and those in the know, were aware that this victory was a failure in itself.

Hjalmvigi was turning, slowly, playing up to the crowd, with an expression of wounded shock. Only when he turned back to Halfdan did his face take on a predatory snarl of victory.

'You are níðingr,' called Orm, addressing the priest. 'All that you have is Halfdan Vigholfsson's to take.'

Hjalmvigi's expression did not change. What had the cursed priest lost? He had nothing but the shirt on his back, and he was already nothing, with no power, place or reputation, no home, allies or money. He had lost nothing. There was nothing for Halfdan to take.

The jarl felt both defeated and angry, and before he knew what he was doing, he had taken two steps, sword still up, toward Hjalmvigi.

'Back down, Halfdan,' called Orm Axebiter. 'Holmgång is done. Any strike given now is murder.'

Halfdan's lip wrinkled. He was sorely tempted just to strike the man down right now. But to do so might come back not only on him, but on all his friends, all the Wolves, and that would not be right. Instead, he continued to grip the sword tight, but lunged at Hjalmvigi with only a pointed finger.

'You have *lost* nothing, but you have also *won* nothing, priest. You were mine before this duel, given by Harðráði, and will be again. And this time there will be no challenge given. You will be handed over to me, and I will kill you. Slowly.'

He could see by the shadow that flickered across the priest's eyes that the man understood, and believed, now, that death was certain, and coming fast.

Halfdan backed away, then turned to Leif, hoping to see a sparkle in the Rus's eye. If there was any instant, clever solution to this, only Leif was likely to come up with it. He was disappointed to see there only irritation and helplessness.

Then he saw the Rus's eyes change. Fortunately he realised what he was seeing before Leif even cried out. Those grey eyes held a warning. The man was looking past Halfdan, past his right shoulder. Halfdan lurched to his left through pure reaction to what he saw, a move that saved his life, as Hjalmvigi's sword swept down through the air a hand's breath from him, right where he had been standing. Without Leif's warning, that sword would have slammed into the back of Halfdan's head, almost certainly killing him instantly.

Halfdan swung without thinking, also a reaction.

Hjalmvigi was too close, his attack's momentum carrying him right up behind Halfdan, and so the swing failed to connect the priest's giving flesh with the sword's sharp blade. However, it was the jarl's fist, bunched around the sword hilt, that smashed into his face, breaking the nose. Hjalmvigi let out a muffled, gurgling cry and fell back.

Halfdan turned, ready to finish this, but his opportunity had gone. Hjalmvigi had staggered back out of reach, while Orm Axebiter, who had started walking over toward the holm the moment the fight ended, was suddenly leaping across the last rope and bearing down on the injured priest. Halfdan watched, impotently, as Orm smacked the sword from Hjalmvigi's stunned hand, then heaved it away with his toe, where the priest's second retrieved it. Hjalmvigi continued to back away, passing rope after rope. Any moment now he would trip over the last and plunge into the harbour.

Halfdan tensed, wanting to lunge for the man, even though he couldn't get there in time, and Axebiter was in the way anyway. The priest was doing it again. He would get away. It seemed incredible that he might, but Halfdan had watched Orm Axebiter disappear into the water in much worse conditions and wearing armour, and yet the man had escaped him to reappear on a ship later. That Hjalmvigi might do the same in just a robe was at the very least a *possibility*.

But the call of Ran's deep, cold hall was not for the priest this day. Even as Hjalmvigi reached the edge of the jetty and teetered, ready to fall, Orm Axebiter was on him, hand sweeping out, and grabbing his robe, bunched at the throat. He held the man there for a moment, and then pulled him back to safety.

Halfdan straightened.

'He is mine.'

Axebiter looked unsure, and so Halfdan turned to see Harðráði and Bishop Aage striding toward him along the jetty. Beyond them, the rest of his friends were on the way, too.

'He is *mine*,' he shouted again, this time with his eyes on the king.

'For my part, you can have him,' Harðráði replied, loudly. 'He is níðingr. *Less* than níðingr. A man who murders and who breaks the ancient rules of Holmgång and the laws of Norway, in defiance of the king? Take the ex-priest and do with him as you will.'

But even as he said this, Harðráði's gaze snapped across the open water to the flagship of King Magnus, his nephew, who stood close to the prow at the sheer strake, watching. Halfdan's gaze joined the Norseman's. The younger king had *best* not interfere now.

Even at this distance, he could see how troubled Magnus's gaze was.

Halfdan took a deep breath, strode across to the centre of the square, and held up his sword and battered shield, high in the air, as he turned slowly, taking in ship after ship, face after face.

'I am Halfdan Loki-born, leader of Odin's Wolves, Jarl of Dragsvik and master of the *Sea Wolf* and *Sea Dragon*. I have fought the wars of the Georgians, the Byzantines, and the Normans, served in the Varangians, ousted a jarl in Angle Land, and the gods walk in my shadow. This *níðingr*, a former priest, banished by Onund of Sweden, cast out by his own Church, guilty now of at least three counts of attempted murder, was given to me by King Harald Sigurdsson, called Harðráði.

Just because the Holmgång has ended does not change that. Hjalmvigi of Uppsala is my property, and any man who wishes to deny that should step forth and meet me on this ox hide now, for I have plenty of fight left in me yet.'

Again, having finished, he turned slowly, lowering sword and shield, but still gripping them, a challenge in every aspect of his being. As he turned, he watched them all. Harðráði nodded, Aage next to him impassive, for though they might both kneel to the nailed god, that was where their connection to Hjalmvigi ended. Orm Axebiter stood strong, holding the priest, waiting, ready to impose his king's will either way. Leif had an odd look of pride, which Halfdan resolved to ask about later. The crews of the ships were uniformly silent, no one willing to step up in support of the excommunicated priest. Even Magnus, standing by the carved dragon of his flagship, looked away, severing all ties to Hjalmvigi in the face of the man's endless treachery.

The Wolves were at the strakes of their ships, hungry, expectant. The crowd on the harbour front were silent, simply rapt, enthralled. Gunnhild, Ketil, Anna, Bjorn, Ulfr, Farlof and Eygrímr were waiting, expectant, watching the crowds.

Back to Hjalmvigi.

Halfdan had a fascinating glimpse then into the mind of a madman.

The man's expression was cycling faster than a whirling child's top. Panic, hauteur, defiance, disbelief, deviousness, self-importance, righteousness, fury, despair... the emotions came thick and fast, and each was visible in its passing.

Then the man's gaze fell on Halfdan and he pulled himself from Axebiter's grasp and smoothed down his robe.

'I acknowledge only the authority of God, and of his priest in this world, the pope. Until God or his Holiness in Rome tell me I am not free, I refuse to accept such a verdict. I am a free man, and this... *heathen*, has no claim on me!'

He turned to walk away and made a strange squawking noise as Orm Axebiter grasped his shoulder and stopped him. Leif was there a moment later, helping restrain the man.

'Well?' bellowed Halfdan, turning again, slightly faster, addressing all present.

Not a single voice raised a reply.

Allowing a wolf's smile to rise, Halfdan Loki-born, jarl and warrior, crossed to the captive priest and stopped in front of him.

'You are mine, Hjalmvigi. You survived *this* day. You will *not* survive the next.'

Epilogue

And after that Loki hid himself in Franang's waterfall in the guise of a salmon, and there the gods took him. He was bound with the bowels of his son Vali, but his son Narfi was changed to a wolf. Skathi took a poison-snake and fastened it up over Loki's face, and the poison dropped thereon. Sigyn, Loki's wife, sat there and held a shell under the poison, but when the shell was full she bore away the poison, and meanwhile the poison dropped on Loki. Then he struggled so hard that the whole earth shook therewith; and now that is called an earthquake.

The fate of Loki, in the Lokasenna of the Poetic Edda

Drip.

Halfdan turned to Leif. The Rus had prime place beside his jarl, with Gunnhild on the far side. In fact, all the core members of the Wolves were at the top table, from those who had been with them since the start, or had been collected as far as Kiev, like Lief, to men like Eygrímr and his followers, brought from Angle Land relatively recently.

The rest, enough men these days to crew two dragon ships, occupied the other tables, the hall heaving and rolling with noise and festivities and occasional boasts and tumultuous belches from Bjorn. Indeed, the people of the villages of Dragsvik and Tjugum, as well as all the surrounding farmsteads in the new jarldom, were gathered around in the autumn air outside the longhouse, similarly feasting and drinking in celebration of their new jarl.

'I have been composing a saga,' Leif said quietly, pulling the leg from a chicken on the table before him.

Halfdan turned to him, eyebrow raised. He said nothing more.

Leif smiled, and took a bite of the chicken, chewing for a while, then dropping it back to the plate. 'I know. Tales are told around the fire, and that is the way it has always been, the old way. I know. The Wolves are all about the old ways. But there are things to be learned from the places we have been, Halfdan. Up here no one writes down the histories, and the problem with that is that every fifth telling of the same story it changes, until eventually it barely resembles the truth. A bit like Bjorn's anecdotes, to be honest. But the Byzantines are masters of writing down their history, and not *just* theirs, but those of their enemies and neighbours, of their Roman forebears, too. I didn't want the tale of our exploits to become an unbelievable thing of legend. I wanted them to be remembered for exactly what they are.'

'You act like we are all on the edge of death, Leif. As though this is our funeral. I personally plan to live a long and very interesting life yet.'

Leif chuckled. 'Well, quite. But now we are here, with a home, and all has changed. We are settled. And it's no good saying we'll just live the old way. Loading up the ships and going raiding is not so easy these days, since every land is a kingdom with an army now. There are no isolated monasteries full of gold and without protection, these days. The world is changing, and we will inevitably change with it.'

Halfdan looked at him sidelong. 'Until the day the hearth and home become a ball and chain, and the whale road sings an irresistible song, eh, Leif?'

Drip.

The Rus frowned. Was Halfdan really thinking this was just temporary? That they had a home, and he a title, but that was just for a rest before they went somewhere else? And if so, where? He shook his head as if to clear it.

'Anyway, the point is that I am writing out our saga. I'm writing it in Greek, I'm afraid. I could do Latin, but my Greek is better. And when it's done, I'm going to lodge copies with the church at Niðaróss and Aage's new church at Hróarskelda.'

'It has certainly been a long and varied road, has it not?'

'Fuck off,' bellowed Bjorn across the room, and they both looked round to see the big man jabbing a finger at a grinning Ketil.

Leif chuckled. 'And in some ways it still is. You realise we are never going to have peace here, as long as Harðráði stays in Vik, with Orm Axebiter. Those two will probably end up killing each other.'

Now, Halfdan gave a light laugh. 'Harald will be off soon enough. Magnus has gone back north, and his uncle will be on him, waiting for the moment to claim single rule, if you know what I mean.'

Drip.

'It's time, Halfdan,' called another voice, and the two men turned to Gunnhild, who had risen from her seat. Following suit, they joined her and walked across to the wall of the great hall. The occupants, to a man, fell silent, watching.

They came to a halt in front of a tableau from a nightmare.

In other times, in another life, Leif might have argued against it, but somehow it seemed entirely fitting. Gunnhild had explained it rather well. Hjalmvigi was the worst of all things, a poisoner. Oh, he'd been a murderer, a betrayer and so much more, but poison was something a true Northman abhorred. Halfdan had given it much thought. He'd fought the urge to gut the priest, Leif knew, because while it might be momentarily satisfying, it was just not good enough. He'd decided the man should die by his own methods. Burning him to death in a house was tempting for the jarl, but in the end he had decided on poison.

It had been Gunnhild who had suggested the specifics.

Hjalmvigi sagged against the timbers of the wall, bound to them with chains, too tight to let him fall. He wore black rags in mockery of the white robes he had worn for most of the time they knew him, and his head was upturned, held there by the presence of a sharp blade beneath his chin that lacerated him when he moved too far.

He was Loki, bound.

Above him, a carved wooden serpent periodically disgorged from its mouth a gobbet of liquid formed from the gradual compression of fungi above, in a press covered in granite blocks. The liquid would repeatedly hit the priest in the face and then run down it. Inevitably some of it made it into his mouth, and gradually, over the day, he had been showing more and more effects of the poison. By noon, his breathing had become rapid. Then he had started to sweat. His eyes had rolled, and then he had lost control of parts of his body, including his bowels. His chin had drooped and only came back to meet the dropping poison when it touched the blade.

But he was almost gone now. He looked like draugr, as though already he should be clawing at the inside of a coffin. Leif looked away for a moment in distaste, but made himself look back. It *was* horrible. It *was* inhuman. It was also perfectly fitting.

Almost on cue, Hjalmvigi, the cursed priest, turned his head as far as he could manage, his wide, pink, bloodshot eyes swivelling the rest of the way to take in his captors. He looked as though he was about to speak, but in fact managed just an excruciated gasp.

The life left his eyes as his chest heaved three times in quick succession and then fell still. He sagged, chin resting on the blade, blood running down the wall.

It was done.

Halfdan nodded in satisfaction, and turned to his men. 'Take this thing out onto the hillside and leave it for the animals. The ones with no sense of taste, clearly.'

And so Hjalmvigi of Uppsala passed from the world. Despite himself, Leif whispered a silent prayer for the man's soul before turning his back on the gruesome sight.

'Right,' Halfdan said. 'Axe throwing now. Nearest to the valknut on the far wall wins a silver arm ring.'

Leif grinned and hurried to find his weapons. The thrown axe was one of his specialities. As he crossed the room, he looked about him. Oddly, this felt as much like home as any place he'd ever been, though that was clearly because of the people in it, his family. The Wolves of Odin, and now they had a home.

He turned to see Halfdan standing with his hands on his hips and his gaze fixed out of the hall's door, where they could just see the masts of the *Sea Wolf* and *Sea Dragon* at the harbour.

A home.

Until the whale road called them again...

Historical Note

As with all the Wolves of Odin books, when it came to planning and writing *Kings of Stone and Ice*, I was faced with a dual task. With all historical fiction, a good tale combines the personal stories of the characters in the saga with a solid view of the historical framework in which it is set. A book written about the adventures of characters that does not tie in with acknowledged history is fantasy, not historical fiction, while a book that explores the history but pays little attention to the story itself is a textbook. Historical fiction seeks to seamlessly blend the two aspects.

With the previous volumes of the saga I sought to do just that. Book one was Halfdan's revenge tale, but in the context of Yngvar's saga and the Georgian civil war of the 1040s. Book two explored Gunnhild's personality in the context of the troubled reign of the Macedonian emperors and empresses of Byzantium. Book three examined Ketil's ego against the background of the Byzantine civil war and the machinations of the Norman lords of Apulia. Book four focused on Ulfr's shipbuilding amid the early troubles of William the Bastard in the Norman court, and book five explored the names and the remains of Dark Age Swaledale, while telling us why Bjorn is what he is. Book six was slightly more troublesome. I had to tell Leif's tale, as the last of the crew to be examined, and put it in a historical framework as usual, while also tying up all the threads of the past five books, for this is the last in Halfdan's current saga.

Originally, the plot of book six had been intended to involve the end of Onund's reign in Sweden but, as so often happens

359

with the plotting of series and their writing, the story gradually strayed from the original plan as it went. By the time I had finished book five, the timing was wrong for Onund's death, and so I went on a little research rampage. What followed was perhaps the most fun and fascinating dot-to-dot puzzle I've done.

Hjalmvigi is based upon a character mentioned only briefly in Yngvar's saga, and the character I portray is largely fiction. He is at this point in Sweden, but excommunicated, and as such, I could do what I wanted with him. And while he needed to be central to the plot, for he is the goal that has driven Halfdan through four books now, he couldn't be the whole plot. The other major loose end I had to tie up was getting *Sea Wolf* back from Harald Hardrada. I knew Hardrada was back in the north at this time, engaged in his new war, and so the research began. Hardrada went to Sweden, to Onund, and Onund was where Hjalmvigi was. Two threads tied together there. But if Hjalmvigi were to leave Sigtun, where would he go? Well, not to Denmark, for the kings were in Sigtun planning to invade Denmark. Yet their enemy was Norway, and, the enemy of an enemy being a friend, naturally Hjalmvigi would flee to Magnus's court. Suddenly I had a war in which the Wolves could find themselves, along with the ever-entertaining Hardrada, with the prize for Sveinn being Denmark, the prize for Hardrada being Norway and the prize for the Wolves being Hjalmvigi. Perfect. And as I worked, things continued to fall into place.

Because then there was Leif. The other characters each had an angle that made it easy to explore their personality, but I just couldn't see what that was for Leif. So, with such an odd realisation, I sat back and reasoned why this was the case. It was clearly because he was out of his depth, far from home, and feeling useless. That, then, was the aspect I needed to explore. And the fresh realisation that he and Hardrada's new wife probably knew each other just played into that. And then that made me think about the rest of the crew too, and the very nature of 'home' and where that concept fit into their lives.

Thus was *Kings of Stone and Ice* born. Apologies for the lengthy introduction to my notes, but I felt it was important to provide something of an insight into the book's background before exploring its contents. Onward into those, then…

We pick up the tale a little on from the Wolves' time in the archbishop's court at Jorvik. We find the crew contemplating what they must do while in Roskilde, at that time the capital of Denmark, on the island known as Zealand, now home also to Copenhagen. Here, as an aside, I will give you the modern equivalents of the ancient placenames in the book, for your map-based edification:

Angle Land – England
Ánslo – now Oslo, capital of Norway
Fioni – the Danish island of Fyn
Hróarskelda – Roskilde, city in Denmark
Jótland – now Jutland, the mainland Danish peninsula
Jótlandshaf – now Kattegat & Skagerrak, straits between Denmark, Norway and Sweden
Kaupang – a ruined Viking town near Oslo
Miklagarðr – then also Constantinople, now Istanbul
Niðaróss – now Trondheim in Norway
Nordmandi – Normandy, northern France
Odinswe – now Odense, on the Danish island of Fyn
Sigtun – still Sigtun, in Sweden
Sjáland – the Danish island of Sjælland/Zealand
Skáney – Scania, the southern tip region of Sweden
Stiklestad – a village in Norway, scene of a legendary battle
Þrónd (Thrond) – Trondheimsleia, a coastal strait outside the Trondheim Fjord
Torpstrand – a fictional island village in the area of modern Karlslunde, Denmark
Ultra Traiectum – now Utrecht in the Netherlands

Though the region at this point still sports only wooden churches, and stone ones have yet to appear, by the 1040s, Roskilde was already a bishopric, and we know that Aage was bishop at this time, though we know little else about him. The churches I have portrayed in the novel are generally conjectural, based on a simplified version of the later Scandinavian stave churches, since we have no image of these early wooden churches to work from. The geography of Roskilde (explored later on, during the war there) is based upon fairly scant evidence, and again a healthy level of conjecture, something not uncommon when exploring the Viking era. I will revisit this subject in due course.

The crew moves on from there to Ales stennar in Scania, the southern tip of what is now Sweden. This monument, one of Sweden's most important ancient sites, remains visitable today. The ship shape of tall stones is an enigma (although similar monuments abound across Germany and Scandinavia), and historians and archaeologists continue to theorise as to its purpose and nature, with one (barking) figure claiming it to be a prehistoric calendar of sorts. Stone ships are often burial monuments, with some cemeteries in Dark Age Germany and Scandinavia sporting numerous smaller examples. The true nature of the great one at Ales stennar is most likely religious, and reflects both ships and the sea. I have given it a purpose and a history in line with one of many possibilities. Interestingly, in exploring the details of the few excavations there, what Leif buries nearby appears on a table of finds.

There is little to tell about the return to Gotland, other than it gives us an insight into the 'you can never go home' nature of much Viking activity. We do get to actually meet Halfdan's childhood friend, mentioned in book one, at last, and I get to introduce the concept of the male magic worker, a rare character even in legend. From there we move to the court in Sigtun. This town appeared in book one, and any details of the royal compound are my own invention, for the archaeology has yet to reveal any data. Similarly, the church there is my own creation, based again on the stave churches of Norway, all of which are later builds. The stone Leif finds within is one of the many Yngvar runestones to be found in Sweden: U Fv1992;157, which was unearthed in the Sigtun area. In Sigtun we are reunited with Hardrada, and meet Ellisif/Elisaveta of Kiev. She is one of history's more unsung and interesting women. She seems to have been beautiful, clever, strong, and in a position of power, and yet, because her husband was even more impressive, she has somehow faded into the background. There is only one source that tells of her time in the north: Stúfr blindi Þórðarson kattar, and that source still gives us frustratingly little real information. I would have liked to have explored her character and timeline a great deal more but, unfortunately, this was not her tale, and other matters took precedence. She remains a character I would love to revisit, however.

As we move into part two, the war begins. We know from Hardrada's saga (pieces of which are quoted throughout the book) that Zealand was their first target, and that Roskilde burns. The geography of the town is based upon a combination of archaeology (the harbour is known) and a reconstruction based two centuries later by Mogens Suhr Andersen and found at https://jggj.dk/RoskildeOP.htm. The village that the crew attacks on the south coast is a fictional settlement of which there will have been many, this one based in the Karlslunde area. The portaging of the ship I have given in less detail in this book, for the minutiae of such has already been explored in book one. This, however, is once again based upon known facts, with guesswork only featuring where the facts are lacking. The use of log rollers is attested in such activity. Arriving in Roskilde, once again the church is based on examples of stave churches. The existence of artwork from the era that combines Christian motifs with pagan design is common enough that the doors should not be considered unusual.

As Roskilde falls, we move to the next stage of the war, with the invasion of the island of Fyn. Hardrada's saga tells us: 'Fiona too could not withstand the fury of thy wasting hand. Helms burst, shields broke, Fiona's bounds were filled with death's terrific sounds.' We have therefore no detail of the war on Fyn, but since Odinswe (modern Odense) was already a thriving town, with one of the five famous 'ring fortresses' of Harald Bluetooth, that seems an almost certain target. Once again, the geography of the early medieval town is troubled, and based on scant evidence. There is, in fact, no evidence currently of a harbour, for the modern port is based on a later canal driven into the town, but it seems hard to believe that a thriving Viking town on an island, only two miles from the water, did not have a harbour of its own. The existence of the Odin grove and its nature are conjecture, based on the little we do know, but the very name of the town seems to tell us that such a place existed.

The Hardrada saga goes on to tell us:

'Thereupon some men were sent off in a light boat, in which they sailed south in all haste to Denmark, and got some Danish men, who were proven friends of King Magnus, to propose this matter to Harald. This affair was conducted very secretly.'

I have expanded on this. Halfdan and his Wolves encounter these men in a light boat, and I have made the 'Danish men' the Wolves, escorting them to Harald. After all, Halfdan is half Danish, and Gunnhild entirely so. Of what follows we are told only 'he accepted the proposal, and the people went back to King Magnus with this answer'. Again, I have expanded on this somewhat, and had the Wolves go back with the answer. This is my conceit to bring the plot of Halfdan and Hjalmvigi into the light of the history once more.

In five previous books about Vikings, I had realised that I had actually had little action involving sailing, which is a sad lack, given how central the sea was to the lives of these people. I have written of storms at sea several times, usually in the setting of Rome, but any storm was going to be different in a longship, especially off the wild northern coast of Norway. In examining the route along the coast, I realised that they would have to sail the Trondheimsleia, and it struck me how difficult a sail that might have been in poor conditions. Even a little research into currents and winds there backed that up. So with a nice, exciting little sea storm scene, we arrive in the fjord at Trondheim. Catapults watch them as they arrive. I will grant you that Vikings and artillery are two words one does not easily combine. They are known to have used siege engines at the siege of Paris in AD 885, though these may have been acquired from the Franks and not their own. But by the 1040s, we have to acknowledge that the world has moved on from the traditional days of the Viking raider, and catapult technology was clearly available. Moreover, as the Viking age fades, the very nature of war and the military changes in Scandinavia, from raiding parties toward true armies.

Magnus had thus far been portrayed in this novel as the enemy. But we ought perhaps to remember that he was a son of Saint Olaf, just as Hardrada was the man's brother, and that bloodline was clearly a strong one. Magnus is remembered to history as Magnus the Good, and his reign was a positive one. Indeed, had Hardrada not interfered, and had Magnus lived long enough, he might well have succeeded in his dream of rebuilding Cnut's North Sea Empire, ruling Norway, Denmark and Britain. What world would we be living in now had that happened, I wonder? But clearly, though Magnus had been the enemy, he had to be clever, and probably likeable. And so the deal is struck, and the Wolves, with Halfdan frustrated at still not being able to strangle Hjalmvigi, sail south once more.

I could not resist having them stop at Kaupang for a number of reasons. The closure of Bjorn's backstory was a bonus, really, for what I wanted there was for Gunnhild to finish her journey. I think of the scene like Luke Skywalker. In *Empire* he left training to face Vader, then went back to Yoda in the third film to finish his training and become a Jedi. Similarly, Gunnhild left Hedeby to chase Yngvar with her training incomplete, and so she too had to find a master to finish her training and become a true völva. And, of course, this scene gives the heroes the way to overcome disaster at the end and save Halfdan.

The scenes that follow, from the evening of breaking pacts between Hardrada and Sveinn, through the assassination attempt and to the landing at Vik, are all expansions on what we are told in the saga of Harald Hardrada. The argument between the two leaders is almost (albeit paraphrased) verbatim from the saga. The assassination I have twisted a little, however. Of it, in the saga, we are told:

'Harald then went away to sleep somewhere else, and laid a billet of wood in his place. At midnight a boat rowed alongside to the ship's bulwark; a man went on board, lifted up the cloth of the tent of the bulwarks, went up, and struck in Harald's bed with a great ax, so that it stood fast in the lump of wood. The man instantly ran back to his boat again, and rowed away in the dark night, for the moon was set; but the axe remained sticking in the piece of wood as an evidence.'

I have played with these details a little, though not in basis. Having the whole thing be a ploy by Hardrada in order to break the treaty and make it look like Sveinn's fault may not be far from the truth. It certainly makes more sense than a genuine attempt by Sveinn, and fits with the lunatic's personality.

Whatever the case, in the saga, Harald immediately loudly blames Sveinn, pronounces the alliance broken, and tells his men to put to sea immediately. The saga tells us they 'rowed during the night northwards along the land; and then proceeded night and day until they came to King Magnus', and this is precisely what I portrayed.

Harald's attempt to bring his people on side at Vik is not from the saga, but it does make perfect sense. The feast is my own invention, as, clearly, is the burning building and the attempt to kill off the Wolves. As an aside at this point, I would like to thank my favourite Viking, Leni McCormick, for her input.

Just once, in this saga, I wanted to have a genuine Scandinavian song. I wanted something for Bjorn to sing, and I asked Leni if she knew of any traditional Norwegian song that was crude or violent or funny, and she gave me the lay that appears in the text. In chapter eighteen, you probably felt frustrated at the sudden burst of Norwegian in the midst of the tale. Here, then, is how the song translates:

> *I rowed my boat out to the Pollock ground*
> *It was in the morning, quite early*
> *Then came Olav from Kårelunnen*
> *And put his boat up alongside mine*
> *So I smacked him with my fishing rod*
> *Now he's knocked out in the back of his boat*
> *I was so happy I started to sing*
> *I was the Pollock ground king*

Thank you, Leni. Genuine Viking entertainment from a genuine Viking.

For the Vik of the saga, I have used the town of Vikøyri to give me appropriate geography. Vikøyri is suitably old and is in the Vik municipality and so fits the bill. Of course, nothing that is there now was there then, and vice versa, and so with so much of Viking history, we need to fill in the blanks. Still, churches, houses, farms and harbours are all staples of the medieval Viking world.

I suspect little needs to be said of the rest of the book, until the very end. The burning of the houses, the murder attempts and the Holmgång are all very self-explanatory, and I think few readers by now will not be aware of Holmgång. As such, I have not delved too deeply into the minutiae here.

The poisoning of Halfdan and Leif deserves a little explanation. Much of Viking history remains vague and uncertain, and two of the biggest mysteries remain völvas and berserkir. We only know the former existed from sagas, although burial sites attributed to these fascinating women have been discovered, and the finds from one are in the British Museum. I shall not delve deeply again here, as I've discussed the subject over previous books. Similarly, I have already discussed berserkir, a fabled group that may or may not have actually existed. The berserkr's traditional image, as seen on the famous Lewis chessmen, is of 'shield biters'. What it was that whipped these warriors into their battle frenzy is still an unanswered question, and a number of possibilities have been raised.

I have chosen to make it an arcane compound of various substances, and have left a bit of mystery in there, but I have included two principal ingredients. One is henbane, which is a plant of the nightshade family. Its inclusion is rooted in the fact that henbane was found among the cargo of a sunken fifteenth-century Danish/Norse ship near Sweden, confirming that the substance was known and used there, and a sixteenth-century Pomeranian witch trial where the accused had used henbane to make a man 'run around crazy'. The more important ingredient for this book, though, is the fungus. There has been conjecture that death cap was used by berserkir, although this seems unlikely, as it would be far too easy to simply die from its use, as it is so heavily toxic. A lesser option, also conjectured, is the fly agaric, which grows plentiful in Scandinavia, is less deadly, but still very potent, and could easily help induce a berserk state. It is also a fungus often misidentified and eaten by accident, which lends well to my tale of it being slipped into Halfdan's breakfast. Incidentally, the antidote Gunnhild takes from the hut and uses to save her friends contains benzylpenicillin and cephalosporin, two types of mould that can be used to lessen the effects brought on by fly agaric. Survival of ingestion of this toxin is common, as long as aid is received in time.

So that, then, is the story of the poisoning and the Holmgång.

Again, I'm not sure how much needs to be said from here on. From the Holmgång, the rest is epilogue. The Wolves are together, their quest and saga complete. They have a place and a home. Whether that will always be enough remains to be seen. There is a lot of future left for the Wolves of Odin, even in the Christian world of the 1040s. But for now, their story has been told. Great Vikings have sagas, and significant portions of this tale have been drawn from them, including those of Hardrada and of Yngvar. But now Halfdan is a great Viking. He has visited the corners of the earth, fought for emperors, met great men, influenced the future, and built an army, a fleet and a home for them. This, then, has been the saga of Halfdan Loki-born, last of Odin's true Wolves. I hope you have enjoyed reading these books as much as I have enjoyed writing them, and should the whale road call again, perhaps you will join the Wolves, and me, as they move on.

Until then, skål. You can drink blaand, I will drink whisky. I am a modern Viking…

Simon Turney
July 2024

Glossary

Aesir – one of the two groups of Viking gods, including Thor, Odin, Loki and Tyr

Berserkr (pl. berserkir) – lit. 'bear shirts'. The berserkers of Viking fame who were overtaken by battle madness in the name of Odin

Draugr (pl. draugar) – the zombie-like restless dead, occupying graves and guarding their treasure jealously

Dromon – a Byzantine warship powered by sails or by banks of oars akin to the Roman trireme or Ottoman galley

Excubitores – an elite Byzantine regiment with an origin as imperial bodyguards, by this time part of the garrison of Constantinople

Freyja – the most powerful goddess of the Vanir, whose realm includes magic, fertility, war and the gathering of the slain to her land of Fólkvangr

Gotlander – one of the three peoples of modern Sweden, the Goths occupied the island of Gotland

Holmgang – an official, ritual form of duel between two opponents

Jarl – a noble of power (the derivation of the English 'earl') who receives fealty from all free men of a region

Karl – a free man. Neither a noble, nor a slave

Katepan – regional governor of the Byzantine empire

Loki – a trickster god, a shape-shifter, who is destined to fight alongside the giants against the other gods at the end of days

Miklagarðr – Viking name for Constantinople, the capital of the Byzantine Empire, now Istanbul

Mjǫllnir – Thor's hammer

Norns – the female entities who control the fates of both men and gods

Odin – most powerful of the Aesir, the chief god and father of Thor, who gave an eye in return for wisdom and who has twin ravens and twin wolves, and an eight-legged horse

Ragnarok – the end of the universe, including a great battle between gods, giants, monsters and the slain who have been gathered by Odin and Freyja

Rakke – A Viking version of a mast parrel, the sliding wooden collar by which a yard or spar is held to a mast in such a way that it may be hoisted or lowered

Rus – the descendants of the Vikings who settled Kiev and Novgorod and areas of Belarus and Ukraine, from whom the name Russian derives (Rusland)

Sax – a short sword or long knife of Germanic origin, known to the Saxons as the seax

Seiðr – a form of magic that flows around men and gods, which can be used and understood by few, the source of divination

Svear – one of the three peoples of modern Sweden, the Svears occupied the northern regions of Sweden, around Uppsala

'Tafl – a Viking board game akin to chess or go, where one player has to bring his jarl piece to the edge of the board

Theotokos [Pammakaristos] – lit. 'Mother of God'. Greek terms of Mary, mother of Jesus

Thor – son of Odin, the god of thunder, one of the most powerful of the Aesir

Thrall – a slave with no will beyond that of his master, often a captive of war

Valknut – a symbol of interlocked triangles believed to bind an object or person to Odin

Varangian – the Byzantine imperial bodyguard, formed of Northmen

Varangoi – Greek term for the Varangian Guard

Völva (pl. völvur) – a wise woman or witch or seeress with the power of prophecy and the ability to understand and manipulate Seiðr